Earth Trap:
Rings Around the World

Other Books by Soma Vira
Published by Space Link Books

Planet Keepers I: Checkmating Aliens
Planet Keepers II: Good Bye Alien God
Planet Keepers III: Nikita's Shadows
Planet Keepers IV: Lord Kito's Revenge
Angel Trails: Double Lives
Angel Trails: Electra Undercover (Forthcoming)
Earth Trap: Rings Around the World
Kuru Trap: The Forbidden Blood
Twin Trap: Operation Space Sword (Forthcoming)

Soma Vira

Earth Trap:
Rings Around the World

Space Link Books • New York

Space Link Books
77 W. 55 St.
New York, NY 10019

Printed in the United States of America.

Produced by BookWorld Press, Inc.
Distributed by BookWorld Services, Inc.
    1933 Whitfield Park Loop
    Sarasota, FL 34243
    24-hour order lines: 800 444-2524
    Fax orders: 800 777-2525

        Publisher's Cataloging in Publication

Vira, Soma.
    Earth Trap: rings around the world / Soma Vira.
    p. cm.
    ISBN 0-9646057-5-9

        I. Title

PS3572.I73E37SP 1996   813'.54
                            QB196-20014

To
Jayant, Prashant, Bharat and Poonam
The Stars Lighting Up My Space

We desire nothing so much as what we ought not to have.

Publilius Syrus: Maxim 559, Circa 42 B.C.

Sooner or later, every war of trade becomes a war of blood.

Eugene V. Debs: Speech in Canton, 1918

Then darkness enveloped the whole American armada. Not a pinpoint of light showed from those hundreds of ships as they surged on through the night toward their destiny, carrying across the ageless and indifferent sea, tens of thousands of young men, fighting for . . . each other.

Ernie Pyle: BRAVE MEN, June 1944

Archimedes was a mathematical machine, that's why it was okay for him to say, "Give me a lever long enough, and a prop strong enough. I can single-handed move the world."
I'm no mathematician. Do not talk to me of Archimedes's lever. Do not talk to me of missiles and killer satellites. Give me ideas . . . Ideas more dangerous than killer satellites, and I will move the world.

General Stanley Stryker:
ESSAYS, UNSTABLE EQUILIBRIUM,
Page 51, 2051 A.D.

Author's Note

This novel is a fantasy-science fiction mystery depicting some of the consequences of international space exploration rivalry in the year 2051. It is a satire on the political and social lives of groups existing on the fringes of society as they shape and reshape their daily lives.

It is, therefore, concerned with relationships at various levels: parental, social and political. Hallucinatory and prophetic. Suspended in space and time . . .

Briefly: in the year 2051, three space ships, Hiroshima Hoku, Titanic, and Volga One, are launched to conquer Mars, casting traps that catch the actions of people whose lives collide and get tangled up across national borders.

NASA is facing an unprecedented problem: Titanic is not communicating! Is it unable to do so because it is in some kind of trouble? Or, has it changed allegiance and hooked itself to some other nation's space ambitions?

The Soviet Union is also feeling trapped. But the disappearance of Volga One has created an even bigger problem for the Royal Emperor's Samurai Society: it has triggered KGB probes, enabling them to discover the secret of Hiroshima Hoku's real mission that no one was expected to learn until it reached Mars.

The flight director of the Chinese space mission wants to escape his trap: the Republic of China is the only country that does not recognize the Candle Runners, a grassroots organization spreading across the globe disdaining global boundaries.

Busy raising new flag-slogans, the Candle Runners don't even realize what kinds of traps are waiting for their young leaders at the international conference they are organizing at Earth Sanctuary, Ayodhya — a city in India that has risen from the ashes of a religion-torn metropolis as a beacon of light for the space-ready human race.

Caught in this time frame, the Titanic captain's family is falling apart: NASA has told them that although they are not sure, it is possible Titanic may have fallen in a black hole.

The captain's twin daughters, seething under their mother's dictatorial behavior, secretly run away to attend the Candle Runners' first global convention in Earth Sanctuary, Ayodhya.

The captain's son, Neil, losing his invention with no hope of recovering it (his mother sent it with Titanic without his knowledge and permission), and, confused by his mother's behavior, leaves home without giving her his new address.

On top of all the problems she's having, the captain's wife, Meera, falls in the clutches of two blackmailers. One tells her Neil isn't her son because when her daughter was born, her husband secretly exchanged her with a son he fathered with some other woman. And, another one demands money, claiming he saw the auto accident in which she mortally injured someone but which she failed to report.

Soon NASA also discovers Hiroshima Hoku's secret mission. They also learn that the day Volga Two reaches its launch pad the Soviet Union will attack Japan.

America decides there is only one solution: stop the Soviet Union — by force if necessary — and try unified international action to solve the problem. As America and the Soviet Union start marshalling their forces, their chief executives are kidnapped by underground leaders wanting solutions on their own terms.

This unexpected coup d'etat, engineered in such an ingenious manner that it totally knocks out all rescue efforts, throws spanners in everyone's carefully orchestrated plans.

To everyone's surprise, the kidnappers choose Meera A'Kash to negotiate their demands. Worried about her daughters, she does what she must. But she is enraged and decides when the crisis is over she'll use the forces behind her to free Earth from the terrorists' traps.

Can Earth wrench control of its life? The story continues in "Kuru Trap," the second novel in this projected trilogy.

Is it impossible? Can it happen? Perhaps. Perhaps not.

Perhaps in some other shape: A mirage is a mirage. It moves, changes shape, disappears, or whispers like a fable.

When does a fable turn into a myth? A myth, into a legend? And, imagination into a mirage of a day-'n'-night descending shockvision future, hidden in currents of time and space?

Space — our new frontier! To nurture this teething baby, can we conceive conditions that'll make it available to all pioneers? Or, would it become an instrument of power in the hands of those who'd have the financial tools to control it?

If we do manage to seed some other planet, would this new frontier cause bloodbaths similar to those we experienced on our Earth in the past centuries?

While working to build permanent space stations, and hoping to achieve interstellar travel, are these some of the questions worth considering? Or is it best to just dedicate ourselves to achieving our dreams, leaving such problems to be solved by the shadows of the new century?

These questions come to mind because in this century, the human mind has learned to rely upon the technical facets of wars and to seek solutions through science and technology. It comes to us so naturally because science is logical and predictable. And technology, understandable and controllable. Thus, the deductive logic says: Wars are not only controllable and containable, they are also, for all time to come, the ultimate solution.

But, what if technology is not controllable? What if it'd keep walking one step ahead of war-sought solutions? What if, falling into enemy hands it can let them win? Are we infallible? Under certain conditions, can we lose also? Is this realization the best memory jogger to make sure that we don't? Or is it merely a mirage? A deliciously enchanting trap?

These are some of the questions: breaking, mending and cementing relationships in "Earth Trap," "Kuru Trap" and "Twin Trap," the three novels in this series.

Needless to say, this story is not an attempt to present an optimistic — or pessimistic — view of our space future. And the doctrines, tactics and policies mentioned here do not reflect any nation's doctrines, tactics and policies. Nor are the characters based on any people living in the present or past. If anyone discerns any similarity between the people in this story and someone they know, it would be purely coincidental.

It may also be mentioned that except where required by the contents of the story, no attempt has been made here to discuss the scientific complexities of the space race and the various nations' politics, strategies and decisions. Our readers will find themselves limited to the same immediate and narrow world in which the characters of this novel, lacking full knowledge of the principles that make the world technology run, live and move, knowing only what they've been taught or have been able to learn by their own efforts.

Last but not the least, no work of this kind can be completed without tremendous advice, help and support from innumerable people. I'm greatly indebted to everyone who encouraged me, helped me and stood by me very patiently. Amongst them, my special thanks to Ramesh C. Anand, Dr. Yogendra S. Goel, Dana Rae Pomeroy (Writer's Edge, Inc.), Dr. Virendra S. Goel, Mrs. Saroj Goel, Kanti Anand and Dr. Ashok Lata Mital. And, to my son Prashant without whose help my laptop wouldn't have worked.

1

Separate
Skyquakes

Meera A'Kash knew she was speeding, but she was late for
her appointment, and the small backwater road was
deserted. To save a lost soul, clutching to a crumbling link, one
has to do what one must, even if it means bypassing the rules.

Her eyes fell on the calendar under the speedometer . . . April
21, 2051. What the heck, she thought. This was not an ordinary,
take-it-or-leave-it year. This was the year 2051. The year of her
triumph. Nothing detrimental, nothing that shouldn't happen,
could happen to her this year. Nothing.

She pressed her foot on the accelerator and her Mercedes
lunged forward. Just then, her phone rang. Switching the
controls to automatic, she pressed the receive button. "Hello?"

"Mom?" It was Neil, and his cracking voice sounded as if he were on the verge of crying. "Mom, Titanic's gone. They can't . . . they can't . . ."

She felt afraid. Fourteen-year-old Neil considered himself a tough nut. Nothing, not even his sister Gopa's taunts, could make him cry. What could be so wrong? She wished she could reach out and touch him.

"They can't what, sonny?" she asked soothingly. "Calm down and tell me. Their tracking system — "

"You're not listening, mom," Neil interrupted. "The spaceship is gone. And dad with it. They're all gone. My experiment, too. Mom . . ."

Her hands trembled as she switched off the automatic controls. The auto swerved, ready to smash into the swiftly looming, leaning tree. Before it could crash into its target, with bare seconds to spare, Meera managed to regain control and stop the car.

With her heart racing, head pounding, she sat staring blindly through her windscreen, the phone lying where she had dropped it in her lap. Slowly she became aware of sounds coming through the instrument. In slow motion, she picked it up. "Neil? What happened? What did they say? Malfunction? Explosion?"

"No, mom!"

"Please, tell me son. Why can't they reach it?"

"It's gone." His tear-stained words came faintly. "No explosion. Nothing. It's just gone. Disappeared just like that."

"Spaceships like the Titanic can't just disappear, Neil. That's impossible. Something must have gone wrong with their tracking system. You know how it is. Just one small glitch and — Hold on. I'll check on my autovision."

"Mom, the monitor is chiming an auto. It looks like NASA's. It is. And two uniformed officers are getting out."

"OK, Neil, hold them. I'm canceling my meeting and coming back. Don't let them leave until I get there, OK?"

"Right, mom. They're at the door." He clicked off the phone.

Meera punched her office number. "Earth Reality," her secretary, Cathy, immediately responded. "May I . . . "

"Cathy, this is me. Listen, I won't be able to keep my eleven o'clock. Call them and cancel it, but don't reschedule yet. Tell them you'll call back. I'll call you later."

"You'll be back by four?"

"Why?" Meera asked impatiently.

"The Candle Runners . . . "

"You can take care of them, can't you!"

There was a small silence at the other end. Cathy knew that Meera never stood up anyone, unless it was a real catastrophe. And right now she was canceling not one, but two meetings.

"Neil OK?" she asked, concerned.

"He's fine. Cathy, have you been watching the news?"

"The news? I don't waste time watching . . . Oh, you mean the Titanic. I watched the blast off. Two a.m. sharp. But since entering the office . . . Why? Something special?"

"I'll call you later." Meera cut off the connection.

Her hand moved toward the small auto-vision glaring at her darkly from the dashboard, but she pulled it back — Neil was alone with NASA officers. Why had they arrived so abruptly? To shatter her hopes and dreams? To wind up everything?

No! Not at the threshold of Vishu's long-awaited triumph! Not at the brink of Earth Reality's achieving what Vishu had visualized, hoped for, for so long. Life wouldn't trap her again like this! There had to be a logical explanation. NASA must have wanted to reassure Neil. They knew how attached he was to his father.

Looking into the dashboard mirror at her worry-streaked face, she scolded herself. "You rabbit-feet! Until Vishu returns, you've got to take his place. Play his role. Take care of the kids. What are you doing here? Neil is alone with a couple of Uniforms! What do they want, to hold him hostage?"

Jolted by the frightening thought, she shook her head to clear her mind and, quickly switching on the engine, backed up, turned and started racing toward her home.

Despite all her efforts to keep her mind calm, it continued burning with questions, repeating them again and again. What had happened? Why had NASA officers come riding on the wind? If they wanted to reassure her, why hadn't they just called? Had Vishu broken his promise and told them about

Neil's invention? Oh God, she hoped not. Anything but that.

The Titanic was the super ship, the twenty-first century's finest space marvel. Even Japan and the Soviet Alliance had envied it. Everyone had been saying that this one ship was capable of doing more than twenty European ships put together. Early this morning, when it had blasted off with its twenty passengers, six crew members, and fourteen specialists, the whole world must have been watching. The sat-vision cameras had rolled and rolled, showing the roof-hitting celebrations in practically every country.

And why not? The United States had done it again. They had again achieved a first. Surpassing all humankind's past achievements, in space or on earth, the Titanic was racing to skywrite unprecedented history on the surface of Mars.

Earlier, the Soviet Alliance had sent an unmanned spaceship, Volga One, to the same destination. And last night, hours before the Titanic roared off, Japan had launched its Hiroshima Hoku, with five humanoid robots.

But the Titanic carried twenty pioneers representing various ethnic groups. Their intention was not just to explore the planet but to set up a colony on Mars. Only the courier ship, Earth Star, would come back for supplies and replacements.

The Titanic was the result of ten years of labor. Ten years of research. Ten years of testing and retesting and re-retesting. Orbiting around the moon for a full thirty days, it had passed the final test-run with flying colors. Its crew worked like the limbs of a living organism. No twenty individuals, living anywhere on earth, could have so much affection, so much regard, so much affinity for each other as the twenty riding the Titanic.

And, before launching it, they had rechecked everything. No other nation was as meticulous, as solicitous, concerning the safety of its astronauts as the United States. Everything had been checked carefully and repeatedly. Not an iota of doubt had remained in any mind, even the most skeptical.

The weather had been perfect. The launch had been magnificent. The starship had risen on its plume of fire and light, like a newborn that knew its rightful place under the sun.

No. Nothing could have happened to it. A computer,

somewhere, must have malfunctioned. They must be fixing it, and, because she was the captain's wife, instead of just calling, they had sent a couple of officers to give her all the details.

Her eyes misted. The auto raced. Suddenly her blurred vision saw an obstruction. She swiftly applied the brakes, but before she could stop, she had hit something. Or somebody.

Horrified, she opened the door. Leaning with one foot on the ground, she looked out; an old man's blood-trickling body, lay face down, crumpled near her left wheel. She couldn't believe her eyes. She had killed a pedestrian? The wife of the captain of the Titanic had mindlessly murdered an innocent person?

Bold newspaper headlines rotated before her eyes in blazing colors: Meera A'Kash Kills John Q . . . Titanic Takes Toll On Earth . . . Glory Blinds Meera A'Kash . . .

Panicking, she slid back on her seat, slammed the door shut and backed off. Veering to avoid the bleeding body, the car shot forward at full speed.

You bloody rabbit-feet! her mind shrieked at her. Call the police. He's probably still alive. You can't let him die like this on a deserted road. Call the ambulance . . .

God, you are something! her shaking breath screamed back at her. What if he is already dead? What if he has a huge family behind him? You want to be sued for millions? You want to be tried for murder? You want to spend the rest of your life trapped in some seedy, rat-infested, drug-curdling prison?

But dear, her shadow remonstrated, your auto left tire marks. They will find you. You'll be labeled a hit-and-run driver for the rest of your bloody life. You'll be caught. You want to face that kind of music? For ever . . . and ever. You better turn. Go back. Now!

Forget it, her searing mind bitterly responded. It wasn't my fault. He should have known not to cross the street in front of a speeding car. He killed himself. I did try to help. I did try to stop the car. He was too fast for me. You know that.

Someone will find him. They'll take him to some hospital. He'll be OK. You'll see. He'll be OK. You've got nothing to worry about. Nothing at all. You'll see . . .

Not bothering to garage her auto, she left it at the porch.

Quickly climbing the few low steps, she crossed the veranda. The front door was slightly open. Wise of Neil, she thought. He is alone with strangers.

As she entered, two NASA officers, looking neat, trim and tall in their blue uniforms, sprang up. She quickly threw a glance around the room to see if it was looking OK — with a young son in the house, she never knew what would be littered around when she came home.

"Please, no need for formality," she said, waving them back toward their seats.

Moving toward her favorite chair, she noticed Neil had given them drinks. That pleased her. But the glasses stood untouched on the almost-empty marble cocktail table. "Please, have something," she said. "If you'd like something else . . . "

"Mrs. A'Kash," the younger-looking officer picked up his glass but put it back before it could reach his lips, "chances are there's nothing wrong. We just came over to — "

"What do you mean, chances are?" she asked sharply. "Is the Titanic OK? Is my husband OK?"

"We have no reason to believe they are not. We are trying our best to re-establish contact."

"What are you trying to tell me?" she blazed impatiently. "Your computers have broken down? Everywhere? On every goddarn tracking station? Globally?"

The two officers glanced at each other.

She couldn't fathom their silent communication. Whatever it was their eyes silently signalled to each other, it was clearly no good. Her mind trembled; if something was wrong, what good would it do to shout at these two messengers?

"If that's the case," she said, trying to simmer down, "why not contact Russia? Or China? Or Japan? Their equipment is as good as yours. Maybe even better. Until you can repair yours, why not use their facilities? Or are political goals more important than twenty specialists? Specialists who are depending upon you to reach their destination . . . "

As she stopped for breath, the older one glanced at his assistant to restrain him and said kindly, "Mrs. A'Kash, I'm sorry, we forgot to give you our names. I'm Sam Oringer from

Space Defense Command. My assistant, Lieutenant Colonel James Miskovitz."

Surprised by the absence of angry reaction in a voice that sounded like a familiar, long-forgotten baritone, she felt nonplussed. Acknowledging the introductions, she nodded quietly.

"When one is alone," the officer was saying, kindly, pleasantly, "one can start imagining things that, in time, may turn out to be wrong. Therefore, NASA feels it'd be best if Mr. Neil A'Kash and yourself would come with us."

"No," Neil blurted out before Meera could reply.

He glared at them. Angrily. Defiantly. Daring them to move him even an inch. "I'm not going anywhere," he shouted. "My dad told me to stay here. Here." Stamping his foot to emphasize his point he screamed, "An' take care of everything until he returns. When he returns, he shouldn't feel that . . . "

"My son is right," Meera supported him. "Besides, what would we do in your office? You've got the same sat-vision we have here."

"True," Sam Oringer nodded and smiled.

Again no protest. Meera was beginning to feel overwhelmed by him. More and more, he was sounding like the father she had often imagined, had always wanted, but never had.

"You're right," the tall, majestic-looking officer was saying, stripes of achieved victories shimmering on his broad shoulders. "But sometimes, peer support — "

"Why do we need support?" Neil demanded harshly, his whole body tense with an anger he had never experienced so strongly. "What's really wrong? Why can't you tell us? We can accept facts. Or do you consider us juvenile freak-outs, who — "

"Please, don't say that," Sam Oringer chided affectionately, just as a loving father would. "It's just that, well, the thing is, at this point . . . Do you know what black holes are?"

"Who doesn't?" Neil asked sarcastically.

"Well," the officer drawled, "as you know, until now they've existed only in theory. We are wondering, if, by any chance, the Titanic has found one."

Admiring Oringer's discreet diplomacy, storing it in his mind for some future time when he might need it, Miskovitz was trying to pass the time by looking around. His eyes lingered on the antiques tastefully scattered around the large living room. It's not a question of money, he was thinking. Lots of millionaires in America. It's the question of how you spend it. The owner of this house, he thought, feeling mesmerized, not only knows about art, but also loves it. As the thought emerged in his mind, his eyes hit on a gigantic oil painting hanging above the black marble mantelpiece. Shocked, as if suddenly awakened from a delightful dream, he straightened up.

The ghoulish painting looked so incongruous amid the other exquisite objects. And what on earth was it trying to flaunt — two halves of a spaceship trying to devour each other? Or three-fourths of the Earth invisible, shrouded by rings of rising hydrocarbons and nitrogen oxides; and the visible fourth, trapped, throttled and bombarded by satellites orbiting around it like hissing snakes, scorpions and cobras.

In the Museum of Ancient History, he thought, I've seen many hideous paintings, especially by that ancient painter who splashed on his canvas those bright yellows and reds. What was his name? Von something, who had cut off part of his ear. The painter of this one, he thought, probably had cut his throat.

The caption beneath the painting flaunted its intent in big, bold red letters: Rings Around the World.

He couldn't pull his eyes away from it. It seemed to have a strange effect on his mind.

The sudden silence in the room caught his attention.

"You mean," he heard Meera gasping, as if she were trying to grasp the meaning of the words that must have been just said, "you mean . . . " As the full import of those words seemed to hit her, she collapsed on the arm of her chair.

"Mom!" Neil sprang to her side. "Mom!" He tried to lift her head. The touch of those cool, caring fingers seemed to give her some strength. She straightened up, pulled him to her side, and, putting her arm around him, held him tight.

"Black hole?" she murmured, trying to find comfort in the reality of her son's presence. "I've only heard the word. If that's what happened, can the Titanic get out of it?"

"But dad told me," Neil asserted before Oringer could reply, "the Titanic can't lose touch. No way. It has that backup computer. If, for any reason, land communications can't reach it, it can talk with its twin unit at Mission Control."

Oringer nodded. "That's right. The fail-safe system was installed for our landing party. On the test-run around the moon, it was tested several times. It worked perfectly."

"So as soon as they get their bearing, they should call you?" Meera sounded hopeful. Color slowly returned to her face.

The officers again exchanged glances. "That's what we're hoping." Oringer smiled encouragingly and added, "If you wish, we can stay with you until we hear something."

"No," Meera said firmly, "there's no need for it. I won't have time for you. I must call my daughters and . . . Well, we thank you for coming. And I hope you will keep us informed."

"Of course." The officers got up to leave. Neil came forward to shake hands and walked them to the front door.

Outside, where he knew his mother wouldn't be able to hear him, he asked quietly, "When my dad calls, would you please ask him about my experiment?"

"What experiment?" Sam Oringer looked surprised.

"Just ask him. Would you? Please."

"OK," Oringer nodded, "I'll ask our people who do the talking."

Neil's face brightened up. He solemnly shook hands and stood watching them until they entered their auto and drove away. As he returned, Meera asked, "Gopa called?"

"Nope. She never calls until she needs money. You know that."

"Don't talk like that about your sister," Meera chided him gently. "Your Granma's sat-vision was probably broken again. I hope it was and they haven't heard the news. Let me call Pooja. She should come back right away."

"I called her."

"And?"

"The lodge-keeper said they'd gone camping overnight, to watch the liftoff. They hadn't yet returned. I told her to call us right away, as soon as they come back."

"Good. Can you give me the phone?"

Tilting the reclining chair, she put her feet up and dialed her mother's number. It was answered on the first ring. "Hello?"

The voice sounded unfamiliar, gruff and brutal.

"Who is speaking?" Meera demanded.

There was a small silence. "I could ask the same," came the reply. The voice at the other end seemed somehow different, more gentle or hesitant. "With whom do you wish to speak?"

"With my mother," Meera said impatiently, "or my daughter. Call them, please."

"Is this Mrs. A'Kash?" The voice sounded relieved, as if a heavy burden had fallen off the speaker's shoulders. "Sergeant Goodhorn here, ma'am. Glad you called. I was trying to find your number."

Meera's pulse beat faster. "What are you doing in my mother's house? I want to speak with her."

"Your mother had a heart attack. I just sent her to that new hospital, Coronary Care."

Meera's hand, holding the phone, shook. "My daughter? Did she go with her?"

"She — " Sgt. Goodhorn hesitated. "Would you be coming here, ma'am? The hospital, I'm sure, would like to know. The neighbors told me you are her only living relative."

"I want to speak with my daughter," Meera shouted.

"Didn't she call you, ma'am? This morning we had student demonstrations at City Hall. Mayor's residence. Lee Chung's. They just wouldn't listen to nobody. The police had to use tear gas and batons. I could make some calls and call you back."

Meera felt numb. She stared at nothing — such things happened in movies, not in real life. They were never real.

They couldn't be happening to her. Not now. She was having a nightmare. She must wake up. Wake up and go to the Mission Control office. And be there when her husband called.

Vishu, my wandering love, where are you? a hidden voice in her mind screamed.

She stared at his devil-may-care profile, smiling from the mantelpiece in its dazzling brass frame. How could he look so detached? As if nothing had happened, as if nothing could ever happen. As if the world would always be full of those benevolent stars that had shone upon them, upon those body-touching, honeymoon Himalayan peaks of bare delight.

"Mrs. A'Kash? Ma'am?" The phone was screeching in her reluctant ear.

Neil was standing near the mantelpiece, his eyes glued to his father's photograph. His mother's voice had been just a sound he had been hearing without really listening. When it stopped, he turned and, seeing her ashen face, got scared. "Mom, what is it? Mom? Granma OK? Mothhher . . . "

Meera glanced at him as if he were some stranger. Then recognition came. She shivered and tears rolled down her cheeks.

"Yes, sergeant," she said in the phone. "I'll catch the first available flight. Could you . . . would you take care of things until I come?"

"Sure, ma'am. As I said, I'll make some phone calls. I'll try to find your daughter."

"Thank you, sergeant. I appreciate it."

"No problem, Mrs. A'Kash. We'll see you soon."

"Who was that, mom? Somebody broke into granma's house?"

"Granma had a heart attack. I've got to go there."

"You can't go alone." He moved and sat on her armrest. "I'll come with you."

"I was hoping you'd say that. Can you call the airline? Book the next available flight while I pack our suitcase."

"Sure, mom, right away."

Walking toward her room, she thought, if I hadn't run away, if I had taken that unfortunate man to a hospital, this wouldn't have happened. This is my punishment. Who says God is not always watching everything?

But Lord, she silently asked, why are You punishing my mother? It was my crime, not hers. I should have had the heart attack. Not her. If I find that victim now, if I confess to the police, would You heal my mother? Would You please help? You know it was an accident. You know I tried to stop. You know I couldn't. You know it was more his fault than mine.

Taking out the suitcase, she opened it.

Then a thought came. She switched on her bedside radio and caught a reporter in mid-sentence, " . . . is critical, but stable. As we reported earlier, there were no ID papers on his body, just a brief, hand-scribbled note on a yellow paper in his shirt pocket. It said, 'My daughter is going to kill me today.'

"If he was so sure, why didn't he report it to police? Why didn't he ask for police protection? Was it his daughter who ran him down on that deserted road? So far, police have no motive, no clues and no suspects. They are asking anyone with any information to call Precinct Forty-five or this special number: 879-2222. All calls will be kept strictly confidential . . . "

Meera switched off the radio. Somehow, she was sure the reporter was talking about her victim. Was he running away from his daughter? His mind elsewhere? Was that why he wasn't watching for oncoming traffic?

How stupid of the police, she thought. They shouldn't have given out the contents of that note. After hearing this, do they expect his daughter to come forward? Where did they keep their brains. Did the man have other children? Neighbors? Should she call the *Tribune's* news desk to find out the name of the hospital? On her way to the airport, should she pay him a visit?

The office had been unusually quiet, but Gen. Stanley Stryker, director of NASA's Space Defense Command, was not able to concentrate on his work.

His eyes were glued to the open file lying on his neat but crowded desk, but his mind was far away, trying to figure out what could have happened to the Titanic on its maiden voyage.

Hearing his secretary's soft voice in the outside office, he glanced up as his intercom buzzed. "Colonel Oringer and Lieutenant Colonel Miskovitz are . . . "

"Fine," he said impatiently. "Send them in."

His door opened, and officers Oringer and Miskovitz entered and saluted. A brief smile hovered in Stryker's worried eyes.

Waving them toward the waiting chairs, he asked, "Why are you alone?"

Col. Oringer's face was a blank wall. "She looks clean."

Gen. Stryker's right-hand fingers beat an impatient tattoo on his desk. "That's no reason, Sam, and you know it. And you also know — "

"Pardon, sir." The elderly colonel sounded upset. "What I meant was, from her response, it was clear she doesn't know anything. If there was a conspiracy, the perpetrators, including her husband, kept it a secret from — "

"Damn it, Sam! That was no reason not to bring her as ordered."

"Quite right, sir. I thought about it. But under the circumstances . . . "

"What circumstances?"

"You had ordered me to keep track of her mother's movements. On our way to her house, we had a call from our office. Earlier this morning her mother suffered a heart attack. As you know, she's the only child. She'd have to go there."

"And when she reaches there," Lt. Col. Miskovitz added quickly, "she'll be facing another problem."

"What problem," the general asked impatiently.

"Her daughter may have been arrested in student riots. Arrested or injured. Or both."

Gen. Stryker met their unflinching eyes. "Heart attack? Was that before or after the news about the Titanic was flashed on the sat-screens?"

The two officers exchanged glances. It was obvious they hadn't thought about that, hadn't connected the two together.

"And who was arrested?" Stryker was asking. "Gopa? It couldn't have been Pooja. It's amazing how different those twins are. They defy the theories of all sociologists. What were the riots about?"

"Didn't get a chance to hear the whole story," Miskovitz replied. "Something to do with those new Japanese robots at Lee Chung's manufacturing plant."

"Let's hear about it." The general pressed his remote and the large sat-screen on the side wall lit up with the image of a reporter standing near a hospital entrance. "So far, no one has called the hospital or police stations," he was saying in his microphone. "Everyone, even a homeless person, carries with him a few items. But this poor victim had nothing except that cryptic note found in his torn shirt: My daughter is going to kill me today. Who is this man?"

The lean, haggard face of a white man, perhaps in his sixties, with dirty, unkempt hair, lying unconscious on a stretcher, replaced the reporter's dark face on the screen. In the background, his Bostonian baritone droned on. "Where is his daughter? Someone knows them. A ten-thousand-dollar reward has been set up for the person who can identify him . . . "

Stryker's dark brown eyes, staring at the face on the screen, had lost not only the cool, detached reserve that generally resided there, but also the anxiety that had been clouding them. He looked horrified.

"Sparky," he whispered.

"Sir?" Oringer asked.

"I must call Herb."

"FBI," Miskovitz whispered.

If Stryker heard the aside, he ignored it. "Did they mention the name of the hospital where Mrs. Heinrich was taken?"

"Mrs. Heinrich? Oh, Mrs. A'Kash's mother." Col. Oringer thought a minute. "No, and we didn't ask. But that shouldn't be difficult to find out."

"Good. Sam, I want you to go there. As soon as visitors are allowed, call me. I want to talk with her personally. I have a feeling — call it a hunch — the Titanic's disappearance has something to do with her heart attack."

"Very good, sir." Oringer pushed back his chair and got up; so did James Miskovitz. As they turned, Stryker called, "Jimmy."

"Sir?" Hearing his name, the youngest officer in SDC turned and stood at attention, waiting for his orders.

"I want you," Stryker told him, "to find out all about Gopa's activities for the past ten days. Report to me directly."

"Yes, sir."

Together, the officers walked out and closed the door behind them. Miskovitz fell in step with his boss. "Sir, did you recognize the face? Who's Sparky?"

Oringer was trying to concentrate and not succeeding. "I have a feeling I should know that face, but I don't. Why?"

Using the side door, they descended the few steps and moved toward the waiting auto. "We may as well take the same flight," Oringer said.

"Why not," Miskovitz agreed. "After dropping you at your residence, I'll make the arrangements. Would you like me to come over to — "

"No. Just leave the flight number on my machine. I'll meet you at the airport. You go ahead. I'll take a cab." Sam Oringer stood watching Miskovitz drive away. Then he retraced his steps, opened the side door and re-entered his office.

Sparky's lean and haggard face was rotating in his mind. He was thinking, if I don't find out who Sparky is . . .

The lodge-keeper, Hansa Shareefa, stood near the window, watching the threatening sky and the occasional truck traversing the isolated highway. She was worried — the sun was now totally hidden. The sky had started crackling. It was getting darker and darker. Any minute it could start pouring. Where were the girls? They should have returned long ago.

Why are you worrying? Angry at the concern she felt, she started scolding herself. Like everyone else, they were just overnight guests. Here today. Gone tomorrow. Never even a thank you note, no matter how good the service you provided them.

But they are teenagers, her other self protested. Because their parents don't care, because their teachers don't care, that's an even bigger reason that someone else must. Because no one else cares, that's why.

Just then, big, fat drops started falling on the windowpanes, and simultaneously, as if on cue, an auto entered the driveway. Hansa gave a big sigh of relief and ran to open the door. Laughing and giggling, the girls poured in. Pushing the door against the howling wind, together they managed to close it, although they were all drenched in the process.

Turning instinctively, fearfully, Hansa counted them. Her heart lurched — there were only fifteen! One was missing. She searched their faces. Which one — the girl with the dark, aquamarine eyes and long, golden hair, the one whose brother and mother had called several times. She was not with them. Where was she? Had they left her behind?

Feeling anxious, she asked, "Where's your friend?"

"Which friend?" one of them asked.

"The one with the long, blond hair. Is her name Pooja?"

"Oh, Pooja. She backed out at the last minute. Didn't want to spend the night in a tent."

"She didn't go with you?"

"Nope."

"Omigod!"

"What happened?" Some faces looked concerned.

"Her brother called several times. Her mother called. I didn't ring her room because I thought . . . Omigod . . . " Leaving them, Hansa ran to Pooja's room.

The room was a mess. The bed was not made. Obviously, she had slept there. And taken a shower. Then what? Did she go for a walk? When? How long ago? When the clouds started gathering and it was clear they'd pour like hell, why hadn't she come back? There was no other motel for miles around. Was she lost? Could she have gotten hit on the highway by a speeding truck or something? Gods above! Why was her brother so worried? Why were they calling? And calling and calling? She must contact them right away.

Running back to her office, she dialed the number Pooja's brother had left, but she only got a recording: "We're sorry we cannot come to the phone right now, but your call is very important to us. At the beep, would you please leave a brief message. We'll call you back. Thank you very much."

The recording beeped, but Hansa sat staring at the tele-unit, wanting to kick it. What good was having a phone? Someone could be dying, but it just keeps repeating, "Leave a message. Leave a message . . . "

What message? That your sister is missing, that her friends left her here, but she isn't here, that the highway is very dangerous and if she went alone . . .

Panicking, she began to dial 911.

2

An Old and
Busy Neighbor

Pooja A'Kash looked at her wristwatch again. She had been
standing there, near the drooping weeping willow, for almost
ten minutes, but the young, yellow-haired priest, sitting yoga-
style in the small clearing, legs crossed, hands on his knees,
hadn't opened his eyes. Hadn't moved a single muscle.

Dark clouds hanging overhead had rumbled and thundered.
Lightning had cracked several times. But not once had he
opened his eyes and looked above. The damp wind, blowing his
moon-gold hair, clearly indicated that the storm was coming
closer. Any minute it would start pouring. Didn't he know he
was going to get soaking wet?

Sitting there, eyes closed, breath controlled, back taut and
rigid, was he lost in his yoga meditation, or had he fainted or

something? Should she go to him and shake him, try to revive him? Or was that a bad idea? Whatever faith he believed in, were there taboos in it against touching women? How could she find out? How could she decide?

But decide she must. Either do something or forget it and run back to the lodging house. It'd be stupid to get drenched and catch cold for absolutely no reason at all.

As lightning cracked again, she shivered and made up her mind. Quickly crossing the small space that separated them, she stood close to him and said very softly, "The storm is getting closer. It's no good to sit here any longer."

His eyelids fluttered and his eyes opened. Clear, blue eyes, limpid and wide. She felt mesmerized. He smiled as if the moment was the only thing that mattered and nothing else.

Gaining courage, she smiled back. "See? Look up there," she said, pointing toward the thick, dark clouds.

"Does nature frighten you?" he asked quietly.

"No." That voice sent shivers up her spine. "But catching cold does."

"Then you shall not catch cold." In one fluid motion, he untangled his feet and stood up, towering up above her. "Shall we run?"

"Where to?"

"To wherever you live."

"That's too far. We'll never reach there. The storm is coming from that direction. See?" To emphasize her point, she gestured toward the gathering clouds.

"OK. Another solution. We run to my tent. Thataway." Without waiting for her reply, he started loping in the indicated direction.

She followed, feeling clumsy and angry. Look at him. So sure of himself that you'd just follow quietly. Not looking back, not even once. Why do you always get caught in such stupid situations?

As if reading her thoughts, he stopped and looked back. "Have we outrun the storm? What do you think?"

"For a few minutes, maybe," she said, feeling out of breath.

"Not very far now. Just beyond those trees." He pointed, and through the foliage she could see a picnic area where a lone van was parked. She started to giggle.

"What's so funny?"

"The space-age tent." She tried to stop giggling, but the more she tried wiping tears from her mirth-flooding eyes, the more helpless she felt. It was catching. He also started laughing.

"Right. Space-age tent. The latest model for A.D. 2051."

Stretching his long arm, he took hold of her hand, and together they ran toward the small, forlorn-looking shelter.

Trying to keep up, she thought, if he lives around here, how in Earth's name am I going to see him again?

They were still a few feet away from their space-age shelter when big heavy drops began to fall on their heads. Both trying to adjust their pace to the other's, they began to run faster. Reaching the camper, they quickly clambered inside, closing the door behind them.

As if angry that they had gotten away from its clutches, the storm unleashed all its fury and started pounding the roof of their shelter. Moving a dark-blue curtain, Pooja tried to peek out the window but could see only the pillars of water pouring down.

"Tea or coffee?"

She turned. He had put water on the stove and now stood combing his thick, moon-gold hair with his long fingers.

"Anything." She settled down on a seat that was right where she was standing.

"Tea, then. The Darjeeling kind. Sugar? Milk?"

"Fine."

"OK." He handed her a steaming cup, took one himself and sat down. "How about introductions? I'm Rahul. The best free-lance journalist this world can afford." He smiled and his left cheek dimpled.

Journalist. She looked at his yellow robes. Reverend-journalist. To check the mirth building up inside her, she quickly took a giant sip of her tea and scalded her tongue.

"Wow! It's hot!" She gingerly took another sip. "Rahul what?"

"Last names are ID tags. I don't like to remember them unless really needed."

"I couldn't agree more." Feeling comfortable, she kicked off her shoes and curled her feet beneath her. "I'm Pooja."

"Pooja?" He put down his cup and stared at her. "Not Captain Vishu A'Kash's daughter?"

"The same." She leaned against the camper wall and smiled wryly. "I don't even need an ID tag, do I?"

"Forgive me." He looked embarrassed and his apology sounded sincere. "It's just that I didn't . . . I wasn't expecting to — "

"I know," she quickly interrupted. "I shouldn't be here. I should be in the Space Mission guest observatory watching the screens and cheering. That's what I should be doing. Not wandering here."

"I didn't mean that. Please don't misunderstand. I really didn't mean that." Quite agitated, he got up, then sat down again. "Have you . . . Where are you staying?"

"In a skytel. Not very far from where I disturbed — "

Not waiting for her to complete her explanation, as if whatever she had to say wasn't as important as what he had in mind, he quickly interrupted. "When did you last watch sat-V or hear the radio?"

She was surprised, not so much by the irrelevant question as by the enormous anxiety written all over his handsome face. "A couple of days ago. Why?"

"Then you don't know!"

"What?" His troubled behavior puzzled her. "What don't I know? By the way, are we doing a crossword puzzle?"

He moved across the camper and sat beside her on the edge of the seat. "You need to know and the sooner you do . . . " He got up. "I'm going to turn on my auto-V," he announced, using the common abbreviated term.

"OK," she said easily, wondering who said that priests, especially the yellow-robed kind, controlled their thoughts so well that no one could read their body language. This one, was he a fake, or was it only when he was doing his yoga that he was a priest? Maybe at other times he was just an ordinary fellow mortal being? A reverend-journalist.

Her tea was not so hot now, and it was easier to hide her giggles.

He was looking for the remote. Finding it, he sat with his finger on the 'on' button. "You see, NASA has a problem."

"NASA's always having problems."

"Not this kind. You see, they think . . . It seems the Titanic has fallen into some space hole. They can't reach it."

"So what? Papa can reach them. The Titanic has that new magnetized computer. They tested it for three days on their moon run. I know. Papa told me."

"But he hasn't."

"So what? He must be busy. He'll contact them when he needs them."

She seemed so sure, so undisturbed, that he wondered if she was so naive that she'd blindly believe anything that anyone told her. Or did she know something that no one else did?

Chief Flight Operations Officer Nikolai Poplavsky stood atop the Glavkosmos Mission Control building and glared at the Baikonur Korolev launch area. Although the most densely pigeonholed space facilities on earth, none of its pads were active today.

But Poplavsky wasn't thinking about that. He could have gotten a better view of the whole complex and all the facilities it provided in more minute detail than any one might want, one by one or altogether, on the operation center's main screen. He hadn't come here to observe that.

In fact, he hadn't come all this way to observe anything. What he needed was solitude to think. And at this time of day, this was the only place where he thought he could get it.

His hopes proved wrong.

Barely two minutes after he had reached the platform, he heard footsteps behind him. Turning, he saw Vladimir Grachenko approaching at his usual jungle tiger's loping pace.

Despite his troubled feelings, Poplavsky smiled. When not wearing the face of director of Manned Space Operations, Grachenko could be quite jovial and friendly.

Right now, however, the familiar countenance facing him looked more like the rocket-fueling mask of Lt. Gen. Leon Kostyszyn of whom he had been thinking lately.

"Can you believe," Grachenko asked without any preamble, "what our American friends are feeding the global news media?"

"You mean about the Titanic?"

"What else?" Grachenko scowled.

"I want to believe part of it."

"Part of it?"

"Yes," Poplavsky nodded, "because if I could, I could believe in my theory for the other part. And I could call Kostyszyn, and — "

"Whoa. Wait a minute." Grachenko waved a stern finger. "We are not talking to anyone in Military Intelligence. When they need us, they'll come calling soon enough. You know that. What do you want to tell them, anyway?"

"It's just a theory."

"I'd like to hear it."

"Well, if NASA is not lying, not hiding some devious plot that they haven't disclosed even to their own people," the flight operations officer said, looking at his friend and deciding he could trust him, "maybe the Titanic has jumped transfer windows, jumped allegiance, and is now flying some other flag."

The Glavkosmos manned space operations director's eyes widened. "You don't mean that. Whose?"

"Just think about it. The Titanic's co-pilot is a second generation Japanese, and the mission specialist — "

"A Chinese for untold centuries," Grachenko finished for him. "But what has that to do with anything?"

"Her captain, the much touted Vishu A'Kash, is Indo-British. Why did he change his name? To hide his British roots? That's worth pondering, especially when you remember that his wife's dear, departed father was a German, and — "

"Why's that so important?" Grachenko asked impatiently.

"The British still don't have their own space facilities. The Americans rebuffed them and refused what they wanted —

equal partnership in space operations. And because they have these strong trade ties with the European Economic Community, they've been actively — and, I mean actively — participating in the European space projects, which we know is European just in name. Essentially, what the German Space Council says goes."

"So?"

"The Titanic was built to orbit Mars. Permanently. It is capable of tricks we haven't even imagined. Suppose the Japs or the Chinese or the Europeans managed to duplicate that secret backup system and hooked it to the Titanic's wonder computer?"

"I don't believe they've got any backup system," the general said firmly. "If they had one, they'd keep it a secret, not proclaim it to the whole world. When they discover we've broken their codes, they love to play such stupid hoaxes. In the past, several times, we got hoodwinked by their devious tricks. But now we are wiser. We don't believe all their propaganda."

"But, suppose, just suppose, this time it's true. That as publicized, they do have a backup system and a secret computer on the Titanic that can access earth comm-systems independently. The Japanese have thousands of fingers in America. And the Chinese — "

"No." Grachenko shook his head vigorously. "The Chinese, despite all their claims, don't yet have that kind of expertise. The Japs have just launched their own robotic Mars-ship. The Titanic is nowhere near their glory-inebriated mind's product. But — "

"But?" the flight operations officer asked.

"I don't know why, but I've been wondering about this upstart rabble-rousers' cult, the Candle Runners. The more I try to forget it, the more it keeps popping up in my mind."

"They aren't just back-fringe outcasts any more, are they? I mean — "

"They've been gaining a lot of ground." Grachenko's weather-beaten eyes seemed to have acquired a faraway look. "I'm wondering if they could have penetrated private corporations engaged in rocket manufacturing."

"I hadn't thought about that." Poplavsky's face turned pale. "We must try to find out. The KGB would know. They must have allowed them that so well-publicized chapter here so they

could penetrate it. Kostyszyn has to know. I must call him right
away."

"No." Vladimir Grachenko's 57-year-old face looked
stubborn. "I don't trust them. You are the best operations officer
alive today. You should be able to find some other way."

"Friend Vladi, your faith in my genius is much exaggerated.
But," Nikolai Poplavsky smiled, and his chest puffed up a little,
"I never give up anything without trying. Let's go to my office."

"Comrade director, our Lop Nor warning station insists our
imperialist friends are not lying. Not this time. They've really
lost the Titanic," advised a Chinese Air Force colonel, entering
Flight Director Mao Ki Tung's office at Shuang Ch'eng-tzu
Mission Control Center.

"Isn't their judgment premature?" asked the flight director. "It
could be just a malfunction in their tangled tracking system. I
don't have to tell you, of all people, that it takes just one
computer to misbehave for their whole imperial operation to get
disjointed. That kind of repair takes time.

"So, to buy time, they're feeding the news media their
imperial lies. Haste kills. If we are hasty, when it's repaired,
we'd have to eat dirt."

In fact, he had been hoping that it wasn't a malfunction. That
the Titanic had really fallen into a hole. Black hole. White hole.
Some unknown, alien civilization's smelly, squalid, penal hole.
That didn't matter. What mattered was that NASA shouldn't
reach Mars first. That was the only thing that mattered.

"They are saying several governments, including New Delhi,
have started sending condolences to Washington. They think we
should beat the Moscow copycats and get our message there
first."

"No way." The flight director's round face turned beet red.
"Fear of some Moscow imperialists is not going to dictate to us
what to do and when. Look at our Japanese neighbors. Have
they sent their condolences? And how about those jumping
birds, what do they call themselves, the Candle Runners?"

"You are right, comrade director," the colonel replied,

impressed. "It may not be worth considering the actions of the dopey Candle Runners, but the Japs should have been the first ones, considering Titanic's co-pilot has a Hiroshima-born father."

"He is no more Japanese than you and I." The flight director smiled and put his feet up on his cluttered table. "I diligently read everyone's bio data," he smugly informed the young officer. "This lizard has renounced his parents. He doesn't believe in Buddhism or Shintoism; in family or marriage.

"He's a hardcore Yank yippee," emphasized Mao Ki Tung with relish. "No doubt that's why he was selected. They're a nation of immigrants. In their space program, every nationality participates," he tried to mimic the American accent. "That's all hogwash. We know the reality. We know the facts."

"True, comrade director," the colonel smiled and nodded. "Your analysis is always flawless. Always to the point. We all know that. But," he continued, "when you dig into it deeper, don't you think they'd be waiting to hear from us, considering their so-called mission specialist is of Chinese ancestry?"

"Bah! Humbug! as the British space operations coordinator would say." Comrade Director Mao Ki Tung moved his massive frame, seeking a more comfortable position in his executive chair. "That boot-licking bastard is more corrupt than a white or black imperialist. If I could manage it, our People's Republic would proclaim a global law for those who serve foreign governments; their westernized children wouldn't be allowed to wear the good Chinese names. Come on. Enough chatter. Let's get back to work."

"Right, comrade director." The colonel saluted and turned to go back to his station, as Mao Ki Tung closed his eyes for a well-deserved rest.

Meera A'Kash was waiting in the police station for Gopa, the daughter she could never understand.

The fault, she had always felt, was her husband's. If he hadn't spoiled Gopa, she'd have been like her twin, Pooja. An impossible thought, she knew, because Vishu A'Kash had definite rooted ideas about bringing up twins.

Soon after they were born, when he was allowed in the birthing room and his glance fell upon them, his first words were, "Holy Churchill! Identical twins! They should never be the proverbial look-alikes. They should grow up to be as different as peaches and apples."

Well, his holy wish had been granted.

Never had two sisters, born to one mother, been so dissimilar and so hostile to each other as were her two daughters. It had been to forget this misfortune, this ever-present calamity, and to distance herself as much as possible from the pain that it constantly caused her, that she had started her project, Earth Reality.

Now Vishu had gone and left her to cope alone with what he had started. And if he had really gone away forever . . .

As her eyes started filling up, she hastily looked around to make sure no one was watching her, found her handkerchief, blew her nose and buried her face in a magazine, which she tried to read though unable to comprehend a single, smudgy word. Finally, after a never-ending eternity, she heard feet approaching. Holding her breath, she looked up, but Sgt. Goodhorn was alone.

"I'm sorry, Mrs. A'Kash, but your daughter is refusing," he said as if it were his fault.

"Refusing what?"

"The bail."

"How, how can she refuse it? She has no right to do so."

"Well, she's saying she's not alone. Scores of others are with her, many of them injured and not getting proper medical care. Either you bail out everybody or nobody."

"That's ridiculous. I don't have that kind of money."

"I took the liberty of mentioning that," Goodhorn sounded apologetic. "Her answer was, you don't need money. All you need to do is to call your friends in NASA."

"Why should NASA care?"

Goodhorn simply stood his ground.

"Sergeant, do you know something? Do these kids belong to that cult, the Candle Runners?"

"Perhaps some do, ma'am. But they don't hate NASA. Not really. I hope NASA knows that."

"I've never taken advantage of my husband's position," Meera A'Kash protested. "And this thoughtless protest of theirs had nothing to do with any space activity. NASA wasn't involved. I cannot call them, hear them refuse and let them laugh at me."

It was not clear if the sergeant had a reply. If he did, he didn't get a chance to voice it because just then the street side door opened and a bevy of reporters wielding mikes and cameras crowded in.

Meera felt scared. Those determined faces clearly said they'd get what they wanted. At any cost. No one would be able to push them back.

She saw a couple of equally determined officers detach themselves from the duty station and walk toward the newcomers. There would be a confrontation. If she didn't decide quickly . . .

Trying to hide her face behind the magazine she was still holding, she moved quickly. "Sergeant," she asked in a muffled voice, "can I use the phone in your office?"

"Sure, ma'am. This way." Goodhorn led her, trying to shield her by his massive body. The reporters, too busy arguing with the duty officers, didn't notice a police-escorted woman disappearing behind a side door.

The lights were dim in the rooftop revolving restaurant to better allow the guests to enjoy the crimson panorama, resembling a glowing Mars landscape, gliding all around them.

Situated on the hundred-and-fiftieth floor of the newest ITT Sheraton, Washington's latest architectural pride was built to resemble the most exotic Martian restaurant one could imagine.

Looking through its transparent walls, one did not see the uneven city skyline enveloped by dense smog. One did not see dying flowers and dirty waterfalls. One saw a bewitching panorama, colorful and alive, as only an imaginative planet can be.

Stryker, however, had not chosen this restaurant to enjoy the capitol's number one tourist attraction. The State Department had told him to meet with the consul general of Mexico, Pablo Martinez. And he was to make sure it wouldn't look like an official visit. Not an easy job where the honorable Pablo Martinez was concerned.

Worse, the whole visit would be a waste if his guest wasn't in a good mood.

From his past experience, Stryker knew that if anything could open up the Mexican consul general's mind it was the Martian tequila served in the Coromandal Bar. So, here he was.

And Martinez hadn't failed him. Dutifully devoting a few minutes to enjoying the evening lights popping up around them in the robotics frontier land, he had concentrated on consuming his favorite drink and reciting with gusto his favorite *masculine* jokes. Finally, they had ordered dinner.

Stryker hadn't bothered to look at the menu. He had cajoled Martinez into choosing for both of them. If this maneuver enhanced the Mexican's ego, he had thought, that would be additional help.

As the waiter collected the menus, bowed and moved away, Martinez caressed his goblet, leaned back and softly asked, "Stan, my friend, how goes Titanic?"

Stryker was taken aback. He had expected questions, but not such a direct, straightforward inquiry. Not from the ever circling, ever polite Pablo Martinez.

He had agonized over this meeting, had cursed the White House, the State Department, the CIA and FBI. He had no reason to do their job for them. They had no right to burden him with it. They had all those slick, oiled, well-heeled special agents. What were they all doing while he was sitting here on thorns and needles?

Pablo Martinez was a diplomat, representing his country's interests. And in his official capacity he had to do and say what was required, but, in his personal capacity, he was a friend — an old friend.

And in his eternally crowded life, where the general had to often offer plausible platitudes to the unbelieving press and to equally, or even more bellicose congressmen and senators, Stanley Stryker had never double-talked with a friend. Never taken advantage of a friend.

Now, hearing the unexpected question, he was startled, but his military training came to his rescue. His face didn't give him away. Twirling his wine glass with his fingers, he smiled. "Please, no Titanic. I'm sure you watched me on your sat-V, giving the story to the news media. Not just once, but several times."

"The official story, yes," the Mexican diplomat drawled. "Now, what about the real story?"

"You surprise me. You think I lied to them?"

"Not lied," said the poker eyes. "Gave them the facts as you knew 'em then. But in the space operations business, facts change every microsecond. Amigo, what are the facts now?"

The Space Defense Command chief stared at his wine as if the answer were hidden there, then looked up. "Can I be frank with you, Pablo? Can you keep it a secret, even from your government?"

"Does that need to be said!"

"Of course not. But these are trying times, my friend. It doesn't hurt to reassure oneself."

"Of course." The Mexican consul general smiled blandly and Gen. Stryker knew the FBI and CIA would get their wish. Pablo would call his government as soon as he reached home.

"Well, you see, I trust you," he said in his most friendly manner, "and I needed to unload myself, that's why I — "

"Invited me to dinner?" Pablo nodded. "Of course. We are friends, are we not? Whenever I've faced such a situation, haven't I unburdened myself to you?"

Stryker nodded, "You're right. I'll tell you what I think. I think they don't know what they are talking about. I don't think the Titanic has fallen in any hole, black or white."

Pablo's round eyes bulged. "Why?"

Before Stryker could reply, the waiters arrived and started placing before them steaming bowls of duck-mushroom soup, pineapple daiquiri salad, and a basket of assorted Italian breads and bread sticks.

Stryker waited until they left. Seeing Pablo attack his soup with unfeigned relish, he felt reassured and picked up where he had stopped. "The Titanic, as you know, has a built-in, fail-safe com-system. If for some reason, any reason, our ground computers fail to access it, it can activate our backup computer unit designed specially for that purpose."

"Even from the depths of a black hole?"

"There was no black hole in its trajectory."

"So, why is it not communicating?"

"What do you think?"

"You tell me."

"You know how hard we tried to make it a joint mission with the Soviet Alliance? You know that, don't you?"

At your terms, the Mexican diplomat silently told himself. But, without saying anything, he simply nodded his head.

"The Japanese also wouldn't cooperate. They wanted to conquer Mars on their own terms."

"If the Titanic has been gobbled by a black hole, they may," Pablo stated matter-of-factly. "I watched the news on my way over here. Their Hiroshima Hoku, loaded with their miracle robos, is performing flawlessly."

"That was one of the reasons," Stryker went on, "our crew and specialists were chosen from our immigrant citizens: a third-generation, Indo-British captain; a second-generation, Japanese co-pilot; a Chinese mission specialist."

"I know," Pablo interrupted. "Like everyone else, I went through the list noting everyone's heredity and background."

Pablo Martinez was feeling sorry for his friend. He was glad he didn't have to wrestle with those kinds of problems. And secretly, he had always admired NASA's efforts over all the other space-venturing nations'.

It was with genuine honesty that he said, "I thought NASA did an excellent job. No major nationality was left out. Even the cults are represented by a Candle Runner. So all the people in the various countries can feel affinity and take pride in Titanic's glory and achievements."

Just then the waiters came back to clear the table and place before them the dishes Pablo had ordered — curried chicken and shrimp with grapes, lobster baked potatoes, almond stuffed prawns, foie gras with Balsamic vinegar and Kashmiri pulao.

The aroma of the spices quickened Pablo's appetite. Digging into his chicken, he said as if there had been no interruption, "If that wasn't done, many ethnic groups may have felt left out. This way, we can really say it's a step for the whole of mankind."

"So, instead of feeling proud of this unique achievement, why are you worrying about it?"

The waiters' efficient and time-consuming efforts had given Stryker enough time to rearrange and collect his thoughts. He spoke slowly, stressing the 'what ifs.'

"What if that attempt, making this flight truly international, has backfired? What if, unknown to us, secretly, one of our team members is more loyal to the land of his ancient blood than to his adopted land?"

"Meaning? What can one do in space?"

"Hijack the spaceship. Attach it to another nation's system."

The Mexican consul general stared at NASA's spokesman. He had expected some gobbledygook that they anticipated he would transmit to his government. But this didn't sound like official nonsense. It couldn't be . . . Was his friend really secretly worried? Was that why he had really called him, to make him a sounding board for his ideas — because no one in NASA would listen to him, or believe him?

"Sounds incredible, doesn't it?" Stryker asked.

"But how? For chris'sake, it's a spaceship. One person can't run a whole spaceship."

"No," Stryker agreed, "but it takes only one person to hijack a ship. Any ship. And the ship's doctor . . . I've heard Candle Runners are capable of inducing mass hypnotism."

Pablo Martinez watched his friend drive his fork into the delicate aromatic prawns, then, without lifting it from the plate, change his mind. The general obviously couldn't take his mind away from his gathering problems to enjoy his meal.

Feeling worse, Martinez put down his fork. His mouth felt dry, and suddenly his appetite was also gone. "What are you trying to tell me, amigo?" he asked. "That a spaceship can be

hijacked? That it can fool, outmaneuver, the ground controls?
That — "

"Not an ordinary spaceship. But perhaps the Titanic can."

"Perhaps?"

"In a way it's a test-run, isn't it?"

"Wasn't that a test-run when it orbited the moon for three full
days?" Pablo asked, almost defiantly.

"Of course it was. But no one suspected it of anything. The
kind of specialists it took on board, they have minds and
capabilities of which we may not have full knowledge. As to
land assistance, the Japanese and Soviet spaceships are just
ahead of it. It can tie itself to either one of them."

"You have a point," Pablo admitted. He carefully placed his
fork and knife together and beckoned the hovering waiter.
"Coffee?" he asked his host. Stryker nodded. The waiter
motioned to his assistant to clear the table and hastened away.

Pablo looked out at the revolving landscape, alive with its
real-looking creatures silently moving past them. When the
waiter brought the steaming cups of Columbian coffee, its aroma
seemed to bring the Mexican back to the real world.

"So," he asked, "what do you propose to do about it?"

Stryker was measuring two spoons of cream into his coffee.

He didn't reply.

Pablo decided to stop feeling sorry for his friend and dug into
his own mind for some concrete suggestion. "Why not ask
them?"

"Ask who?" Stryker spoke as if he were ready to wash his
hands of the whole thing.

"Whoever you are suspecting — the Soviets, the Japanese."

"Can't do that. You know that."

"No, I don't know that. Why? Why can't you ask them?"

"First, if any one of them is involved, they won't admit it
until the Titanic reaches Mars. And secondly — "

"Yes?" Pablo asked.

"If our theory is wrong, if none of them is responsible and
something has really happened to the Titanic, then any such
inquiry could — would — be considered an accusation. It could
— would — lead to all sorts of misunderstandings, threats."

"I hadn't thought of that," Pablo nodded, agreeing.

Stryker glanced at him thoughtfully. "I was thinking maybe you can help."

The Mexican consul general had expected that all along. So finally, it was here. The real purpose of this dinner. He braced himself. "How?"

"It's just an idea. Just something I thought might give me a peg to move on. You don't have to accept it."

"I know that," Pablo said, but he thought, lies, amigo. What lies you're capable of. If I don't accept it, tomorrow what would happen to our pending trade treaty negotiations and to that aid we're hoping to get for that stalled spaceport?

"What I was thinking is this," Stryker said slowly, measuring each word. "Your country's ambassador to Moscow? He is your brother-in-law, is he not?"

Pablo nodded.

"I've heard how charming he is. And how influential. The Russians really like him."

"He brags a lot, but most of it's true."

Stryker glanced at his longtime friend and thought how lucky he was to have chosen the military for his career. He'd never have succeeded as a diplomat. The kind of pressures it imposed, the compulsions, the impositions that it required, would have driven him crazy overnight.

"Could you," he asked, "mind you, not in your official capacity, but as a favor to me," he paused, stressing the word *favor*, "could you ask him to make some off-the-cuff, discreet inquiries?"

Pablo Martinez didn't respond.

Looking at Pablo staring into his coffee, Stryker cursed himself for accepting this job. But he had to do it. He continued, "You know what's always said: The KGB treads fearlessly where even air fears to enter. If someone has done some mischief, I bet the KGB knows. And socializing . . . one drink too many . . . someone in Moscow would be willing to talk."

"I'm not so sure of that. And I don't think the KGB is so omnipotent. But, supposing my brother-in-law can dig up some facts about the Russians. That would still leave the Japanese and the Europeans. And your ship's doctor's brothers-in-arms, the Candle Runners."

"I have a feeling — call it a hunch — if anyone of them has done something, the KGB would know."

"Maybe. But one thing's for sure. They won't know if the Candle Runners are somehow involved."

For that I have a possible source, Stryker silently thought. *Our missing captain's, Vishu A'Kash's, wife. The so innocent-looking Meera A'Kash. The one who claims to hate politics but creates a global network called Earth Reality.*

To Pablo, he said nothing.

Pablo Martinez was gazing outside at a moving tableau of Martian settlers hunting Shegotas, a kind of desert sheep-goat sporting a camel's hump, developed recently by the Japanese through genetic engineering for their protégé, the Egyptians.

"I wonder," he said softly, as if to himself, "I wonder, facing this situation, what Ray Bradbury would have done."

"Pardon?"

"Ray Bradbury." Looking at his host's startled face, Pablo smiled, "The science fiction wizard. The one who created real live, twentieth-century Martians. You ever read him?"

"Sure. When I was growing up."

"Since I can remember, he has been my mentor. My guru. Any time I face a ticklish situation, I try to look at it through his visionary eyes, and — "

"And?" Stryker asked, really curious.

"I find a superb solution. For example, this restaurant."

"What about it?"

"One day its owner sat down and wondered, if Ray Bradbury wanted to own a restaurant, what would it look like. Presto! Washington got the first revolving Martian restaurant."

"You own this restaurant?"

"With my wife and my brother-in-law. You see, he and I were pals before my sister hooked him. He introduced me to . . . "

"And you've just reintroduced me. Tonight I'll curl up with a couple of Bradbury's mind-sizzling masterpieces."

"And I'll call Oscar. Between the four of us — "

"Four?"

"Three of us and Ray Bradbury. We'll figure out a way to beat the KGB at their own game."

Feeling relieved, Stryker looked through the clear glass wall; after a ravishing, mind-grappling chase, the robo-hunter had hooked his prey; his spiked arrow had pierced the robo-Shegota's water-loaded hump.

3

No. Not My Child.
No Way

In the police station, at the fringe of the swarming pack of ragged students chatting and laughing and pushing and shoving while awaiting to collect their personal items from the duty officer's desk, Meera A'Kash felt like an alien. Some of the students were very tall, and she was craning her neck to look for her daughter, Gopa, who hadn't come out yet.

Always first, she was thinking, when the trouble is about to begin. And always last when someone is trying to sort out the grisly, messy situation.

She felt somewhat relieved as the outer door opened and Col. Oringer walked in. At their first meeting, he had made a mark upon her troubled tenacity. He had felt like someone whom she could trust and lean upon.

Forcing a smile to her face, she moved toward him, but before she could reach him, she saw him getting waylaid by her self-appointed guardian, good old Sgt. Goodhorn. "Colonel, sir, can I have a word with you, sir?"

"Of course, sergeant."

Meera A'Kash hesitated. Should she join them or not?

Goodhorn moved toward her with the colonel just behind him. "Ma'am, would you please excuse us for a couple of minutes?"

"Of course, sergeant. Looking at these kids, it seems to me I'll be here all day anyway."

"I know, ma'am. It feels that way. But we'll be through soon. Believe me."

She smiled. "I believe you."

Goodhorn led the colonel to an inner office and indicated a chair. Ignoring it, Oringer moved to the only window in the room. "Well, sergeant, what's on your mind?"

"Sir, during routine investigation, I learned something. I can't figure out if it's important or not. And if it is, should I tell Mrs. A'Kash or not."

"Is that so? What's the problem?"

"You see, just before her heart attack, Mrs. Heinrich had a phone call. In fact, it could be that's what brought on . . . "

"How do you know that?" Oringer asked quickly.

"A neighbor was visiting Mrs. Heinrich."

"The same one who called 911?"

Goodhorn nodded. "Mrs. Heinrich's arthritis was acting up, so the neighbor picked up the phone for her. She said that Mrs. Heinrich said hello, looked surprised at what was said at the other end, listened a couple of minutes, then shouted, 'No, not my daughter. No way,' and collapsed."

"And since she hasn't regained consciousness, we don't know who that caller was?"

"We traced the call. It originated in Titusville. But it was made from a phone booth."

"And Meera A'Kash lives in Titusville. And she is Mrs. Heinrich's only daughter," Oringer said softly, thoughtfully gazing out the small window.

Sgt. Goodhorn knew the comments were not directed at him. He simply waited.

Finally, Oringer turned. "What could Meera A'Kash have done that was so shocking? From all that I've read about her in our files, she seems like an exemplary woman. Only the other day I was saying to my assistant that they don't make daughters like her anymore."

"That's what the neighbor was telling me. That's why she kept repeating that remark to me. At her suggestion, we got a court order and searched through Mrs. Heinrich's papers.

"That was before Mrs. A'Kash arrived," the sergeant explained. "We looked and looked, but we couldn't find any reference to any other daughter, adopted or surrogate."

"Hmmm."

"I noticed another thing. Mrs. A'Kash's middle initial is M, but nowhere could I find what the initial stands for."

"How's that important?"

"I don't know. It just seemed peculiar, that's all. True, people don't always use their full middle name. But in documents, it's generally spelled out. In her case, it was omitted even on her wedding certificate."

"Could be just one of those quirks. Some people act funny about their names. Look at her husband. How he changed his."

"I read somewhere about that," Goodhorn nodded. "Gave up his father's name and invented one for himself."

"The height of creativity, isn't it?" Oringer smiled. "Well sergeant, let me think about it. Meanwhile, let's move. Mrs. A'Kash must be getting very impatient."

"Yes, sir. Right, sir."

Gopa A'Kash had finally reached the sergeant who was handing out the students' belongings. Meera first noticed her daughter's clipped, boyish-looking hair. Then the purple T-shirt, bearing slogans in big, bold, black letters, and patched blue jeans, which were more white than blue and frayed at the knees.

Next to her stood her famous companion, Sharky, an unkempt, bearded man, his muscled arms and feet covered with multicolored tattoos of butterflies and killing sharks. As always, Meera couldn't decide which was her stronger reaction —

disgust or frustration.

She remembered when they had first received Sharky's photo from Gopa. She had thrown it at her husband. "Look at that! Why don't you do something about it? Next thing we know, she'll have her whole body splotched."

Throwing the photo in the wastepaper basket, he had laughed. "Don't worry. She won't."

"No?" she had stormed. "When I called her, she gave me a long lecture. 'Mothhher! You don't know anything. Tattoos are the earliest known art forms. All the ancient cultures — Mesopotamians, Egyptians, American Indians, Chinese, Japanese — all of them love them. Really, mom, they're safer than getting your nose fixed. Specially since the '80s when the first electric tattoo machine was invented by that genius, Samuel F.O. Reilly. You check it out. Everyone gets them — military men, politicians, actors — '"

"All true." Wanting to close the argument, Vishu had interrupted. "But your daughter won't have them. Take my word."

"What makes you so sure?"

"A tattoo, for most people who get them, is a kind of psychic crutch to inspire hope, to repair a crippled image, to keep noxious emotions at bay or to reduce the gap between their hidden self and their cravings. For some, it's a kind of pictorial quest for self-definition, to ease their sense of inadequacy and isolation. It offers them a clarified picture of their diffused ego, giving them a tangible promise of their perceived identity. Some people have deep feelings they can't articulate. So they do it graphically. Pictorially.

"Your daughter is a very vocal person with healthy emotions. She doesn't need symbolic crutches. You should know that."

Maybe he was right, but Meera A'Kash had lain awake many nights wondering what she'd do if her vagrant daughter disfigured her young body with those ugly permanent marks.

Noticing Gopa's place in line, Meera moved toward her, but Gopa saw no need to wait for her picky mother. Grabbing her purse and umbrella, she hooked her hand in the tattooed man's elbow and waved. "Bye, mom."

"What do you mean, *bye*? You're coming with me."

"Nope. We have things to decide. It doesn't end here. It's just the beginning."

"Not for you, dear. You're coming with me."

"Don't be stupid, mom! Try to understand. The politicians must be rescued from the clutches of their dreadful reality. You can't confront them because you grew up with them. But, we — "

"Now listen, young lady — "

"Don't 'young lady' me, mom! I'm not Pooja. Come on, Sharky. Let's go."

Sam Oringer had returned. Feeling his presence, Meera controlled her temper with an effort. "Wait, Gopa! Listen. Until your papa returns, you must stay with me."

"Nope. If papa wanted that, he'd have told me. I'm to stay with granma."

"She's in the hospital."

"I know. I was told. Until she's released, I'll stay with friends. Come on, Sharky. Let's go. It's getting late." Without giving Meera a second look, they moved briskly away, hand in hand, and didn't look back.

"Children!" said Sam Oringer, looking everywhere except at Meera A'Kash. "Can I drop you somewhere, Mrs. A'Kash?"

"Colonel, I'm very grateful to you for all your help," she replied, looking for something in her purse. In reality, she was buying time until she could regain her composure. "I don't have words to thank you. Really, I don't." She looked up and smiled at him. "It was nice of you to bail them out. I hadn't expected such a quick response."

"Well, it was just a coincidence that I was here visiting a friend. When they got your call, they left a message at my hotel. And, knowing how important it was to you — "

"You dropped everything and rushed over. I really do appreciate it."

"Only doing my duty, Mrs. A'Kash. Shall we go?"

She glanced at the now empty room and seemed to sigh, "Why not." Turning and walking beside him, she glanced up. "If you're staying a while longer, I'd like to invite you for dinner. You and your friend."

"I'll ask her. You sure I can't drop you somewhere?"

"Well, I was going to visit my mother. If it's not out of your way."

"Not at all. Which hospital is it?"

"That new one. Coronary Care."

"Good. It's on my way. In fact, I'd like to come with you and pay my respects to your mother."

"She's in no condition to receive visitors."

"That's OK. We were here a long time. She may have improved. The doctor may allow a brief visit."

"Let's hope so." Meera A'Kash moved toward where he was holding the auto door open for her and got inside. Closing it, he took the driver's seat. The air-auto moved swiftly on pillars of air, not touching the road.

Gen. Stryker was jogging alone on the secluded beach when another man overtook him. Without changing his pace, Stryker glanced at him. "Hi, Herb. What's the latest?"

The FBI director spotted a lonely looking bench at the rim of the rising tide. His mind imagined his toes digging into the sand under it. His tired feet seemed to yearn for it. He indicated it with a long finger. "Shall we sit?"

"Why not."

They moved toward it. "Since last we talked," Herb Caine said, "we haven't made much progress. As you know, our man disappeared from Barcelona about seven months ago. His credit card charges indicate he went to Bonn, Germany, but he stayed there only a couple of days. Then he flew to Bombay and from there to New Delhi. And there, his trail disappears."

"Why? American credit cards are accepted all over India."

"He transferred his account to a New Delhi bank and cashed almost half of it. Since then, no withdrawals have been made; his credit card hasn't been used."

"And his mail?" Stryker asked.

"Collecting at a box number at a New Delhi post office."

"Well? Why not go through it? It may provide a clue."

"We can't." The FBI director kicked the sand angrily with his jogging boot.

"Why not?"

"He had dual citizenship. The Indian government is very strict about any foreign intervention in — "

"Their citizens' rights." Stryker completed the statement for him. "When it suits them, right?"

Herbert Caine furiously kicked the sand again.

"So? Why not let the CIA or state department go to their counterpart in India, whatever they call them there?"

"That would mean letting them know we suspect him. About the Indian intelligence boys, I don't care, but — "

"But?" Stryker asked impatiently.

"Our news media would learn about it."

"So? You have to tell them anyway. You can't let him lie in the hospital as John Q."

"We have to."

"You can't do that." Stryker looked horrified. "He's lying in a general ward like a pariah. He — "

"He's a bachelor, remember? There is no record anywhere of his having an illegitimate daughter, or an adopted one. Where and when did he acquire this mysterious daughter? Why did no one — absolutely no one — know about it?" Caine asked.

He couldn't remain seated any more. Stretching to his full height, Caine started pacing back and forth, back and forth. "Why did he quit his research so suddenly, without any reason, without saying anything to anyone?"

"Why did he transfer his residency to India?" The FBI man glared at Stryker, as if he suspected it had been done on his orders. "Come to think of it, why did he maintain dual citizenship? Why did he so cleverly cover his tracks? Why did he go to Germany? Was he working for the Gestapo? Where was he for the past five months, until the day he turned up on our street, knocked out by an unknown . . . "

"I can also think of lots of questions." Stryker glared at Caine angrily. "That doesn't mean we can let him lie in a public ward, like an indigent homeless beggar. Just now you spoke of India's pride in their citizens. Don't we have any, especially for a citizen who was one of our most precious scientists. Who was — "

"Not was . . . is," Caine reminded him, planting his feet near Stryker's. "I know how you're feeling because I'm feeling the same. No. Even worse. Because it has to be my decision. But until we find out about this daughter — until we learn why he thought she'd kill him — and if it was she who tried to kill him . . . "

Stryker couldn't remain seated either. He took off his shoes, waded into the edge of the water and came back with the invading tide. "I think you're making a mistake."

"Why?"

"You're underestimating our press. They can probe and reach where your special agents can't even — "

"I won't deny that." Caine slumped back down on the bench. "But I can't take that risk. If he's a foreign agent, if the Titanic has fallen prey to a conspiracy, his accident, so soon after its disappearance, may not be a coincidence. By the way, have you heard from your friend, the resourceful Pablo Martinez?"

Stryker ignored the question. "So you won't let me identify him?"

"Not yet, general."

"And what if someone else recognizes him, as I did?"

The FBI director stared at him. "You're right. We must move him. Right away." He turned quickly and started jogging back in the direction from which he'd come.

"And make sure the press doesn't learn about it." Feeling helpless, angry and frustrated, Stryker shouted at his back, "Because if they do, they'll chew you alive."

Herbert Caine heard but didn't look back. Raising one hand, he waved and increased his pace.

Just then the phone in Stryker's pocket beeped. He took it out and turned it on. "Stryker."

"General?" It was Sam Oringer. "Can you find a doctor for me? A lady doctor? And quickly?"

"Tall order, Sam. I can try. Why?"

"I'm calling from the hospital. I'll explain later. How long will it take, sir?"

Stryker wondered what kind of an illness Sam Oringer had that needed the immediate services of a lady doctor, but he stifled his curiosity. "I'll go straight to my office and make a few calls. Today's Saturday, you know?"

"I know, sir. Can I call you back about five?"

"You got into an accident or something, colonel?"

"No, sir." In the phone booth, Oringer impatiently glanced at his wrist watch. "Got to go now. Thank you, general. I'll be in touch." The phone at his end clicked off.

Stryker stared at the small unit in his hand, then, pushing it back into his pocket, he looked longingly at the sparkling ocean, sighed and started putting on his shoes.

Vladimir Grachenko, Director of Soviet Manned Space Operations, never liked to visit with anyone in Military Intelligence, and Lt. Gen. Leon Kostyszyn topped that list. But protocol demanded politeness. And that's what he was trying to do right now. Be polite.

"But, comrade lieutenant general," he was saying, "I don't understand. Why should you worry about an old, retired, to all accounts, half-crazy — "

"Suppose he's not retired," Kostyszyn snapped. "Suppose we've been fed lot of propaganda? He was engaged in very sensitive, secret research in Barcelona. We know that. Germany has very close ties with Spain. We know that. Suppose, he was — is — a double agent. Suppose the Japanese robo-ship has roped in the Titanic. For almost a year now, Bonn and Tokyo have been exchanging delegations, but their trade negotiations aren't getting anywhere. We know that. Suppose, they aren't trade — "

"Aren't we making lots of assumptions, comrade?"

"No. We are not," Kostyszyn snapped. "The university claims he disappeared without telling them. As far as they are concerned, he died long ago. Follows, they're not paying his salary. Who is? He wasn't a rich man. How has he managed all his expenses for the past seven months? From Barcelona, he went to Stuttgart. From there to Tubingen. On to Bombay and New Delhi. There, someone remembered credit cards are traceable. Who's paying him all that cash? As soon as the

Titanic disappeared, someone knocked him off. Who? The Japanese? The Germans? Our friends, the so-perfect Indians."

"There was that note in his pocket about his daughter's intention to kill him," said Grachenko, squelching his anger. No sense in locking horns with this bull, he decided. It would lengthen this brief meeting.

"And you believed that?" Kostyszyn's laughter sounded very harsh in Grachenko's impatient ears. Harsh and mirthless and cruel. Was he born like that, he wondered, or was it his position that had made him such an insufferable person?

"How many such false notes are planted all the time?" Kostyszyn was sneering maliciously. "You don't know."

No, I don't know, Grachenko thought silently. But I don't work in your department, do I? Do your own dirty work. Don't drag me in. I'm not interested, and I don't have time.

"Well," he said pushing his chair back, "I'm sure you'll soon find out. Now, if you'll excuse me.

"Wait," the lieutenant general commanded, "I didn't call you here to give you this inside information."

"Then why did you call me?"

"Orders from General Kikilo himself. He said that I must ask you to do two things. First, work on Volga's computers. Make them talk with Hiroshima Hoku — "

"That's impossible!" Grachenko sputtered with anger. "Our spaceship was not designed to spy on another."

Kostyszyn smiled. "General Kikilo doesn't believe in the word *impossible*." You know that. Secondly, Volga Two must be launched within — "

"Volga Two isn't ready. And until Volga reaches Mars — "

"Comrade director," Kostyszyn said with a nasty sneer, "I'm not in the habit of questioning my general's orders. He wants Volga Two to overtake Hiroshima. Mars is still way off. Before they reach it, Volga Two must cancel Hiroshima's tractor signals and take over the Titanic for the glory of our motherland."

"And suppose Hiroshima Hoku has nothing to do with the Titanic's disappearance?"

"Then Volga Two will be the first manned orbital ship, won't it?" Kostyszyn said with a hungry lion's look lurking in his beady, grey eyes.

Lt. Col. James Miskovitz looked at his broken image in the lobby's cracked mirror: unpolished shoes; faded blue jeans, frayed severely below the knees; clean, but unironed, shirt, with a frayed collar; carelessly shaven face and uncombed hair.

He felt funny. Even in his college days, he had never dressed like this. But duty was duty. And, who knows, it might be some fun. Besides, it'd be more than worth it if it gave him a chance to briefly know one of the celebrated twins. He moved to the door and rang the bell.

"Come in," a thin, shrill voice shouted from inside. "It's open."

Cracking the door, he saw a littered room and a thin, freckled girl, with large, horn-rimmed glasses, sitting behind a littered desk. "Well?" she asked.

He hesitated. "I want to join your organization." He said the first words that came to his mind.

"Why?"

Before he could answer, he was saved by a tornado of storming feet. *Freckles* jumped up, "They let you go. We won!"

"No, we didn't," a man's angry voice behind him blared. Turning, Miskovitz looked at him and thought that, despite his murky tattoos, with a bath and shave and clean shirt, the speaker could look quite handsome.

"They let us go," he complained loudly through his scraggly beard, as if he wanted not just the beings in this room, but the whole world to hear, "because it was very embarrassing to have the world's topmost hero's favorite daughter in detention."

"No. That's not true and you know it," the young girl beside him shouted. "What's the matter with you?"

Her photographs don't do her justice, Miskovitz thought. She is so much prettier. If only her golden hair weren't so closely cropped — even shorter than many boys'. And if, like all these other geeks, she wasn't wearing that stupid, purple T-shirt, proclaiming in such ghostly words, 'Earth is for humans, not for robots'.

"I had to coerce the fucking police officers," she was shouting. "I had to blackmail my mom — "

"OK, OK, cool it!" the horn-rimmed girl shouted. "Don't you know Sharky? Don't you know he likes pulling your legs? Both of 'em."

They all laughed. Taking advantage of that, the horn-rimmed girl gave a small push to Miskovitz. "Here. He wants to join us."

"Why?"

"How would I know, Gopa? You're the membership director. You expect me to — "

"No, I don't," Gopa A'Kash snapped, then turned toward him. "Come. We'll talk in my office."

Following her, Miskovitz entered a small windowless room, containing a table that left very little room for the two rickety chairs. Gopa took one and gestured him to the other. In the same motion, picking up a pen, she pulled a yellow pad toward her. "Your name?"

"James Miskovitz." He spoke solemnly, not revealing any sign of the smile that wanted to burst out at her very official manner and demeanor.

"High school dropout?"

"I did join college," he hesitated, "but . . . "

"Why do you want to join our group?"

"Isn't your cause worth joining?"

She put down her pen, leaned back against her chair and steepled her fingers. "Perhaps it is. Perhaps it is not. What's your niche?"

"Niche?"

"Your pet concerns? What do you believe in?"

"Well . . . " He again hesitated. Sam Oringer had done him a major injustice. He should have prepared him for this interview.

"None," she scribbled on her yellow pad. "I knew that. At first glance, I knew that. What can you do?"

"Well . . . " His face started turning red; this was really embarrassing.

But Gopa wasn't looking at him. Scribbling on the pad, she asked, "Are you a worker? An organizer? An administrator?"

"I guess, I could . . . could do anything you want me to do."

"One of those." She laughed, a sweet, tinkling laugh. "OK, you just stick by me until we find your niche."

Relieved, he smiled. "I'd like to buy a T-shirt. One that says 'Even animals don't have barriers — black and white horses race together.' Where can I get it?"

She sighed. "We can't use 'em anymore."

"Why?"

"Price of our freedom. They banned them. Banned the name of our organization."

"Sorry to hear that. I loved that name — EBCO — Earth Barrier Crashers Organization."

"I coined it." Her lovely aquamarine eyes sparkled with pride. "Since this morning, since we agreed to give it up, I've been thinking of a new name. How about, EESO, Earth's Egg Savers Organization?"

"Egg Savers?" he sounded dubious.

"Well, you see, everything germinates from the . . . sort of an egg, and if we can . . . No, that doesn't sound right."

He nodded and she continued. "ERO, Earth Reality Organization, would have been perfect. But my mom got hold of it first."

"She doesn't have a monopoly on it. With your persuasive powers," he looked at her encouragingly, "you could even persuade her to share it with you."

"Naw. I couldn't do that. Not as long as mom remains at the helm."

"Why?"

"Well, she's kinda . . . kinda . . . she's funny. My joining won't do a thing because as long as she keeps her meddling fingers there, her Earth Realty will suffer from arterial fibrillation."

"Excuse me?"

"My papa wants me to be a doctor, a spaceship doctor," she said proudly. "He explained once that every organization has a heart. It may be a strong heart. A corroding heart. A malevolent heart. Whatever kind it is, it delineates . . . it . . . it stamps its work. Mom's Earth Reality suffers from arterial fibrillation; its heart beats strongly, but erratically."

"Well? Why don't you offer to be the doctor, and fix it?"

"I could. I would have, specially after papa left. But under the new circumstances, I don't think it'd be possible."

"What circumstances? We'll find the Titanic; it's just a question of time."

"Oh, I wasn't thinking of the Titanic. I meant other . . . other circumstances."

At this first meeting, he thought, I can't ask "what circumstances." He said supportively, "No matter what, I believe in one thing — and, I'm sure you do, too. No matter what they are, circumstances can be conquered."

"Not these ones." She threw a defiant glance at him. "You see, I got myself pregnant."

He was surprised. "I didn't know you were married."

"I'm not. You know Commander Kodama? It's his baby."

"Commander Kodama?" Miskovitz asked. Understanding dawned in his eyes. "Oh, the Titanic's co-pilot. What's wrong with that? Your mom will understand that."

"No. She won't. You see, I didn't know him. Met him only once." She lowered her eyes. Her glowing face suddenly looked very sad.

What happened? he wanted to ask. Did he force himself upon you? The question was so crude, so personal, he couldn't voice it.

She raised her face. "Once, when he came to see papa, I was in our backyard, decorating the swing with roses and water lilies for the cookout party. He came and stood looking at me. I sat down on the half-decorated swing and asked him if he could give it a little push. He sat down near me and kicked the earth with his toes . . . He has very long legs, you see. So un-Japanese.

"Anyway, he started to talk — how he's the only child, how if something happened and he didn't come back his family's name would vanish from this earth and what that would do to its history, and to his father and mother."

"But that's not what his bio says." Miskovitz objected. "He doesn't believe in family. When he took American citizenship, he even renounced his parents. He doesn't believe in anything, not even religion. He is more American than all Americans.

He — "

Gopa interrupted him, afraid that if she didn't, he'd just go on and on and would never stop. "That was only so his family would let him go. If he hadn't, they wouldn't have allowed him to go on this mission. Listening to him, I felt so bad, I said, 'Commander, let me have the honor of giving you a child. I know you'll come back, but if you don't, our child will continue your family name.'"

"And he agreed?"

"Why shouldn't he have?" she asked angrily. "It was a fair offer. Without any ties, any commitment. I was a virgin, so his parents would have no objection to the child's bearing the family name."

Miskovitz stared at her. What had motivated her? Pity? Fears generated by her father's imminent departure? Dreams of publicity . . . and Cmdr. Kodama! Such depraved lies! Forgetting all ethics, he had taken advantage of a gullible teenager's sentiments. Scoundrel. If James ever found him . . .

"I haven't told my mom yet. I can see her face when she hears it. 'Gopa,' she'll scream in that mocking tone of hers. She loves to scream, you know. 'Gopa,' she'll scream. 'How could you! You didn't love him. You didn't even know him. How could you! Just see somebody, and like an alley cat . . . Pooja would never have done it, even if he had forced himself upon her. I wonder if you're really my daughter. Because a daughter of mine could never do such a thing, never. No. Not my daughter.'"

Gopa's expression had been changing and her eyes had been filling up. Unable to continue, she put her head on the table and buried it between both her hands. She began to sob softly, but her whole body heaved.

James Miskovitz, the ever resourceful lieutenant colonel, renowned in NASA and SDC for his quick wits, didn't know what to do. What to do with his eyes. What to do with his hands.

Then, as if galvanized by some strange inner force, he moved around the desk, picked her up and sat down with her in his lap, gently dabbing a long finger at her tears.

She didn't resist. Sobbing intermittently, she lay inert in his arms. Holding her so close, feeling breathless by her touch, by her soft, cool fragrance, feeling strangely emotional, as he had never felt before, he gently touched her golden hair with his lips. She felt shay and hid her face against his solid chest.

Then her arms rose, as if without her knowledge, and circled his neck. That simple gesture of her limp body brought forth from deep inside her a new torrent of sobs. Unable to say anything, unable to move, he just held her, giving her time to get rid of her anger, her sorrow, her frustration, and he wondered how much grief, how much yearning, had accumulated in that young heart for the mother she had, but didn't have.

Then an idea came to him. "I have a new name for your organization," he said.

"What?" she asked, between sobs.

"Hope you like it."

She looked up at him. "Tell me."

"ECO," he said hopefully, still dabbing at her tears.

"ECHO?"

"No. ECO. Earth Colors Organization."

"Earth Colors," she murmured softly. "That sounds beautiful. ECO — that would rhyme with ECHO. We can make good slogans. Write songs."

Color returned to her cheeks, and her lovely aquamarine eyes sparkled. "That's good, James. Very good. Fantastic. Let's tell Sharky." Holding his hand, swinging it, she moved toward the door. "You found your niche."

"I have?"

"Yes. You'll join our think tank. Sharky will be so jealous," she laughed. That tinkling, winsome laughter invaded the outer office as they emerged and eyes turned toward them, including Sharky's, who was sitting alone in a corner, sulking.

The implant behind his left ear ticked twice.

That meant he needed to call them. But it was a routine call. There was no emergency.

Rahul punched the road display on his dashboard. A wide shoulder, where he could park his van for a few minutes, was coming up. He checked the camper video; curled up on the back seat, her head cradled by her left arm, Pooja was fast asleep.

He parked and, picking up his small packet, got out. Just below the slope there were several bushes and small trees that would provide good cover. He moved toward them. Then, as an afterthought, he turned back and opened the hood of the van so that a passerby wouldn't bother to stop and investigate. Leaving a few tools near the front tire, he again moved toward the bushes.

It was a good spot. Quickly erecting his inflatable tent, he went inside, seamed the opening and pressed his implant. Within minutes, the holo of a senior elder appeared before his eyes.

"Greetings, Rahul," the elder one said. "You got your first task done. And in a short time. We are pleased."

"But I didn't do anything. I was trying to figure out what to do and it happened by itself. Just like that."

"That's the way life works, Rahul. Something that is supposed to happen finds an excuse and happens. Now, the real tough part of your assignment begins. Make sure she goes to Ayodhya with you. And make sure she thinks it's her idea, not yours."

"No problem. Consider it done. Can I take a bit more time, sir, and say hello to my mother?"

"Sure, why not." The elder's holo disappeared, and the next instant, his mother was smiling at him.

"Good to hear from you, Rahul," she said. "Your first time away for so long. I hope you're not feeling too homesick."

"Mother, I need your blessings about something."

"Oh, what's that?"

"Pooja. I want to ask her to be my oath-mate."

"Wrong idea, son. She's not for you."

"That's what *you* think. Tell me, what will the elders do, when I do it?"

"The question won't arise because you won't do it."

"I'm telling you, I will."

"You won't, Rahul. No child of mine would do something they shouldn't and create unnecessary complications. No way. Farewell now, my son. Have fun." Before he could reply, before he could say a single word, her holo disappeared.

Folding up his tent, he strode toward his van and wondered what she had meant by *complications*.

4

The Torn
Rainbow

Watering her office plants, Cathy wondered if she should call Meera and give her the message her favorite daughter, Pooja, had left. Standing work orders dictated she should, but if Mrs. Heinrich was on her deathbed, would it be wise to burden Meera's mind with another problem, especially when . . .

Just then the door opened and a couple of tall guys walked in. Cathy put down her pitcher. "May I help you?"

"Blowtorch was sick. He couldn't come," the one with tousled blue hair, blue shirt and blue jeans said. "You typed it?"

"Nope." She moved to her desk and stood against its edge, trying not to stare at the blue tattoo peeking through his open shirt collar. "My boss — "

"Isn't yet back," interrupted the one with green hair, green shirt and green pants. He scowled. "So what. Doesn't she call you?"

"What does calling have to do with it?" Cathy's cool wanted to run away. "She has to sign them. I can't sign for her."

"Did we insist on signatures? Did we?" They both started together, but the green one let his friend continue. "We got to leave tonight. Gimme her number. Let me call her."

They looked belligerent, and Cathy was frightened. She was alone in the office, and she had heard stories about the Candle Runners. "OK, OK. Don't get riled up," she said stoutly, wondering what that whole tattoo looked like. "I'll call her."

She dialed her own number at her empty apartment and let it ring and ring and ring. "She's not answering." She replaced the phone. "She must be at the hospital."

Just then the phone rang. As Cathy picked it up, the blue one stretched his long arm across the desk and pressed the audio. Not daring to switch it off, Cathy said into the phone, "Earth Reality."

"Cathy, Meera here. I'll be there tomorrow. Call Blowtorch. Ask him to delay — "

"Mrs. A'Kash." The blue one leaned over the speakerphone. "So good of you to call. You know these airlines. We can't afford the flight change penalty. We must have th — "

"Cathy, who is speaking?"

"I didn't get your names." Cathy glared at the strangers, feeling angry and helpless.

"Snow Flower here, Mrs. A'Kash," the blue one said into the speaker. "Remember me? I was with Blow last time we met."

"Sorry, Snow. Can I speak with Blow?"

"As I was telling Cathy here, he was a wee bit unwell and seeing we got twenty hours of straight flight — "

"I understand," Meera's distant voice said. "Tell you what. I'll send the papers by messenger. That OK?"

"That'll be just fine," Snow Flower smiled. A big, wide smile. "Blow is at the office: 592-2029. When we get back, we'll invite you to our big splash."

"I'll be looking forward to it," Meera A'Kash replied.

"Meanwhile, I wish you luck. Have a good trip. May all clouds fear your sunshine."

"May sunshine shoulder you always," returned Snow cheerfully. Both men waved to Cathy and, taking long strides, walked out the door, closing it behind them.

"Oh, Meera, I was so scared," Cathy said into the phone as soon as the door closed.

"Why? What happened?" Meera sounded concerned.

"They wore blue and green. The stories!"

"Falsehoods. Spread by vicious, malevolent people," Meera laughed. "Surely, Cathy, you know that."

No, I don't know that, Cathy silently said to herself. But on the phone she laughed, "Sure. I was just kidding. So, what do you want me to do?"

"Are the papers ready?"

"Of course they are."

"Fine. Call the temps. Ask them to send someone for a week. A pleasing phone voice a must. Then call Blowtorch. Tell him you'll meet him at the airport with all the documents."

"You really want me to go with them?"

"Who else can go, Cathy? I'm stuck here. I tried to delay them. You heard me."

"Sorry, Meera." Cathy did feel bad for being difficult. "I just feel I shouldn't take your place since you're coming back — " She tried to sound cheerful. "Your mother feeling better?" She felt like saying, since you're coming back, you can go tomorrow. One day's delay doesn't mean anything. But she didn't say it.

"No," Meera was saying. "She's still in coma. That's why I can't go. Colonel Oringer has a friend, a psycho-cardiologist. She's taking over. When I'm needed, she'll call me right away."

"That's good. As long as there's breath, there's always a chance. By the way," Cathy said, "I may meet Pooja there."

"What? She's come back? No, don't take her with you."

"Sorry," Cathy said feeling guilty. "I should have called you. She phoned yesterday. Said something about joining Earth Corps, then hung up before I could ask anything. I made some calls. Seems they're workaholics. Got chapters in twenty countries and growing. They are also sending a delegation."

"You must have misunderstood." Meera sounded very confident. "Pooja wouldn't join anything without my permission."

"I hope you're right."

"What do you mean, you hope I'm right?" Meera shouted. "What did she say exactly?"

"Her words were," said Cathy, nettled, "'tell mom I've joined Earth Corps. I'm traveling with them. Tell her not to worry.'" Meera's secretary recited the message in a crisp, staccato manner, resenting the fact that she'd been on the receiving end of her employer's anger through no fault of her own.

"That's it?"

"Yes, then she hung up. Didn't give me a chance to say a word."

There was a heavy silence at the other end of the line. All Cathy could hear was Meera's breathing. "Well, I've got to call the temps before they close," Cathy said, "and then go home and pack."

"OK, Cathy. And Cathy, can I ask you a favor?"

"Sure, boss. Anything."

"If Pooja is there, would you call me right away?"

"Sure will."

"I wish you a good flight," Meera said, trying to sound cheerful, but the pain in her distant voice was unmistakable.

Cathy felt sorry for her — children do grow up. Didn't Meera A'Kash know that? Was she one of those who couldn't accept the fact? "I wish you the same," she said. "I'll call you," she added soothingly, "even if she isn't there."

"Thank you. I appreciate that." Meera A'Kash's sad voice was quiet. The phone connection was severed.

It was a hellish, mind and soul splintering nightmare, one that had no beginning and no end, one that demanded action and wouldn't allow it, that clamored but had no voices. There were mind-boggling colors, blinding colors: dark purples, blazing blues, hellish greens, smoldering reds, colors that collided, blended and blinded but wouldn't let him close his eyes.

And sounds. Sounds that deafened, that curled and moved through his fingers but would not be caught. Sounds. Sounds and colors that savagely choreographed . . .

Stanley Stryker woke up sweating.

He looked at the alarm clock, went to the bathroom, then went to the kitchen. Making himself a large mug of hot chocolate milk, he drank it in big gulps, almost scalding his tongue. Then, returning to bed, he switched off the light and tried to sleep again.

Tossing and turning and feeling exhausted, he finally dozed off. But the dreams assaulted and sparked his mind again. He was in the cockpit of Soviet Spaceship Volga, chained to his seat so tightly he couldn't move. All his viewports were bolted. He was trying to stretch his fingers, but he couldn't reach the switch that would allow him to access Mission Control. He couldn't move his head. He couldn't move his eyes. The only thing he could do was to stare at the Titanic, tumbling helplessly in junk-littered space, not very far behind.

Its crew, straining against their restraint belts, were shrieking, howling and convulsing. Someone aboard the Soviet ship, painted black top to toe, was reporting, "It worked. Our plan worked. They are all dying. Our poisoned food capsules worked." Somewhere, there were cheers, howls, drumbeats and a voice in his eardrums shrieking,"Press the button. Now. Shoot. It's now only space debris. Get rid of it. Shoot. Now shoot . . . " A robot arm was pushing his elbow, but he clenched his teeth and folded his fingers, tighter and tighter, till they broke, cracking like dry twigs . . .

But, no! That must have been a dream. He was not in the Volga. He was in the Titanic, arguing with the ship's doctor. "You're a Candle Runner. Light them with your candles. Revive them. Give them your soul light . . . You're the ship's doctor. Revive them. Dammit! Do it. Do it or I'll squeeze out your bones."

The ship's doctor was laughing, howling, dancing around him, naked from the waist up. Her multicolored hair, alive and hissing, was lashing and biting him, making him dance on his palms. But, no. Her throat was in his hands. He was squeezing it, and it was coming apart within his crushing, blue-steel fingers. Her blood-dripping flesh and bones, turning into black and red, tongue-rolling snakes, wrapped themselves around his legs, his back, his neck, squeezing and squeezing and squeezing . . .

Stryker shrieked and woke up again.

The previous nightmare he hadn't been able to remember. This one he did, with all its gory details. He shuddered. I must record it, he thought. If I do, I may not have it again.

Picking up his dicta-unit, he started speaking into it. Why? Why am I having such satanic nightmares? Is it some kind of psychic phenomenon? Is it because that's what happened? Food poisoning is not impossible. If they all died, in their death throes, could they have hit some controls that simply disintegrated the ship and our cameras didn't catch it? Is that possible? I must check the last footage again, enlarging every small speck of it. And I must have the food capsules tested. Could they have been poisoned? When and where? And by whom? Could it be the work of foreign agents?

He stopped and stared at his dicta-unit. It seemed to shimmer and say, "Aren't you just being stupid and morbid. If the food were spoiled or poisoned, and the crew and passengers died, the life-support readings would have told you. The cameras would have told you. The recordings never stopped. They just abruptly ceased. You know that. You know that very well."

"Yes, I know that," Stryker told the machine, "and I shouldn't have recorded my stupid ravings. So here goes. I'm erasing. But I'm going to get the food packages investigated anyway."

He pushed away the dicta-unit and pulled out his exercise bike from a corner. He rode vigorously in preparation for the coming day.

Entering her mother's house, Meera A'Kash looked for Neil. The kitchen table held the remains of a light meal, but he wasn't there. Nor was he in the living room. "Neil," she called. "Neil, where are you?"

He didn't answer, but the doorbell rang. Again he went out without his keys, she thought, amused. Mom is here, so why bother. You've got to grow up, son. Thinking she must talk with him, she quickly moved to open the door. But it wasn't Neil. On the steps stood an old woman in loose, hanging clothes, the flesh of her cheeks drooping down to her chin. The putrid smell that wafted in almost gagged Meera.

Revolted, she hastily stepped back. "My mother isn't here," she said, trying to close the door.

"I know," the old woman smiled, placing her gnarled, blue-veined , throbbing hand on the door frame. "I came to see you."

"Why? I don't know you."

"And I don't know you," the hag said, as if that settled the score. "But it'd be good for you listen to me. As they say, time well spent is time — "

"I'm very tired. I need to go to bed," Meera said, trying to close the door again, hoping that when it was about to close on the old woman's hand, she would withdraw it to avoid getting hurt.

The woman extended a large, dirty boot in the crack. "You want to go to bed? When your son isn't home?"

Meera felt scared. "What have you done to my son?"

"Nothing . . . Not yet."

The old woman leered and her leathery, beady, gloating eyes crinkled. "Not yet," she repeated. "So far, I just made sure he wouldn't be here when we talk."

Meera's heart throbbed wildly. "What's your problem? Say it quickly. I'm listening."

"It's not my problem, honey. And if I can't come in . . . " She started to turn and move away.

"When did I say you can't come in?" Meera's frustration was mounting with every passing minute. She stepped back and the old woman shuffled in and plunked herself on the large sofa, pulling the soft cushions behind her elbows and back.

"OK, tell me," Meera said, standing a few feet away, as if by not sitting she could hasten this revolting ghoul's sob story.

Deep inside Meera's mind was the thought that as soon as the crone left, she must call the sofa cleaners.

"Manners, manners," the old woman was acridly reprimanding. "Don't I get something to drink?"

"No, you don't, because I'm tired and not feeling well."

"OK. First, good news. Your daughter is doing well."

Meera realized anger wouldn't help. It would only amuse and satisfy this contemptible, wretched ghoul. To get rid of her, she must humor her. "Which daughter?" she asked patiently.

"Neelam, the third one."

"You've come to the wrong house." Meera felt relieved. "I don't have a daughter called Neelam."

"You do. It wasn't an easy birth. You had a Caesarean."

"Yes, I had a Caesarean section. That was for Neil."

"No, it wasn't." The bluish lips smiled and the leathery eyes crinkled. "They never told you? Neil isn't your son."

The woman was clearly mad. "What are you talking about?"

"My daughter was your nurse. She told me the babies were switched."

Meera A'Kash slowly sat down in the nearest chair. "No one can do that. That's criminal."

"It's not, honey, not if the father wants it done and if he pays handsomely. Very, very handsomely. Very generously."

"You are out of your mind."

"Am I? Have you ever checked your husband's checkbook?"

"Why should I? I trust him."

"The worse mistake a woman can make, love. Well, I'll be goin'."

"Wait. What proof do you have?"

"The birth certificates. The real ones." The woman pulled out a couple of crinkled sheets from her pocket. "These are copies. The originals are safe in a secret locker, and only I know its location. The hospital has only forgeries."

Meera took the papers. Recognizing her doctor's signature, she stared at them. The old woman snatched them back. Taking out a small phone from her pocket, she dialed it. "We are through. Neil can come home now."

Replacing the phone, she laboriously started getting up.

Meera halted her with her sharp gaze. "Why are you telling me this? What do you want? You want to blackmail me? If I report it, you'll go to prison for the rest of your life."

The old woman didn't answer. She started toward the door, but Meera moved swiftly to block her way. "Where is Neelam?"

"Tell you, hon, I'm tired. We'll talk some other time."

"No. Tell me now. Who is Neil's father?"

"Your husband, of course," the old woman cackled, as she opened the door and went out.

Meera went after her to stop her, to get more information. Attempting to avoid her pursuit, the old woman tried to move faster. Just then, Neil came running, climbing two steps at a time. When he noticed the old woman, he tried to avoid her, but it was too late. They collided. The old woman tumbled down the brick steps. Hitting the railing, her head cracked open and she lay bleeding, dying on the cement walkway.

Neil looked horrified. "Mom, I didn't mean to hit her. Honest, mom, I didn't."

Meera stared at him, this child whom she had loved, nursed and cuddled. He wasn't hers? Her husband had duped her? Cheated her for him? For this gangly boy, he had deprived her of her newborn daughter? Given her away, without her knowledge, before she had even seen the crying, pouting, eye-blinking newborn, the lovely, reddish face? And he'd not said a single word about it? For fourteen long — very long — very together-living years? Why? Why? And this ghastly woman? Why had she never come to her before? Why now . . .

"I'll call an ambulance," Neil said, moving past his mother, but his words didn't reach her ears. She was staring at the crookedly folded body, lying motionless on the walkway — was it true?

Could it be true? Vishu, her husband — the one who had such an honest face and such candid, captivating eyes — was he really capable of such ghastly deception? And this old woman? Where was she until now? Why had she decided to leave her dirty hole and seek out Meera now? Why . . .

She moved down to look at the old woman's face, to stamp it in her memory so that she'd never be able to forget it and suddenly realized that the crone's motives and timing didn't matter. If she died, Meera might never find anyone else to answer all her questions. Questions that wouldn't wait, that shouldn't wait.

She turned and quickly started climbing the steps to go inside and call the ambulance. She had hardly reached the door when she heard the siren and the screeching of tires. Turning, she saw two paramedics in white uniforms taking out a stretcher and another one kneeling near the woman checking for life signs. He stood up, saw Meera and moved toward her.

Before he could say anything, Meera spoke up. "I don't know anything about it. I just came home and saw her lying there. I was just going to call you. Where are you taking her?"

"You know her?" the paramedic asked.

"No, but she fell in front of my house. I'd like to do something. Whatever I can. Send her flowers."

"She won't need flowers anymore," the paramedic said. "She's dead." He got in the van and drove away, taking the unexpected, unwelcome stranger's lifeless body with him and turning Meera into a living statue, who had no ground left under her feet.

In the austere conference room, Gen. Stanley Stryker and FBI Director Herbert Caine were waiting for the others. Stryker wanted to ask Caine to sit down. He wanted to tell him that his constant pacing from one map-crowded wall to another, from one shuttered window to another, was buffeting his nerves. But it seemed too much of an effort.

He shuffled the papers in his files, not really reading them, just glaring at them.

"Dammit, where are they?" Caine growled. "Last night I had a nightmare."

About their not showing up at this meeting? Stryker thought, but didn't say anything aloud.

"I never have bad dreams. My wife always feels jealous. She says, 'If I worked in your kind of job, I'd have nightmares day and night.' I never believed her when she told me how real hers were. I thought she was imagining them, making up stories. Now I know. They were too real."

Stanley Stryker, the glaring statue, still didn't say anything.

"I dreamt I was in the Titanic," Caine scowled at Stryker as if it were his fault. "It was so real. Even now, even in this daylight, it still feels spooky."

You think you're the only one who's having nightmares? Stryker wanted to complain, but he didn't. Any such complaint, he knew, would only incense his beleaguered friend's tormented feelings. He merely looked up.

"We were all singing loudly and drinking — vodka and champaign, whisky, French and Italian wines and Martian cocktails.

"And," Caine said, "Commander Kodama was choreographing a new space dance, provoking everyone to join him. I was determined to dance with Shakti, the ship's doctor, but she was running all over the ship, lighting lamps and candles of all shapes, colors and sizes, and the candle burning on her forehead kept burning me, making me more and more inflamed.

"Suddenly a very large asteroid loomed ahead." Caine's slender body visibly shuddered, but it seemed he hadn't noticed it. Not losing a single breath, he continued, "Everyone worked frantically and we veered just in time to avoid a collision, but we lost contact with Houston. The captain assured us there was nothing to worry about. As soon as the asteroid passed, contact would be restored. The words were hardly out of his mouth when a missile hit us. The ship lurched. All the lights went out. Through the viewports, I could see other zeroing missiles. Why? I thought. Why are they attacking us. We're not a warship. Some went astray, but one hit and the ship rolled violently. I swayed from side to side and shrieked, and then my eyes opened and I found it was my wife shaking me, trying to wake me up . . . "

Stryker remembered his own nightmare. "Must have been real bad," he said sympathetically. The previous night's images of his own hellish quagmires swirled in his mind.

"Bad," Caine growled. "That's not the word for it. And the worst part of it is, I can't forget it. All morning it's been haunting me. Do you think it's possible? Could something like that have happened?"

"Like what?" Stryker asked absent-mindedly, distracted by

his own troubled thoughts.

"That we lost contact with it because some space debris blocked our tracking system's eyes? And then, before it could get out of that object's shadow, it was hit and destroyed?"

Stryker looked at him thoughtfully. "I have thought about it and tried to simulate it. When this meeting's over, if you wish, you can view the simulations."

"If something like that happened," Caine's eyes looked very determined, "I know whose missile it was."

"Whose?"

"The Soviet Alliance's."

Stryker shook his head. "Don't be paranoid. Don't you remember? By that last treaty we had — what year was it — all the space missiles on all sides were destroyed. We constantly monitor the space. If there were any — even one — we'd know about it."

"Maybe it wasn't a real missile. Space debris can be armed, I know that much." Caine glared at him as if daring him to refute it. "And lots of the debris floating out there belongs to our conniving friends. You know that."

Before Stryker could reply, the door opened and White House spokeswoman Irena Chalmers walked in. Her dark brown eyes and husky, highbrow face clearly indicated that her Scottish blood was up in flames.

"Once, just once," she said, throwing herself in the nearest seat, "I wish someone would tell me something beforehand. Is that too much to ask?"

"Join the club," Stryker smiled, not because he wanted to but because he felt he should. "What happened?"

She ignored him and turned toward Caine. "You must have known. I wouldn't accept that you didn't. Why didn't you tell me? The president . . . " She choked.

The FBI director knew the kinds of moods Irena Chalmers was capable of. He stopped pacing and leaned on the back of the chair facing her. "What is it, Irena? What happened?"

"Sparky. That's what's happened. Sparky."

"Oh." Both Stryker and Caine exchanged glances. That enraged Irena Chalmers more than anything else could have.

"You knew!" she shouted. "Both of you knew! That bugger lying there in that murky hospital in a coma is Sparky. Both of you knew that! And you didn't tell me! Why? Give me one reason, just one."

"Well," Caine drawled, "there wasn't any reason."

"Reason?" she charged indignantly. "Reason? Isn't learning something before the reporters do reason enough?"

"Reporters?" Caine asked horrified.

"Yes, the reporters. And don't keep repeating my words like a parrot." Suddenly she simmered down and asked him sweetly, "So, nobody's told you? You'll learn it from the evening newspapers? Is that it?"

"Irena," Stryker barked authoritatively, commandingly, "would you stop talking in riddles?"

"I'd love to." She glanced at their troubled faces. "In your heavenly wisdom, you moved him to a secret location. At this secure haven, a cleaning woman recognized him. it seems he had rented a studio just next to hers. Eager to get the ten-thousand-dollar reward, she called the *Tribune*. The reporters raided his studio. They didn't find much, except his passport and his diary."

"His diary?" All blood suddenly drained from Caine's face. He approached Irena, turned her chair to face him and stood there as if she were hiding it. "Where is it?"

Irena leaned back in her chair and steepled her fingers. "How do I know? Shouldn't you?"

"Young lady, if you think it's a joke —. "

"No. I don't think it's a joke," she shouted back, "and don't *young lady* me, Mr. So Clever. After what I've just gone through at that impromptu, that . . . that hilarious press briefing, I'm not in a mood to . . . "

Without waiting for her to finish, Caine angrily stormed out of the room.

"Caine has been under heavy pressure, Irena," Stryker said soothingly. "This Titanic problem. That must be the reason he forgot to call you. All of us make mistakes."

"Don't you think I have pressures?"

"Of course you do. Perhaps worse than ours." The expression

in his eyes belied his feelings. "Why not share them with me."

"Oh, no! I'm not falling into that trap." She smiled. "Want to know what his diary says?"

"What?" Stryker asked, hoping his unbecoming curiosity didn't show.

"One of the WKTB fatties waved it under my nose. Then she read a portion of it in that shrill voice of hers: 'Guru Mata told me to beware of my daughter. That's why I never married. That's why I underwent a vasectomy. But guru Mata was right. No one can escape one's fate. I was under a terrible shock when I learned I had a daughter. Now that I have found her, should I plead with her not to kill me? She doesn't even know me. Why should she want to take my life? Or should I just accept my fate?'"

"That's it?" Stryker asked.

"Oh, there's probably more. We can all read it in the evening paper."

"Did they mention the daughter's name? Who is she? Where does she live?" Stryker asked, thinking if they've found her . . . if some good comes out of this fiasco . . .

"You kidding?" Irena scoffed. "Don't you know how these black crows love their scoops?" She glanced at her wrist watch. "Only a few hours to wait. Maybe they'll print an extra edition."

"I doubt it. It's not that important. By the way, do you believe in this mumbo jumbo?"

"What mumbo jumbo?" Irena asked absent-mindedly.

"All this fortune telling? Fate? Reincarnation?"

"Do you?"

"I asked you first."

"I'm an agnostic. I believe in nothing and everything. But we aren't talking about me."

No, we are not," Stryker agreed. "You possess a brilliant mind, just like Sparky. I simply wanted your opinion."

She leaned back in her chair and lit a cigarette. Blowing smoke rings, she thoughtfully looked into them. Indecision clamored in her eyes.

"Before coming here," she finally said, as if talking to herself, "I had to call on the president. He told me that Sparky is brilliant

— could have won the Nobel Prize. He must have met this guru Mata when he was doing his doctoral thesis in India. That was an impressionable age. He may have believed it then. But why he continued to believe it, that's what I don't understand."

"There's another possibility," Stryker said thoughtfully.

"What?"

"Someone may have planted that diary in his room."

"Why would anyone do that?" When Irena smiled, she really looked charming.

"To mislead everyone," Stryker sounded very serious. "Suppose, somewhere along the line, Sparky tripped and became a double agent. Suppose he was running and they found him.

"They had to kill him in such a way that it could not be traced to them. They knew he had lived in India. This mumbo jumbo is one thing in which many people believe, even in our country. Wouldn't this hoax be the best camouflage?"

"Are you just passing time until the others arrive," Irena asked, "or are you serious?"

Before Stryker could reply, the phone rang. He picked it up. As he listened, his eyebrows went up. "What is it?" Irena whispered.

"You're free to leave." Stryker replaced the phone in its cradle. "This meeting's canceled."

"Why?"

"Caine is flying to India. He's already left for the airport. And — "

"I knew it." Irena thumped the table. "He is violating the rules. He is not telling us everything he knows. I must speak with the president."

"If I were you," Stryker said softly, "I would not. At least not yet."

"Why?"

"What the president doesn't know, he cannot be accused of taking, or not taking, any action upon . . . "

"But he's the head of our government, commander of all forces, and chief executive of our nation. He is . . . "

"Irena, your patriotism was one reason you were chosen for this job." Stryker gently put his hand upon hers, quieting the blows being rained on the table. "But, you need to learn patience. Curb your enthusiasm. If you don't, you'll only hurt your president, not help him. Not at all."

Irena glanced at him and pulled her hand free. "I don't agree with you," she said firmly. "But I'll think about it."

"That's good enough for me. I trust your judgment." Stryker closed his file and got up.

"f you're not doing anything," he said nonchalantly, "perhaps you'd like to come with me and watch us create a simulation."

"Really?" she exclaimed. "I'd love that."

In her enthusiasm, it didn't occur to her that the space defense command chief had invited her to sidetrack her — to make sure she wouldn't immediately run to the president to tell him right away about Herbert Caine's sudden and unexpected decision to rush to India himself. Something that he was not supposed to do. Something that he should not have done.

But Stryker firmly believed that sometimes, if circumstances demanded, you had to break the rules.

The FBI director was good at his job. Not just good. Really topnotch. If he feared something, if he believed that something needed to be done, that he needed to take care of himself, then it was best that as few people as possible learn about his trip.

Irena Chalmers, he knew, had a good head upon her shoulders. After seeing the simulations, she would be quite capable of putting two and two together and keeping her mouth shut without being advised to do so.

5

Double Exposure

Stryker was busy analyzing Volga and Hiroshima Hoku's flight trajectory simulations when Sam Oringer walked in. "General. Sir, we have a third problem."

Stryker looked up at him, "Let's not start counting them, colonel." His worried eyes belied his light tone. "Everyone else is doing it for us."

"Not this one, general. Everyone's saying it's your baby. Miskovitz has resigned." He offered a typed sheet of paper.

Stryker took it, but didn't look at it. "Why? You burned coals under his feet?"

Despite his worries, Oringer smiled. "Not me, sir. His sleeping conscience. He has joined ECO, this new brotherhood of Gopa's bunch."

"Humph! Where is he?"

"I told him he couldn't leave without completing his last assignment. I reminded him that you had given him a job with orders to report to you personally. He's waiting outside."

"Good," Stryker said, placing the resignation carefully on top of a pile of papers near his hand. "Call him."

Waiting, Stryker thought about it — if handled properly, this unexpected development could turn into a God-given break. Planning his strategy, he was staring at his screen when he heard the familiar words, "Reporting, sir." He looked up and saw Miskovitz standing at attention. The lieutenant colonel, about to resign, was not in civilian clothes.

In fact, his bearing couldn't have been more military. His uniform had a razor-sharp crease and his shoes looked newly polished. He stood at attention, eyes and muscles under proper regimental control as if a newly graduated cadet reporting to his first officer.

Deep inside his mind, Stryker felt relieved. This young officer may have fallen victim to the charms of that flamboyant teenager, but he hadn't forgotten his responsibilities. That was a good omen. A real good sign.

He smiled. "At ease, James. You, too, colonel. Have a seat." He waved toward chairs and waited until they sat down. "Your report, James? Hope you discovered something."

"Well, not exactly, sir." Miskovitz was feeling very uncomfortable; Oringer knew there was nothing to report. And, he had submitted his resignation. If Stryker needed a report, it was the colonel's job to brief him. What was the need to drag him here?

Controlling his frustration, he dutifully recited in proper, measured tones, "General, per your instructions, I conducted a thorough investigation. But at every comer, I drew a blank. If the Titanic is missing because Captain A'Kash planned mischief, he didn't mention anything to his children."

"Good," Stryker said amiably. "I'm glad to hear that."

The comment took Miskovitz by surprise; he had expected hard looks, tough questions. Disbelief. All night, thinking about it, he hadn't been able to sleep. The general had no questions?

Not even one? If Col. Oringer had been sitting in that chair, James knew he would have been grilled and grilled and grilled.

"But," Stryker was saying, "I'm not so happy about this other item." His hand fell upon the resignation that Miskovitz recognized. "Why, lieutenant? Sam working you too hard? I know he can be ruthless."

"No, sir. No, not at all." Without looking at his boss, Miskovitz stammered, "Well, sir, if you want to know the truth, it's just that . . . it's really personal."

"When you work for your government," Stryker said as kindly as he could, "nothing remains personal. I'm sure you know that."

James Miskovitz, the immaculate, enthusiastic, conscientious lieutenant colonel, nodded. He was feeling very tense and awkward, but no way could he let them know that. "You're right, sir," he replied promptly. "Sorry, I spoke without thinking. It's nothing that I need to hide. You see, sir, until now I've been living my father's dreams. And," he quickly added, "it's not that it was against my wishes. On the contrary, I was proud to follow in his footsteps. And I felt greatly honored when I was selected to serve under you in the SDC. But a time comes . . . " Glancing at their stern-looking faces, he hesitated.

"Yes?" Stryker encouraged him. "Go on, son. Your worries are my worries. I may not be able to do anything about them, but I'd certainly like to hear about them."

Miskovitz wanted to take a deep breath, but he controlled the urge. "It may sound absurd to you, sir, but I feel a time comes when . . . when one must take one's life in one's own hands. When one must do what one would like to do. And, one better do it before it's too late."

Stealing a brief glance at Sam Oringer's stony-looking face, he took that breath he had been controlling in his chest. "I feel that time has come for me, sir. I feel, in fact I know, my life will have more meaning if I serve my country some other way."

Saying all that nonstop, almost in one breath, he glanced apprehensively at Stryker, expecting anger and reprimands. Enigmatically, the general was looking pleased.

"Good," Stryker nodded approvingly. "Everyone has the right

to decide about his life's pathways and crossroads. But that's no
reason to quit. You can keep your job and join the ECO."

"Sir?" This was something so unexpected, so startling,
Miskovitz couldn't believe his ears, couldn't believe he had
heard right. "You don't mean it."

"Course, I mean it." Stryker smiled his most charming smile.
"I can't afford to say things I don't mean."

"But . . . but general, sir, in ECO I have responsibilities. I
need to spend time there. Go places . . . "

"Those of us who wish to serve our country often have to
wear two hats, lieutenant. It's nothing new. If you have enough
stamina, enough fortitude, enough vitality and courage . . . "

Vitality and courage? Stamina? Fortitude? Miskovitz gaped at
the fatherly face of the person he had always admired so much.
What was he talking about? He knows me inside out. He knows
I don't lack these attributes. Why is he having doubts?

"Sir? I don't understand."

"I will explain, Jimmy. In today's world, everything's
intertwined. Anyone — a person, an organization, a government
— can do a good job only if they have adequate knowledge.
ECO is a baby organization. Industry's nasty attitude toward it is
proof enough of how much it's needed for the protection of
what's important to our world. We'd like to help it grow.
Working with them, you'd be able to let us know their needs,
their concerns . . . "

Listening, Miskovitz's face had started turning pale. As
understanding came, scraping his chair back, he shot up like an
unleashed jaguar. Forgetting discipline, he angrily lashed, "No!
You want me to be your spy? No. Never."

"We are speaking of a function, lieutenant, not of a word that
has acquired unsavory connotations," said Stryker, ignoring the
outburst. "ECO is a new name, but the group's original goals
haven't changed. And they're similar to many others, such as
Earth Watchers, and Candle Runners. In our free society, we
need such organizations, just like a living body needs air and
water. Do you know why?"

Miskovitz shook his head and Stryker answered his own
question. "To keep us on our toes. We humans are a highly

charged species that loves to indulge in self-propulsion. Don't you think so, colonel?"

Sam Oringer nodded and Stryker continued. "While seeking self-advancement, some of us forget the parameters of our civic responsibilities. When an inner clique, blinded by selfish motives, snatches the reins, an organization — no matter how good its ideals — gets converted into a dangerous tool, capable of destroying everything that you and I may be aspiring and working for. However, if timely precautions are taken, these elements can be spotted before they get out of control. It's only people with your background and training who are capable of handling such an enormously discretionary job."

Keeping his facial muscles under tight control, Miskovitz listened quietly to this long speech, but in his dark brown eyes betrayed a kaleidoscope of conflicting emotions. He lowered himself back into his chair but didn't say anything.

Stryker realized he was teetering on the brink. If left to decide by himself, his thoughts could push him either way. Therefore, choosing each word with utmost care, he proceeded with caution. "Everyone receives training. It's essential for any job. But it's not training that spells one's success or failure. It's the other ingredients, and often, until one faces a situation, one doesn't know what one can or cannot do."

Miskovitz glanced up at Stryker as if he expected him to continue. Stryker smiled. "You just said you want to serve your nation better. I liked that. When I was your age — how long ago was that Sam? About thirty years ago? That's what my dreams were made of.

"Tell me, James, what better way do we have to serve than to make sure that our ideals, which strengthen our nation and safeguard our global concerns, do get a chance to survive and prosper? And if, as sometimes happens, some misguided persons blinded by dangerous ambitions start walking the wrong roads, they get caught before they can do much harm?"

"General," said Miskovitz slowly, "I never realized . . . this never occurred to me."

"It's not always possible to think of everything by oneself. That's why it's good to work together."

Miskovitz glanced at Sam Oringer, who, all this time, hadn't said a single word.

Finding encouragement there, he glanced back at Stryker. "Sir, if I agree to it, I'd have freedom to use my discretion?"

"Meaning?"

"I won't be spying. I will report to you only what I think should be reported."

"If I didn't believe in your discretion, lieutenant," Stryker responded, "would I have given you this opportunity?"

"Sorry, sir. It's just that I don't want to disgrace my uniform. I don't want to promise something that I may not be able to deliver."

"If your father was here," Sam Oringer said, "He'd have been very proud to hear that."

Miskovitz's face brightened. "OK, sir, it's a deal. And I promise I won't waste SDC time for ECO work."

"Don't worry about that, lieutenant. If you need time, let Sam know. He'll work it out. In fact, now that I think of it, your request couldn't have come at a better time."

"Sir?"

"Well, I've been reading about this mammoth meeting of world organizations. If I didn't have this Titanic problem, I'd have liked to attend it. Is ECO sending a delegation?"

"Yes, sir, they are. In fact," he hesitated. "Gopa and Sharky and all were insisting — "

"That you go with them? Good. I'd like you to go. When you come back, tell me what I missed. Take lots of pictures. Sam, can you get him a working camcorder? With lots of film?"

"Sure can, general," said Oringer enthusiastically. "When he returns, we'll throw a party. Let everyone enjoy what they feel they are missing."

"Good," Stryker said, dismissing them. They got up and saluted.

Acknowledging, he turned toward his waiting screens.

Gopa didn't feel like having breakfast. Eating alone was no fun and food was nauseating her. Pushing away her plate, she thought of watering her plants. As she neared them, the miniature roses, nestling in gleaming brass pots, seemed to nod and bow. She bent over them, affectionately caressing them, and they seemed to whisper, Walk lightly on untested feet.

"Huh? Sounds fascinating." She wagged a finger at them, "What does it mean?"

You tell me. The rose buds shook under her loving fingers.

You tell me.

Since morning, since she had woken up, this uninvited conversation had been going on in her mind. The words changed but centered on the same theme. Whichever way she turned, it followed her. She had tried to shake it off but it wouldn't go away. Like a helpless listener caught in a closed elevator with two talkative strangers, she was caught in that maddeningly compulsive dialogue.

You love him?

Why should I love him? I love Sharky.

But, you don't want to get married to Sharky.

For Earth's sake, talk sense! Marriage is a coward's way of handling a hormone-generated necessity. It's outmoded. Finished! Sharky and I agree; if we remain free, we'll have a better relationship. And less chances of separating. Ever.

Sure! That's why you are carrying another person's child?

That's different and you know it. He was feeling miserable. For the sake of my papa, I wanted to cheer him up. So I offered to be a surrogate mother. Happens every day. Our world has thousands of surrogate mothers. I didn't do anything new.

Except that now you've met someone who may not want to marry someone who so easily catches another's child.I offered it as a psychological pill. A placebo. I really didn't think I'd get pregnant. I mean, people have to try. Again and again and again and even then, they can't conceive. No one gets pregnant the first time.

And, I'd never done it before. Why did it happen to me? Why? Thick tears welled up in Gopa's smarting eyes.

Well! Don't be such a crybaby! Sharky isn't so bad. Until this stars 'n' stripes flaunting chatterbox showed up from nowhere, Sharky — what was it you used to call him? The old faithful —

he was your moon and sun and stars and heaven.

Was is right. Forget 'old faithful' and all that. Now he seems so boring, so clumsy, so . . . transparent, so . . . narrow-minded . . . so pungent . . . so . . .

Stop it! You're going to run out of adjectives. And don't forget — Mama is going back today. Time to tell her about it.

I'm not going to tell her. Let someone else tell her.

Someone else? Who? Sharky?

You kidding? They're not capable of talking to each other.

Then? Who else is there?

I know. I'll call Neil. What are little brothers for? Brushing her tears, Gopa moved toward the phone.

Climbing the steps, Meera was just clicking her keypad when she heard the phone ringing. Dropping the suitcase she had just purchased, leaving the door open, she rushed to grab the receiver. As she was about to pick it up, the clamor stopped.

"Who could it be?" Neil came up behind her. "Cathy and Pooja aren't here and Gopa never calls."

"Don't be a wise guy," Meera snapped, her voice cold like ice. "Drink your milk. Then finish packing."

"Mom? What's wrong?"

"What do you mean what's wrong? What's this new habit you've acquired of always questioning me?" Her facial expression matched her voice. "Get going. It's getting late."

"Mom, you never talk to me like that! You talk like that with Gopa, but not with Pooja and never with me. What's wrong? What have I done wrong?"

Meera stared at him; was he really not her son? Had she really nursed, cuddled and loved, with all her senses, with all her dreams and hopes, someone else's misbegotten child? Had her husband of twenty years really cheated on her so brazenly?

"I always listen to you. You knew I didn't want to give my experiment to the Titanic. You gave it to dad without my permission, but I didn't say nothing. Now it's lost. Perhaps forever. But I never blamed you. Not once. Did I?"

Meera wasn't listening. Staring at him, she was thinking

about her husband of twenty years. They had lived together all that time and never, not once, had Vishu said a single word, given any indication of how horribly he had wronged her. Was that possible? Meera cursed the strange, pig-headed woman, consigning her to bum forever in hell! Why had she died without giving Meera valid proof? Without giving her all the facts.

"Mom?"

"You are still standing here?" she barked, so unlike the previous Meera. "Do you want to come with me or do you want to stay here alone in this wretched house?"

Neil felt like saying he'd prefer to stay here alone, but that didn't sound wise. Dad was away. Before leaving, he'd told Neil to act like a man. To take care of mom. "You won't disappoint me, son," he had said, giving Neil a final hug.

Suddenly, he envisioned him — trapped in a damaged spaceship that was violently tumbling in space. Tumbling and tumbling. All its life-support systems conking out, one by one. Nothing that its captain could do, nothing that its co-pilot could do . . .

Afraid that Meera would see the tears in his eyes, Neil turned quickly, picked up the suitcase and ran up the stairs to his room. Throwing his clothes in it, he thought, I should call Gopa. Persuade her to come with us. She can straighten mom out. Her constant presence would take care of mom. Serve mom right . . .

Meera stared at his disappearing legs and started rebuking herself. What's wrong with you! If your husband betrayed you, how's that this child's fault? Why are you punishing Neil for Vishu's treachery? Or, to be more exact, for your own mistake? Why did you never question it when your husband started coming home late? Every day. Day after day. Why did you never wonder when so often refusing sex, he feigned sleep? If you had watched the warning signals . . .

The phone started ringing again.

She thought of not answering it, but it could be Pooja. Or the hospital. She picked it up. "Hello?"

Upstairs, at the first ring, Neil had stopped packing. Hearing Meera's voice, he quietly picked up the phone and covered the mouthpiece with a clammy hand.

"Is this Mrs. A'Kash?" the caller was asking.

"Who is speaking?" Meera asked somewhat impatiently, not recognizing the voice.

"Mrs. A'Kash, when are you coming back home?"

"Who is speaking, please?" Meera asked again.

"I have the trump card," the strange voice snickered. "Color footage of a speeding Mercedes and an old man bleeding in the road."

Meera's hand trembled. Her heart palpitated. Impossible! The road was deserted! No one had witnessed that accident. But anyone could throw stones in the dark. Thanks to her husband, the whole world knew her. The whole world could find her phone number.

No doubt this person, whoever he was, was trying to play a con game. He wanted to blackmail her. She should give him no rope. She should act normally and not let him think he could frighten her.

"I'm not interested," she said quietly. "At Earth Reality, we don't try to collect funds by evoking sympathy."

"I could have given it to the police. Or to SDC. I could have put it on television — the bleeding picture of the dying man whose diary says his daughter is his killer."

"So, call his daughter. Why are you calling me?" Meera snapped, pushing as much anger as she could in her trembling voice.

The phone went dead.

Meera stared at the mouthpiece in her hand. Who was the caller? What did he want? Money? It suddenly occurred to her that her mother's number was unlisted. How did he get this number? Did her unfortunate victim die? When she got back, should she go to the police?

Would they believe her if she told them she wasn't able to report the accident because she had to rush to her dying mother?

Upstairs, Neil quietly replaced the phone. He was baffled — what bleeding old man? he wondered.

Had his mother killed someone and not reported it, just like any nervous teenager? Was that what was driving her mad? Was that why she was behaving so irrationally?

Dad was right, he thought. Mom needs a man's firm hand. What a shame he had forgotten that and screamed at her like a juvenile. He should be gentle with her. And firm . . . tender, gentle and firm, just like dad . . .

He decided to finish his packing quickly and then go help her pack.

Stryker was in his backyard, planting the bougainvillaea that should have been planted two days earlier. They had started to wither inside their jute packing and, if not taken care of right away, might not survive. From the corner of his eye, he noticed Rosa Butler, his housekeeper, coming out of the kitchen door carrying a small stool and his phone.

"Rosa," he said in annoyance, "I thought I told you not to bother me. To tell them I'm not at home."

"I've been doing that, sir. But this is from the White House." She sounded apologetic, as if it were her fault. "The president, himself." She offered him a paper towel.

Quickly wiping his hands, he took the phone. "Mr. President? What a pleasant surprise."

"General," the president's voice came, cool and angry. Obviously he was not in a mood for pleasantries. "I don't believe in coincidences."

"Neither do I, Mr. President. What's on your mind?"

"The wife of your vanishing, trick-playing pilot," the far-off voice carried a sharp edge, like a newly sharpened razor's cutting bite. "It's she who tried to kill Sparky. And don't start arguing. It's a confirmed fact. There's no doubt about it."

Stryker took a deep breath and leaned against the stool. "How do we know that, sir?"

"Trust the FBI," the president sounded cool. So cool that it spelled disaster for anyone who might have the audacity of facing him that minute. "The tire tracks at the accident site belonged to a Mercedes. It seems they methodically checked every Mercedes in Titusville. The blood on Mrs. A'Kash's tires matched."

Stryker whistled. The honest-to-goodness, loving-hearted,

self-appointed correction officer for the planet's rowdy elements was a hit-and-run killer? Then he remembered something. "But sir, if that's the case, we can stop worrying. That means it was just an accident and Sparky's cover was not broken."

"You don't know all the facts."

"But I do, Mr. President. Mrs. A'Kash had an appointment that morning with a potential client. She was on her way when Neil called her about the Titanic and she turned back."

"I know that."

"Then you know, sir, it couldn't have been anything but an unfortunate accident."

Hearing silence at the other end, Stryker thought he should explain. "Her return trip was unexpected. Unscheduled. At that time, she was not supposed to be on that road. No one had any way of guessing she'd be there, at that precise moment. Too bad she didn't report it. Must have panicked. That's the only — "

"Don't jump to conclusions, general. That's not like you." The president's distant voice was still cool and even. The fury and anger in it were almost visible.

"Sorry, Mr. President. I was only — "

"You remember that much-touted diary?"

"Sparky's? Yes, of course, sir."

"That was not the only thing they found. They found other items. If you put two and two together . . . There's a possibility — " the president hesitated. There was a slight pause.

Stryker's heart took a slight tumble. "Yes, Mr. President?" he asked with baited breath.

"She could be that daughter."

The phone almost fell out of Stryker's hand. Meera A'Kash?

An illegitimate daughter! The Titanic's captain's wife! The president of Earth Reality! He shook his head to clear his mind. "I'll call Coronary Care right away. If her mother's out of the coma — "

"I've called a meeting of all the department heads. No excuses acceptable. Tomorrow. Nine o'clock. Sharp."

"I'll be there, Mr. President . . . " Stryker hadn't even finished speaking when the connection was broken and the line went dead.

Flight Director Mao Ki Tung had always taken lots of pride in his mission control facilities at Shuang Ch'eng-tzu. So what if they were not as comfortable and richly appointed as those of the Yankees? His funding went for functional purposes. So what if there were not as many buildings, spacious and filled with miscellaneous space paraphernalia, as the Soviets had? What had those Russian imperial powers given up in terms of trade treaties to fund their facilities?

So what if they were not robot, powered by glittering machines, as was the case with the upstart, copycat Japanese imperialists?

So what?

They were efficient. They were reliable. They were living proof of what an edifice built upon simple, honest, hardworking people's money could look like. Should look like.

They were exactly what a people's republic could afford and maintain and be proud of.

Tung firmly believed that if the American spaceship had been a Chinese spaceship, flying under his control, it would never have managed to disappear like the Titanic had.

But for the past few days, his pride and self-esteem were constantly being punctured by a strange, unexplainable kind of apprehension. Something was wrong. He wasn't able to place his finger on it and that was no good. Mao Ki Tung believed in keeping things in their proper place, under his control. Because of this unidentifiable apprehension, he had decided to summon his range safety officer, Col. Han Ha Fong.

"Comrade colonel, what do you think?" he asked as Han Ha Fong appeared, saluting and looking inordinately apprehensive. "Why has it been so quiet, as our Soviet imperialist friends would say, on the space queen Titanic front?"

From his past experience, Col. Han Ha Fong knew that no matter what answer he gave, it would displease the honorable flight director. Therefore, as always, he decided to play it safe. "Comrade director, I'd be flattered to hear your analysis."

"Well, if you ask me," Mao Ki Tung mused, leaning back in

his chair and steepling his fingers, "you know I don't like to speculate, but wouldn't it be logical to assume that it could only be due to one of two reasons?"

"It most certainly would, comrade. May I ask the reasons?"

His audience was good. Attentive and polite. What more could one ask? Tung beamed. "One, they've found it, but they are not releasing the news, so that no other mishap has to be reported until it attains orbit around Mars."

"Possible. Quite possible." Fong sagely nodded his greying head.

"Two, they've really lost it, but they don't want to admit it, so they keep the whole world guessing."

"Possible," the captive colonel nodded again. "Possible."

"So how do you think we can find out which one is correct?"

"Have you thought about it, comrade director?"

"Have I thought about it?" The question was so ridiculous, Mao Ki Tung laughed. "Colonel, what do you do if worms are clinging inside a bowl and refusing to come out?"

"What would you do, comrade director?"

"I'd light a fire under the bowl. That's what I'd do."

The mission control director rubbed his hands in anticipation, as a vision of worms crawling out of a bowl crowded his mind. "I could call a press conference, accept our responsibility. It was unfortunate, yes, but — "

The suggestion was so ridiculous that, forgetting protocol, the wide-eyed colonel blurted out, "Why would they believe us?"

"Could happen. Like them, we also have lots of space junk floating around out there. We don't know how, but one of them armed itself — "

"Pardon, comrade director," at the risk of losing his job, Col. Fong decided to defer, "if we do that, we'll be a global joke. Especially later, when we'll have to confess that our admission was a mistake. And," seeing determination in Tung's calculating eyes, he quickly added, "although we've made inroads, quite significant ones, I'd say we still don't really know how the imperialist mind works. It could trigger war. Perhaps world war. Our Mars ship should be ready soon. Can we risk that?"

"Yes. There's that," Mao Ki Tung agreed. "We are not afraid

of war. But according to our comrade chairman's philosophy, we should not be the ones to trigger it or to fire the first shot.

"And, as you say, our coming space launch . . . " He reflected. "Then, what can we do? How can we cut through this news blackout?"

Fong desperately tried to think of an item that would be so interesting, so scintillating, it might divert Mao Ki Tung's one-track mind. Like a sailor holding onto a floating straw, he hesitatingly ventured, "Comrade director, what do you think about this global meet in India?"

Tung's small, round eyes showed interest. "I seem to remember reading about it somewhere. What is the purpose of this meeting?"

"These are the clubs that have sprouted all over the globe during the past forty or fifty years. You could put them in two groups: those who are always boycotting something and those who are always saving something."

"Oh, yes." Thoroughly amused and aroused by this description, Mao Ki Tung slapped his belly and laughed. "Environmentalists, paleontologists, race relations bigots, equality-opportunity singers, all that back-to-the-hunter-gatherer-mousy-crowd. And all of it spearheaded by that spineless, imperialist mouthpiece, the so-called United Nations."

"Everyone's talking about them, comrade. From what I hear, they're now not limited to the so-called middle class and lower middle class. They're making heavy inroads into governing classes. They can't be lightly dismissed anymore."

"Why?" For the first time in a long while Mao Ki Tung felt curious about something that was not directly related to his job. "What has changed?

"I think you've heard wrong, colonel. We know everyone hates them. I mean, everyone who shoulders the responsibility for clothing and feeding this world. Keeping people alive is more important that worrying about dying trees. You know that. Don't you realize they're always under someone's hammer . . . ridiculed, beaten, jailed . . . Are you keeping wrong company, comrade?"

This time, Col. Fong was not intimidated. Ignoring the jibe, he countered, "I've heard that it all started to coalesce when they banded under the name Candle Runners. At this meeting, that group may be named the *umbrella* under whose wing all the other clubs would function as a single, multi-unit entity."

"So? The real purpose of this meeting is to plan a common platform?" Mao Ki Tung asked.

Col. Fong nodded. "The U.N. will be there, of course. And scientists and industrialists — in fact, anyone who can afford to go and can get permission. No one wants to be left out."

"Who's representing us?" A dim hope flared deep in Mao Ki Tung's mind. If no one had been chosen yet, perhaps he could pull a few strings.

"No one." Col. Fong's expressive eyes looked sad.

"Why?"

"Our government doesn't believe in all that crap. You know that, comrade director."

"It's not a matter of belief." Tung was suddenly angry. "It's a question of legal representation. If the whole world is being represented, why should we be left out?"

"Even if our government should change its mind, we won't get permission to participate."

"Who can deny us permission?" Insulted, as if someone had denied him his birthright, Tung pounded his desk and shouted, "Who can dare to offend the only true communist government?"

"The organizers, Earth Reality, the U.N. Environment Commission, ECO, all of them." Seeing Tung ready to eat him alive, Fong was undeterred. This was one topic on which he could say whatever he wanted, one conversation that could not threaten his job.

Keeping his poker face intact, he continued. "They've been very selective. I've heard that even the topmost American news media — the *New York Times*, *Time* magazine, the famous TV networks — were not able to get permission."

"You know," Tung smiled, remembering something, "New Delhi calls it discrimination. They won't allow it."

"The Indian government has nothing to do with it, comrade director. It's being held in Ayodhya, the place they've been calling Mother Earth's Sanctuary."

"I know. The holy city in northern India, the so-called birthplace of their Lord Rama. Hiding behind their blind decades."

Fong nodded. "Your memory is good, comrade director. You also remember how they came up with the breakthrough idea of building not a mosque or temple, but a huge monument to all Earth life. All Earth religions. And — "

"I remember," Tung interrupted with a nod. "In fact, when the decision was made, I was an exchange professor at the Indian Space Technology Institute. Being there, I read all the propaganda about the glory of it, and how it was all made possible due to the blessing of the God-king Rama and his disciple, the Monkey God."

Having achieved his objective of diverting Mao Ki Tung's Titanic-obsessed mind, Col. Fong did not want to linger. He got up, hoping his boss' mind would be so busy he wouldn't notice his leaving without being formally dismissed.

Tung looked up. "Yes, comrade colonel, you are dismissed. You've given me much food for thought. Candle Runners or not, the slavish Indian government's cowardly objections not withstanding, I'm going to make sure that our great republic is represented at this historical global get-together."

The colonel stopped in his tracks, curious. "How will you do that, comrade director?"

"I'll offer to start a chapter in Beijing." Mao Ki Tung's beady, watering eyes were gloating, absolutely gloating. "They'll be honored. They'll be flattered. They'll be delirious with happiness, overcome with glory at finally succeeding in converting us. The invincible Chinese. The ones who they believed they'd never be able to convert. They won't be able to refuse that offer."

Col. Fong was impressed. "And the members will be of your choosing. Fantastic, as they'd say in America, comrade director. No one else, no one else in the whole of China, would have thought of such a splendid strategy."

"Since you like the idea, colonel," Mao Ki Tung said majestically, "when I select my committee members, you will be my first deputy."

6

Cocoons Also Crumble

Pooja A'Kash typed the last word, switched off her laptop and locked her fingers together, stretching her hands above her head. Leaning back, she strained the muscles of her shoulders and back, enjoying the stretching exercise.

The cool grass under her naked feet felt like a soothing, invigorating cushion, while the trees overhead rustled softly in clean, fragrant air. Somewhere, not far away, mynas, robins and bulbuls sang and chattered. Emotions, new, strange, the kind she had never experienced before, the ones that almost frightened her by their intensity, surged in her mind.

I never thought the sky could look so blue, she thought. I'm so glad I came to this land where my grandmother was born. If I hadn't come, I'd have never learnt, never known, how, why, legends are born. Legends that can be mine, that can course in my blood and make my mind roam . . .

Behind her a cheerful voice asked, "All finished?"

Turning, she saw Rahul smiling at her. The rays of the departing sun played upon his wide forehead, upon his unruly golden hair. In the late evening's rosy light, he looked like a starman come down to earth. If I imprison him in my arms and suffocate him with my kisses, what would he say? What would he do? she wondered.

"Not finished? Then let's download only — "

"It's finished." Making two tiny fists, she rubbed her eyes and looked up at him again. Tall and regal, he still looked like her dream prince on a white horse. "What's your rush? Why don't you read it first? You may not like it."

"If that's what I thought," he leaned over the laptop and set it to print what she'd been typing almost the whole afternoon, "do you think I'd have let you spend so much time bending over this old machine? Let's see."

Picking up the first sheet that came out of the printer, he read the headline. "All Roads Lead to Ayodhya This Month." He whistled. "I like it. No. I love it. Just beautiful. Why don't you read it to me?" Grabbing the other sheets from the printer, he offered them to her.

Stepping away, she folded her hands behind her back and shook her head. "Nope, I wrote it. You read it. Your job."

"OK," he nodded agreeably. "I'll read it. But don't you go away. You need to hear it."

Ignoring the lonely chair, he gathered all the sheets and made himself comfortable on the rug lying near the laptop. "Take the chair," he invited.

She plunked down beside him, wondering if, finding her so close, he might pull her even closer and hold her. If he did, should she move away or give in?

But Rahul was concentrating on locating the first sheet that had gotten mixed up when he had so impatiently gathered them.

Finding it, he relaxed and started to read softly as if wanting to enjoy every word of it. "When I told my brother, Neil, I was leaving for the Candle Runners' convention, he sounded concerned. 'Aren't you worried about their non-refrigerated spoiled food? About drinking their filthy water? About their beggars who waylay you in broad daylight? They're maniacs. You'll get sick. You'll get hurt. Don't go, Pooja, he had said.'

"It is a shame, I wanted to tell him, that India still has that connotation in our country. If you want to worry about violence, aren't there as many lunatics and cutthroats in our small town or in any city in the world? For any American, this fabulous global convention could be a journey into a past that still exists, like a magic hop into another time, another history, another rhythm, another mood.

"I've been here only two days. So far, the feeling I've been getting is one of being in the center of a space opera. To walk into Shanti Nikunj is to see not only the Shiva fountain and the outdoor cafes, but also the rippling water-wind flag of the Earth Spirit, the star-spangled banner that's our pride, the hammer and sickle of the Soviet Alliance, the mystical globe of Brazil, the colorful and enticing flags of all the one hundred and fifty nations, flying side by side and on sale at a souvenir stand, like a geography lesson come to life.

"In the Nikunj, Earth Corps cadets — girls and boys, eight to twelve years old, dressed in the eye-catching costumes of our world — guide you to wherever you want to go: the convention hall, Nehru market, Epicland, the Earth Spirit Temple, the ancient city, the lovely Saryu beaches. If you don't understand their language, their little fingers tug at your heart and walk you — "

Rahul stopped reading and glanced at her. She was sitting quietly, her chin supported on her knees, her manicured fingers making invisible circles in the thick lawn grass.

Hearing him stop, she looked up at him, and, in her expressive eyes, he again saw those emotions that he had been trying to ignore all the time — ignore and forget — whether he was with her or away from her.

"And you say you've never written anything before?" he asked lightly, teasingly.

"Well, term papers and things. What everyone writes. Never

anything for a journal or newspaper."

"Well, it's beautiful. With practice, you'll be able to beat the best of them." He glanced at the second page. "Is it all *joie de vivre* and poetry, or have you touched upon some nitty-gritty items also?"

She smiled. "You mean items like the unseen, unnoticeable, elaborate arrangements for the personal safety of the participants, the almost round-the-clock rehearsals by the various ethnic groups for the dance and drama pageants for late evening fun, the marvels of modern electronics that allow non-attending members to participate in all the debates and voting, the special arrangements for pale aborigines from the Americas, who take off their clothes, fry their skin, pour down their throats huge amounts of coke and beer and — "

"Wait. Wait. Enough," he laughed. "I don't think I need to read the rest of it. Soon they'll be space-loading us with their mind-boggling demands anyway. Let's send it."

Watching him transmit the article to the editor's desk at the World News, she asked him quietly, "Rahul, can I ask something?"

He glanced at her and knew what was coming. He had been fearful of this moment, had tried to avoid it, delay it, but, like any inevitability, it had quietly tiptoed in. It had arrived, and the best he could do now was not to be nervous and field it as best as he could.

"If I say no," he responded, staring at the laptop as if it required all his attention, "you won't ask it?"

"OK, I won't."

"Hey. What's that. I was only kidding. You know that. Come on, don't be such a *chui-muyi*. What's on your mind? If you won't tell me, I won't take you to Epicland."

That threat worked. Believing him, she started to speak but stopped without saying a word. She hadn't realized it'd be so difficult because she had phrased it many times in her mind — not just in her dreams, but also when fully awake. After all that preparation, it had seemed very simple. But now when the time had come to say it, it didn't seem so easy. "Well, you see . . . no, it's nothing. Let's forget it."

No, he thought, we are not going to forget it. Because if we do, it will always linger between us, making both of us increasingly uncomfortable. No sense in making life more difficult than what it has to be.

He rolled up the printed sheets, closed the laptop and turned toward her. "You remember what you once told me?"

"What?"

"That you don't know why but you like to tell me things that you never tell anyone else."

She nodded, her cheeks flushed.

"I liked that. And just now I was only teasing. By now you should know me. I'd like to hear your question."

"It's nothing really. I was just wondering, when two people are so close, as we have been . . . If it had been someone else, he'd have tried his best to seduce me. I may have rebuffed him, but he'd have tried anyway. But . . . "

"But, I haven't?" He ruffled her thick, golden hair affectionately. "That's because we are two different species."

"What do you mean?"

"Well . . . how should I put it? You are not yet eighteen and I'll soon be twenty-five. When you are not yet eighteen, a life-form who is nine years older belongs to a different species."

"If I was Gopa, you wouldn't have said such a thing."

"What makes you say that." He didn't just look and sound surprised, he was surprised. He had expected a protest, but not this kind.

"Gopa has so many boyfriends, she doesn't know what to do with them."

"You are her twin, as pretty as she is, even more attractive. More sophisticated. Better looking in every way. You can have even a higher number of gawking admirers."

"Nope." She shook her head vigorously.

"Why not?"

"My mom says that first you fall in love, then you have a boyfriend."

"And you've never fallen in love," he said incredulously and wondered if she were going to give him that *you're my first* routine.

"A couple of times. But when I told her, my mom said it wasn't love. It was just me growing up. Just my hormones."

"I feel sorry for your mom."

"Not for me?" She sounded surprised. "If she hadn't drummed that into my head, drilled and drilled since I was that high," she indicated with her hand a couple of feet above the ground, "I'd have learned, like anyone else, how to behave with boys. How to make friends. How to — "

"That you'll learn, I promise you." He took her hand and pulled her toward him. Gently touching her chin, he lifted up her face. "But, for us, no falling in love. No living together. No tears. No fighting. OK?"

"OK." She smiled. "Who needs that anyway."

"Fine. Then let's pick up our bathing suits and find those aborigines of yours on the Saryu banks. Amongst them are hiding your friends." Holding her by her waist, he picked her up and planted a light kiss on her nose. She laughed, struggled to get free, then threw her arms around his neck and returned his kiss. Tentatively at first, then confidently. Boldly. Passionately.

"Hey," he said laughing. "Remember? No falling in love. Come. Let's go to the beach."

Gopa was sitting at her dressing table combing her hair and softly humming an old love song when Sharky burst in the room. Snatching her comb, he shouted, "This stubble is not worth combing. Comb your wig."

Gopa didn't understand. Neither the unexpected, startling fury, nor the strange remark. Since they had arrived here at the convention, Sharky had been like that — burning hot and cold unnecessarily. Ascribing it to his work pressures, she had tried to ignore it.

At home, when he lost his temper, the tactic had always worked. No reason why it shouldn't work here.

"What wig?" she asked, trying to snatch back her comb.

"The one you had on yesterday, riding the dragon boat with that stranger. Laughing and giggling and talking. Your wig falling all over him. What were you doing? Smoking crack?

Ingesting speed? What was he telling you? How many — ”

"You dope!" she shouted. "You know I don't smoke. And I wasn't riding dragon boats and you know that, too. I was in the auditorium, working with the techs, trying to speed up those changes that you and your buddy, James, concocted. Barely two weeks left for the opening day and you want such stark, radical changes. The stupidity of it. The — ”

"Don't change the subject. Who was that Lothario?"

"You tell me. Who were you ogling with your near-blind eyes? It wasn't me. You're getting blinder and blinder. How many times have I asked you to get contact lenses? They could even give some luster to the jungle you call your face. Make you look better."

"You scheming, conniving, Space-Throw-Away! Don't talk to me like that! Never talk to me like that! Never. Never . . . ” Flinging her comb at the mirror, cracking the glass, he stalked toward the door.

His grand exit was marred. He collided with Miskovitz, who was rushing in. Cursing loudly, Sharky pushed him aside and ran out.

Barely avoiding falling, Miskovitz straightened up. "What was that all about?" he asked, straightening his tie.

Gopa tossed a haughty glance at him, then threw back her head and started laughing.

"Gopa . . . Gopa?"

Suddenly, she slumped in her chair, put her head on the dressing table between both her hands and began to sob hysterically.

In college, Miskovitz had spent all his time with computers and biospheres. He never had time to learn about female tantrums. He wanted to help her, but didn't know how.

He walked toward her heaving form, sat on the edge of her dressing table and tried to lift up her head. "Gopa? What's wrong?"

She looked up, her eyes swollen and red. Then she spoke and there was no rage in her voice, no sadness, only lethargy, absolute and dark and all-pervading. "Everything."

Hearing that and seeing her like this, his eyes misted. All his emotions, all his feelings, raced to the core of his psyche, tugging it, wanting to blind it. Helpless questions raced through his mind — what could he do to tear out the arrows that were boomeranging through her mind, coursing through her heart?

He wanted to touch her face, brush away those tears, but he dared not. He knelt down near her and softly murmured, "That's a lot."

As if his proximity was too much, as if at this moment she couldn't cope with it, she got up, moved to the narrow bed and sat down on its edge. "Did Sharky ever tell you?"

"What?"

"He sermonizes it to everybody. He's very proud of it."

"Of what?"

"He has worked out an entire theory to prove that the idea of marriage is absolutely irrational."

"He has a lot of company. Many think like that today."

"Ah. But he is the leader, the chief honcho of that twenty-first century anti-marriage night patrol. He doesn't even want to speak the word, marriage. That's demeaning. He calls it 'powering the kitchen sink.'

"And do you know what he preaches is the price, the terribly derogatory, horribly uncivilized aftermath, of getting chained to this category for routinely blinding lust for nightly power?"

Feeling totally helpless, Miskovitz simply looked at her.

"He believes that this shackling lust is much worse than those maligned items like smoking crack because it doesn't just enslave people's minds and emotions. It does much worse. It automatically chains them to routine, trivial aboriginal tasks, like laboring for food and creating unwanted children, preventing them from devoting their intellects and urges to our planetary causes and inventing the much-wanted new Earth system for urgently needed items such as sun shields for ozone subliming or robotics deconstruction."

I must somehow get her off this track, James thought. He asked a safe question. "Where has he gone? I came to get him."

"Important?"

It wasn't, but he had to keep her mind on this track. If he failed, she might revert to her beating rage and frustration. The child growing in her belly, he knew, was partially responsible for these tantrums. He said with believable conviction. "Very."

"OK, let's go find him. When he runs like this, he always shoots for his auto."

She moved toward the door and Miskovitz followed her. "If he took an auto, we'll never find him."

"Oh, yes we will. Cheenoo's idea. We just fixed it this morning. Anyone who borrows an auto must punch a destination into the main computer. No matter where the auto goes, the garage computers can keep track of it."

"Fantastic." Miskovitz's face brightened. "That will help a lot when the convention gets started. Let's test the system."

Walking rapidly, almost running, they reached the garage and Gopa accessed the computer. "Shucks!" she exclaimed, staring at the printout on the screen.

"Well?" Miskovitz asked.

"He went to Khar-Dooshan Shamshan. You know how to — "

"We don't have to know. Just punch it in your auto."

"I forgot. These new Japanese autos are handy after all," Gopa reluctantly admitted. "OK, Let's move."

She started punching data on the check-out screen — their destination, their names, and the ID of the auto standing next in line. Miskovitz got into driver's seat and programmed their route into the auto's memory board.

As Gopa finished programming the computer, the garage door slid open. Moving quickly, she took her seat near Miskovitz and he pressed the ignition key. The auto rose a few inches and swiftly moved on cushions of air, sailing like a majestic boat.

Gopa settled back. "With these new airwheel autos, they'd never have to maintain their roads, would they?"

Miskovitz had pulled a map out of the side pocket and was poring over it, "Space alive," he said, "this carnival area is big. It must have taken years — "

"It has," she interrupted, glad to be the guide. "It was started when they were still wrangling over the Earth Spirit Temple's blueprint. And they keep adding new attractions."

"I can't recognize any of these names."

"All are based upon ancient mythology: Ramayan,

Mahabharat, the Bible, etcetera," Gopa explained. "This one, where we are headed, is one of the most popular ones."

"Why?"

"Dunno. Maybe due to the kind of magic inherent in its story or the kind of participation it allows. It's based upon an episode in the Ramayan."

"You know the story?" Not only did Miskovitz want to keep her mind off their earlier conversation, but he was also truly interested.

"Some." She smiled at the memory. "King Ravana's brothers, Khar and Dooshan, leading their ferocious army, rolled out in their magnificent chariots to kill Lord Rama. Not wanting to kill them, he advised them to go back and not die unnecessarily.

"Looking at him, standing there barefoot and alone, armed with only a few arrows in his shoulder *tuneer*, believing he could alone, all by himself, defeat their ferocious army, Khar and Dooshan made fun of him, laughing at his naive and audacious remarks and ordered their army to attack.

"Lord Rama had no choice. He had to fight. Invoking Lord Shiva, he shot a divine arrow into the midst of the advancing army. The air, emanating from the divine arrow, swished all around the army, creating an atmosphere in which every soldier saw in every other soldier's face, Lord Rama's face. Believing they were killing him, within minutes the soldiers ferociously killed each other while Rama simply stood there, watching and feeling sorry for them."

"Nice story. Plausible." Miskovitz nodded. "Could be done, you know. Mass hallucination. Mass hypnotism. But," he asked, "how do you participate?"

"Easy. Before the fight begins, you are given the evil soldier's uniform, a Rama mask, a bow, and as many arrows as you want. You can't aim at Lord Rama. That's against the rules. You try to kill as many robo-soldiers as you can.

"If you get hit, their rubber arrows do not hurt you. But, if your steel tipped arrow touches a robo-soldier, it immediately tumbles to the ground. For each hit, you get a point. Ten, you win the bow and arrows. Twenty, you win the evil uniform. Thirty, you carry away your Rama mask."

"Whew!" Miskovitz whistled. "I'd like to play that game. Carry away a few masks."

"Impossible." Gopa sounded amused. "Those robo-soldiers love to kill each other. They don't give you much chance. During the past three years, since it's opened, no one has managed to win a mask. And it's not for lack of trying."

"Ah, no robo-soldier is yet born that can match wits with yours truly," James Miskovitz drawled and Gopa laughed.

The main gate was open, not surprising since they knew Sharky had preceded them.

Leaving their auto in the parking lot, they moved toward the ticket window and were surprised to find it closed until Gopa remembered that the park remained open throughout the weekends and closed on Mondays.

"In his mad fury," she said, "Sharky forgot."

"What?"

"They're closed on Mondays."

"Oh. If nobody's around, we should be able to find him right away." Miskovitz moved toward the entrance.

The gate was open, and, entering the arena, he was surprised to find a grand fight in motion with arrows flying and robos falling . . .

"Sharky knew how to activate it?" Miskovitz asked.

"Must have." Gopa was equally surprised.

As they moved toward the scene, the robos stopped, "Sharky," Miskovitz called. "Sharky," Gopa joined him, "Sharkeeey . . . Sharkeeey."

There was no reply. Stepping cautiously amongst the fallen robo-soldiers, they moved toward Lord Rama's dais. Then they saw him, lying face up. In Sharky's hand was an arrow, the steel tip burrowed in his neck. Around its edges, his blood had trickled and coagulated.

Gopa's feet froze as an involuntary shriek escaped her lips and hung in midair. Miskovitz stood transfixed, muscles tightening, eyes rebelling. "Suicide?" He whispered, "Why?"

As if a spell were broken, Gopa moved a step forward, hesitated, then moved back. "There's nobody here. We need to call somebody."

"Right." Miskovitz searched his pocket. "I don't have my phone. You have yours?"

"No." Gopa shook her head. "There must be one in the auto."

"Right. Let's go."

"No. You go," she said. "I'll wait here."

He didn't want to leave her alone. She was in a vulnerable mood. The psychological trauma he had witnessed earlier clearly indicated it could be very dangerous to leave her with her oathmate's body. But strange emotions lurked in her eyes and arguing with her seemed even more unwise. He quickly retraced his steps to the auto.

Gopa knelt beside Sharky's inert body and lifted a tattooed hand that had been thrown to one side in the death throes. "Sharky, why?" Holding the lifeless limb in both her hands, she murmured softly, rebelliously, "Why? Had you again started taking marijuana? Is that why you were asking me about it? I got you to stop it. Why would I do it, Sharky?

"Or did you really think I was having sex with somebody? But, you know me. I wouldn't be friends with anyone else!" Making a fist, she shook it in his face. "I wasn't. But even if I was, so what? That was no reason to get your beef up. You set the rules, remember? Remember your theory of Powering the Kitchen Sink?

"You insisted we were free. We'd never, never behave like those other couples . . . blinded and shackled and doomed by sex and power. You forgot that? Why? Why? Dammit! Tell me why . . . "

She got up and moved back, kicking at the robos. "Why did you do it? To remind me that I wouldn't survive without you? Killing yourself, were you killing me? When I gave you that poem, 'Bathed in your shadow, I can take on anybody. Even conceive an outlandish stranger's child . . . ' did you really believe me?

"If you did," she knelt beside him again, once more taking his hand and kissing his lifeless fingers, "you were right. Without you, I'm just a fish without water. How am I going to go on living, my friend? What happened to your tough armor? How could you . . . Why . . . Why did you crumble like this? Like . . . like an old, flimsy cocoon?"

Behind her, feet sounded. Releasing his hand, she stood up and stared at the newcomers with fixed, dry, smarting eyes.

The one in the blue police uniform stood near Sharky's head, not touching him, just looking down at him. Then he turned toward them. "Was he left-handed?"

"No," Gopa said. "Why?"

"The arrow is in his left hand."

The park warden, in a green uniform, breathed hard. "Murder?"

"He had no enemies." Gopa felt angry at this insult.

"That's right, officer," Miskovitz ventured. "He was very popular. People loved him. I know that."

"Nevertheless — " The hawk-eyed officer stared at them, at each face, assessing. Probing. Determined to pierce through their masks. "That's his left hand." He made a half-circle and stood at the body's feet.

"He did that, used his left hand," the Park warden stuttered, "purposely."

"Nonsense." Gopa blurted out. She felt all eyes watching her. That made her more angry. "Why would anyone who was dying do that?"

He tried to assess her. "To implicate somebody."

That hadn't occurred to Hawk Eyes. Startled, he looked at them. Gopa, cheeks flushed, fists tightened, was staring at the two officers defiantly. Miskovitz was staring at the body that had convulsed in expelling its last breath. And the park warden, cool,detached, had his thoughts written clearly on his expressive face. Here was another junky, another day. Ah, well. All in a day's work.

But he made no further comment. "All right," the officer said, "you two can go. When the preliminaries are over, we'll call you."

As Gopa and James Miskovitz turned, they heard the screaming wail of the ambulance coming toward the grounds.

Meera A'Kash was fixing a scotch and soda for Sam Oringer when the phone rang. She moved a few paces and picked it up.

"Hello?"

It was a woman's voice, gruff, scratchy, sounding more like a man who had a bad cold. "Neil is staying here tonight."

Meera was surprised. "Where is *here*?" The phone went dead.

Meera's face turned pale — where was Neil?

She recognized the voices of his friends' parents, homes he went to visit. But he never stayed there overnight. If it got late, no matter how much they asked, he insisted on coming back.

She looked at her wrist watch. It was not yet seven. Not late at all. They didn't even need to bring him home. He could have come by himself. Then why? Where was he?

And why hadn't he called himself? He had left without telling her when she wasn't at home and had failed to leave a message for her on their video-diary.

Oringer realized something was wrong.

She had refused his dinner invitation on the pretext she hadn't told Neil she would be out and wasn't sure what time he'd be coming home. She had repeated that she needed to wait for him and keep his dinner ready. Without her, she had insisted, Neil wouldn't eat. Now it seemed he wasn't coming.

Should he say something? he wondered. What?

She turned toward him. "Colonel, is it just me, or has everyone raised such obnoxious, intolerable kids?"

"That was Neil?" he asked.

"He didn't leave a note where he'd be. And now someone calls and says he isn't coming home. He doesn't even have the . . . the . . . to call me." The drink she was fixing spilled over the edge of the glass and she pushed it away. The glass fell and splintered. She stared at the broken pieces.

Oringer stepped gingerly amidst the wreckage. "Let me."

Picking up the shards, he dabbed the bar countertop with napkins.

"That Gopa," staring at his efforts as if not comprehending what he was doing she continued, "I thought she behaved that way because Vishu spoiled her. I was wrong. They're all the same. Pooja, she runs away with some punk without telling me . . . and . . . and . . . " She was going to mention Neelam, the daughter she'd had, but never had. Remembering just in time that it was a space-gone secret, she stopped and bit her lower lip. Tasting blood, she grimaced and dabbed it with a napkin.

Since Neil wasn't coming home, Oringer wondered if he should repeat his dinner invitation. It didn't seem wise. In this mood, ordinary conversation would be impossible. He'd return not much wiser and the general would get mad at him for wasting another evening without producing any concrete results. Besides there was no need for him to listen to her bitching and act as her psychoanalyst.

He glanced at his wristwatch and spoke as if he had just remembered something. "Mrs. A'Kash, I'm sorry. I was expecting an important call and forgot to call-forward it. I just remembered. Can I have a rain check for another evening?"

His courtly manner amused her. "Sure, colonel. I'm sorry about tonight. Everything suddenly seems to be piling up on me. I hadn't realized how many things my husband was taking care of. I guess I was taking it for granted. And now that I have to . . . I'm sorry, I completely forgot you were coming over. These kids . . . even Neil, specially Neil." Moving abruptly, she fixed herself a drink and poured it down her throat. Then fearful of being alone, she offered him one.

"I can't believe what's going on," she said quickly, as if confiding a secret. "Neil's father's life is in jeopardy. We don't know if he's alive. But the only thing this ungrateful brat is crying about is his stupid invention. Keeps blaming me — if I hadn't sent it with his father, he wouldn't have lost it. I'll bet that's why he's not coming home. To teach me a lesson. Wants me to beg forgiveness. Can you believe it?"

"Let him sleep on it a few days. When he gets over it, he'll realize his mistake."

"I bet he won't. He's his father's seedling. As obstinate, as one-track-minded, as God could have ever conceived. I'm going to stop caring, too. Why should I care!" She picked up the drink that Oringer hadn't touched and swallowed it.

"I'll call you. Tomorrow." Oringer decided to beat a hasty retreat. "Have a nice evening."

"Same to you, colonel," she said to his retreating back.

As the door closed behind him, she moved and picked up her

husband's photo. "Vishu, where are you? Are you really gone or have the world's computers gone mad? Am I a widow or a wife?"

She put the photo back and went to the bar, then changed her mind and walked to her bedroom to pick up her wedding albums from the bedside shelf. Opening one, she remembered the first night of her honeymoon — the open sky, and the stars, and . . .

We'll have an unconventional honeymoon, Vishu A'Kash had declared, on the mountaintop, under the stars, with no one, nothing, except the whispering winds around us . . .

They had gone to Kashmir and had spent their first night on the mountaintop, naked under the stars, like the fabled Adam and Eve.

Near dawn, when sun's first rays had woken her, seeing his sleeping face smiling in some beguiling dream, she had promised herself that she'd always sleep next to him. She'd never sleep in a separate room, a separate bed. No matter what job he took, no matter where he went, she'd always stay by his side.

"Lord Vishnu," she had silently prayed, "on this first morning of my new life, grant me just this: to get up every morning and upon opening my eyes, the first thing, the very first thing, I will always want to see is this face. This face that is now mine. Only mine. Smiling like this, dreaming, perhaps of the exciting, lifting, life-breathing sex we shared together all night . . . "

And she had kept her promise. Until the day he left in that cursed spaceship, they had never fought at night. She had never slept in a separate bed.

How many times had she pleaded with him. Please, do not name the ship Titanic. Why is this name so important to you? No. I'm not superstitious. And you know it. But some things are just not done. This is one of those. I have a premonition, a bad feeling. For a long time I haven't asked you for anything. This one small, silly request you must accept: Do not name your ship Titanic.

But he had only laughed and teased and then flown away in that never-returning spaceship. And since that night, she hadn't been able to sleep in their bed.

Perhaps fate had been merciful to her in that she'd had to go to her invalid mother's bedside, to keep a sleepless vigil, night after night. But, no. Fate hadn't been merciful at all. If she hadn't gone to her mother's house, that strange, old woman wouldn't have been able to plant those poison seeds in her mind.

Or was it only she who was at fault? If, instead of worrying so much about her daughters, she had kept track of his doings . . .

"Vishu, husband mine," she spoke softly to the picture of his boyish face, laughing in the sun, "is Neil really not my son? Do I really have another daughter? Neelam? I like that name. But would I like her? Would she like me? Considering the actions of your children, whom I've cared for all their lives, I doubt it. But if she exists, I must find her. If only because when you learn about it, it will hurt you that, despite all your secrecy, I learned about her."

Closing the album decisively, she replaced it and moved to pack her suitcase; if Neil thought he didn't need her, that was just fine. She'd leave him alone. The best way to learn is by making mistakes. She'd leave him a note — a message on their video-diary — and enough money to buy his ticket. If he loved her, had any feeling for her, he would call. She would come back. Or he could come over there, to his grandmother's house. He knew how to reach her.

Right now, she couldn't afford to wait for him. She'd go away. She must go away. She must leave. Because in this house, where she had never been alone, she wouldn't be able to spend this long, black, wretched night all by herself. This night or tomorrow's soon-coming night, or all the other cruel nights that would follow.

She picked up Neil's photo to take it with her. Neil, she said softly to the picture, I don't know if you are my son. Why you are behaving in such a horrible manner? And why am I feeling so guilty leaving you here. You don't care . . . none of you care.

How secure I used to feel here. What a mistake that was. This house wasn't a perfect shelter. It was just a fake, brittle cocoon. And it has suddenly, without any warning, fallen apart, leaving me feeling exposed like . . . like a naked exhibit, lying in an open auction case for the world to see and stare at and despise and reject and . . . and kick around with lofty disgust.

The ringing of the phone in the other room broke her chaotic lamentation. "Neil?" her mind cried and she ran to grab that lifeline before it could stop ringing.

But it was that menacing, cruel voice. "Mrs. A'Kash, we're not greedy. We want to be kind. We'll sell you your victim's negative for a paltry twenty million. Tomorrow, we'll let you know where you can drop the money."

Before Meera could breathe, the line was disconnected.

The phone fell from her hand, but she didn't notice. Her eyes moved toward the photo of her missing husband. Before they could reach it, they hit on that strange painting on the wall — Rings Around the World.

She stared at it. Strangulating strings? Choking the world? Her world? Wouldn't that be the best way? The easiest, the least messy way? Tie strings around her neck and, kicking away the world, drop away in that unseen void where no one would be able to find her?

7

Stones That Ripple

After the long, hot drive on the unpaved, dusty road, the sight of the small village, nestling under thick, shady trees, seemed so refreshing that Herbert Caine almost forgot his parched throat. As soon as his tight-lipped driver stopped the auto and without waiting for him to come around and open the door, Caine opened it himself and jumped out.

The few seconds it had taken hadn't seemed time enough to even blink his eyes, but hearing giggles, he turned and found himself ringed by a swarm of barefoot, scantily clad children. Behind them, in the distance, female heads were peeking through the painted doors of their small huts, and men stood warily under the trees in small, scattered groups, watching him silently.

The place that had appeared deserted just a few minutes ago suddenly seemed hot and alive with suspicion, curiosity and adolescent mirth.

Caine turned toward his taciturn driver, loaned to him by the consulate, "Ask them if anyone here speaks English."

"You are not in America, sir," a young boy, twelve or fourteen, said in his lilting Indian accent. "This is India." His chest seemed to expand a bit. "We have two France-returned — "

"Hush," a young girl, perhaps his own age, closed his mouth with her grimy hand. "You got no eyes. Doesn't he look exhausted.

"Sir," she addressed him politely, "we got no bottled water. Would you like some fresh fruit? Or Indian beer? Pepsi? World Coke?"

Caine smiled. Had he just gotten lucky or were the stories about Indian villages just that — stories?

"Everything sounds great," he replied. "Anything would be OK, if it's not too much trouble. I am thirsty."

"No trouble. Come." She grabbed his right hand and, half walking, half skipping, started toward a shady grove, where he could see some people smoking hookahs and playing cards.

The other children didn't give up their prerogative of escorting him. Some fell in a few steps behind, others skipped ahead, all chattering in their native language.

Caine could have understood most of it if he had made the effort, but other things were on his mind. The girl seemed the leader of the group and perhaps was used to fielding questions. Caine wondered if she would give him a few answers before they reached her home.

"Can I ask you something?" he said politely.

"Why not?" she smiled up at him.

"How do you know I take bottled water?"

"Why, everyone knows that. All of you who come here . . . "

"You mean others like me are here?" His pulse beat faster.

"Not right now. But they do come. All the time."

"Why? What's so special here?"

"Nothing," she giggled. "Nothing. Just our world-famous guru Mata. Everyone wants to touch her feet and hear her divine words."

"That's the reason I've come also," he quickly admitted.
"Would I be able to have her *darshan* today?"

"No. I'm afraid not."

"Why?" His heart sank — following that mysterious woman's trail, he had traveled to city after city, town after town. And now at last, when he had clearly reached his destination . . . They had reached the shady mango grove. Seeing them, the younger adults stood up as a sign of respect, but the older ones didn't move their eyes from their games and their hookahs and the tobacco water pipes they were sharing.

Still pulling his hand, his guide moved toward one who was surrounded by many children. Coming nearer, Caine saw the reason; with a small carving stick, he was showing them how to dig a map in the soft ground. Fascinated, the children were enthusiastically assisting him.

"Bapu," she said, trying to make her way. "Bapooo."

"Yes, Chimpoo?" He looked up, saw the stranger and smiled. "Sahib, welcome. Chimpoo, did you give your guest some Coke?"

"He just came, Bapu. He is also looking for our guru Mata."

The geography teacher said something to his group, placed his carving stick carefully in what looked like an unfinished lake, and got up. "Come, Sahib. Too noisy here. We'll sit in that corner over there. Chimpoo, would you remember to wash your hands before you touch the fruits?"

She giggled, nodded and skipped away.

Following his host, Caine looked back and saw that the children had again started carving their earth map, mischievously jostling each other.

Chimpoo's father was saying, "Our honorable guru Mata has always been popular with foreigners. Young or adult, they all adore her. Her powers must be increasing, for now she has started attracting other countries' officers also. You are from the American consulate, aren't you?"

This was news! Others were looking for her? Why? From which countries? If he asked, would the villager tell him?

"I'll tell you," said the teacher, as if he had read his mind.

Dressed in a white shirt and creased khaki shorts, he was moving briskly but with restraint, like a leashed athlete, to keep pace with Caine's tired feet. Guiding Caine to a solitary-looking chess table, he waited until Caine took a chair, then moving to one opposite him, he leaned upon its back.

"Since you're an American," he said pleasantly, "I can tell you. It's privileged information, but we don't hide anything from Americans," he laughed. "First we had the high-flying Japanese, then the thick-booted Chinese, followed by the portly Germans."

Stopping, he glanced at his guest, whom he had been expecting for the past two days. He had known he'd come. Americans were sometimes late, but never remiss . . . In the end, they generally succeeded in getting what no one else could even touch.

Noticing his host's expectant eyes, Caine realized some kind of response was expected from him. He didn't know what to say. One wrong word and this seemingly cordial camaraderie could blow away like a frail whiff of smoke, even before it had gotten underway.

He wished he had brought a consular officer with him. If he asked who came after the Germans, would that be inappropriate?

It could be, he hypothesized, that guru Mata had gone away somewhere because she didn't want to meet all these foreigners. If he asked about that, would that be insulting her?

The village teacher turned around the chair on which he had been leaning, lowered himself leisurely, stretched his bare feet to their full length, crossed them at the ankles and leaned back.

Trying to find the sky through the thick green foliage, he remarked softly, meditatively, "Nowadays, the young ones' horizons are changing more rapidly than they ever have."

Platitudes! Why? Caine glanced at his host.

"America today is the same enticing country it was in my father's times. Perhaps even more glamorous, even more prosperous. But today's young ones . . . "

"Have you been to America?" Caine asked. It seemed to be the safest question at the moment.

"I was born there."

"Oh, I hadn't realized . . . "

The middle-aged, young-looking teacher laughed and sat up with his hands on his knees, steepling his fingers. "And my dad. And his parents. Some of my family members are still there."

"But you came back."

"Not me," he shook his head. "My dad. He is a doctor. Loves setting up new hospitals, especially in remote villages."

"And you?"

"I'm a doctor, too. But, aren't we straying?"

"Yes. We are." Caine decided to be frank with him. There was no other way. "I came here on a hunch. Now all this activity that you've described makes me wonder if my wild theory wasn't really so wild after all."

"We are very helpful folks around here," the village doctor said laconically. "That is, if we like the people."

"I noticed that," Caine nodded. "And maybe you can help. It's a long story, but I'll try to tell you briefly. One of our scientists was hit by an auto. He was never married, had no children, but in his diary, he stated — no, repeated many times, with stubborn conviction — your honorable guru Mata's prediction that he, the scientist, that is, would be killed by his daughter. I came here to consult with guru Mata to see if, in her calculations, there's room for another person? Or must this person — the one who hit him — be his daughter?"

"He was hit by a woman? She claims to be his daughter?"

Caine shook his head. "We don't know who hit him. Despite a reward, so far no one has admitted anything."

"A hit-and-run driver?" The village doctor smiled. "What's so strange about that? When I was there, all the news media used to spew off statistics — how many more people were being killed by autos every day than by . . . "

"There's more to it," Caine admitted. "Fragments of paper were found in his room, letters written, or half-written, torn in small pieces, then burned in a wastepaper basket. On the ones that could be salvaged, we found names of places in Germany and India, and amongst them, one name stood out."

"And?" The teacher-doctor's eyes were glistening with curiosity.

Was he just hungry for a spicy story, Caine wondered, or was there more to it? Hiding his concern, he continued. "Of course, some names are very common. And it could be anyone's. But it could be the name of our famous space mother-in-law."

"You mean that fellow's who disappeared with the Titanic?"

Herbert Caine simply nodded.

The village doctor whistled. "Like everyone, I read the news stories. She was born in India, wasn't she? Married an architect, who was born in Germany but had taken Egyptian citizenship and never gave it up, even when he got his American green card."

Herbert Caine nodded, "Your information is correct."

"Earth save me! That explains the bevy of foreign autos making such frequent runs for our village?"

"Not really."

"Why? And don't tell me no one else had access to those burnt papers."

Just then, Chimpoo came over with a friend, carrying bowls of fruit and a tray of beverages, the glasses filled with ice. Smiling shyly, they offered Caine a choice of Coke, iced tea with sprigs of mint leaves, fresh orange juice and lemonade. He picked up a glass of orange juice. The cool liquid not only relieved his thirst, but some of his tension also started ebbing away.

He leaned against the back of his chair, sipped his juice and spoke more comfortably. "You're right. We have made snooping such a fine art, the whole world has become like a big family. Everyone knows what everyone else is doing. No. The reason I said that was because there are theories."

"Such as?" His enigmatic host prevented any immediate response by waving toward the bowl of fruit. "Try this . . . Lakhnavi Kharbooja, named after the city where it originated, in Lucknow. A kind of cantaloupe. Our specialty. We are very proud of it."

At a New Delhi restaurant Caine had tried a mango and not liked it. He picked up a small piece of the alien-looking, soft, white fruit and put it in his mouth gingerly. It had a very delicate, fragile aroma and, as it touched his taste buds, it almost melted in his mouth. He quickly wanted to have another one. And then another.

Emptying his plate, he leaned toward the table to refill it. "Delicious," he said. "Never tasted anything like it. I wonder why don't we grow it in Florida."

"Maybe it doesn't like Florida."

Caine laughed. "As I was saying, there are theories. One says that the diary and those torn papers aren't real, that they are forgeries and were planted."

"But why?"

Caine shrugged, "theorists' job is to throw pebbles in placid pools and create ripples. My job is not to trace the pebbles. I only try to read the ripples."

"You should try to read the pebbles also. Especially those that don't create ripples. Those are the ones that can be real dangerous, like . . . like internal injuries. Unseen, but always there. Like kidney stones that can kill, if not treated in time."

Caine stared at his host's silent, enigmatic face. "You could be right. What particular stone are you thinking of?"

The village teacher-doctor steepled his fingers and gazed at the horizon, then brought his eyes back and fixed them upon Caine's face. "Guru Mata is under very strict surveillance."

Caine was startled. "Why? Isn't she just another one of your saintly spiritual gurus? A kind of walking psychiatrist who heals people's pain by listening to them patiently?"

"Yes. Just a simple spiritual soul — a penniless guru — at whose feet they bow for advice and guidance before they do anything — fix marriage dates, launch election campaigns, take overseas trips, lay foundation stones . . . All of them . . . highly placed politicians, industrialists . . . "

"I've heard about it." Caine didn't need to hear the whole list. "Never gave it much importance." That was obviously a mistake, he thought, and added, "The Secret Service always gets blamed, but it has responsibilities. If she has such links, your Secret Service did the right thing. We'd have done the same."

"I didn't say it was the honorable Indian Snoopers," the village doctor smiled. "They goofed. You will probably learn about it anyway, so I'm not telling you a state secret. She was being tailed by the KGB."

Caine sat up and stared at his host's poker face. "Why? Why should they be interested in her?"

The doctor stared at the green leaves hanging over his head, as if asking them whether or not to reply. "I myself just learned of it the other day," he said softly, distantly. "Her father was a Russian. She never relinquished her Soviet citizenship."

The CIA should have known that. We're supposed to keep track of overseas Soviets, Caine thought. We goofed. But, thanks to this talkative stranger, I can now salvage the situation.

"I need to talk with her," he said, hoping his urgency wasn't showing. "Can you arrange a meeting?"

"I would if I could, but it's impossible."

"Why?" Caine remembered Chimpoo's words.

"The KGB. They were here first. They whisked her away before you could say, 'Come with us, please.'"

That, of course, was not surprising. "So she can be reached only at the Soviet embassy?"

"The embassy? When they can take her to the heartland?"

Of course! And if these simple villagers broadcast this fact to everyone who fluttered here before him, it really didn't matter because the KGB would hide her in some secret shell anyway. Blast it!

And in all this, he thought, looking at his enigmatic, athletic host, where do you fit in? Do you by any chance belong to the KGB? And were you waiting here for me? And did I fall into your trap and tell you more than what you had hoped to hear?

Again, as if having read his mind, the teacher-doctor spoke, softly and serenely. "No, I'm not a KGB stooge, Mr. Caine."

Hearing his name, the FBI director was startled. "You know who I am. You've known all along."

The undecipherable doctor smiled. "You yourself said that the world is now an open family, where everyone knows — "

"Everyone's secrets," Caine wryly jumped in. "And may I ask, where do you belong? The Indian Secret Service?"

Just then, Chimpoo and her friend came running and, reaching them, halted to a dead stop. "Bapu?"

"Yes, Beta."

"Amma is asking if sahib would stay for dinner?"

"No, Chimpoo," Caine replied before her father could. "I have to rush back. Would you please thank your mom for me and tell her I'd like a rain check."

"A rain check?" she giggled. "I know about that." She turned, grabbed her friend's hand and they dashed back.

"You have a lovely daughter," Caine said, turning toward his host. "Was she born in America?"

"I also need a rain check," he said, smiling. "My students are waiting for me. We need to snowcap those mountains and fill the lakes and rivers with blue water. I'll walk you to your auto."

Caine got up; there was no sense in pressing. If this fellow was born in the United States, finding out about him wouldn't be difficult. And it could wait.

He didn't realize how erroneous that assumption was.

At the Shaung Ch'eng-tzu Mission Control Center, Flight Director Mao Ki Tung was slashing through his office, from one map-decorated wall to another. "I wasn't mistaken about them, was I?" he demanded. "I've always said those dumb Indians are still slaves to their imperialist British masters, haven't I?"

He glared at Col. Fong as if despite his being a mere underling, that opinionated officer had dared to defy his authentic, time-tested theory. "Haven't I?"

Col. Fong decided the time for behaving like an ancient, dug-up, ceramic soldier was over. If he didn't come up with a proper answer, it could result in dire consequences for his career.

He nodded with proper respect and maximum possible enthusiasm. "Yes you have, comrade director. Always. Everyone knows that." Enough. From his past experience, he knew there was no need to ask the reason for this thundering reminder of the director's oft-repeated theory. It would be revealed soon enough.

He was right.

"Those dumb idiots! They've denied my offer," Mao Ki Tung shouted at the maps, at the roof, at the world in general. "I broke my own rule. I didn't wait for their offer. I made the offer first. And those dumb idiots . . . " he slashed his fists through the insult-ridden air.

"You know, comrade director, what they say in the darkforces-ridden-West: 'There's more than one way to skin a cat.' Why not use their own poison potion upon them?"

Through the haze of his cosmic anger, Tung saw a faint glimmer. "What?"

"A very simple ruse. Let's present them a dragon boat."

"A dragon boat?" Tung kicked a wastepaper basket and it went flying, scattering items in its path, just like his runaway thoughts. He was dreaming in terms of leading in all the debates and processions, not in terms of stupid dragon boats.

"Yes, comrade director. You remember our annual Hong Kong International Dragon Boat Races?"

"Yes, a relic of the long-gone British Crown. What about them?" His eyes said: Trying to sidetrack me, Fong? You won't succeed.

"I'm sure you know that this ancient regatta commemorates the death of poet Qu Yuan, who threw himself into the ocean as a final protest against the ordinances of his noble government. Legend says that defying the wrath of their emperor, the local fishermen raced out in their boats beating the mighty ocean waves with their fragile oars to frighten away the great white fish and prevent them from eating their hero."

"So?" Not getting the drift of this conversation, Tung's tone was suspicious.

"An apt theme, don't you think, to bless the rebel's cause? Memory of a defiance, blessed by religious trappings. They have a suitable river. You supply the history — a three-thousand-year-old legend.

"Pageantry — Buddhist monks, scattering rice along the Saryu banks, invoking the protective spirit of Qu Yuan for a safe regatta and successful convention. Please the Tibetans. Charm the U.N. Supply a theme that'll reverberate not just at this convention, but that will also be repeated in all the future ones during the coming centuries. Unsurpassable Chinese victory, comrade director."

Col. Fong stopped, but other unspoken words hung like freshly woven garlands in the room's expectant air. He thought, if you'll do this, Mao Ki Tung, in earth's history, your name will become immortal. You will become immortal.

"Yes," Mao Ki Tung breathed hard. "A worthy thought. We shall consider it. If our comrade chairman will allow the expense of transporting a huge boat . . . "

"The boat need not be transported. Only two items would be needed: carved dragon heads and dragon tails. Fishermen along India's Malabar coast make beautiful boats. If we tell them the boat is for the convention's inaugural race and give them heads and tails as gifts, they may not even charge for the boat."

Mao Ki Tung's expression had been changing. Moving back to his desk, he positioned himself in his executive chair. "Yes, comrade Fong," he stated deliberately, "it's a worthy idea. Here's what I want you to do. Jot down the few points that I should take up with our comrade chairman. As you know, at times he can be very obstinate. Very illogical.

"And," he wagged a fat finger, "this is one of those times. But putting our thoughts together, we should be able to convince him. Let me have them as soon as possible. Yes? Within an hour."

Inwardly relieved at having managed his dismissal from Mao Ki Tung's august presence so easily, Col. Fong saluted and was about to withdraw when a young lieutenant colonel burst into the room unceremoniously. "Comrade director," he said breathlessly, "you must come to the operations room right away."

Tung's heavy eyebrows climbed to his receding hairline. "What did you say?"

The lieutenant saluted and stood at attention, "Permission to report, comrade director. We all saw it. Just now. The Soviet Volga. Volga One. It disintegrated in space. Just now."

Tung's mind reeled. He didn't know whether he should be happy at this new setback for the arrogant Russians or grieve for the communist world's loss. "The Japs," Tung surmised. "No doubt, they are responsible. No one can stop it now. There will be war. We must prepare for it. Colonel?"

The senior colonel was still there. Again jumping to hasty conclusions, Mao Ki! he was thinking. I know what a powerful manipulator you are. I'll pray to Buddha you don't succeed this time, just this once. Because if you do, this time it won't be just a war, it will be a global war. A chemo-nuclear war. Then, only the nuclear cloud will remain to remember your immortal name . . .

"Colonel," Tung was saying, "get the tape ready for replay. I'll be there. First, I need to make a few calls. If I can't start these centurion stones rippling," he added ominously, "my name's not Mao Ki."

Stryker was staring at the screens — playing and replaying tapes of Volga and Titanic's flight paths — together and separately. Separately and together. What was the missing link, the one item that could be responsible for their destruction?

Was it one and the same reason in both instances? Or were two discrete factors holding the clues?

Did Volga's destruction mean the Japanese were not responsible? Surely they wouldn't take steps that pointed at them so conspicuously!

Or would they? Because by doing so, nobody would suspect them.

Wasn't it time to make some phone calls? Time to ask a few questions? Why hadn't the Russians called? Were they waiting for us to call first?

Stryker wished Sparky would wake up from his coma and provide some answers. He wished that Meera's mother would regain her speech so that he could talk with her. And, above all, he wished that his friend, Herbert Caine — his alter ego and sounding board — was here so they could talk and thrash around ideas.

Why was he spending so much time in India? Why was he stuck there? That wasn't his style. He worked fast, wrapped up riddles quickly and left the loose ends to be mopped up by his staff.

What had gone wrong? Stryker wondered. Why such a silence at his end? Was his assistant telling the truth when he said that she hadn't heard from him?

Somehow, that didn't seem right. Not at all. No matter where he was, no matter how unreachable, Caine always found ways to keep in touch. Why was his staff making up stories?

Then there was this other problem. The problem of his having those nerve-wracking nightmares. In his pre-Titanic days, he used to sleep so soundly that Melody, his ex-wife, used to complain he slept like a stone. She always worried that in an emergency if she needed to wake him up she wouldn't succeed until something unthinkable had happened. To make her feel better, he used to invent dreams. Dreams and nightmares that she wouldn't believe.

Now, hardly a night went by without his waking up in the middle of the night, sweating, screaming, not wanting to go back to sleep again, horrified at what his fiendish nightmares had conjured up. And the worst part of it was that he couldn't talk about them. If he did, they'd advise him to report to the department psychiatrist. And that would go on his official record. No, he couldn't mention those dreams to anyone. Anyone. Except his buddy, Pablo Martinez.

But a dark curtain had fallen around Pablo. That was, to say the least, bewildering and stupefying. Why in earth's name was he maintaining such a silence? Why wasn't he returning calls? Official requests left at his office and personal messages left on his videodiary remained unacknowledged. Why?

They used to talk so often. When they did not find each other, they faxed jokes or riddles, with time limits for receiving solutions. Now the time limits seemed to have no meaning. They had all expired. His fax at home gave him no anagrams. It had itself become a riddle, a stony extension of their moribund friendship.

Why? Because Pablo didn't want to contact his brother-in-law and check the winds in Moscow?

But he had accepted the request in his usual, cheerful manner. Not by a single action, by a single word, had he given any clue that he didn't like it. Wouldn't like to handle it.

In fact, remembering his matchless guru, the legendary, science fiction maestro, Ray Bradbury, he had hinted he'd use some unusual, previously untried unheard of methodology.

Then, why? Why had he gone into such mysterious

seclusion? What kind of ultimate riddle was he posing? And if he couldn't find the answer, would that mean the demise of their precious friendship?

Stryker shivered; the problems were taking their toll. An unbearable, prickling toll. He shouldn't let them. What was the solution? Call Melody? Invite here for dinner? Or . . .

"General?"

He looked up. His secretary, Mona, stood near, with a phone in her hand and a worried expression on her dark ebony face.

"Call from the White House, sir. 'Urgent,' they said."

He took the phone. "Stryker."

"General, would you please hold for the president, sir," a charming, female voice said.

Almost immediately he heard the familiar voice. "Stan, thought I would let you know. I just had a call from Moscow on my yellow phone."

Stryker's mind reeled, dark images swirled, one of his nightmares was coming true? Imagine bad things and they'd happen.

He curbed his thoughts. "Does that mean we need to trouble our Marines, Mr. President?"

"Didn't get time to find out. Someone said, 'This warning's all you get, Mr. President. This is Yellow Alert.' Then the line was cut off. Weird!"

"Did you recognize the voice, sir?"

"You know, I recognize some of them, those whom I've met. The Soviet president. The Russian Republic's president. The Presidium chairman . . . But this one I didn't. I've given the tape to Herb's assistant. By the way, he's coming back. Day after tomorrow."

"Thank you for telling me, Mr. President. If you have a few minutes, may I ask you something?"

"You never need permission, Stan. You know that."

"Has someone called Glavkosmos?"

"When Volga One joined our Titanic, the State Department should have called. As always, they dithered. If we call now, that may be construed as a response to their Yellow Alert."

"Not necessarily," the SDC general said confidently. "I've

met their Vladimir Grachenko at several international gatherings. He's stubbornly apolitical. Has a sensible head on his tough, unbending shoulders. Quite jovial and friendly, too, when he's not wearing the mantle of the director of Manned Space Operations."

"Fine." The strong, deep baritone held a soft chuckle. "Why don't you call him. But, Stan, be prudent. Very cautious. If there has been some kind of a sudden coup there, if heads have rolled, your Vladimir may have toppled. And, Stan?"

"Yes, Mr. President?"

"If there's something I should know, you will call me back?"

"Of course, sir. You know I will."

"Good," said a soft sigh and the line was disconnected.

Stryker waited for a few seconds. The phone, silent but ominous, remained inert in his hand. What was happening in Moscow? Could an item like the crumbling of a space machine cause the fall of a political alliance?

That shouldn't be logical. Or possible.

But wasn't he thinking in terms of the system he knew? A democratic policy.

Could he really guess what would happen within the elusive and mysterious Soviet Alliance where, despite an emergence of some democratic threads, the ancient communist elements were still holding onto their early roots? There, democracy was not an invulnerable life source embedded in the very core of its people. There, it was still an uncemented shell castle in which if just one crucial shell toppled the whole castle could come crumbling down.

Well, he'd have to find out. The president had thrown the ball into his court.

He looked up to find his secretary, who had discreetly moved away. "Mona," he called.

"General?" Moving quickly, gracefully, she came over right away and took the phone from his hand.

"Check my office. Blanket it, you know, as usual. I'm going to make a few phone calls."

"Yes, sir. Right away." She moved quickly, efficiently on her high heels, with her usual graceful movements.

For a few seconds, he watched her undulating, receding back. She has become such an essential part of my office life, he thought. I don't know what I'd do without her.

Then, withdrawing his mind, he turned toward the screens where two familiar images were frozen in space and time. The tiny speck that was Volga One, inexplicably, unaccountably, crumbled into little shards. And the Titanic, another tiny speck, one minute there, the next minute gone. Without leaving any residue. Any sign.

Sighing, he gathered his papers and got up, fighting dark thoughts. If a military takeover was underway in Moscow, if heads were getting lined up to be rolled — and Vladimir Grachenko's head among them — who was the most likely successor? Lt. Gen. Leon Kostyszyn?

If that was the case, it wasn't a phony Yellow Alert. A Red Alert could follow. With a war. Not just a war, but a global war. A hungry war that could not be contained, that would turn into a world-consuming, chemo-nuclear war.

So, his nightmares weren't just nightmares after all. They were real. Real and strong foreboding of the future to come . . .

The blood surging in his veins rushed to his temple, and he quickened his steps.

"All clear, sir," said Mona as he entered his office.

Quickly stepping out, she closed the door behind her.

8

Thunder Days/ Nuclear Nights

An usher in a gold-braided blue uniform directed Sam Oringer to Meera A'Kash's table.

Walking toward her, he noticed that she wore tennis shoes and tennis shorts, but there was no tennis racket at her table. The drink she had ordered seemed untouched. And she wasn't paying any attention to the couple of pairs playing on the side courts with amateurish gusto.

As he came closer, he saw she was clenching and unclenching her fists and her face looked older — drawn and haggard, with unnatural lines creasing her forehead. He felt alarmed and quickened his steps.

The grass was thick and his shoes weren't making any noise. Only when he reached her table did she look up, sensing his presence. Seeing him, her tired eyes lit up with unfeigned pleasure.

"Colonel," she said extending her hand, "thank you for accepting my call. Thank you for coming."

He took her hand in both of his, squeezed it affectionately and sat down next to her. "If I say I often wait for your call, you may misinterpret it," he laughed as if it were a joke. "So I won't say it. But tell me, how long are we going to keep up this colonel business. What's wrong with my name?"

She seemed surprised "I . . . I never thought about it, you being in SDC and all. And," she stole a glance at him, wondering whether or not to say it, "and somehow, from the first day I saw you, many times I get this feeling of . . . sort of glimpsing my long-lost father."

"Oh." He leaned back. "I didn't know I had reached that point where one starts invoking a fatherly image. I — "

"Please, don't misunderstand." Afraid she had insulted him, she quickly interrupted. "You don't look old. Not at all. It's just that I've always missed my father. And, colonel — "

"Again, remember, not colonel, just Sam. Nowadays, even kids don't call their parents 'mom' and 'pop.' At least my son doesn't."

"You have a son?"

"Of course. I married. Fathered a child. Got out unbloodied through a stormy divorce — like any true-blooded American."

She smiled. "I never heard it put that way. You make it sound almost like fun."

"Almost is right. Tell me, are we going to sit here and drink or play a game or two? I warn you, I haven't played for a long time. I've gone rusty."

"And I haven't played since my college days. Period. But my mother bought all of us — Vishu, myself and our children — life memberships at this country club, and this seemed as good a place as any to waste some of your time."

"Forget my time," he declared, waving at the waiter to get him a drink. "How's your mother?"

"Still in a coma. It was very kind of you to put her in your friend's care. Combing the world, I couldn't have found a better doctor. I'm not worried about her."

But we are, me and Gen. Stryker, Sam thought as the waiter came over to take his order. If that wasn't the case, he wouldn't be here, wasting his time.

"I wish," Meera continued as soon as the waiter walked away, "I was lying in that hospital in her place."

"No you don't," Sam protested.

"Yes, I do. You know why? Because I think the only lucky people are those who can go crazy. You know something else? I never used to have nightmares. Now, I do. Almost every night. Can you tell me? Am I a widow or not?"

Sam Oringer didn't know what to say. He put his hand on her small-looking hand, lying listlessly on the table. "Believe me, I wish I knew."

She pulled her hand away. "And there is this thing about this fourth child."

"What fourth child?"

She looked at him searchingly. "You mean you don't know? The department doesn't know?"

"Doesn't know what, Mrs. A'Kash?"

"I thought it was Meera?"

"Sorry," he said smiling, "habits die hard, don't they? Meera it is. So tell me, what it is you think we don't know."

"It could all be lies, just an attempt to blackmail me."

Sam Oringer had worked hard at learning how to present a poker face, how to manifest a fatherly image, but she was making it very difficult for him. Perhaps, he thought, the best approach would be to keep quiet. Say as little as possible. Now that she had started, perhaps she would go on.

He was right. She drained her glass in one defiant gulp and put it down decisively. "An old woman came to me with a mad story that Vishu wanted a son and was convinced I wouldn't be able to give him one. So he got another woman pregnant and switched my daughter with her son. If it's true, Neil isn't my son and I have a daughter, called Neelam, somewhere in this world."

Oringer stared at her. Was that why she had called him? To present him this crooked story? Why? To start divorce proceedings? Is that what this was all about?

"In life," he said slowly, cautiously, "anything's possible. I'd like to talk with this woman."

"She's dead. Fell down the steps and died on the spot."

Another story? Oringer wondered. Or could she be telling the truth? It sounded so strange. Like no duplicity can.

"In my nightmares," she was saying, "every night I kill that old blackmailer in a different manner. And that's not the only person I kill."

Oringer was feeling sorry for her, but he feared that if he made a wrong gesture, spoke a wrong word, he might silence her. He kept his face immobile and his eyes sympathetic.

"That day, when Neil called about the Titanic and I heard him crying I decided to return home." She pressed both her palms against her eyes, as if to blot out what those horrified eyes were seeing. Removing them, she glanced at Oringer defiantly. "I braked the auto right away. I did," she stated almost belligerently. "But that maniac was determined to commit suicide. He ran under my wheels like a crazed animal."

Like a crazed animal . . . Determined to commit suicide. Oringer's breath almost stopped. She couldn't be talking about Sparky, could she? That day, in that area, was that the only auto accident . . .

But Sparky was never married. There was no record anywhere of his ever having any child, even an adopted or surrogate one . . .

And she was certainly not his daughter. There was no ambiguity about that. Her birth records were verified before Capt. A'Kash was chosen.

So it was just an unfortunate accident. And that weird forecast and absurd note, planted or not, had nothing to do with it.

What if there were a science for forecasting the future? his doubting mind asked. The CIA was not infallible. Were they shadowing Sparky every minute — day and night? Of course not. What if she was an illegitimate daughter?

Suddenly, he wanted to shake her and ask her the critical question. Who was it, Meera, that you almost killed? Was it Sparky? Are you his daughter? Was it him on the phone when your mother cried out, "No. Not my daughter. No way . . . " Is that what he was doing on that road at that time, coming to you, to plead with you to spare his life? . . .

Hiding his agitation, keeping his poker face intact, he quietly said, "I'm sure you did. And called an ambulance?"

"No, I didn't." She looked embarrassed. "I guess I panicked. I saw bloody newspaper headlines slashing me apart. I guess I'd have called the police after reaching home, but when I arrived, you were there. Then, as soon as you left, the call came about my mother. Getting ready to leave, I heard on the news he was in some hospital. Since he was alive — .I'm not defending myself. I should have called the police, but one thing led to another and I never got around to — "

"Who was it? The victim the media are calling John Q?"

She nodded. "And sometimes — no, often — I think that if I hadn't run away, if I had picked him up and taken him to hospital, I wouldn't have been the cause of the third death."

"What?" Startled, Oringer sat up.

"My secretary, Cathy. She didn't want to go to India. She was worrying about plane crashes. She was imagining herself dying in some dirty hospital, dehydrated by diarrhea caused by dirty water and spoiled meat. She fretted about opium-blinded hooligans, about gang rape and riots and fights at that open convention. Was she having premonitions? I didn't worry about her. I worried about my life's work. About the accolades I'd receive. I pushed her, forced her to go. And she got killed."

"Cathy? Killed in India? That must be investigated."

"Nothing to investigate."

"What do you mean, nothing to investigate!" His shell was not indestructible. Suddenly, without any warning, it fractured and he spoke harshly, angrily. "If an American is killed overseas, that is a very serious matter. It must be looked into right away."

"I had told her not to break her journey, to go to Ayodhya by airplane. In Bombay, she decided to take a train with the others. Wherever the train stopped, she saw people on the platform, waiting till the last minute, then running to catch it. That seemed a lot of fun to her. They told her not to try it, but she wouldn't listen. Twice she succeeded. The third time . . . "

"Oh, my God!"

"The security guards fluttered red flags. Someone pulled the chain. But by the time the train could stop, her body was so mangled, they thought it'd be merciful for her kin in America if they didn't see it. They gave her a Christian burial and sent condolences to me. To me, who had killed her!"

"It wasn't your fault," he said gently. "You're being too hard on yourself."

"Am I? Until now, I had never realized it. But there is something seriously wrong with me. That's why my husband flew away, to a place from which he wouldn't have to return. That's why my son has taken shelter in some stranger's house and refuses to speak with me. That's why Pooja . . . " she choked.

"What happened to Pooja?"

"I hope nothing. It's just that I don't know where she is. How she is. She hasn't called. Not even once. It's never happened before. When she was away from home, she used to call five times a day. Vishu used to tease me, 'Are you still breast-feeding her? Is that why she misses you so much?' Cathy had promised me that she'd try to find her, take care of her. She couldn't even take care of herself . . . and Gopa . . . "

Oringer didn't dare say anything, but he wondered what was coming next. No wonder she was looking so haggard. So spent. How much could a person take? There are limits.

"Thinking about it, I can't seem to breathe. If they're together, what kind of bad example is Gopa setting right now for Pooja — Pooja, pearl of my eyes, who never moved a finger without my permission . . .

"Disturbed about her papa I suppose, wanting to be a daredevil desperado like her sister, she went away with this stupid group, without telling me where she was going and when she'd be back."

Oringer couldn't take emotional racking. That was one reason for his divorce. He picked up his untouched drink and poured it down his throat, without wanting it, without tasting it.

"Colonel, people look at me and envy me. 'She has more than anyone can want in one lifetime,' they say. 'A world-famous husband, who adores her. Lovely home. All the wealth of her mother. Adoring children . . . '

"What will they say when they learn that my mother didn't love my father? That's why he was never home. That's why I never had a brother. Or a sister. That's why he left all his wealth tied up in all kinds of trusts. My husband had another lover. My daughters hate me. My son is not my son. I'm alone. Absolutely alone. I have nothing. In this whole goddamn world, there is not a person, not a thing, I can call my own. Colonel, what's going to happen to me? What am I going to do?"

Her misery wasn't feigned. It was real. Whatever she had done, or had failed to do, it didn't diminish the guilt and anguish that was giving her such fiendish nightmares. Waking and sleeping. Eyes open or closed.

Oringer shivered. His fracturing shell, which he had been trying very hard to hold together, suddenly crumbled and fell apart under that fearsome load.

"The first thing you are going to do," he said gently, but firmly, "is to give me whatever information you can about that old woman. Her story sounds ridiculous. Without proof, I wouldn't believe it. It may be just a pack of lies that she cooked up to blackmail you. But if she was telling the truth, if Captain A'Kash has another daughter, she is our responsibility.

"If she exists," he asked hesitantly, "if we can find her, would you like to meet her?"

"If she lives, she is my daughter. I should like to meet her. But, in my nightmares, either she has died or she considers me a demon and refuses to see my face."

"Well, that's the second thing you're going to do — stop torturing yourself like this. If she's alive, we will find her. That'll be the time to decide whether or not you should meet her. Ask any parent. Everyone has some child problem; it's just a question of degree. That's no reason to have nightmares."

"There's something I didn't tell you."

Oringer looked at her, concerned, involved. He wasn't worried any more about what his expression might or might not convey.

"Someone's called twice. Wants twenty million dollars."

"That old woman's partner?"

"No. He says he has a photo of that accident."

"Oh!" New questions tumbled through Oringer's mind. A third coincidence? Someone just happened to be there, at the right time, to snap the right kind of photo? No kidding. Didn't it prove that the accident was plotted? And that the plot succeeded? Could this be the person who might have planted that note in Sparky's shirt pocket and that diary in his apartment?

Keeping his thoughts to himself, he quietly said, "Just one more suggestion."

"Yes, Colonel?"

"You will come with me to meet with General Stryker."

"General Stryker?"

"My boss. He has an uncanny ability to see through all kinds of mysteries. What no one can guess, what no one can solve, he can. And does."

"OK, if you think he can help, I'll come. But you may regret it."

He looked surprised, "Why?"

"I may replace him as my father figure."

He laughed, got up and offered her his hand.

His dreamless sleep disturbed, Rahul thought there was an earthquake. His bed was shaking violently. Coming slowly awake, he realized it was Pooja trying to wake him up. "Rahul, Rahul. Please, wake up. Rahul, Rahoool. Pleeese . . . "

"Pooja, what the . . . " He sat up groggily. "What's the time?"

"Soon it will be five."

"So," He groaned and tried to hide under his sheets again. "what's this early morning ruckus? We're not going anywhere so early today."

"Rahul, please. Gopa is in some kind of trouble."

"Gopa?" His sleep fled. He sat up straight, his mind and eyes absolutely clear. "You forgot what we had agreed upon when I agreed to bring you here?"

"What?" she asked wide-eyed, fearful of having done

something wrong.

"That you will not be seen with Gopa. If you see her coming, you will run and hide."

"Oh, that?" She looked very much relieved, "I haven't broken my promise." She glared at him accusingly. "How could you even think I would!"

"Then how do you know she's in trouble?"

"I can see it. Envision it. Rahul, please. She . . .

"Oh, Pooja! For Pluto's sake! It's five in the morning, too early for breakfast stories. Let me go back to sleep."

"You don't believe me, do you?"

"Believe what?"

"That she's sitting in a boat, planning something horrid. If you don't do something right away, soon it will be too late." Pooja was looking at him pleadingly, grief written in her large expressive eyes and across her tear-stained face. "If you won't listen to me," she promised him, "you'll regret it. Forever. And I'll never speak to you again."

Rahul suddenly wondered if he had allowed himself to be burdened by a teenager who was suffering from serious psychological problems. If so, what would be the right way to deal with her? Should he humor her?

He sat up and dangled his feet over the side of the bed. "OK, tell me about it."

"I just told you." She sounded extremely exasperated. "She's somewhere on the river bank . . . "

"Not that part," Rahul shook his head. "The other part. Why do you think you can envision her?"

"I always have. Ever since I can remember."

"Meaning?"

Pooja heaved a big sigh. "OK, I'll tell you something I've never told anyone, not even my mom.

"I don't remember my papa ever caring for me. My first memories are of my papa taking care of Gopa, feeding her, teasing her, playing with her. And me lying alone in the crib, trying to reach out to her mind, to catch how it felt to play with one's papa." She looked at Rahul, trying to ascertain whether or not he was believing her.

"I remember," she continued, looking at him defiantly, "that to read her mind, I needed to see her — face, her arms, her legs. But as time passed, I didn't need to see her or be near her. I could feel her mind any time I wanted to."

Rahul couldn't decide if he should believe her. Not wanting to frighten her, he asked solemnly, "Does she know you can do that?"

"I don't know. She doesn't like me. We never talk, unless politeness requires it."

"And yet you are worried about her?"

"She's my sister," Pooja said simply, as if that explained it all.

"OK." He moved toward the bathroom. "I'll go to the convention dorms, although I wonder what they'll say if I go knocking and ask them if one of their leaders is in her bed."

She didn't hear the ridicule in his voice. "Please, hurry."

"I will." He peeked out the bathroom door, his shaver grazing his cheeks. "If you promise me something."

Another promise; her morning eyes looked angry.

"Until I return, you will not move from here. You will not call anyone. You will not talk with . . . "

"Oh, my!" Despite her worries, she laughed. "No liberties?" She gave him a mock salute. "Yes, commander, sir. Your orders will be obeyed, sir."

He smiled and entered the shower.

James Miskovitz was knocking at Gopa's door. Every morning before breakfast they went jogging. Most of the time, it was Gopa and Sharky who woke him up. The previous night, remembering Sharky wouldn't be there, he had set his alarm so that he could be at her door before she awakened, so that first thing in the morning she wouldn't miss Sharky's voice.

Not getting any response, he tried the knob. The door was not locked. It opened easily. Entering, he noticed that her bed hadn't been slept in.

Worried, he looked around and noticed a piece of paper on her dressing table. It was a simple note: I'm gone. Don't come looking for me. You won't find me.

Oh, Gibraltar! James Miskovitz's heart raced to his mind. Where had she gone? In this strange country, where was he going to go looking for her?

Check the garage, his mind said. He quickly moved. Outside he noticed a young man pushing his Honda and peeking at door numbers. "May I help you?" James asked.

"Perhaps you can," the young man replied. "I was looking for Ms. Gopa A'Kash."

So early in the morning? Miskovitz thought. "Why?"

The young man hesitated, checking out Miskovitz, wondering whether or not to trust him. Finally he said, "It's personal."

You're kidding, Miskovitz thought. If this guy knows her well enough to have personal business — not just so early in the morning, but any time of day — he would have known who the man was.

"She's never available this early," he said. "You can catch her later, in the convention hall."

"You don't understand. I have a problem."

"Tell me."

"OK." The young man seemed to have made up his mind. "I'm a free-lance reporter. I was told I'd need her permission to cover the convention. I'm sure she's a very busy person. Later, I may not find her. So I thought . . . "

A good story, Miskovitz thought, but not good enough. "Fine," he offered cordially, "I can give you an appointment."

"I'd rather ask her myself," the young free-lancer, if that's what he was, insisted. "Won't take more than a minute. Is she here or at the river bank?"

Miskovitz stared at him.

"Someone said I might not find her at home because last night she was seen going toward the river. That somehow didn't seem right. If she went for a moonlight swim, she would have returned, wouldn't she? Have you checked her room?"

"You want to write about her private life?" Miskovitz felt the kind of burning anger he rarely experienced.

"Please, don't misunderstand me. I'm a friend. I don't want her to face any adverse publicity. That's why I've come. You can believe me."

"Why?" Miskovitz looked belligerent. "Why should I believe you?"

"If she is missing," the stranger pleaded, "let me help you find her. If she's not, I'll just say 'hello' and be gone before you can say 'good-bye.' "

"All right." There was something in the reporter's voice, in his clear, guileless eyes, that made Miskovitz change his mind. If Gopa was in trouble, he might need help. If this fellow had foul motives, he'd find a way to deal with him later.

"She's not here," he admitted, "and there's an ambiguous note on her table. Perhaps that means I do need to find out what she's doing. What makes you think you can help?"

"As I said, I've reasons to believe she may be somewhere on the river. I've got a Honda. It goes where autos can't. You're her friend. She may not listen to me because she doesn't know me. If we can find her, I'll need your help to bring her back."

The words sounded ominous. Was this young man, for some reason, trying to lure him away from here? Or did he really know something and sincerely want to help?

There was only one way to find out — go with him and start the search. The river was as good a place as any other. Considering Gopa's love for water, perhaps it was the most likely place.

"OK," Miskovitz replied, "let's go. But on one condition."

"Name it." The stranger moved to start the engine.

"Trouble or no trouble, it'll not get to any paper."

"I'd like you to remember your words," the young man said, as if he was afraid Miskovitz was the one who'd want to report it, and Rahul wanted to be sure he wouldn't do so.

"Let's go," Miskovitz replied, suppressing a smile. Swinging his long leg over the back seat, he remembered to ask, "Did your friend say which road she . . . "

"No," the stranger spoke loudly, his voice coming over the Honda's roar. "But it doesn't matter because we don't need to search on any road. We need the river."

Why? Miskovitz wanted to ask. How did he know that? What made him so sure?

Somehow, it didn't seem the right time to ask. He decided to stifle his curiosity and keep his mouth shut.

At this time of morning, the streets were deserted. They saw only an occasional night watchman going home a little late, or a sweeper cleaning the street with his long, palm bristle broom. Miskovitz knew a shortcut. He guided the stranger, and the Honda scooted down the narrow path, awakening the sleeping birds who rose up in the graying skies, raising a loud cacophony of protests. Soon, they saw the majestic Saryu, and as they came closer down the river bank, they saw the power boat gently lolling on the calm waters. In it sat a lone figure, her head touching the wheel, hidden between her hands, perhaps sleeping, perhaps not. Hearing the roar of the Honda's engine, she lifted her head and stared at Rahul.

"That's her," Miskovitz said from behind him. Rahul braked his Honda and they got off. Seeing Miskovitz, Gopa stood up in the boat, waved her hands and shouted, "I told you not to come. I told you . . . " Quickly dropping down on her seat, she switched on the engine and started reversing the boat.

"Gopa, wait," Miskovitz shouted and started running toward her. Before he could reach the shore, the boat was in the middle of the river and speeding away.

"What does she think she's doing?" Rahul muttered angrily.

"She lost her companion yesterday in a freak accident."

"If they were so close, she shouldn't have been left alone." Rahul didn't know which he felt stronger, anger or frustration. Suddenly, a thought struck him and his face turned white. "Do you know," he asked hesitatingly, "does she . . . smoke?"

"Not that I know of," replied Miskovitz, feeling a dark, strange apprehension. Did she? Or didn't she? What did he really know about her? Almost nothing.

"What do we do now?" he asked, feeling totally helpless.

"We must find a guard station," Rahul replied calmly, matter-of-factly. "There must be one here. Which way?"

"I think this way." Miskovitz pointed upstream. "Let's go."

They remounted the Honda and soon saw the station. Hearing the roar of the motor, a guard came out, rubbing his sleepy eyes. He must have been sleeping in his uniform; it looked rumpled and there were no shoes on his stockinged feet.

"We need a power boat, quick," Miskovitz said.

The guard wasn't impressed by their sense of urgency. "No power boat," he said yawning.

"What do you mean, no power boat?"

"You understand English?" the guard sounded angry. "No means *none*. Not one. *Samjhe*? Understand? Zero. None."

"Aren't you supposed to have one?"

"We do. We have. A few hours ago, someone stole it."

"Stole it?" Rahul asked.

"You two descended from parrots or something?" the guard snapped. "Since they announced that dragon boat race for inaugurating their crazy convention, no boat is safe in this area. They've all been rented or borrowed — with or without permission. What's your problem? Want to get a head start?"

"We saw a friend going down to the river," Rahul said.

"She's sick and may not be able to control the boat. We must reach her."

"You want to rescue somebody? Why didn't you say so in the first place? Let me call the helicopter."

"Helicopter?"

"Damn Yankees! You guys are worse than parrots." From his waistband he took out his mobile phone, pressed a few buttons and spoke quickly into the mouthpiece. "They will be here," he said smugly. "Soon."

"A helicopter can't rescue a sick girl speeding away in a speed boat," Miskovitz shouted angrily.

"Maybe not in America. This is India. And this is our Ma Saryu. We know her. You should see it during the monsoons. You should see how many fishermen our helicopters rescue."

"Fishermen want to be rescued."

"Ah! But the cattle don't." They heard the roar of the helicopters above their heads and the rest of his words were almost drowned. "You should see how many we rescue."

Two helicopters touched down and a couple of yellow-uniformed rescue workers got out. The guard ran toward them, telling them what was happening, all the time pointing toward Rahul and Miskovitz.

Rahul said, "Why don't you — . I'm sorry, I didn't get your

name. I'm Rahul. Why don't you go with them? I'll try to find a boat and follow."

"Good idea. I'm Miskovitz. James. See you later."

He quickly moved toward the helicopters. The rescue workers didn't have any objection to his flying with them. In fact, they welcomed the idea.

Soon they saw her, steadily going downstream. Hearing the noise of the helicopters, she looked up.

Knowing she had seen them, the co-pilot in Miskovitz's helicopter dropped a ladder. Flailing both hands, Gopa angrily told them to go away and stubbornly pushed her speedometer to achieve the maximum speed. As her boat careening on the deep waters, the co-pilot immediately pulled his ladder up.

Biding time, keeping pace, both helicopters hovered above her.

Miskovitz wondered how much gas she had. How long would it last? Looking behind, he saw a moving speck on the stream, approaching their position rapidly. He hoped Rahul had found a boat. That distant dot on the waters, he hoped, was him and the watch guard. If they caught up with her . . .

His thoughts broke; the co-pilot was handing him a megaphone. Miskovitz quickly decided what to say. "Gopa," he shouted in the friendliest tone, "let me come down, please. You know me. I won't criticize your plans. I only want to talk with you."

The speedboat behind them was approaching fast. Gopa saw it and realized what it was. She pushed the throttle forward, trying to coax more power out of her speedboat's engine."

"Keep talking to her," the pilot said to Miskovitz. "But don't say anything that may prompt her to leave her seat. I'm going to try something."

"What?" Miskovitz asked.

"Just keep talking," the pilot barked. "Hold her attention. She must not move."

"Gopa, I'm sorry, we got worried," Miskovitz shouted in the megaspeaker. "That was foolish. We should have respected your orders. You are very intelligent, very organized. I know that. Will you forgive me?"

The last words were hardly out of his mouth when a laser beam streaked down from the helicopter and pierced the back portion of the boat, making a hole clear to its bottom. Gopa screamed and stood up, the boat wobbling under her feet.

Water started gushing in the boat, wetting her shoes, her legs, her dress. She looked behind her. The boat chasing her was still far down river. If she jumped right away, before they could come near her, she could swim to the bank and run, hiding in the tall sugarcane fields lining the road.

She looked up. She looked behind. She hesitated. The water rose toward her knees.

"Shall I drop the net?" the co-pilot asked.

"Wait," the pilot said. "That engine is still running. It has to stop before we do anything. You don't want to scare her."

Gopa quickly pulled off her shoes and her waterlogged dress. Stretching both her hands above her head, she poised for a second at the rim of the boat. Then, without looking up again, without looking behind, she jumped into the fast-flowing river. At the same instant, the co-pilot dropped a heavy, steel mesh net.

Dropping around her, the net immediately started closing up under her, scooping her into its folds. As soon as it closed, the helicopter crew quickly pulled her up.

Rahul, who was aboard the other boat, which was now quite near, saw the rescue. He quickly threw a hooked line and taking the sinking vessel in tow, the rescue boat turned and headed back.

Rahul looked up at Gopa, motionless in her steel cage, being carried away by the speeding helicopter.

Pooja has some questions to answer, he thought. And he needed the answers quickly. He hoped Pooja would cooperate.

9

Through the Cracks

Vladimir Grachenko was trying to concentrate on his Volga salad and broiled swordfish, and was not succeeding. He was determined not to let anything disturb him while he was eating; he would not think about Volga One or Volga Two. Or, Hiroshima Hoku. Or any other item related to confounded space. But his mind was not obeying him.

Lt. Gen. Kostyszyn had sent word that he would be in Grachenko's office at 9 a.m. Sharp.

Not, "Would you have time?" No "please," just that he'd be there. That was Kostyszyn's way. Had always been. And Grachenko had never liked it. A few times he had thought of telling the superegoist — who seemed to believe that even the Supreme Soviet should bow down to him — what he thought of him. But common sense had prevailed and he had kept his opinion bottled up.

The worst part of it was he knew what was boiling in Kostyszyn's crackpot mind. What he was coming to demand. And he knew what his reply would be. Word for word. He knew how this nasty meeting would end. Then why was his restless mind repeating, again and again, the whole scene that would be played out?

Angry with himself, Grachenko was taking it out on the swordfish, jabbing and pushing it with his fork unnecessarily.

Approaching him, his secretary noticed his mood and hesitated. Grachenko looked up. "Yes, Tanya?"

"Call from Washington, comrade director. General Stanley Stryker. Should I tell him to call back?"

"Of course not." Grachenko dropped his fork and touched his napkin to his lips. "I've been expecting his call. Just because he delayed it, I won't keep him waiting." Quickly taking the phone, he rumbled into it, "Comrade Stryker, how's your world treating you?"

"I could ask the same, friend Vladi, since our boats seem to be running in the same direction."

"Not really," the director of Glavkosmos Manned Space Operations replied. "We know what happened to our Volga One."

There was a brief silence at the other end. Then Stryker asked softly, tentatively, "Not Hiroshima Hoku, I hope."

"Let's just say we've only declared a Yellow Alert. And some of us are hoping — at least, I am — that it will be canceled. That it won't be upgraded."

"Humph!" Stryker wondered what to say.

The cryptic remark told him that the situation was salvageable. But that was not the information the president of the United States was expecting from him. It was better than nothing because, in tactical terms, it indicated an urgent need for the toughest action that could be taken without actually declaring war — the possibility of an upgrade to Red Alert was very much there. But, it was not probable.

"Anything new on the Titanic?" Grachenko was asking.

"You must have analyzed its flight path. What do you think? I'd like to know your opinion. That's why I'm calling."

You want to fool me, Stryker? Grachenko thought, as a smile lit up his swarthy face. "Well," he drawled, "if you ask me, I think some mysterious force was at work. Twenty-first century spaceships can't blink out like fusing light bulbs."

"That 'mysterious force,' as you put it, was not, by any chance, Volga One, was it?"

"Comrade Stryker." Grachenko's voice sounded very much aggrieved. "Is that an accusation? Our General Kikilo is just waiting to hear it so he can jump to Red Alert."

"Just kidding, friend Vladi. You know how we Yankees love to kid around. By the way," Stryker added softly, "it should be very easy now for General Kikilo to decide about canceling or continuing this unexpected Yellow Alert."

"If I had said that," Grachenko smiled, "you'd have protested, 'How's that?'" He quickly pressed a button under his chair's arm. Before he could remove his finger, the door and windows had swiftly closed and glowing red light circled their frames indicating the safety net was on and operational.

During all his years of occupying this chair and those before it, Grachenko had never used the surveillance cancellation device because the danger was that if Kostyszyn's men were snooping, they'd immediately come running, armed with dangerous questions. Tonight, knowing how the American talked, he had only one of two options: either disconnect the phone right away or blanket his room.

His sudden curiosity had overpowered his usual caution and he had recklessly, spontaneously, taken the risk that, in his saner moments, he'd never have taken. Now it was done. Whatever happened, he'd have to accept the consequences. But at least for the time being he wouldn't have to watch his every word and he'd be able to enjoy the rest of this conversation.

"Your intelligence services really are the best," Stryker was saying. "They scooped up that holy woman, what's her name, before anyone else could even say, 'Let's get her.' Now . . . "

Grachenko laughed. "Not such a glorious scoop. She called them, asking for protection, demanding her citizenship rights."

"What?" Stryker was really surprised. "She was in no danger. The Indian government gives complete freedom to its citizens."

"That was the problem," Grachenko laughed again. "Too much freedom. Suddenly, like so many others, she got very much afraid of it. She demanded the qualified freedom that only the Soviet Alliance can provide its citizens."

Stryker couldn't believe it. However, during all the years he had known him, Grachenko had never lied to him. He might not answer a question, or he might reply in a roundabout way, but he never lied.

So, what was this mysterious woman up to, when she used the only foolproof strategy that could have fooled the three-eyed KGB? "I admit it," he grinned. "Our system is no Utopia. It has its faults. The reason I mentioned the possibility of an 'easier decision' was because I was thinking that now Kikilo could consult Her Holiness and, based upon her forecast . . . "

"Our general doesn't believe in all that hocus-pocus. I'm sure you know that."

Stryker nodded as if Grachenko could see him. "But, among us," he stated cheerfully, "there are many who do believe. So, with our comrade general's permission, can I send one of my officers to consult with her?"

Grachenko couldn't believe his ears. "During the Yellow Alert?"

"Why not?" Stryker asked blandly. "It's not a political demand. It's a personal request, evoked by faith and religion. We know it's not scientific, but we believe in it. In this respect, we aren't as enlightened and modern as you are, you know."

"If you put it that way," Grachenko said thoughtfully, "I can ask him . . . "

"So? When can I call you back?"

"I'll call you. Tomorrow afternoon soon enough?"

"That would be fine, friend Vladi. As the Candle Runners, ours and yours, say, 'May all clouds fear your sunshine.'"

"I wish you the same, friend Stan. May your sunshine shoulder you always. Wait for my call. After lunch, our time."

The phones simultaneously clicked off. Immediately, Stryker's buzzed again, as if his secretary were waiting for the line to get free. He pressed the intercom. "Yes, Mona?"

"Colonel Oringer's called three times, sir."

That was unusual. "What's the problem?" he asked.

"He didn't say, sir. Just wanted to know if he could come over right away."

"So, why did you let him call three times?"

Stryker's voice had an unusual edge, and Mona decided it must be due to his Glavkosmos call. "I wasn't sure how long your phone calls would take, general," she said apologetically. "Should I call him now?"

"You know *him*, Mona. He must be here already. Check his office, or . . . " Stryker stopped when he heard Mona's pleasant voice through the speakerphone. "Good morning, colonel. How good of you to come. The general is waiting for you."

"Thank you, Miss Marshal. Would you please tell him I have Mrs. A'Kash with me."

These were the words Stryker had been waiting to hear since the day the *Titanic* had disappeared. He had almost given up hope in view of Oringer's reluctance, or inability, to make it possible. Delighted, he switched off the speaker phone, quickly strode to the door and opened it. "Sam, I've been on the phone. Sorry you had to call several times."

"No problem, general. I knew you'd be here, since you like to get your work done early before others arrive. I just wanted to make sure because Mrs. A'Kash was with me. I left her in my office. If you don't have time, I can — "

"Of course I have time. Mona, would you bring her up, please?"

"Yes, sir. Right away." Moving quickly, she left the office. The general stepped back from the door he had been solidly occupying to let Sam Oringer enter his office.

"So, tell me," Stryker demanded, standing against the edge of his desk, "how did you manage it?"

"She has so many problems, general." Wanting to tell Stryker some basic facts before Meera's arrival, Oringer spoke rapidly. "Someone's told her Captain A'Kash was two-timing. Someone else is blackmailing her. Her children . . . "

"Did you say blackmailing?" Stryker asked.

Before Oringer could reply, they heard the tap of high heels and voices outside the door, followed the next instant by a light knock.

"General," Mona asked, "may we come in?"

"Yes, of course," Stryker replied and moved to greet the visitor. "Mrs. A'Kash, what a pleasure. I've heard so much about you from your husband, I feel as if I know you."

"I'm honored, general," she smiled, but her voice told him how miserable she was feeling. "I wouldn't have dared to waste your time. But," she glanced toward Sam Oringer, who was standing quietly nearby, "Colonel Oringer thought you wouldn't mind."

"Mind? I'm delighted. Why not make yourself comfortable? Mona will get us some drinks. What would you like?"

"Drinks? So early in the morning?"

"One gets used to certain words. I mean tea or coffee . . . Coffee? How about you, Sam? Coffee?" Stryker asked. Seeing the colonel nod, Mona stepped out of the room to fill the beverage requirements.

Meera's eyes were roaming over the mementos and career achievement awards scattered around the room. On the mantelpiece, she noticed a small package, wrapped in Titanic paper, tied with that special, star-studded blue ribbon. It reminded her of something. "General, if you don't mind, may I ask you something?"

"Why not?" he said graciously. "Answering questions is my job."

"That blue package." She pointed toward it. "Is it the one I gave to my husband?"

"No. This is an experiment we didn't get time to check out, so it wasn't sent on the Titanic. But I don't recall Captain A'Kash requesting clearance for anything. What did you give him? He must have left it here in the storage room."

"I wish he had," Meera said pathetically. "I wish I hadn't forced him. He never listened to me before. Why did he break his rule for that package? If he hadn't, I wouldn't have lost my son." Tears brimmed in her tired eyes and she turned her face away to hide them.

Stryker was appalled, not by her misery, but by the fact that something had been placed on the Titanic without their knowledge. Without their permission. How was that possible?

His face, however, didn't betray his feelings. "I don't understand, Mrs. A'Kash," he said, as if his only concern was her problem. "If you gave something to your husband, why should it upset your son?"

"Well, you see, he was working on something that he wanted to submit through his school, but he missed the deadline. So I told Vishu that it was not logical for him to deprive his son of the honor. The only reason to submit it through the channels was so that the school would gain some mileage out of it. We didn't have to worry about that. When he sent it back with the other items, we'd inform the school."

"And Captain A'Kash agreed?" Stryker asked, puzzled, but not showing it.

"Well, at first he didn't. Started quoting all sorts of rules. He seems so obnoxious when he starts sounding like a living rule book. So I got angry and told him how horrible it'd be if, from the first Mars flight, scores of children would get back their experiments and his own son wouldn't. Now, I wish I hadn't forced him."

"So, Neil should be happy. Why is he angry?"

"Well, as I said, he didn't want to send it. And then, it seems, when it was wrapped, his working notes weren't removed. He thinks I did that purposely so that he wouldn't be able to repeat the experiment until the original one comes back."

Stryker was trying to understand her; was she that manipulative or that naive? If it was the former, he had a big problem on his hands. If it was the latter, it could be worse. "What was the experiment?" he asked quietly.

Either she didn't hear him, or she considered the question unimportant. "I can't figure it out," she said. "Any time I needed anything, he used to jump and run. I never had to say anything twice. When we were at home, he used to sort of wander after me.

"Now, anything that I say, he twists it around. He insults me. He ignores me. And, if I say something, he stares at me as if I was a stranger. General, as they grow older, do all children get so cruel? Or is it just me who was born with such a bottomless, black kismet?"

"He is angry for losing his pet project, Mrs. A'Kash. Any child would be. What was the project?"

"I don't know. He refused to bring it home, so I picked it up from his school and gave it to Vishu without telling him. I told him when he was replaying his father's boarding tape. He threw a tantrum and ran away to his room, then he refused to talk about it. I asked and asked but he wouldn't tell me. And when the Titanic disappeared, he . . . " She choked and couldn't continue.

Stryker's mind was a battlefield of questions, but he suppressed them all. Very quietly, not giving the slightest indication of how he was feeling, he said pleasantly, "I'd like to ask him about it."

"I don't know where he is. One day he left home in my absence. That night, someone called and said he was staying at their place, then disconnected the line without giving me her name and phone number. Since then, I haven't heard from him."

"He must be attending classes. Did you try his school?" Oringer asked.

She looked crestfallen. "I didn't even think of that! I've been having so many problems, been so worried, it just . . . "

"It can happen to anyone," Oringer said soothingly. "Don't worry about it." He turned toward Stryker. "General, I can't say Neil and I are friends, but he will recognize me. Should I try to contact him?"

"Yes. And tell him I personally want to congratulate him. That's why I want him to come over to visit with me."

Meera panicked. "Don't tell him I'm here. If you do, he won't come."

"I'll remember that, Mrs. A'Kash," Oringer said. He looked toward Stryker and, getting his silent permission, quietly left.

In the few minutes Stryker had when Sam was talking with Meera, he had decided upon a plan of action, "Mrs. A'Kash — "

"Meera, please," she interrupted.

"Fine," he accepted. "Meera, we suddenly have a lot of work

and we're short of hands. Would you like to help us out, as a volunteer, of course." He smiled. "There won't be any pay."

"I'd be greatly honored, general. But I'm afraid I won't be any good. I don't know anything about the space sciences. Never studied them."

"You know, Meera, I've never understood something. Why do people think we only need scientists here? The kind of support staff that we need . . . Could you help me with a non-routine job? It should be quite simple for a person like you."

"Yes, general?" she asked eagerly.

"What I'm going to tell you is very confidential. You are not to mention it to anyone."

"I will guard it with my life, general."

"I believe you. You see, everything sent on the Titanic was photographed. It needs cataloguing. Can you do it for me?"

If an officer like Capt. A'Kash took something on board without our knowledge, he was thinking, could someone else have done the same? And, if they dared to break the rules, were those items responsible for whatever it was that happened to the Titanic? He had to find out. And soon.

Meera had been expecting a sizzling assignment, not a librarian's job. But, one thing can lead to another, she told herself. If she did this job well, it could lead to others. Important ones. That's why he was giving it to her, to test her. To find out how good she was. How thoroughly, how neatly, how fast could she do this mundane chore. If she excelled at it, proved herself worthy . . .

"If it's not appealing to you . . . " Stryker was saying.

That tone frightened her. Afraid he might change his mind, she quickly interrupted. "Sorry, general. I was trying to remember if anything was pending in my office. When can I begin?"

"After lunch," Stryker said, "because first I want you to tell me about these things that have been bothering you. Colonel Oringer said something about a blackmailer . . . "

Scared, Meera gripped the hands of her chair, then chided herself. What was the matter with her? That's why she'd come here, wasn't it? To seek his help? If she didn't tell him the same things she'd told Sam Oringer, how could this man help her?

"Well, general," she said, bracing herself, "perhaps, it would be better if I begin at the beginning."

Stryker merely nodded — he knew when not to be a distracting factor.

It was easier to say it than do it.

Meera wondered where to begin — when the wheels that had brought her to the present roads had started rolling. When she agreed to marry the would-be captain. When she got pregnant with Neil. When she had been almost forced to establish Earth Reality. When that old man ran under her wheels like a demented, wild deer.

James Miskovitz was watching the young doctor, attired in a rumpled white uniform, tackle his percolator. He must have been on night duty because his eyes looked reddish. Tall and lanky, he moved with graceful ease and his brownish face seemed to have a special kind of charm. Despite the early morning stubble crowding his dimpled cheeks, he looked very handsome.

If his bedside routine is as impressive, James was thinking, his patients must love him.

The doctor poured steaming coffee into a large cup. "Black? With cream?"

"No, thank you," Miskovitz said. "Its aroma is tempting, but I'll take a rain check. I just had breakfast."

"Coffee is taken after breakfast. Come on, try it. My special blend." Placing the cup before James, the doctor poured a second one for himself, plunked down in his chair and relaxed, warming his hands around his cup.

Watching him, Miskovitz changed his mind. He picked up his cup. The coffee was really good. It seemed to say, "Don't worry. All things work out.'

Noticing the tension ebbing from his visitor's body and face, the doctor nonchalantly pulled a file toward him. "The nurse told me you wanted to see me about Miss A'Kash."

Miskovitz nodded. "That's right."

"She's OK. I can release her any time you want."

Miskovitz didn't understand that statement. If he said, 'No, don't release her,' would they just keep Gopa in the hospital? What kind of a hospital was this!

"Are you related to her?" the doctor was asking.

"No. Both of us are members of ECO, attending the Candle Runners' convention. She's our vice president."

"I see." The doctor made a notation in his file and looked up. "Perhaps that explains some of the things."

Not to me, Miskovitz thought. The doctor didn't volunteer any further comments.

He may have finished his duty, Miskovitz thought, but my day is just beginning and I can't sit here all day. He decided to be blunt. "Did you talk with her about it?" he asked. "Had she gone to the river to commit suicide?"

"It's not as simple as that." The doctor looked straight into Miskovitz's eyes, as if he wanted to penetrate his deepest, innermost thoughts.

It took him only seconds to make up his mind. "If I knew something about your relationship, we could talk about a few things."

Miskovitz understood the doctor's dilemma — he didn't want to reveal his patient's condition to someone who might not be entitled to it. That was fine, but it made his job more difficult. What, and how much, would he have to reveal to gain the doctor's confidence? He quickly came to a decision.

"Doctor," he started, choosing each word with care. "I'm sure you know that her father is missing in space and her mother is in America. She had an oath-companion. Yesterday, his body was found with a steel arrow in his neck. I haven't known her very long, but during the brief period we've known each other, we've become good friends. And here, in Ayodhya, I'm the only one she can count upon."

"That's what she told me," the doctor said, apparently satisfied. "You seem like a sensible person. I'd be willing to release her in your custody, but you have to be very careful. She's a timid and insecure person and needs lots of support and caring."

Timid? Insecure? Gopa? Miskovitz gawked at the doctor.

He smiled. "I know what you're thinking. She acts tough. Talks tough. Controls everyone around her. But that's a front she's been putting up to hide her real self, and finally, it's started taking its toll. I think the fault is mostly her father's. Perhaps, to a certain extent, her mother's also. Nothing we can do about that. What we can try to do is see that the dual personalities she had been developing do not keep ripening. Somehow, these two personalities have to merge so that she can become a whole person and not a schizophrenic."

Miskovitz stared silently at the doctor. Finally, he said, "So, what's your advice? What should I do?"

"Not much. Just be yourself. But now that you know about her condition, don't start treating her with kid gloves. Just behave as you always have. That Sharky, despite all his faults, was good for her. By the way, she didn't mention it to any of you, but she knows he was murdered."

"He was? Why? By whom? Does she know?"

"Her future may depend upon answers to these questions," the doctor said quietly. "Therefore, I didn't rush into them."

He moved, as if the meeting was over. "I'd like to see her again," he said as if he was making a request, but it sounded like an order. "If possible, every third day."

"I'll make it possible," Miskovitz said with confidence.

"Good," the doctor said smiling. "Let's go find her. Just give me a few minutes to change these dirty clothes." He moved toward his closet. As he pressed a panel and the large door slid back, Miskovitz's glance fell upon a large painting, leaning against the side wall. He stared at it.

"Doctor, if you don't mind . . . " he said, feeling breathless. "That painting, It seems very familiar!"

"Really?" The doctor pulled it out and looked at it at arm's length. "I never thought I'd hear those words from anyone."

"Why?"

"Because it's one of four. Only someone who may have seen the others . . . "

Suddenly Miskovitz realized what was wrong; the painting was upside down. If turned around, it would look like that enigma on Meera A'Kash's mantelpiece, Rings Around the

World. He breathed hard. "I've seen one, although not exactly like this one, unless you're holding it upside down."

"I'm not." The doctor smiled, putting it against the wall. "It's in four pieces. Each part is complete in itself, but not really complete, unless the four are joined together."

"Interesting idea," Miskovitz said. "Do you know the artist?"

He nodded. "My cousin." Pride lurked in his cheerful voice.

Miskovitz was delighted. The time had finally come for his crowded questions to be answered. "Could I, may I, doctor, it's like my impossible dream come true. I'd like to meet him."

The doctor shook his head. "Impossible."

Miskovitz was crestfallen, "Why?"

"Navy commanders are hard to find at any time. You have a bigger problem. Right now, she's on the Titanic. If you'll excuse me." Taking a fresh set of clothes, he disappeared into his bathroom.

Miskovitz stared at the painting.

Since the day he had seen its twin in Meera A'Kash's house, he hadn't been able to forget it. In his idle moments, he had tried to sketch it. In his dreams, he had argued with its creator about its colors, its composition, its theme.

What was its theme? Why was it in four parts? How did one of them reach Meera A'Kash? Where were the other two?

The doctor emerged from the bathroom looking as if he'd had a full night's rest. "Let's go. Gopa may be in the children's ward. She loves kids. That's a good sign."

Miskovitz didn't hear him. He asked, "Why four? Why aren't they together?"

"What?"

"These paintings? You said there are four. Why aren't they together?"

"Some kind of hocus-pocus conceived by my cousin. When the four come together, something is supposed to happen."

"What?"

"I've no idea. I'm not a Candle Runner."

The doctor's voice and face clearly said that he didn't believe in any of it. And, he didn't want to talk about it.

"This way," he said, striding briskly. "Do you hear her? She has a lovely voice. The children adore her."

The doctor was right. Surrounded by kids, Gopa was reading a story. They were so much absorbed in it, no one looked up when the two men entered the ward.

For a few minutes, they stood quietly listening. Then the doctor glanced at Miskovitz.

He gathered up his courage and called softly, "Gopa?"

Startled by his voice, she glanced toward him and her eyes lit up with unfeigned pleasure. "James! So nice of you to come. This fable is fascinating. I never read it before."

"It's checkup time for the kids," the doctor said. "Their physician will be here any minute. Would you like to finish it for them some other time?"

"I'd love to," Gopa said, closing the book and giving it to an older child. "What do I do now?"

"Come with me," Miskovitz said. "I've got the outline typed that you had dictated. But I think the three of us — you, me and Rahul — should go over it once again."

"OK," she said and nodded. She looked at the doctor, a question in her eyes.

"I think that's a good idea," he answered her unspoken inquiry. "Tomorrow, if you're in the vicinity, why not stop by? It'd be a pleasure to see you."

Before she could reply, Miskovitz spoke up. "I'll check her schedule and let you know."

Gopa giggled. "Didn't I tell you? He's a great secretary."

"You're lucky." Despite the fact that he was very tired, the doctor smiled his most charming smile. "I've been looking. Can't find one."

"Ah, but you can't steal mine." She moved and hooked her hand in Miskovitz's elbow.

"No harm in trying, is there?" The doctor tousled her hair and asked Miskovitz, "You know your way out?"

"Yes, doctor. And thank you again for the coffee. That was real good. Would you give me the secret of your special blend?"

"I'll think about it," the doctor replied, waving a quick farewell. The next instant, he disappeared through another door.

Miskovitz escorted Gopa toward the exit. She walked quietly, without saying anything, and Miskovitz decided not to breach her thoughts. He opened the door of the auto for her. She got in and took the seat next to him.

Starting the engine, he got out of the hospital's main gate.

Only then did she say softly, tentatively, "James?"

He glanced at her and smiled.

"You think I went there to commit suicide, don't you?"

"Am I crazy or something, that I should think such a stupid thing?" he asked belligerently. "Have I no brains? Do I look that dumb? That's what you think of me?"

"Then, what do you think?" she asked, not looking at him.

"I think, now that Sharky is gone, your responsibilities have doubled." He thought it best to state the fact, let her get used to hearing it, and he needed to know her reaction. "You went there to plan your work in peace. And you got mad at me because I disobeyed your instructions and disturbed you when I shouldn't have."

"You're partly right," she said, putting her hand in his arm and moving closer. "Actually, I was very much disturbed."

"If it's not real personal, can I ask about what?"

"I should have told you. One item, as you can guess, was Sharky. What you can't guess is that I think that security officer was right. Sharky was murdered."

"Why? He may have had enemies there. Not here."

"He had received two threatening notes. When I asked, he pooh-poohed them and stuffed them in his pocket. The other night, I went through his pockets, but I couldn't find them."

"We'll look again. If we look together, we'll find them," Miskovitz said confidently.

"Or we'll let the CIA earn their bread," she said, dismissing it. "The second item is what really blew my mind."

Miskovitz put his free arm around her tiny waist and drew her close.

She didn't move away. "You know Cheenoo? Who he is?"

"Who doesn't?" Miskovitz smiled. "The most vocal, the most colorful of personalities. The best flute player in any part of the world. The leader of the Japanese delegation."

"That's only secondary right now. More important is the fact that his mother is a senior officer in the Japanese space program."

"So?"

"That evening, when we returned without Sharky, you went away somewhere. I was alone when Cheenoo came to my room, looking like the face of death. I thought that with hearing about Sharky, maybe he also feared for his life, so I tried to humor him. What he told me . . . " Her voice shook and she nestled against him.

He didn't know how to soothe and comfort her. "He has also received threatening notes?" he asked.

"No. He said that all our efforts for trying to improve humanity's chances upon our rapidly decaying earth are useless. There's no sense in our trying because soon it won't mean anything. He wants to round up his delegation and go back."

"Did he say why?"

"He said that he had done something very un-Japanese. He wanted to call his friend, but his mother was on the line. He should have put down the phone right away, but, feeling curious, he listened. And he learned something that no one in his family knew, or would know, until Hiroshima Hoku reaches Mars."

She took a deep breath. "The terrible secret he learned that fateful day was that his mom belongs to the emperor's Royal Samurai Society. Not just belongs, she is an officer in it."

James Miskovitz whistled. "I thought all such clubs were banned long ago."

"They were. Hers was also, but it went underground and survives."

"So? How does it concern us? Like the other nefarious cliques, it's not sabotaging our efforts."

"Not directly. Only indirectly, which is worse."

"Don't talk in riddles," he said impatiently. "If Cheenoo is upset about his mother's social life, that's no reason to — "

"Scientists, who have programmed Hiroshima Hoku's robots, are this club's officers. As soon as it attains orbit around Mars, it's going to broadcast a message to Earth. As near as I can recall, Cheenoo said the message will be, 'Our emperor is not a symbol. He is our *Tenno*, the heavenly sovereign. From today, his flag flies over Mars. Earth must recognize him as the one and only ruler. Any nation that balks will be removed from the face of the earth.' That's the gist of it, anyway."

Miskovitz's breath almost stopped — if it were true, it followed that it was Hiroshima Hoku that had somehow scooped up the Titanic. It was Hiroshima Hoku that had destroyed Volga One.

This was not a question of spying upon the convention. It was a matter of human rights and freedom. Of world safety.

He'd be derelict in his duty as a world citizen if he didn't immediately send this information to Gen. Stryker. At this point, even if the general was powerless to do anything, he should at least know. That was absolutely imperative. There could be no other choice.

"If you were with me," he asked, "would Cheenoo be willing to tell me about it?"

"I don't know. He may have already gone back."

"I hope not." Miskovitz mentally crossed the fingers of both his hands. "Let's go to his room right away."

He pressed his foot on the accelerator, and the auto zoomed like a reckless racing car, driven by one determined to win.

10

Mirage Shackles

On the spacious Saryu banks, it seemed as if every nation of the world was giving final finishing touches to their boats — boats of all colors, shapes and sizes, from sailboats to speedboats, rowboats to dragon boats. Those who had never handled a vessel before were trying to learn the skill in a river teeming with all kinds of daredevils. Professionals and amateurs alike were spraying each other, laughing, gossiping and singing their favorite songs, trying not to jostle each other, but not succeeding.

After much debate, the details of the inaugural race had been worked out to everyone's satisfaction. Blessed by twenty-one Buddhist priests, the dragon boats would inaugurate the race. Then tribal Shamans and fifty-one priests of the various

denominations — Hindu, Muslim, Sikh, Jewish and Zoroastrian
would shower blessings upon the various kinds of hand-powered
boats. After that race was won and lost, eleven Christian priests
would anoint the third, and last, contest for engine-powered
speedboats.

On the fringes of the crowd, Rahul and Pooja were busy with
their colorful sailboat. Pooja had never participated in a boat
race. Excited, humming softly, she was polishing the oars.

Rahul decided this was the right time to tackle the touchy
topic. "Pooja," he asked, "are we friends? Real friends?"

She stared at him with her large, expressive eyes. What kind
of a question was that?

"Friends talk about everything. Share thoughts, right?"

"If that is so, Rahul, I have a question."

"Shoot."

"When you want to ask something, why do you keep
circling? Why don't you just ask it?"

"Because," he said slowly, "because, I'm afraid of losing your
friendship."

She smiled, moved a little and leaned against his back.
"Everyone's your friend. Why worry about me?"

"You mind if I answer that some other time?"

"It better be soon," she threatened, "or I'll stop answering
your questions."

"That's a deal. Would you answer one now?"

"As you say, shoot."

"You said you can envision your sister anytime. Can you
reach your mother also?"

The answer came readily. "I've never tried."

"How about your father?"

She hesitated. "Why do you want to know?"

That was his answer — she could. Did distance affect her
endeavor? If he asked, would she tell him? He decided to try.
"No one can figure out if he's still alive, or not. D'you know?"

This time, there was a long silence. Finally, she said, "I think
he's OK."

She paused for his reaction. When none came, she softly
continued. "When Titanic disappeared, the images grew very

dim — faint, wobbly, uncertain. I began to fear I had lost him. But then they began to get better, sometimes stronger. Maybe it's those times when he's thinking of us. He is sad, but not worried. He is OK."

He's not worried? Rahul wondered. Doesn't he know, because he's not communicating, the whole world is worried? If he is a traitor, fine. But at least, he has to let us know.

"Does he know how much all of us are worried about them all?"

"I don't know. He's too far away for me to read his thoughts. I just get a sort of vague feeling."

"Can you tell if he's a prisoner or something?"

"I don't know. But I doubt it."

"Why?"

"One day, I heard him talking with Neil. He was telling him, Mars is going to be a cruel place, son. Just like early Earth. No matter what they say now, all the nations who get there will fight for the largest share. During those wars, I'd rather die than be enslaved by anyone. When that happens, you'll have to assume command here, and take care of your mom and sisters."

Words are easy, Rahul thought, but when the time comes, dying is not. Why that pep talk? So that his son would talk about it? Often repeat his words. So he'd retain the free world's goodwill. And if the sabotage failed, ignorant of his foul deed, everyone would welcome him back with open arms?

He wondered if he should disobey orders, call the elders and ask them about it.

If he did that, they might get angry and recall him. There was no need to take that risk. At least, not yet.

"Pooja," he said, turning her around so that she faced him, "I want to ask you a favor."

"You may not get it, but you can ask," she responded mischievously.

"You remember your promise that you'll keep away from Gopa?"

"I haven't broken it. You know that. And I thank you again for saving her life."

"I shouldn't have asked for that promise. That was a mistake.

I want you to forgive me and break it."

"No need for apology. You got the pledge so easily because I don't want to go near her anyway."

"You two belong together. Sisters shouldn't be separated, especially twins. It's against the law of nature."

"Law of nature or not, we can't be together."

"Why not?"

"She hates me. Despises me. She won't talk with me."

"I don't believe that."

"Believe it," she said belligerently, her aquamarine eyes blazing as she moved away from him.

He pulled her back. "Why? Give me a reason. just one."

"She thinks I'm mama's pet."

"Well, you are not mama's pet anymore, so that objection is gone."

"That's true," she agreed. "Well, if it'll make you feel you've atoned for your mistake, I'll meet her."

"Good. Let's go."

"Right now?" she looked dismayed.

"Why not? This's as good a time as any. Perhaps, even better."

"Why better?"

"Considering she's been so busy, chairperson of her gang and all, if she didn't have time to get her own boat, we could invite her to share ours. She may like it."

"She may," Pooja agreed. "She loves sailing. OK, let's go. Where are my *chappals*?" Jumping up, she started looking for her sandals. "I still think it's a mistake," she added cheerfully. "You may regret it, with all your heart." Giggling, she took hold of his hand and ran toward the parking lot where his Honda was parked, dragging Rahul with her.

Gopa was not expecting anyone.

She was surprised by the knocking at her door. Opening it, she couldn't believe her eyes — there stood Pooja, looking uncertain, with a handsome stranger just behind her, looking even more uncertain.

"Pooja!" she exclaimed. "What are you doing here?"

"Following in your footsteps, sister dear. Meet my friend, Rahul."

Gopa didn't move her eyes from her twin's face, didn't even say hello. In harsh, mocking tones she asked, "Mom sent you to get me?"

"Nope," Pooja replied, trying to sound as friendly as possible for Rahul's sake. "Mom doesn't know where I am. I came with Rahul."

"Guilty as charged," Rahul said with a smile, "but only of accompanying her. Coming was her own idea. In fact, I tried to dissuade her. Did my best. That's the truth. Scout's honor."

Gopa grinned. "So, mom got what she deserved." She moved back from the door. "Do come in. How's Neil?"

"I have no idea." Pooja settled in a faraway, solitary chair and Rahul pulled one next to her. Looking at the twins together, he felt mesmerized; they were so alike, but so different, one looking like a born rebel yippie, with her close-cropped hair, a loud T-shirt proclaiming current slogans and faded, frayed jeans. The other looked like a lost fairy-tale princess, who had perhaps slipped in mud and dirtied her beautiful dress while trying to find the proper road.

"You didn't call him?" Gopa was asking, leaning upon the back of a chair facing them.

"I called a couple of times. Once, I got the video-diary, the second time, mom picked up. I didn't want to talk with her, so I disconnected. That's why I didn't call again. You know mom — when she's home, no one can run fast enough to beat her to the phone."

Gopa laughed. "I know." She moved her chair and sat down. "Well, tell me. Are you hitting all the tourist spots?"

"We came to invite you to the dragon boat race. We were able to find a sailboat. Why not join us? It will be fun."

"I wish I could, but ECO has its own boat. I have to . . . "

"Of course," Pooja said, getting up. "I understand. So we'll be going now. Rahul?"

He was surprised at the sudden summons, but before he could reply, Gopa spoke up. "Oh, why not stay a while? I don't have to attend this evening's meeting. I can ask someone else to chair it for me."

"Well, you see, Rahul is a free-lance journalist. We still have to finish today's work. Rahul, we must leave."

He didn't understand Pooja's wanting to run away. After the initial shock, which was quite natural, considering the previous relationship, Gopa was behaving quite nicely.

Did it mean the problem in their relationship was Pooja and not Gopa? Considering what she had told him about her father favoring her sister, it was quite possible.

If that were the case, should he do something about it or would the elders consider it *unnecessary interference*?

"Miss A'Kash," he said, "I'm guilty of — "

"Miss A'Kash?" Gopa's eyebrows arched up to her shaggy hairline. "What's wrong with my name?"

"OK," Rahul said smiling, "before we leave, I must tell you something. I had a selfish interest in wanting to meet with you. My editors have been asking me — "

"I don't give interviews," Gopa interrupted. "That was Sharky's job. Now I have to find someone else." Her voice suddenly cracked and her eyes filled with tears. "Please, excuse me for a sec." She ran quickly to her bathroom.

"Sharky was her oath-companion," Rahul told Pooja in a low voice. "He was killed just a day or so ago."

"Sorry," her voice sounded contrite. "I didn't know."

"Why not invite her to our place?" he whispered.

"She won't come," she whispered back.

Just then Gopa.returned. "I have a bad cold."

"It's this weather. Everyone's getting it," Rahul said, dismissing the apology. "Gopa, I wasn't talking about interviewing. I need news stories. My editors are very hungry. Since you can spare some time," he said invitingly, "why not come to our place? Believe me, it'd be a big help."

Why not, Gopa thought. She really didn't feel like attending the meeting. And Pooja had cared enough to come find her. Besides, who knew where James was. He'd said he had to go out of town on a personal errand and might not be back till late.

Rahul watched the indecision playing on her face. The fact

that she didn't immediately say no encouraged him. "I'd be honored if you'd check the accuracy of some news items I've collected. Firsthand info is better reporting."

He glanced for support toward Pooja's silent, expressionless face. Not finding it, he added, "And perhaps you'd like to send an item under your own byline."

That sounded exciting and Gopa's face brightened. "The honor will be all mine," she said pleasantly. "Would you give me a minute. I need to appoint a chairperson and leave a note for James." She moved quickly toward her phone.

Stryker was waiting for Herbert Caine. When he returned from India, they had talked briefly over the phone, but they had a lot to discuss. They had planned an evening of golf.

It was almost six-thirty, and Caine hadn't yet arrived. It was getting very late. Stryker needed to return to his office for his call from Grachenko. Impatiently, he again looked at his wrist watch.

Just then, Mona peeked in. "General, a messenger just arrived from Lieutenant Colonel James Miskovitz."

A messenger from Miskovitz! Stryker was startled. "Jimmy is back? Why? The convention hasn't even begun."

"Our lieutenant is still there, general. He has sent a messenger, someone from our New Delhi embassy."

"Jimmy sent a messenger?" Stryker repeated incredulously. "Who does he think he is, the Prince of Wales? OK, send him in."

"Mr. Caine is also here, sir," Mona said, keeping the door open for the FBI director.

As soon as Caine entered, she moved to her desk and called the receptionist to send in the courier. As he entered her office, she realized he was no ordinary courier. He was a vice consul. Surprised, she quickly moved to escort him to her boss.

Stryker was also surprised, but it didn't show on his face. After the introductions, when his visitor was seated, he asked jokingly, "All the telecom workers in India are on strike?"

The visitor didn't smile. With a dour countenance, he said,

"General, we were very skeptical. However, since he is your man — we checked his credentials carefully — and because he kept insisting — nothing else would satisfy him — we decided to humor him. I still think we made a mistake."

Stryker realized he was facing a reluctant courier. "You have something for me?" he asked noncommittally.

The vice consul took a small white envelope from his pocket and placed it before him. "We could have faxed it. We could have put it in the diplomatic pouch . . . " It was obvious that he was feeling insulted for having been entrusted this job.

Stryker picked up the envelope and turned it around. It carried the U.S. ambassador's red seal. "That's it?" he quietly inquired."No other message?"

The vice consul apparently didn't trust his voice. He merely nodded.

"Thank you, Mr. Consul. I really appreciate your taking the trouble," Stryker said cordially. "As long as you're here, why not have a mini vacation? I can arrange it."

"Thank you, general, I appreciate the thought, but I have lots of work on my desk. My flight leaves at ten. I must rush back to the airport."

The two men shook hands, and the vice consul walked out, indignant and full of anger. They're just desk jockeys like anybody else, he fumed. Just because they have a glamorous job — floating spaceships that are mere junk, that get lost — they think they can waste the public's money any way they want, take whatever liberty their whims demand. Why send only a senior officer, such as himself, ten thousand miles to deliver a personal letter on a routine flight? While they were at it, why not hire a special private jet to run their personal errands? The embassy employee was totally disgruntled with his current mission.

Stryker didn't immediately open the envelope. Staring at the red seals — five on one side, five on the other — he wondered why one seal hadn't been enough? The fellow sealing it had nothing else to do? Or had everyone over there suddenly gotten crazy bees up their bonnets?

"Can you believe it?" he asked Caine, who had remained silent all this time. "That young James Miskovitz. He didn't mail it." He waved the envelope in the air. "He forced them to send an officer of the embassy to deliver it. How melodramatic can one be!"

"Before you start passing judgment," Caine said quietly, "why not read it? I remember that fellow. I think he has a very sensible head on his shoulders."

"That's what I thought also," Stryker said, tearing the envelope open. "That's why I sent him there."

He started reading the handwritten letter, and Caine saw his eyes turn dark as his face turned white. He read it twice, then just sat staring at it.

"Well?" Caine finally asked, when he could no longer endure the suspense.

Stryker stared at him, then slowly moved his hand to offer him the letter. Caine reached out and started to settle back to read it. His back never touched the seat. Shooting up, dropping the letter on table, he thumped it with his fist. "I admire that young man's presence of mind. Best way to send it. If I was in his place, I'd have run myself. Since he is a delegate, it would have created lots of speculation."

"And just think," Stryker mused, "if he hadn't rebelled, I wouldn't have thought of sending him. What a stroke of luck. I can't believe it."

Caine was reading the letter again. "You know what it means? This is the reason for the Yellow Alert. I wonder if the KGB only suspects or if they know? And if they know, how much and what?"

"And you know what else it means?" Stryker's eyes looked sad. "Civil war in Japan. You know how strong the anti-imperialist factions are there. Here, our world is splitting in two, especially in Hawaii — those who support the imperialists and those who do not. The bottom line could be a holocaust. Despite the gradual arms reduction in the late twenties, everyone still has enough missiles to blow up the world."

"I wonder if we should check with our chief of joint command," Caine murmured.

"Check what?"

"To see if there have been any unusual troop or battleship

movements of the Soviet army and navy."

"Calling would make them suspicious," Stryker said. "Trigger deployment of our forces. And if the Soviets haven't yet done anything, that would certainly get them started. Shouldn't we first consult with the president?"

"You know the president," Caine protested. "He'd call a meeting of the department heads, probably even invite senate and congressional leaders. After an hour or two of debate, a majority of them would vote to hand this letter over to the U.N."

"You no longer believe in majority rule, Herb?" Stryker asked sharply.

Caine didn't reply, and Stryker continued, his voice shaking with anger, "If that's what they'd suggest, wouldn't that be the best way to handle it? Don't just sit there. Tell me. Wouldn't it?"

"I'm thinking," Caine said quietly. "The Candle Runners are not banned in the Soviet Union. They must have sent a delegation to this convention."

Striker just looked at him, trying to understand where his thoughts were leading.

"Through this consul, we must send a message back to Miskovitz. He should contact the Soviet Candle Runners' leader."

Stryker's face brightened. "Good idea." He pressed the intercom. "Mona, would you find out which airline the vice consul is flying and send someone to pick him up?"

"He's still here, general," Mona replied.

The next minute she was standing just inside the door. "He was looking so aggravated, I thought his trip would be absolute torture. I advised him to take a shower and have dinner. I promised him that he wouldn't miss his flight, that we would get him to the airport in good time. Pamela is with him."

"Mona, you are a gem. A real gem. Would you call Pam, ask her to bring him over? No. Don't do that. Find out where he is. I'll go. But first, give me an envelope and our SDC seal."

"I need to take a letter, sir?"

"No. It's just a brief, personal note. I can scribble it. We don't want the busy consul to miss his flight."

OK, sir. The seal and envelope. I'll find out where he is and be back right away."

Stryker pushed a pen and pad toward Caine. "Would you write it? I'll call our New Delhi ambassador."

"Miskovitz is *your* man. I think you should write it."

Without any comment, Stryker retrieved his letterhead.

Mona came back. "General, the consul is in the cafeteria. Seems like he's feeling better."

"Good." Stryker pushed the note in the envelope and wrote on it in large letters, EYES ONLY. LIEUTENANT COLONEL JAMES MISKOVITZ. Picking up his seal, he smiled. "I'm going to seal it just as securely as he did."

Placing that envelope inside another one, he addressed the second to the New Delhi ambassador and sealed that also.

"Coming?" he asked Caine.

"I should be going," he replied. "Lots of work on my desk."

Stryker looked dismayed. "But I didn't get a chance to talk with you"

"Important?"

"Very. New developments."

"OK. I'll wait here."

Stryker strode quickly to the cafeteria.

As he entered, he saw Pamela saying something and the consul laughing. Reminding himself to order flowers for Mona, he walked to their table. Noticing him, looking confused, the consul stood up. "General, I . . . "

"Please, be seated," Stryker said. "The ambassador took so much trouble. The least I can do is to send him a thank you note. Can you take it for me?"

"Certainly, sir."

"Good. I appreciate it. Have a nice trip back." Giving him the note, Stryker quickly headed back toward his office.

On his way, thinking about Grachenko's promised call, he remembered something.

"Herb," he said, entering his office, "I just realized something. Yesterday, when signing off, Grachenko used the Candle Runners' greeting. You know the one, 'May your sunshine shoulder you?' Does that mean he may have secretly joined them?"

"I doubt it," Caine said. "The Soviet government . . .

"You're right. Well, what I want to tell you is really your stinker. Someone called Mrs. A'Kash, mentioned a photo of that accident and demanded twenty million dollars. And someone else informed her Neil isn't her son and — "

Herbert Caine sat up straight. "What did you say?"

"Long story," Stryker said. "I was trying to make it short.

"An old woman told Meera a strange story. It seems Captain A'Kash was told by some doctors that he couldn't have a son by his wife. So he got himself a son by some other woman and switched the children at birth. The daughter born to Meera was named Neelam. And, she's alive."

Caine stared at his friend. "I don't believe it."

"I didn't want to believe it either, but Meera is convinced she was told the truth. She wants to find her missing daughter."

"You know such things can't happen in the Soviet Alliance," Caine looked and sounded depressed. "Some people just can't accept the discipline that freedom requires."

"Funny. You're the second person to say that!"

"Who was the first?"

"Your friend, the holy guru Mata. According to Grachenko, she was scared of the absolute freedom that India gives its citizens. She asked the KGB to pick her up."

"And you believe that?"

"Of course. Every word."

"Christ! Aren't you naive? Grachenko must be laughing at you right now for being so gullible."

At this unjustified remark, Stryker couldn't resist a sharp rebuke. "Did you leave your brains in India? Don't you realize that using such a tactic, she used the only ploy that could have fooled the KGB and you missed it? Shame on you!"

"You're right. I'm tired. My body hasn't yet adjusted to the time change." Caine yawned and stretched. "Back to the A'Kash problems . . . When the blackmailer calls, let us know the details of the pickup. The rest is up to us." He stood up. "Sorry about the golf."

"My fault," Stryker said. "First came that courier. Now, I have to wait for Grachenko's call. Why don't you wait, hear what he has to say, then it'll be easier to decide what to do. We can't depend upon the data we may get from the Soviet Candle Runners. They have only *qualified freedom*, what your guru Mata requested."

Just then the intercom rang. "Call from Glavkosmos Mission Control, general," Mona's voice announced.

"Fine," he said, put it through." He left the speaker on and Vladimir Grachenko's voice came through the black box, loud and clear. "Comrade Stan, I just wanted to tell you that guru Mata is not available."

"They denied my request?" Stryker asked angrily.

"Ah. The English language. 'Not available' does not mean 'request denied.' It means what it says: She can't be reached."

"Why?"

Grachenko heaved a sigh. "I'm not supposed to tell you, but I will. Just let me keep it short. Since she asked for her birthright, security was considered superfluous. She was put on a regular flight. It made its scheduled stop at Karachi. The security officer accompanying her reports that she went to the ladies' room and never came back. If he had thought she was up to something, he'd have alerted the trappers, but . . . "

Stryker threw a quick glance at Caine and asked, "So what are you doing about it?"

"Not my department," replied Grachenko gruffly. "And the KGB doesn't confide in me. I've got to go."

"Before you do, can I just ask a brief question?"

"It better be brief."

"Have you heard from the Royal, or Something, Japanese Emperor's Club?"

Grachenko knew Stryker had purposely used the wrong name. But only yesterday he had taken a risk he shouldn't have. He'd been lucky. Perhaps because it was late at night and they weren't listening. A second time, his luck might not hold out.

Breaking the silence, Stryker asked, "Just thought I'd ask. Our co-pilot, Commander Kodama has a Japanese father."

"He does? Then you shouldn't have entrusted your precious cargo to him. Volga Two is calling me. Got to go. Bye." The phone clicked off.

Stryker switched off the speaker. "You don't know his coded dialogue. What he just said was that they know about the conspiracy, and Volga Two is being programmed to take care of it."

Caine leaned back and steepled his fingers. "That means their Yellow Alert won't be upgraded until it is on the launch pad. Do you know how much time we have?"

"No. So much has been happening, I didn't get a chance to . . . but that can be easily remedied." He pressed the intercom. "Mona?"

"Yes, general?"

"What's new about Volga Two? Have they announced a date?"

"Not yet, sir. Last I heard, they were projecting it within a week. Should I call the news service?"

"No. I was just curious. Thank you." Switching off the intercom, he said, "So we have a few days of breathing time."

"Maybe not that much," Caine replied. "But at least we can sleep on it. Can we meet tomorrow on the jogging trail."

"Jogging trail it is," Stryker nodded. "The president will be furious if he learns we knew about it, didn't tell him and waited for their Red Alert."

"As long as I'm alive," Caine said leaving his chair, "that can never happen. Never. If a Red Alert is to be declared, it'll come from us, not them. If the situation warrants it, I may even advise first strike."

His eyes and face looked so threatening, his body language seemed so ominous, Stryker shuddered. But he let it go and said nothing. He never tied himself to any rigid, unyielding statements. He liked to keep his options open.

Before going home, he thought, I should check Meera's cataloging efforts. That's one item I must discuss with Herb tomorrow morning on the jogging trail.

Telling Mona to close his office and go home, he strode in that direction.

The interstellar spaceship streaked ten degrees off the north pole, like a lightning flash, jettisoned an aeromobile and zoomed away.

No one was there to see it. If someone had noticed it, he would have thought it was a flash of lightning in the overhanging black clouds or a shooting star.

The aeromobile plunged nose down through the thick ice until it hit a white plate, undistinguishable from the ice around it. On impact, a hole opened in the plate, the aeromobile plunged in and the trapdoor closed behind it. Lights glowed inside the vehicle. A door opened in the ice facing it, revealing nothing but total darkness behind it.

Steep stairs dropped down from the vehicle and five figures quickly clambered out. Their spacesuits indicated the bodies were humanoid. On their foreheads, numbers glimmered in the dark.

Number Five took the lead. He counted seven steps, groped for and found a wall, and touched a panel. A portion of the wall noiselessly slid away. The interior glowed with a soft white light, and, as the last body entered it, the door glided back in its grooves.

Seven was looking around at the draped furniture, the machines. "Remarkable." His voice came through his spacesuit. "In Earth time, this place has been closed for almost five thousand years, but not a sign of any bacteria."

"So we can remove our suits," said Eleven. The voice had a tinkling, female quality. "No need to keep them on for twenty-four hours as ordered."

"No," said Five, "not until the unit has been fully recycled. We cannot take any chance. I'll get on it. Nine, activate the system. Seven, you locate the catalysts. And, Eleven, you know your job."

"Give me something else," her voice sounded petulant. "The lab can wait. They haven't abandoned hope."

"If they hadn't," Five snapped, "you wouldn't be here."

"Well, that's not exactly right, is it?" Seven intervened. "Our first priority is to wait and watch. That's why no drastic steps have been taken so far. That's why we need to — "

"The more you keep hoping," Five stated as he moved toward

his station, "the more it'll hurt. Why not accept the inevitable? Since earth was seeded, no other species has inflicted so much abuse upon this planet. Remember the reports? How carpet bombing has turned whole cities into rubble. Along how many roads run miles and miles of blasted dugouts — how many forests have been reduced to acres and acres of scorched stumps? I remember the tears in your eyes when you saw those crumbling graves, all that remain of . . . "

Watching him, Eleven thought only how cruel he was. If he found out how she'd ditched the primary directive, how, breaking all the rules, she'd been secretly sending all those dreams, what would he do? But wasn't a species' life more important than her own future career?

"Stop it!" she shouted. "We all know why we have to reopen this station that was closed permanently. But — "

"But, what?" asked Five angrily.

"This younger generation is different. They are trying. Given a chance, they may — "

"May!" Five scorned. "A good, noble word! But the worst possible mirage — the one that forced us to take this journey. Seven, you still standing? How about finding out what they're doing?"

"Waiting to ask you," Seven retorted haughtily. "Which ones? The one in Egypt or the one in that trouble spot, Japan?"

"Didn't they say we must keep a special eye on that most visible one . . . what's her name?"

"Bhagawati Mata?" offered Eleven helpfully.

"Yes," Five grunted. "You know, I don't deny it. They do deserve credit. Despite all the obstacles, they managed to throw many of the right switches. If, against all odds, they succeed, we will return without anyone knowing we were here. But I think it's wishful thinking. I think this species has readied the point of no return, and, when it's all over, new life forms will be needed. We don't have much time left. Come on. Move."

Seven moved, but Eleven held her ground.

Five realized a different approach was needed to persuade her. "I didn't mean to shout at you," he said contritely. "Good of you to remind us that there's still a chance. Nonetheless, you need to be ready. If those flimsy efforts fail and the humans follow the dinosaurs . . . "

"Dinosaurs!" Eleven spat the word. "How you love to recall those unfortunate, ungainly two by fours. Why can't you face the fact? There is no such thing as a perfect species. If you can't save this one, how do you know the next one won't be worse?"

"Again, you are right," Five nodded. "Logic says we should. But you know the prime directive. We can't interfere in any species' life cycle. We cannot stop its extinction. When it dies — no matter how its life cycle ends — the only thing we can do is to seed new life. Don't you think, Eleven, it's you who needs to accept the facts?"

She tried to cool down and match his tone. "You've read that amongst them are many whose dreams are dominated by the theme of one planet. One space program. Why don't we . . . ?"

Five didn't know what to say. He simply stared at her.

She stamped her foot and moved towards the room that no one else — not even Two — was allowed to enter. "Back to the drawing board, back to the drawing board," she muttered unhappily. "If they only knew how much it hurts to see your best creation die.

11

If the Mirror Cracks

In the Space-Gym Room, Neil A'Kash and Sam Oringer were playing a space version of football. Oringer had played it before, but he was not doing much better than Neil. As Neil scored another point, the score card on the wall enunciated in a female voice, "Game Over." They glanced toward it. Forty-one against forty. Neil had won again by a single point.

Using the handrail against the wall, Oringer moved toward the boy and shook his hand. "This is the first time you've played. With practice, I bet you can tackle our best players."

"I can play again?" Neil asked eagerly, his bright eyes shining with anticipation.

"Why not?" Oringer replied. "We have a Junior Scientist's Club. If you join, you can come here any time. But," he added, "you may not want to."

"Why not?"

"Because the club has rules. It requires — "

"I belong to lots of clubs. I know how to keep secrets."

"If we doubted that . . . " Oringer liked the enthusiastic outburst. "The problem is that juniors must choose an associate, a senior scientist, and share their dreams and inventions with him."

And get a chance to learn from him, Neil thought as his enthusiasm soared higher. "I'd love to do that."

"When the time comes, you may change your mind."

This consistent doubt about his integrity hurt. Anger blazed, in Neil's clear hazel eyes. "I'm an honest person. No one doubts my word."

"You've already refused once."

Neil looked surprised. "When?"

"When General Stryker asked you about your invention."

"Space alive! He isn't a scientist. And he can't blame me for Meera's stupidity."

"Was he blaming you?"

"Not using nasty words, but his eyes, his expression, his tone, everything said what a reeking dipstick I was."

"Sorry. I didn't know that." Wanting to soothe the boy's feelings, Oringer added, "I'm sure he didn't mean it that way. He's been having too many troubles, too much on his mind."

"Oh, I know that. When adults have troubles, they can't think straight. They make too many mistakes."

"Sticky wickets, aren't they?" Oringer nodded pleasantly. "I'm thirsty. How about a drink? Coke? Punch?"

"You have a cafeteria here, too?"

"There are mixed opinions about it. I think you should sample it before you sign for membership." Oringer turned and started moving.

Neil looked at the football, nestled in its cradle, and reluctantly followed. His eyes lingered upon the various types of space items being tested and worked on in the rooms through which they crossed. Everyone working on them looked so busy, so happy.

How wonderful it would be, he thought, if I could come here every day. Work here. Play here. Maybe they have a dorm and I won't have to live at anyone's home.

They found a table for two, near a window, and a waiter handed them menus. Neil glanced through it. "Golam Punch?"

"Why not try it?" Oringer said. "If you don't like it, we'll order something else. Two," he told the hovering waiter, "and two Martian Chikaroos to go with it."

"Yes, colonel." The waiter smiled, collected the menus and walked away.

Oringer turned toward his guest. "So? Are you working on something new?"

"Well, not really. You see, Meera sent all my notes with the experiment, so I'm trying to do it all over again. It may turn out to be the same thing, but something entirely different."

"I know what you mean." Oringer nodded understandingly. "Must be something very complicated."

"Not really. My teacher posed a basic question: What if solid matter can be picked up like sound waves . . .

"A little far-fetched, isn't it?"

"Not really. You know what a magnet does?"

"I'm not a scientist," Oringer said, genuinely interested. "You'll need to explain it to me as you would to a layman."

"I'm not good at explaining," Neil admitted. "My teacher, Mr. Zero Truex, can. We can go to his lab." He looked at his watch. "He'd still be there."

"As soon as we finish our Golam."

"Can he pack it for us? Why waste time here?"

"Good idea," Oringer approved. "Neil, you're my kind of guy. We'll take one for Mr. Truex also." He beckoned the waiter and gave him the order, telling him to rush it.

The waiter hurried away. As they waited, Oringer asked nonchalantly, "By the way, Neil. The first time we met, when I came to your house, remember?"

Neil nodded and Oringer continued. "I heard you calling your mother 'mom.' Today, you've been saying, "Meera.'"

"That's because she's not my mother."

"Come on, Neil. Just because she forgot to ask you — "

"Oh, it's not that." Neil looked away. He picked up a fork and examined it, then dropped it. Finally, he made up his mind. "She was behaving real funny. So one day, when her phone rang, I . . ." He banged the table. "Ask her. She won't deny it. Ask her."

Oringer didn't know what to say. He just looked at the 14-year-old, who was obviously in pain and confused.

"You don't believe me, do you?" Neil asked. "But it's a fact. You see, when we returned from Granma's, I opened the letter."

"Granma wrote you before her stroke?"

"No. The one my dad gave me when he was leaving. He said not to open it until his death was confirmed. But Meera was behaving so strange and the Titanic was gone for sure . . . "

"What did the letter say?" Oringer asked softly.

"That just because Meera wasn't my birthmother, that didn't mean I shouldn't take care of her. Since I'm replacing him as head of our household, it's my responsibility to take care of my sisters and my stepmother."

"Does it say who your mother is?"

"Nope," Neil shook his head.

"Can you show me the letter?"

"Nope. Dad is, officially, still alive. I wouldn't have opened it if mom hadn't started behaving so wacko."

"You're right," Oringer agreed. "That's wise. But it says you need to take care of your mom. Why have you abandoned her?"

"I haven't. It's she who can't stand the sight of me."

"Not true," Sam said sincerely. "She was under a severe shock, not responsible for her actions. You know that. First, your dad disappeared. Then her mother was stricken and almost died."

"And, she almost killed a pedestrian," Neil nodded. "But she wasn't letting me be nice to her."

"It must have been difficult," Oringer said kindly. "In your place, I don't know what I'd have done."

Neil looked at him, grateful for this understanding. Just then the waiter came with their takeout package, and Oringer signed the check. Then, putting both hands on the table, he looked into the troubled teenager's eyes. "Neil, I'm not a wise person. In my life, I've made too many mistakes. They've taught me one thing."

Neil didn't move his eyes. Considering it a good sign, Oringer continued, "Our relationships are very fragile things. They are like . . . like small, clear mirrors. You know, once a mirror breaks, you can't put it back together."

Feelings clouded Neil's eyes. He lowered them. When he looked up again, they were clear. "Thank you for teaching me that, colonel," he said gravely, with respect in his breaking voice. "As long as I live, I'll try to remember that."

"Try — that's a good word, son," Oringer said. "That's all we can do. Come on. Let's catch Mr. Truex before he goes home."

"That lab is his home. More than that dinky place where he showers," Neil said, getting up, his voice back to normal. Picking up the Golam package, he took hold of Sam's hand as if it were the most natural thing in the world.

Sitting at a comer table, Stryker noticed the actions of the two, and one of the creases started receding from his forehead.

Lost in thought, he entered his office. Mona looked up. "General, I was just going to go looking for you."

"Problem?"

"Had a call from Mr. Caine's office. They're going to interrogate Burt Ward. Would you like to watch it on your office monitor or go over there?"

"Burt Ward? Oh, yes. Meera A'Kash's friend. I think I should go there."

"I'll order your auto, sir."

"No. Wait. Call a cab. I want to know what's going on in the world."

Mona smiled. "OK, general." She picked up her phone, but before she could dial, Herbert Caine walked in. "Sorry, Stan, I changed my mind."

"Not going to talk with him today?" Stryker asked.

"No. About you coming over there. Anyone who saw you there would wonder why the SDC general is present at a routine —"

"Fine. You can send me the tape later."

"I can do better. I've brought him here."

"Here?" Stryker was surprised. Bringing a criminal to SDC

headquarters? Herb should know better than that.

"Left him in Pam's office," Caine was saying. "He's a sorry sample of humanity. I'm wondering about him."

"Wondering what? That he won't admit anything?"

"Oh, no! That doesn't bother me," Caine said confidently. Where would you like to talk with him?"

"Well? How about that small office next to the library? Mrs. A'Kash isn't there. Mona?"

"I'll tell Pam, sir." She picked up her phone.

Entering the selected office, Stryker glanced at Burt Ward, the description Herb had given ringing in his mind. It seemed appropriate. Standing quietly near the window, almost not breathing, Ward looked like a ghost of a man. If they had entered the room without knowing he was there, they might not have noticed him.

His eyes were not frightened, but they were not a blind man's eyes either. It seemed as if there were a curtain upon them through which one could not see.

God Almighty, Stryker thought, if this man's a spy, it'd be impossible to peek into his mind. No wonder Caine was worried.

The general took a side chair. Behind him, Caine closed the door. Leaning informally against a chair, he said without any preamble, "Mr. Ward, would you tell us what happened? And please, don't rush. Take your time."

Burt Ward looked at their faces, one at a time, as if he were assessing them.

Is he wondering at whose hands he'd have a better chance? Stryker thought. To whose emotions he should appeal. "You may sit down," he offered amiably.

"It's OK," said Ward, standing his ground. "Not much to tell. This old creep rents a room in my hotel. Looks so poor, I wonder if he pays his bills. So I keep an eye on him. These kinda dips leave at night when everyone is asleep. So, I check. He talks in his sleep. I get curious. Give him lunch. Once he starts talking, he can't stop. All about a daughter he's never seen. And how, with much difficulty, he found her. And now that he knows where she is, he can't get near. At her house there be watchdogs. At her office, her secretary turns him away. Won't even let him wait. And her phone is unlisted. No way to talk with her. When he sez who she is, I get angry. She's got so much money, and her father can't even eat. So I decide to help. I call her office and set up an appointment under a phony name — you know, to make sure she's there."

Stryker nodded. He was admiring Ward's succinct style. Mentioning facts, without saying much. Herb was right, this man could be very dangerous if it were a clever disguise, if he weren't just a low-income rooming house owner. Herb's people must have started checking his background. It wouldn't hurt to ask the CIA guys.

"That morning," Ward was saying, "two boarders git in a stupid brawl. Sorting 'em, we git late. Driving, I like to listen to me sat-V. Suddenly I'm listening to her. She's comin' back. I'm on the other side of the highway. See? I tell this one-track-mind father I must find a place to turn. He turns hysterical, starts raving about her wild dogs. Orders me to stop. Sez, if he stands in the middle of road, she'll see him and stop. Then, she got no choice. She must give him an ear. His talk sounds logical. I pull under a tree. He gits out, runs an' gits hit."

Stryker nodded, "It sounds true. But — "

"It sounds true, 'cause it is true."

"But," Stryker continued, as if he hadn't interrupted, "that doesn't solve the problem. Blackmail is illegal. You know that?"

Ward laughed. A soft, slippery laugh. "Those ugly words git only to what you can't git away with. You know someone who hasn't done illegal? You haven't?"

Stryker ignored the question. "If we prosecute you, Mrs. A'Kash would have to appear in court. We don't need that kind of publicity. If we let you go, you'll talk about it, which will be worse."

Ward's deadpan expression didn't change. "A bit of cash ken solve all problems. Sure you know that."

"What I know is this," Caine spoke for the first time. "A blackmailer is never satisfied. No matter how much he gets, no matter how much time he keeps quiet, sooner or later — sooner, most of the time — he resurfaces and then, once again, one has to solve the same problems all over."

"Then what you wanna do?" Ward asked dispassionately in a neutral voice. "Kill me an' throw my body to sharks?"

"No." Stryker studied him and made up his mind. "If you'll return the negatives and photos to me and promise to keep your mouth shut, I'd be willing to offer you a job."

"What kinda job?" Ward sneered. "Sweeping your office?"

"That depends upon your qualifications, doesn't it?" Stryker smiled. "Tell me, what you can do?"

"I own me own business. I don't need your fuckin' job."

"Language, please," Caine said a little testily. "Don't destroy the good impression you've created. Just tell us in plain and simple words — do you wish to cooperate or not?"

"Greens cooperate. Not me."

"Fine." Stryker scraped back his chair and got up. "You'll stay in a good hotel tonight. Tomorrow, we'll talk again."

"No hotel," Ward said quietly. "If you want to hold me, you charge me. If not, you let me go."

Stryker didn't hesitate. He turned toward Caine. "Charge him."

Caine merely nodded. He opened the door and motioned to the security men waiting outside. "Take him."

Stryker moved to the window and stood staring at nothing. Caine finally took the chair he had been leaning against and spread his feet under the table.

"If we charge him," Stryker said, "Sparky's cover would be broken."

"What other choice do we have?"

Stryker heaved a sigh. "If we can find out whether someone sent Sparky to his place, or whether it was just coincidence that he stayed there, would that give us a leg to start?"

"That's it," Caine sat up. "That's the solution."

"Solution? No. I was only . . . "

Caine stood up. "If the doctors would give me five minutes alone with Sparky — just five — I'd ask him if he was referred there by someone. He'll nod, 'yes,' and we'll charge Mr. Know-All with international espionage."

"What would that do?" Stryker was puzzled. "Sparky is in no condition to answer any questions. You know that."

"If I say he answered and nodded," replied Caine, "he did. And that would give us a closed hearing. Cover intact. Period."

"Are you sure?"

"In life, can we be sure of anything?"

"Don't turn philosopher on me," Stryker sounded angry and frustrated. "I'll call the hospital. Let's go."

Opening the door, they heard running footsteps.

In these offices, no one ever ran. Curious, they waited as a security guard came sprinting up the hall and stopped in front of them. "General, the prisoner was just shot."

"How? Who . . . " The men moved quickly.

Keeping pace, the sergeant breathlessly narrated the event. "His guards were taking him to the waiting van. Suddenly, two men came out of nowhere, pumped several bullets into them and him and got away in an auto that came racing in to pick them up. We were at out post. It all happened before we knew what was happening. We weren't cautioned to expect anything, general!"

Outside, they saw an ambulance picking up the wounded officers. Stryker and Caine walked toward Ward and stood staring at his body, now covered by a white sheet.

"Who'd want to silence him?" Caine whispered.

"Does it mean Sparky was maneuvered to that spot?" Stryker muttered. "Was it a devious plot that succeeded, despite all odds? Perhaps," he stared at Caine, "that guru Mata does hold the key, if we could find her."

"We will," Caine said with conviction. "We will find her." He strode toward his auto. Halfway, he turned and glanced at Stryker who was staring at Ward's body being lifted into the ambulance, his face a mirror of his feelings. Caine swallowed the words he was about to say, entered his auto, and, ignoring the seat belt, turned on the ignition. As his glance fell on the rear mirror, an auto parked on the other side of the street seemed familiar.

"Is it the same auto that was behind me when I was coming here?" he asked himself, then answered his own question. "Stop it! Don't be paranoid! You've got no reason to worry."

He pushed the accelerator, not realizing that he would have been wise if he had worried. As he moved, a cab and a couple of

autos moved behind him. Before he could turn the comer, the
auto waiting in the shadows merged into the traffic, following
his vehicle.

Rahul had left half an hour ago. For that thirty minutes, the
two girls hadn't spoken a single word, hadn't even looked at
each other.

Gopa sat on the windowsill, leafing through magazines. Pooja
sat with her laptop, flipping screen after screen, as if she were
alone and busy, doing work that couldn't wait.

Finally, Gopa couldn't take it any more. "Have you called
your brother?" she asked sarcastically.

Pooja didn't even look up, as if she hadn't heard. So Gopa
repeated, "Have you?"

Pooja typed furiously. "What brother?"

"What a short memory you have!" Gopa sneered. "The one
you always flew to defend, even before I got a chance to say a
single word. That brother."

"He isn't my brother."

"So? Now that you've learned to be independent, you don't
even want to recognize your family?" Gopa laughed
contemptuously. "What would Mom say if she was here?"

Pooja didn't reply, as if it was below her dignity to pay any
attention to such a remark.

Gopa dangled her feet, glared at her sister, then stood up
swiftly. Throwing a magazine over the laptop screen, she stood
with her hands on her hips. "Damn it! Talk to me."

"Not until you learn to talk properly."

"And who is going to teach me?" Gopa snarled. "You?"

"You better believe it."

"What did you say?"

"Now that dad is gone and you can't stand mom, who else is
there?"

"My brother, Neil. You may not know it, but he loves me."

"Ha! And ha!" Pooja mocked. "You'd better give up that
delusion. He isn't your brother."

This was the second time Pooja had said that and there

seemed to be a twang of truth in her words. Even in anger, one
didn't say such a nasty thing. Gopa stared at her. "Have you lost
your mind! Why isn't he my brother?"

"Because he is not," Pooja said smugly, "So I'm the only
family you got. And you don't want me. So you got nobody."

"Why isn't he our brother?" Gopa repeated like a wintry
blast.

"Because," Pooja replied, relishing the word, "because he is
our half-brother."

"What are you talking about?"

"When dad was leaving, he gave me a letter."

"He did not."

"He did." Pooja smirked with unfeigned pleasure.

Gopa's anger was ready to burst. It was only her father's
memory that stopped her from hitting her sister. "If he was
leaving any letter, he'd have given it to me."

"But he didn't," Pooja sneered. "So, all that affection for you
was just a show-off. He didn't love you. He loved me."

Gopa didn't hear the hateful remark. Her mind was moving
like a straw caught in a whirling tornado. Dad had left a letter.
And that letter said that Neil wasn't their brother? Was that
possible, or was Pooja making up the story to rile her? No, no
one, not even Pooja, could make up such a nasty story.

"Where's the letter?" she asked quietly. Too quietly.

Pooja saw her ashen face and got scared. Gopa wasn't going
to get sick, was she? "In my room," she replied hurriedly.
"Remember the holes we dug in our closets? There. In my
closet."

"What did it say? Tell me. Every word."

"I'm not supposed to have read it. Not until he's dead."

Dead! Gopa sprang at her. Furiously pulling her long hair, she
shrieked, "But you disobeyed him? You read it?"

"Ouch! Let go! He was so grossly dramatic about it!" Pooja
remonstrated. "'Open it only after I've died,'" she mimicked
him. "'Don't open it alone. Make sure Gopa is with you. Make
sure Neil is not at home . . . ' I opened it as soon as I saw him
stepping into the van that had come to pick him up."

At any other time, Gopa would have hit her for mocking and

ridiculing her father, but the shock had stunned her. After what she had recently gone through, this seemed like the bullet that would kill her. She stood frozen, staring at the stranger who claimed she was her sister.

Through the window, Pooja heard the sound of the approaching Honda. She realized she must salvage the situation before Rahul stepped into the room.

Moving quickly, she took Gopa's hand and pulled her to the windowsill. "This letter is very brief, sis," she said, putting her arm around Gopa's shoulder. "It only says that, for an important reason that we aren't old enough to understand, he had to father a son with another woman. And because mom gave birth to a daughter at the same time, he switched the children. That our sister is a very affectionate person and, when the time is right, we will meet her."

"Dad! Cheating on mom? Cheating on Neil? Keeping such a horrible secret closeted inside his chest for our whole lives?" Gopa whispered. "I can't believe it."

"He isn't here," Pooja said soothingly. "He isn't coming back. You don't have to believe it. Just don't think about it."

"But I will think about it," Gopa protested. "There's a girl somewhere. Neil's age. Our own sister. We don't know what she looks like! We don't even know her name!"

"Why worry about it?" Pooja could hear Rahul outside the door. She hugged Gopa as affectionately as she could. "We've got each other. Back at home, we've got mom. Isn't that enough?"

Just then the door opened and Rahul walked in. Seeing them, sitting so close together, eyes brimming wet, looking like two faces of one caught in a broken mirror, his face brightened.

"Since I've seen you two together," he said cheerfully, "I've been wondering that if both of you start wearing similar clothes, how am I going to recognize you?"

"We should do that, Gopa," Pooja giggled. "His punishment for bringing us together."

Gopa was trying to recover. "Rahul, I need to go back. When James returns, if he doesn't find me there . . . "

Rahul realized everything was not as smooth as he had

imagined. But then, wasn't he being naive in believing that years and years of feelings would change in one brief meeting?

"He won't worry," he replied soothingly. "We left a note, remember? But I know that lots of work is waiting for you so if you're ready, let's go . . . Pooja," he turned toward her, "I've got something for you."

"What?"

"A letter. Your mother mailed it to our New York office. I just got it." Taking it out of his pocket, he handed it to her.

He had hoped she'd share it with Gopa. Say something like, 'Let's read it together. It's for both of us.' But she didn't even open it.

He sighed inwardly. Time, he thought, time.

Gopa was at the door. He followed her and helped her settle on the Honda. As they left, he wondered if he should ask her if she also had the ability to reach her father. If she did have, Rahul wondered whether she would admit it to him or not.

Behind him, he heard her quietly sobbing. "Gopa! Why are you crying? I'm sure Jim is OK."

"I just learned something."

"What?" he asked worriedly.

"I have another sister. And Neil isn't my brother. He's only my half-brother."

"Pooja told you that?" he asked. "Did she also tell you your dad's alive?"

"She doesn't have to tell me that. I know that."

"You do?"

"Don't ask me how," she said quickly. "I'll tell you, but not right now."

"OK," he said. "Can we talk about the news story I want from you?"

"What did you say?" Gopa asked, as if belatedly hearing what he had said earlier. "Pooja told you dad is alive?"

"Why does that surprise you?"

"I didn't know she believes in guru Mata."

"What has guru Mata got to do with it?"

"She's the one who told me."

"What?"

"When my dad was chosen for this mission, I wanted to run away from home. guru Mata was attending a Candle Runners' carnival. Having heard of her fame, I went to her, hoping she'd be able to persuade him not to go. But she changed my mind. She told me."

"What?"

"That's confidential."

Rahul decided it would be unwise to push. "Do you see her often? Guru Mata, I mean?" he asked.

"Not so often. We don't have to meet." Pride was evident in Gopa's voice. "She says I'm her *Kanishka*, the little finger on her right hand. We often talk. In fact, she's going to call me soon."

Is that so, Rahul thought. The whole world was searching for that slippery soothsayer. And this teenager, living in cracked mirrors . . .

Suddenly he wanted to find the resourceful James Miskovitz.

The Honda flew . . .

12

Shadow
Rings

The range safety officer, Col. Han Ha Fong, was worried. Two days had passed and Flight Director Mao Ki Tung hadn't stepped into his mission control cubicle even once. He hadn't summoned Fong to his office. Worse, no one had heard his decretory voice shouting razor-sharp orders. It felt like someone had died and no one wanted to admit it.

He didn't know about the others, but secretly, Fong was worried. If Tung was sick, someone should summon a doctor. If he wasn't sick . . .

To knock at his door without being summoned was like tying a noose around one's neck and pulling it until one's last breath was gone. But he decided to risk it.

Standing before Tung's door, Fong lifted his hand to knock

but pulled it back; lifted it again, then hesitated and pulled it back again. Finally, mouthing an unspeakable oath through clenched teeth, he forced his knuckles to tap.

"Enter," said the familiar, peremptory voice.

"Comrade director?" Opening the door just a crack, one foot inside, Fong said respectfully, "I'm sorry to intrude, but — "

"Ah! Comrade Han! I was just thinking of calling you. Come in. Come in."

For violating the protocol, Fong had expected a rebuke. Anger. Instead, he was being addressed not as a subordinate, but as an equal. By his personal name. Surprised by this uncharacteristic, unexpected welcome, he stood rooted at his spot, clutching the half-opened door.

"Comrade colonel." Tung's arm moved invitingly and his cheerful voice boomed with pleasure. "At ease. Have a seat. We have to discuss something important. Very important."

So, he knows! Fong thought. That's why he has secluded himself, to plan how to maneuver the chairman and party chiefs. There had apparently been no reason for Fong to be concerned.

"Comrade director, you've heard about it?" Getting hold of himself, he asked, "What's our spot? What are we going to do?"

"Not much," Tung replied cheerfully. "You're going to stay here. I'm going to go there."

Col. Fong was appalled. "To the war front?"

"What war front?"

"Isn't that what we're talking about?"

"I was talking about the dragon boat race and my decision to go there. What were you talking about?"

Fong's discomfort increased; Tung must have heard. No way he couldn't have. At this critical point in the life of the nation — in the lives of the people who made their home in the country riding the center of the world — how could he be thinking of childish dragon boat races?

Or was it possible that, because he had secluded himself, he hadn't yet heard? He didn't know about it?

He decided to venture one tiny toe into the logic-chopping quagmire. "The Soviets have decided to attack Japan. Which side do you think we're going to join?"

"Ha! The Russians!" Tung laughed.

"Our intelligence reports cannot be doubted. You've taught me that, comrade director."

"So I have." Tung nodded. "Never got a chance to teach the other half. The age of international wars is over. This is the age of ideology, of battles over issues.

"Let me name just a few." As he talked, he counted on his fingers, folding them one by one. "On the social side, there's surrogate motherhood, subterranean ghettos, extended families owning a maximum of one child per family. On the political side, we have econo-city conflicts, ethnic freedoms, global warming, colonies on the moon and Mars."

"Yes, colonies!" Fong breathed hard. "That's why the Soviet Alliance— "

"What's the matter with you today, colonel! Having the wrong kinds of nightmares? We don't have to worry about our copycat neighbors. You should know that."

Col. Fong stared at his boss. Just two days ago, sitting in this very chair, he had declared he would push the party to declare war, or, failing that, change his name.

"In fact," the skin-shedding lizard was saying, "just the other day I sent a congratulatory cable to our comrade chairman telling him how wise he was in turning down Tokyo's request for us to contribute to their space effort. They were capable of launching only lifeless robos. Volga Two will carry fifteen professional cosmonauts."

He looked searchingly at his subordinate's troubled face and smiled. "I'm not supposed to tell you, but considering your patriotism, I will. We're negotiating with Moscow. Out of the fifteen, at least two may be Chinese. Our flags — Soviet and Chinese — will fly first over Mars."

So! When the missiles start flying, ours will ring Hiroshima, Fong thought. "I heard that the Soviet Navy . . . "

"Naval exercises," Tung retorted impatiently, "just as the news media reported. Now, about my passport. Since the party has denied it, you have to find someone in the ghettos. I understand the ones they produce look so real that no one can tell the difference."

Fong stared at his chief. Mao Ki Tung, the man who was itching to advise the party chairman to start war preparations, wanted to buy his passport on the black market. Sneak out of his motherland like a criminal.

Could the mere circumstance of having his name associated with the convention have created such damage, such havoc, to his dependable ideals? It didn't seem possible. But how could he deny what he was hearing? What he was seeing?

Did the party know about this abrupt change, this derogatory transformation? This unthinkable, imminent treachery?

"You are going to defect?" he asked softly.

Tung laughed again. "Candle Runners don't need to defect. They are world citizens. They can go where they please. That's the unwritten universal law. Surely you are aware of it."

"But, you are not a Candle Runner," Fong replied, putting a lot of stress upon the word *not*. "Your membership request was not accepted. Considering our political clout, they had to agree to give us Observer status, but that's all you got."

Tung pooh-poohed the distinction. "What political clout?" he scorned. "Politics had nothing to do with it," he said disdainfully. "The acceptance came so quickly due to our history-shaking suggestion about the inaugural race. When I reach there and offer other such world-shaking ideas, they'll beg me to join them." His face clearly said how much he was relishing the idea.

"Since I'm giving you the honor of being in virtual charge here during my absence, can you arrange my passport," he asked belligerently, "or do I need to find time myself?"

Fong was not so naive as to believe the promise of such an unheard of promotion. He knew it was not Mao Ki Tung's to give. In fact, when the party found out about his defection, the flight director would immediately lose the chair he was so comfortably occupying at the moment.

According to the unwritten rules, Fong should inform the party about this treachery right away, right now.

But Tung had done him a few favors. And if the director was out of the way, that might indeed open some doors for Fong. "Your wish is my command, comrade director," he said respectfully. "As soon as I'm dismissed, I'll work on it."

"You're dismissed," Tung said cheerfully. "And, colonel?"

"Yes, comrade director?"

"I can depend upon your discretion?"

"I have no eyes. No ears."

"Good." Without waiting for Fong to leave, Tung stretched his feet over his table and closed his eyes.

Walking towards his auto, an idea struck Fong; all this whimsy was not real. It was merely a hoax. The party wanted Tung to spy, and the deception had to look authentic. It would work only if the Candle Runners believed Mao Ki was a traitor. That's why they had coached the flight director. And that honest officer, who was not capable of committing a perfidious act even in his dreams, was merely practicing his role, making Fong his sounding board.

A broad smile lit up Col. Han Ha Fong's swarthy face — this was the only explanation. There could be no other reason, he told himself stoutly. He was pleased that he had been able to figure it out, all by himself, without anyone's help, without it being spelled out for him.

Feeling proud of serving under a boss to whom the party had handed such a delicate job, whom the party trusted so much, Fong started whistling and, with light steps, raced to his auto to fulfill his small part in the vast, scintillating conspiracy.

In her temporary SDC office, Meera A'Kash had spent more than five hours rechecking the anomaly she had discovered by chance. They couldn't have made such an obvious error, she was thinking. She must have punched a wrong key somewhere and she'd better find her mistake before someone came along.

But even after redoing the calculations three times, she hadn't been able to find the source of her error.

Her head started pounding and she started cursing herself. Why had she taken this stupid job about which she knew nothing? If she did it right, no one would say one nice word. If she made one error — just one small mistake — they'd curse her to the source of the Ganges, for ever and ever.

She heard footsteps approaching, and Gen. Stryker walked in. "Meera," he said without any preamble, "I have some news for you. Some good. Some not so good."

"First, the not so good."

"Oh, no. You've been working hard. First, I want to cheer you up. Your Colonel Oringer — "

"My Colonel Oringer!"

"Sorry," He smiled, pulling a chair over and sitting near her. "Our Colonel Oringer had a heart-to-heart talk with Neil. It seems there's a misunderstanding. He ran away because he thinks you don't want him any more, because he isn't your son."

"Hogwash! He doesn't know."

"But he does."

"Who told him?"

Stryker hesitated; all their efforts would fail if she learned Neil had eavesdropped on her phone conversation. I better caution Sam, he thought, and said, "I don't think Sam asked him that. But, he understands your problem and is willing to be friends."

There was no answering smile on Meera's face. "Just like that! What about his horrible behavior? No apology for that?"

"Isn't apology a two-way interlink, Meera?" Stryker asked gently. "Have you considered your own behavior?"

"I was distraught; my husband was missing, my mother was on her deathbed and this witch wanted to blackmail me."

"He's just a child, Meera, but he is very intelligent. If you had explained to him, he'd have understood."

Meera glanced at his smiling face and stern eyes and realized she must agree. If she didn't, he might put her in some loony bin. "Perhaps," she said haltingly, "you are right."

Stryker looked pleased. "Here," he said, offering her a piece of paper, "that's his phone number. Will you call him?"

She nodded and tucked the paper in her purse. This is *good news*? she thought. If being forced to grapple with the presence of a boy who was not her son was good news, she wasn't sure she was ready to hear the bad news.

Stryker relaxed. "The other item," he said, "is about the fellow who got hit by your auto."

Her face turned pale. What about him! she thought and then silently scolded herself. Whatever it was, she'd have to accept it. Show a cheerful face.

Averting her eyes, she asked, "He died?"

"Oh, no! He's healthier today than he was stretching his dimes in that God-forsaken rooming house. But — "

"But?" Fearing the worst, her heart pounding, she glanced at him.

"He has lost thirty-nine years of his life."

"Please! No jokes!"

"Who's joking?" Stryker looked surprised. "I'm only telling you facts. When he woke up, his first words were, 'Where am I? Call me a cab. I'll miss my flight.' He remembers his life before that flight, when he was flying to India to work on his doctoral thesis, but nothing from then on. His memory stops there."

"How's that possible?"

"The doctors have a word for it, but I don't remember it. They explained it to me. There's something so traumatic connected with that flight that, to heal itself, his mind has blanketed out anything and everything pertinent to it."

"Oh my God. The poor soul. Can a hypnotist help him?"

"We'll have to try everything, but it's going to be a tough job. We can't let the news media find out about it."

"Why?"

Stryker hesitated, then looked at Meera carefully. "Considering you're working here and you are part of our team, maybe I can tell you, if you can keep it a secret."

"Of course, general. I've got that much common sense."

"I'm sure of that, otherwise I wouldn't have mentioned it," he said soothingly. "You see, he's one of our topmost scholars. For reasons I don't know myself, his identity had to be changed. It's a horrible thing to consider, but they say it would be easier to let him die than to let his cover get broken."

"But the doctors have ethics. They never reveal what a patient tells them. And you have your own departmental — "

"That's not the problem. The problem is that someone reliable has to be with him all the time because, in such cases, the patient can remember things unexpectedly. And if he remembers but forgets his oath of secrecy, talks with somebody . . . "

"I see." Meera nodded. "I see your problem. But you are a very creative person, general. I'm sure you'll find a way."

"Thanks for the vote of confidence." Stryker smiled. "But I need to decide right away because the hospital wants to release him. And the only solution I can think of seems impossible."

"Why?" she smiled. "Your disciple, my husband, often told me what you taught him, that no matter how impossible something seems, one must not give up because there are always possibilities."

"Well," he confessed, "I feel ready to eat my words, unless," he looked at her hopefully, "unless, you can help me."

"Me?"

"I need a nondepartmental guardian for him. And right now, you are the only person I have whom I can trust."

"Oh my God!" Her large, expressive eyes bulged. "You don't mean it!"

"I never say anything I don't mean." He frantically searched his mind and found the answer. "You see, this confounded convention has drained all my resources. Everyone I can trust — even my buddy, Pablo Martinez — everyone is right now in Ayodhya, playing the Savior of the world."

The way he said it made her laugh. "I never took nursing courses. And you say Neil wants to come back. Children babble."

"Not Neil. He's not a babbler. He's the second person I can trust. And you don't have to be a nurse. Just be a friend. Talk to him as you would to any normal person. Just be careful. Don't talk about his daughter."

"The one who was supposed to have killed him? Well, at least this once, life proved guru Mata wrong. There may be other instances that we don't know about. She's not so omnipotent after all."

"Oh, I don't know," Stryker mused. "Isn't losing two-thirds of your life like dying? Or even worse?"

"He will recover."

"Let's hope so," Stryker sighed. He searched her face. Seeing indecision playing hide-and-seek there, he realized a little extra push was needed. "By the way, I forgot to mention that the department has to pay for the guardianship."

Meera felt embarrassed, "Oh, I can't accept that."

"You'll need to. We can't let anyone work for free. If we do, there will be so many questions. All of us would get in trouble."

Meera looked at him and saw only honesty and sincerity on his earnest face. There was no subterfuge in his guileless eyes. He looked as if he really needed help.

And she needed the job; the money Vishu had left wouldn't last long. If the Titanic was gone, his salary would stop. They might give her a pension, but that wouldn't even pay her Earth Reality expenses. She had no qualifications for any kind of decent-paying position.

If she didn't want to find another husband, the only way for her to support herself would be to find a job. For that, she'd have to enroll in some business school. Even after completing it . . .

The gods were being kind to her. If she refused this offer, she might never get another one. Since they'd be paying her, she could hire a nurse.

"General, it seems like a humanitarian thing to do. Being associated with Earth Reality and all, I can't say no. I'll be honored to take care of your friend."

"Good." Stryker's worried eyes lit with unfeigned pleasure. "I'll call the hospital. Mona will take care of everything, so your time won't be wasted." He got up.

"General, one minute, if you please," Meera said hastily. "I need to tell you something."

"What?" Stryker turned, feeling apprehensive; had she changed her mind and found an excuse?

"These items that I'm cataloging. This morning, I noticed something. Since then, I've been checking and rechecking, but I can't figure it out."

"What is that?" Stryker asked, his hopes awakened; had she found something that might provide a clue?

"You see this robo-server? When it came off the assembly line, its weight was logged at ninety-five pounds."

"Ah, yes, my *kangaroo*. There were so many arguments

against sending it." He remembered and smiled. "But finally, we — me and Captain A'Kash — won. But I agree, it's a lot of weight when . . . "

"Your logistics are beyond me, general. What I'm wondering is, what am I missing? Because, you see, here, at its prelaunch weighing, it weighed two hundred and five pounds."

Stryker kneeled and stared at the figures. There was no denying it, her statement was correct.

"Its real purpose was not to do routine chores," he wasn't so much telling her as thinking aloud. "That was just a side benefit. The crew would have done those. But on their space walks they'd have needed more supplies than they could carry. It was to trundle those, like a maneuverable storage unit.

"That's it." he said, looking at her. "Some smart alec, wanting to play a joke, hid some supplies in there rather than storing them where they should have been stored."

"I thought of that, general. So to make sure, I rechecked. Several times. You told me that each scheduled item was weighed and is on this list. If something was inside the robo, it wasn't weighed separately. It's not on this list."

Stryker heard her, but inside his mind a suspicion clicked — why had she suspected that the weight difference could mean something stored inside the robo? A humanoid robot didn't have storage capacity. If he asked her, would she tell him?

He didn't have to ask. She smiled, "Maybe you got a stowaway abroad the Titanic, general."

He glared at her. "What makes you say that?"

The look frightened her. "Only kidding, Sir."

"But you knew it had storage space?"

"Of course, I knew," she said nettled by his suspicious look. "Vishu was always teasing Gopa, saying she could come with him and no one would know about it."

"He talked about it? Broke the rules?" Stryker felt his blood pressure rising. "He was under oath."

"Where Gopa was concerned," Meera spoke sharply, "no oath had any meaning for my husband."

Stryker heard her, but the words didn't really register. Colliding thoughts played havoc in his mind. Was that why

Vishu had supported him so passionately to get kangaroo approved? Because he wanted to take something with him secretly? What was it? A computer that could link with Hiroshima Hoku?

Was their exalted captain, the one who hated his father's name, really Tokyo's secret dagger, a Trojan horse who handed their superprized ship to his alien masters? Is that why he had insisted on getting Commander Kodama? . . .

He wondered what action he should take. Call Miskovitz and ask him to bring the Japanese Candle Runner right away? He'd rebel. Tomorrow was the dragon boat race. And right after that, meetings and debates.

Should he fly there himself to meet them?

Or should he wait until the convention was adjourned?

The last option seemed most logical, but did he have that much time? Volga Two would be heading toward the launch pad soon. All reports said the lights in Glavkosmos never dimmed. Work was progressing round the clock in three full shifts. When Gen. Kikilo wanted something, Gen. Kikolo got it. Always.

What about Sparky? Could he be holding the key to this mystery? Should he ask a hypnotist to probe his mind? Was his amnesia real or was he faking?

"General?"

Mona's voice fell distantly in his ears. He looked up.

Efficient, but unassuming, looking trim and neat and lovely as usual, she stood with a phone in her hand.

"The consul general has broken his silence, sir."

"The consul gen . . . " Stryker's eyes lit up with the brightness of the midday sun. "Pablo?"

The expression on that face, so close, yet so far away, the face that she had always adored, was Mona's reward for bringing the news. She smiled. "Would you like to take it here, sir, or in your office?"

Forgetting the Titanic and its captain and its kangaroo, oblivious of Meera, he took the remote from Mona and moved toward the adjoining office, which was vacant.

"Amigo," they heard him saying and knew he was trying his best to suppress his excitement. "How flies the black crow?"

The door closed behind his back. Mona smiled at Meera, waved and strode away.

Meera felt like she was the only one in the entire world who was not moving, who was fixed in time and place like an unbreakable ring around vicious objects that were ferociously winging inside her hollow sphere, scorching her. Scorching her. Burning her. Tempting her to torch them. Torch them, one and all.

She sat staring at the terminal. Who had Vishu taken with him in that kangaroo? Was it Neil's mother?

Pooja sat in a corner, observing the hubbub as the last minutes ticked away at a giddy, intoxicating pace. She was watching it, but her mind was elsewhere, roaming backwards into the past: Who was Neil's mother? Had her papa left a letter with her also? With her or Neelam? If so, had he mentioned the twins? When she had read that letter the tenth time, watching the sat-screen in her solitary motel room, she had felt numb. She had decided to close her mind and forget it. But Gopa's questions had awakened her mind. If she thought long enough — if she analyzed every face stored away in her memory — would she be able to recognize that one face that had taken a sister from her?

Papa was a very social person, she remembered. He loved to give parties and brought home everybody he met, even the people he met just once. But he was not a philanderer. I never saw him flirting, she thought. Unlike so many other men, wanting to show off how debonair they were, he never kissed ladies' fingers.

If that were so, did that mean he'd have brought home the mother of his only son, or did it mean he'd not have dared to do so?

Had he? When? Who was this mysterious woman? When and where and how had he met her? Had he ever brought her home? Did he tell her about us? Does she know us? If I met her somewhere, would I recognize her?

Her reverie was broken by Gopa's frantic voice. "Pooja, can

you come here?" She was waving a glittering banner at her. "Can you hold this for a minute?"

"No. I can't," Pooja shouted back, "because I know it won't be for just a minute."

She saw Rahul's expression, and she knew what he was saying in his mind. 'Oh, for God's sake!'

Let him say it, she thought furiously. She wouldn't let him dictate her actions. She wouldn't let anyone dictate her actions.

"Gopa?" she heard Cheenoo calling. The voice sent shivers through her veins. Everyone had been looking for him, but no one had been able to find him. Now, suddenly, out of nowhere, he was there. And he was not looking for her. He was looking for Gopa. Shucks.

She quickly moved. "Sorry, sis," she said sweetly. "I'll hold it."

But Gopa's hand was empty. Someone had taken the banner and whisked it away. Cheenoo's attention was riveted on Gopa.

"No matter how we do it," he was insisting, "no matter how late it is, Gopa, we must sit down somewhere quiet for half an hour and review tomorrow's agenda."

"More important is our platform." The one called Blowtorch inserted his face between them. "We still have to thrash out a few points."

"Gopa," Miskovitz called from a distant corner, "does Trinidad go before Spain?"

Before she could reply, an electrician ambled over. "Miss A'Kash, if you need another screen . . . "

"Space above! Can somebody take care of him?" Gopa looked around. "I can't be everywhere at the same time."

"No?" Rahul arched an eyebrow.

"No," she retorted. "The Gopas of this world have only two hands and two feet. That's why God invented the Rahuls, who move on wheels. I thought you knew that."

"I did," he replied cheerfully, "until you started borrowing my wheels. Now, I don't even know where to look for them."

"Serves you right," said Miskovitz behind him. "Come to my office later. I'll intro' you to a *four-eye.*"

They laughed, but Blowtorch's friends didn't think it was

funny. "To you guys everything's fun an' games," one whined. "Well, lemme tell you, it's not. Blow is right. Can we meet at nine sharp, your office?"

"No one here wants to be bright-eyed for tomorrow's race?" Gopa asked, looking around.

"You're nuts, Gopa." Blowtorch snapped. "Eight hours of shut-eye not enough for you? What are you? A suckling kid?"

There was sudden silence.

Blowtorch looked at the amazed, horrified and angry faces, then looked very sheepish. "Shucks, Gopa. I'm used to talking to my gang. I forgot you're a lady. Meant no insult."

"No insult taken, Blow," Gopa said sweetly. "You are the bearer of my mother's manifesto. You talk any way you wish. Nine it is. OK?"

Feeling embarrassed, he nodded. Pulling Miskovitz's hand, she stepped away. "James, Spain may not like that. Rahul, what do you think?" She turned for his opinion, but he wasn't around. He'd gone away with the electrician.

Cheenoo came over. "Shorty's in the front row. That's only fair. Why not alphabetize the islands separately?"

Approving the suggestion, someone clapped and others joined in. Someone added music to the applause by turning on the stereo. A few boys got hold of girls' hands and started a brisk *moon-a-rama*.

Before anyone could grab her, Gopa swiftly stepped aside and moved in search of Rahul, but she couldn't go very far.

"Gopa," someone called over the slam-bang music and kicking heels. "There's a phone call for you, long distance."

"Can you take it?" she shouted back.

"Can't. Sez it's personal. Sez it's about Rings Round the World."

"Space above! I'm coming, I'm coming. Can someone find Rahul?"

"I will," Cheenoo said. "Have no fear, Cheenoo's here, with dragon's wings that needs no wheels."

Laughing, Gopa ran toward the phone.

13

Twenty-One
Ways to Kill

Blowtorch was bursting to hang them, one and all. During the past twenty years it had never happened. Any time he spoke, it was considered an order and his gangmates fell upon each other to give life to his words. This evening, he had asked twice, and no one had volunteered — an unprecedented revolt that he didn't know how to deal with.

If he asked a third time and failed again would that mean he had lost his leadership?

Gnashing his teeth, he considered their reluctant faces and barked a third time, "Have the gutter dogs eaten your entrails! Where are your guts? Who can do it?"

Snow Flower, the blue one, had also been gathering anger. He couldn't take it any more. "Forget it, Blow. Just forget it. Don't even think about it."

"Oh, yeah."

"Yeah. You didn't listen. You blew Sharky. You pay for it or not, she's a separate matter. You can't do her in."

"Geekus Crow. You pining for her giblets. Why that jerker's so goddamn precious — "

"Watch it, Blow." Opal Fire, determined not to get involved, lost her cool. "She's the *first space daughter*. You can't — "

"You watch it, Opal. Just 'cause you're a twirl . . . "

"Stop it!" In the back row, Snake Mahdi shot up. "Tell me, what if you snuff her? She has a twin. You bash her up. There's that Earth Core jerry, Rahul something, and behind him, that ex-SDC gollumpus, Miskovitz, and behind him . . . "

"He'll nuke 'em all," Opal sneered. "Forget Green Earth. He'd reign all by himself on cinders."

Blowtorch glanced with dismay at his jeering crowd. He felt choked, asphyxiated. To prove that he was a modest son of Mother Earth, with no ambitions, he had taken modest accommodations. There were only ten of them in his room, but it seemed very crowded. Is that why I'm feeling suffocated? he thought. Is that why my brain feels addled? He had to get hold of himself.

"Guys, listen. Listen," he said, changing his stance. "Ye know me, ye know me long time. How many times ye rip me thet I dig sanctity of life more than it's healthy an' wise? Ye remember thet? I'm not sayin' ye snuff her. There's more than one way to kill. For example, when memory goes, one is as good as dead." He dangled a piece of paper. "Here's a list of twenty-one ways. Ye got good minds. Ye can think of many others. So, 'bout it?"

Wall Walker, the green one, hated counterblasts, but he knew that sometimes one had no choice, except to break one's rules. Turning his back toward Blowtorch, he faced his gang. "Guys, this is our fault," he said pleasantly, as if it weren't a stormy meeting, but a garden picnic. "We're havin' this rubbing, 'cause we forgot somethin'. Even the chairman of China gets a max two turns. Past nineteen years, we done no elections. It's time to call for one."

"What kinda talk is thet?" Blowtorch shrieked. "I conjure up our name. Ye know thet! I got us goin'! Made us a global joint, ye know thet! an' these green . . . these devil-feet-lickin' horde of groupies wanna steal my baby! This bunch that don't know anythin' from nothin', they don't want to reckon my name! Gimme any credit! Just 'cause I don't talk like 'em — all honey an' gooey — just 'cause I got no college . . . "

He choked, cleared his throat and stated belligerently, "They refusin' me seat on the Universal Committee! Is that fair? Tell me, ye all, is that fair?"

Opal felt sorry for him. "You forgettin', Blow," she said kindly. "It's not *us* any more. It's now all-out. Not even countin' that ol' U.N. crowd an' the new alligators we boast — you're not the only one with brains."

She turned abruptly. "Come on, guys. We got to eat before thet nine o'clock meeting."

They got up like one body and moved towards the door. Noticing he wasn't moving with them, Snow Flower turned. "Remember it, Blow? Jus' remember it. That ole, legendary hotshot, Gandhi, the one who liberated this holy cow country . . . they didn't make him the first president. They killed him."

Sparky was in the backyard helping Neil prune and fertilize the tiny rose bushes. During the half hour they had been together, Neil hadn't said a single word.

Sparky decided to puncture the oppressive silence. "I see only you and your mom, Neil. You have no one else?"

Neil put down his shears and sat back. "Funny you said that. Lately, I've been just wondering what the word, 'having,' means."

"Why's that?"

"Well, you see, I got a grandmother, lying in a hospital, who doesn't recognize me; two sisters, who ignore me; and one, who perhaps doesn't even know I exist. I got a mother, who's really not my mother; a father, who may be alive or may have been blown to bits; and an experiment that — "

"An experiment?" An image flickered in Sparky's mind, but before he could catch it, it flickered away. "What kind of an experiment?" he asked excitedly.

"Well, you see, the Titanic has this backup computer that can reprogram software in the landing party's com-units. Well, we thought, what if we could design a device capable of scooping them up from down below? My teacher thought my prototype had possibilities. Meera sent my unfinished unit on the Titanic."

"Why?"

"So that we'd have a space-returned memento from the first Mars flight."

"You didn't tell your mother it was unfinished?"

"Yes, I did. She didn't listen. Day an' night," he choked. "She was such a different person. Since her Earth Reality got — "

"Earth Reality?"

"An organization dad encouraged her to start. As it grew, she started spending all her time on it, started spending all my dad's money to promote it. Dad had started saying that if she didn't slow down, he'd have to declare bankruptcy."

"And now that he won't be coming back — "

"Oh, he'll come back all right. At least, that's what Gopa, the older twin, told me."

"How does she know that? He told her something he didn't tell anyone else?"

"Nope." Neil smiled and picked up his discarded shears. "She believes in this fortune-teller who told her that dad would earn the kind of fame no one ever has. And he'll live longer than thousands of others."

"You told me she's a very intelligent person, brilliant student and all that. She believes in such stupid talk?"

"In India, everyone does. Even the topmost scientists. They have thousands of fortune-tellers. Gurus, they call them. This one that Gopa believes in is exceptionally popular. Bhagawati Mata, mother incarnate, they call her."

Bhagawati Mata! Again, an image flickered somewhere inside Sparky's mind. Again, he wasn't able to catch it. Feeling uneasy and disturbed, feeling it was very important, he asked earnestly, "Can I meet her?"

"Who? Gopa? Why not? When she returns — "

"No," Sparky shook his head vigorously. "No. I meant this

celebrity? If she's so good, perhaps she can see the past also. Mine." To hide the intensity of his feelings, he laughed as if it were a big joke.

"No. You can't."

Sparky felt very angry at this unequivocal statement. It appeared that even this little boy wanted to exercise some sort of authority over him.

Suppressing his fury, he asked quietly, "Why?"

"She's disappeared. No one can find her."

"She may escape government lackeys. She may elude newsmen. But I'm nobody. She earns her bread from people like me. If I go to India," Sparky said with confidence, "people will find her for me. You said that in India, dollars can do anything."

"But you won't be allowed to go to India."

Again that word, *allowed*. Sparky lost his temper. "Why? Am I a prisoner?"

Neil glanced at the man's infuriated face and wondered what to say. Everyone — Col. Oringer, Gen. Stryker, his mother — had told him to be very careful, not to say anything, not to ask anything that might, in any way, remind Sparky of his past life.

They had explained to him that if he made a mistake and because of something he said Sparky got a shock, he might plunge into catatonia and lose the rest of his memories. Become a vegetable. Neil felt sorry for him. He would never do anything to hurt him. That was why, while with him, he spoke as little as possible.

But he couldn't be impolite. He had to answer his questions.

Why had they given him such a tough job? It wasn't fair. When Meera returned he would tell her she could hire a nurse. He didn't want to baby-sit.

"It's not healthy to think like that," he replied carefully. "And before you think of going places, you should get better? Get used to going out? You know, going everyday to the office and things."

"I wasn't a no-good piece of shit. I was a dean's list student." Sparky cooled down a bit. "How old am I now? Fifty? Sixty? I didn't get so old without doing something, without holding a job. Why don't they tell me where I was working? Send me to my office. There, in familiar surroundings, I'd start remembering."

"Maybe," Neil offered helpfully, "they don't know where you were working."

"You don't believe that," Sparky laughed disdainfully. "In this day and age? When they even know what you're thinking at any minute? No, sir. They know that all right. They're just not telling me. Why?" He glared at Neil, as if it were all his fault. "Maybe I was a criminal, the kind they don't dare lock up in an ordinary prison. That's what it is. I was a criminal, who — "

"That can't be true," Neil said sternly. "You shouldn't think like that."

"I remember something about it. The jails were overcrowded. There was talk about it. Secret experiments. A way for selective erasure of memories . . . That's probably what they did because I was in their eyes a criminal, one they couldn't afford to keep alive, but couldn't kill."

Neil looked horrified.

"Don't feel so petrified, son." Sparky smiled. "Growing older means learning about cruelties. There are many ways of killing, some of them quite legal according to any court of law. This is just one of them."

"This is worse than killing," Neil said rebelliously. "Live like a vegetable? Like my poor old granma, pegged to a breathing machine? I'd never let them do that to me. I'd rather die doing something worth doing, like my dad."

"Didn't you say he'll be world-famous and die of old age?"

"He is world-famous. Is there anyone today who can match his fame?" Neil asked, his bright eyes a raging storm of conflicting emotions. "And this mind snatcher didn't say old age. She said, 'longer than thousands of others.' Many children die even before they are born. Do they get counted in the dying thousands? The day he stepped into that damn-blasted machine, hadn't he lived longer than them?"

"You have a point." Sparky nodded. "Everything's relative, isn't it? That's why I think it's wrong of them to imprison me in this house. As you just said, I'd prefer to die than live this life. Memories never take retirement, Neil. They do so only when

you die. I do not want a living death. I want to move around and
take my chances. Either live or die, not both. Not this. This is
not life. Haven't you heard it said so often, one's mind is a lamp.
If it goes . . . As your Keats, or was it Shelley, said, 'When the
lamp is shattered, the light in the dust lies dead.'"

"Shelley," Neil softly murmured. "But you forget. He also
said, 'He lives, he wakes — 'tis Death is dead, not he.'"

Sparky heard, but the words were like a distant echo. He dug
his fingers in the soft earth and softly, mournfully, recited:

"He has out-soared the shadow of our night;

Envy and calumny and hate and pain,

And that unrest which men miscall delight,

Can touch him not and torture not again . . . "

Neil understood his feelings. But he had never thought about
them — about the brutal shards that might be constantly
stabbing this mysterious man's dark misery. A misery that was
dark and solitary, eating his guts day and night.

Feeling sorry for Sparky, Neil thought about it and something
clicked in his mind. "I think there's a way," he said, hope
shining bright in his large, expressive eyes.

Sparky just looked at him.

"Meera was planning to attend this convention in Ayodhya.
She couldn't go because of my granma. But no one expects any
change in granma soon. If we convince her that, in granma's
condition, a few days won't matter. It won't take much doing,
you know. She was dying to go. And then you go with her as her
— "

"Secretary." Sparky's eyes glistened with unshed tears.
"Brilliant, Neil. Fantastic! You are a priceless fellow. Can the
rest of these bushes wait? Can we go talk with her? Right now?"

"She went to see this detective she's hired, to find her
daughter. When she returns . . . "

Just then they heard the Mercedes entering the driveway.

Dropping their shears, they grinned conspiratorially and
moved toward the house.

Cheenoo looked at their faces, silent but eloquent, expressing

their collective feelings like sharp images in a clear mirror. "I
still think, before you decide anything — "

"Why can't you believe?" Gopa asked, her large eyes
shimmering like pools of life-breathing pledges. "For you, James
broke his cover. Told you who he is. He's guaranteeing — "

"Everything," Miskovitz said. "I told you. When I joined
ECO, they didn't let me quit. My boss, General Stryker, is a very
influential person. He can do anything. Anything. He just has to
flick a finger and they'll come running."

"OK," Cheenoo nodded. "I leave me in your hands."

"That's the spirit," Gopa smiled. "Now, about tomorrow. We
all agree about the items we're going to get adopted?"

"Except the spherical structure," Pooja, who hadn't spoken so
far, suddenly spoke up. "You're pitting it suddenly, without any
warning. They won't accept it."

"Pooja." Rahul chided her softly. "Uninformed opinion."

But Gopa looked intrigued. "Why, sis? Why not?"

"We're just kids. Adults find us useful for running around,
taking care of their chores. When it comes to decisions, we don't
count." Pooja felt like a lighthouse-keeper facing errant kids
bent upon dashing headlong into a killing cyclone.

"There will be big guns there. U.N. people. Industrialists,
whose job, mom told me, is to devise invisible webs to control
the threads of administration. They love their pyramids. In the
name of efficiency, their webbing lets them hold on to their
power and crush anyone who dares dream of climbing up. If you
think they'd let you snatch their power base, you're nuts."

They looked at her with surprise. How could dreamy-eyed
Pooja, lost-in-a-jungle princess Pooja, be harboring such
thoughts? That was not just startling. It was unimaginable!

Miskovitz was the first one to recover. "Bravo, Pooja! Your
concern is valid. There will be objections. Tough ones. This is
the right time to think how to tackle them."

"It's the proverbial Eve problem, isn't it?" Cheenoo said.
"How to make Adam eat the apple? How to rescue the rusty
wheels mired in outmoded grooves and make them run on the
new tracks?"

"True," Rahul nodded. "But Eve tried."

Miskovitz agreed. "They say there are twenty-one ways to hit a target. We need only one."

"OK." Pooja settled back regally in her seat. "I'm the nutty, cranky chairman. You convince me."

Rahul smiled. "Gopa, it's your brainchild. You give it first shot."

"OK." Gopa stood up as if she were facing an audience. "Madam secretary general, observers, friends, we're proposing a global unit to represent associations like Earth Reality. Not a supervisory body, only a coordinating agency, connected by communication networks. Let me explain on this board."

Picking up a pad, she put a dot in the middle and started drawing circles around it, joining them by radial lines so that it started looking like a spider's web, designed to motivate and attract others to enter it.

"It's an idea we borrowed from twentieth-century executives, who called it Circular Management System. You see this dot in the center? It's the coordinating unit. These circles around it are local associations, the self-motivated teams. And these radial lines are team members. This system works better because it doesn't box anyone. It allows everyone to connect with everyone else in any direction. As the teams interweave, new directions emerge for a broader use of everyone's talents.

"This system is free of problems that petrify the pyramid system, such as a determination of one's value by the position one holds on the ladder; the waste of talents because one can occupy only one position; and feeling stymied by pressures that block progress when everything must move through *proper channels* — an intrinsic trait inherent in the rigid, paper-crazy, slow-moving bureaucracy.

"It can't be emphasized enough that this flexibility will be achieved without lowering morale or hierarchial positions — problems plumbing the pyramid system due to its rigid ups and downs, resulting in the pickle stew that occurs when one is shifted to a position that seems like a demotion and causes psychological problems.

"In the proposed system, because there won't be any *up and down* one can serve in any position, even in more than one organization, without worrying about higher or lower status. This will benefit all. The teams in the various organizations will have access to talents which are, at present, imprisoned within the hierarchial cages. And the locked, frustrated workers — "

"This is not the U.S. Senate, Ms. A'Kash," Pooja said bitingly. "Why not come to the point."

"The point, your honor, is that the proposed unit will not be concerned with where people stand or how they are ranked," Gopa said proudly. "It will give everyone in every organization equal status and opportunity for exercising their talents. You see these circles? If you move from one point to another, from here to say here, you are not higher or lower — inferior or superior — to the person next to you. You are just working with each other, doing your job that you like best."

"I see that," Pooja nodded grudgingly.

"Our business world would love this free-flowing, multiconnected mode because it would mirror the pathflows of their technological networks — their computers' circuit boards — allowing faster workflows for their multiconnected trading needs.

"No doubt the traditional pyramid style of command was suitable for the boundary-locked, military-based administration, but now it's outdated because it's excessively slow and muscle-bound for our fast-moving, planet-wide econo-systems. The multinational common markets initiated in the closing years of the past century are now an established fact.

"You can check. Any unit trading across national boundaries will tell you that, like the other archaic traditions, the old system is now only an atrocious straitjacket, one that hinders growth and progress. For our business tycoons, the web of inclusion is more practical than the ladder of exclusion that was first developed to keep the pharaoh and his human swords on their thrones. Your honor, I rest my case."

"Not yet," Pooja smiled. "You forgot something."

"What?" Gopa asked, surprised.

Trying to imitate her sister's scholarly voice, Pooja offered, "In the hierarchial structure, because you can't go over your boss's head, information flows up or down. Since access to information spells power, one hides it and hoards it, to gain personal glory and advancement. This leads to administrative abuses. In the proposed unit, because there would be endless points of contacts and information would flow freely, management will remain closely tuned to the needs of those whom it'll serve."

"Wow!" Gopa exclaimed. "I didn't know you were thinking about that, Pooja!"

"Wasn't." Pooja shook her head. "Won't take credit for something I didn't do. You see, I read your notes."

"Really? That was good. Gave me a chance to rehearse my speech."

"I think you need to modify it."

"Tell me," Gopa invited.

"Don't be so negative about the traditional structure. They're sitting on it, and tough criticism would alienate them. Although our world is accelerating toward the point where it will become a close-knit econo-unit, national boundaries will remain. Politics will govern who trades with whom. Entrenched political habits are not easily shaken. They're not just their bread and breath, they're like their birthright.

"Why do you think your system didn't gain wider acceptance during the past sixty or more years? It's not just that their hierarchical system and our spherical system are mirror opposites of each other. It's much more that. During the past centuries, armies and flags followed the traders. Your system threatens the high-flying bureaucrats who feel that it may destroy the national boundaries, which won't be acceptable at all.

"It's not that they don't know. They do know. Just as kings had to make way for elected parliaments, administrative systems that served those primitive systems must change to keep up with the changing world. But they want to delay the change into the future as long as bureaucratically possible. As mom says, they need to be prodded, pushed and inspired.

"Therefore, first, praise their system. Tell them that the hierarchial system was good because it valued position. It motivated one to strive harder because it rewarded individual achievement won by competition. But — and this is your big *but* — but, this is the twenty-first century. We have outgrown the system that was needed by the earlier polities, clan leaders, city-states, kingdoms.

"Today, to deal with the exigencies necessitated by the global technological networks serving the multinational trading communities, our developing, thrusting economy needs drastic changes in the traditional system.

"The proposed system would be a logical vehicle for serving these needs; its circles of affiliation — webbing the community, dramatizing the values of staying close, using one's talents fully — would lead to feelings of fulfillment and being a whole person. And team members, free of psychological pressures and motivated by each other's approbation, will strive harder than any goaded, self-motivated worker in the previous system."

"Previous. Good word. I like that," Rahul approved.

"Fantastic," Cheenoo chimed in.

"What else?" Miskovitz asked.

Gopa had been nodding in approval. Offering her the file, she said, "Since you've been thinking about it, Pooja, why don't you finalize it. It'd be a big help."

Before Pooja could reply, there was a timid knock on the door and an Earth Corps cadet, dressed like a firefly, walked in. "They calling you," the 5-year-old girl said breathlessly. "Please, aunty Gopa, come quick."

Gopa kneeled to reach the eye level of the courier and put one hand upon her shoulder to soothe her. "Who's calling?"

"Aunty Urmi. An' Fireflies. They refusing to be last ones."

"OK, let's go." She got up and took her hand. "You guys coming?"

They were moving toward the door when Snow Flower walked in. "Blowtorch here?" he asked.

"Nope," Gopa said. "Don't lose him now. He has to inaugurate the dragon race. If he sleeps late . . . "

"I can't find him." Snow Flower looked worried. "You guys are going the wrong way. Meeting room's thataway."

"We've still got ten minutes," Rahul said. "Why not come with us? We're going to the Fireflies' ballet."

Snow Flower tagged along. "Found a name for it yet?"

Pooja laughed. "That's Urmi's headache. Why don't you throw in a suggestion? You've got till breakfast. Then it goes to the printers."

"Maybe I will." Snow Flower nodded, looking lost in thought.

They started to leave — Pooja with Cheenoo, Rahul and Snow Flower sort of walking together, each lost in his thoughts. Gopa fell in step with Miskovitz. "James, can I ask you something?"

"About time," he said, taking her hand and pulling her close. "Considering all your questions are now for your doctor friend."

"I'm serious." Glad that he was feeling a little jealous, she smiled and nestled against him. "On the evening news, when that Chinese hustler was extolling the high points of Volga Two, I noticed that you weren't looking at his face. You were staring at the wall behind him. Was his face so repugnant to you?"

"Oh, it had nothing to do with his face. I was just . . . It's a long story," he ended lamely.

"How about a synopsis?"

"I was just . . . I was admiring the painting behind his back."

Gopa didn't understand. OK, he was admiring a painting. So, what was the big deal? Why be so mysterious about it? "What was so special about it?" she asked.

"Supposed to be four of them. I was looking at the third one. If I can locate the fourth —

"Yes? Then what?"

"I don't know. I wasn't able to learn that part. When the four come together, something is supposed to happen."

"I thought you were the practical kind. You didn't believe in such things."

He laughed. "That firefly bunch is the best," he said, trying to change the subject. "They never complain. Someone inciting them?"

Changing the topic, James? she thought. OK! I'll trip you when you're not thinking. "Whatever it is," she answered mischievously, "you'll need to solve it."

Entering the rehearsal hall, they stood just inside, quietly watching the chaos on the stage.

Someone spotted them and ran toward them, followed by others, including 17-year-old Urmi, the writer-director of the ballet that was to be the grand finale of the convention.

"Gopa aunty," the hero of the fireflies sequence shouted, "we won't accept it. At the last minute, these guys — "

Just then, the lights went out.

"What the . . . these techs, they promise but can't deliver! Someone got a candle. If this happens during — "

The lights came back on and so did the huge screens that were located all around the convention arena. They showed an unfamiliar scene: an office with a huge desk, an empty chair and a proudly fluttering flag displaying stars and stripes. Above it all was the presidential seal on the back wall.

"Fellow citizens of our world," a deep, somber voice announced in the background, "the president of the United States."

The tall, lean, familiar figure entered the room, took his chair, and, not wasting any time, started speaking immediately in a deep, friendly tone. "Friends, countrymen, neighbors. I'm sorry for interrupting your schedules. But I had no choice. You are facing a critical emergency and informing you through proper channels would have taken more time than what we have . . . "

"He found the Titanic," someone snickered.

"Hush." anxious voices muttered.

" . . . From a reliable source, we have learned the Soviet Alliance is preparing to invade Japan. After committing this act, which is contrary to all international laws, they wish to claim that they had to do it to stop Tokyo from snatching Mars as their colony . . . "

"Poppycock . . . You wanna pick a fight . . . Elections coming up?" Laughter and a babble of voices rose above the president's words.

"Hush. Hush, listen to him," shouted the others.

Enslavement of a free nation cannot be allowed. If they have a reason to believe that the Japanese intend to violate the space treaties, the complaint needs to be investigated through established channels. Hiroshima Hoku won't reach Mars for months — ”

"How about the Titanic?" someone shouted.

"Gone! Swallowed by his budget deficit," another voice snickered.

"There's no need for this predacity. Therefore, I'm asking Moscow to withdraw their troops and submit their complaint to the United Nations. If this is not done within twenty-four hours, they will be forcing us to declare war."

"No!" Everyone in the hall screamed, in almost one voice.

"We do not want a military confrontation," the somber face on the screen continued, "but, as President Abraham Lincoln once said, 'Those who deny freedom to others deserve it not for themselves.' For the protection of your liberty, we will not hesitate to do what we must.

"If this warning is not heeded, if they do not assure you right away that they're withdrawing their missiles, they'll be forcing us to launch ours. Our troops are always ready. If they force us to declare war, may God forgive us and save us all."

The president rose. The screens turned blank. Flabbergasted, dumbstruck, the crowd assembled in the rehearsal hall stared at each other.

Then voices rose again. This time, there was no shouting and laughing like before, only hushed, frightened questions. "Has he gone mad? Who does he think he is? The emperor of earth? Naw! He won't do it. He's just talking. He's not the only one with missiles. There are others. Europeans, Africans. They won't let him. Listen to him! To save us, he wants to kill us all."

Suddenly, the screens lit up again and the announcer's voice came through loud and clear. "We apologize to our listeners. We are not able to resume our scheduled program because the Republic of China has requested equal time. Please stay tuned."

Again the viewers in the hall saw a table and a flag and a familiar face. But the words, striking their ears, sounded harsh and cruel. "Beijing is not surprised by the imperialist ultimatum. This we must say: Although our alert, Soviet neighbors did not seek our help, we would like them to know, there's no need for them to heed this cowardly warning.

"As free nations, we have every right to protect our territorial interests. And we stand, shoulder to shoulder, beside our brave comrades. The imperialist America must know that every fourth person in the world is a Chinese. And we are calling all our children. We are giving proper forms and instructions to all the airlines; any Chinese who enlists will be given free passage.

"Sons and daughters of China remember what your ancient, teacher, Confucius, taught you. 'To know what is right and not do it is the worst cowardice.' Come home, comrades. Your country needs you. Your ideology, your way of life, needs you."

The screens blanked out again, but only for seconds. The newscaster came back. Someone switched him off.

Absolute silence clouded the hall. It seemed as if no one was breathing. Shuffling their feet, they started to move and the hall began to empty.

Gopa looked up. "Should we cancel the dragon race?"

"Why should we?" Rahul asked. "Their fights should not stop us. On the contrary, we should think of ways of stopping them."

"They're just bluffing, aren't they?" Cheenoo said. "Like so many years ago I read in some history book — what was his name — President Kennedy . . . did during the Cuban missile crisis."

"Kennedy," Miskovitz said. "He succeeded only because Moscow didn't call his bluff. If they don't back out this time . . . History rarely repeats itself."

"Was it Cicero who said, 'History is the witness of the times . . . the messenger of antiquity'?" Pooja's face showed her concentration on remembering correctly.

Seeing her twin's calm acceptance of the facts, Gopa regained her strength. Holding her hand, she said, "No, sis, we're not messengers of antiquity or onlookers writing history. We're something entirely different. We're making history."

She smiled and her voice again sounded natural. "Come on, guys. We'll be late for that nine o'clock meeting. Where's Urmi?"

Gopa looked around the large room and saw the director sitting on the stage, surrounded by her students. Hearing her name, Urmi got up and moved toward them.

"Enough about killing and gloom and doom," Gopa told

them, pushing lots of warmth and enthusiasm into her booming voice. "Come on, fireflies. Let's show them what you can do, how much cheer and sparkle you can put in their rat race lives."

Surrounded by them, holding their hands, she climbed on the stage, and, around her, the ballet started to take its shimmering shape again.

14

Until Missiles Cloud Over

Blowtorch was missing. Only fifty minutes left before the Candle Runners' dragon boat was to inaugurate the race, and the founder of the organization that was to be launched this day, as the cornea of the voluntary organizations engaged in various types of cathartic, revitalizing work, was nowhere to be found.

Snow Flower and Snake Mahdi had searched everywhere. Opal Fire and Wall Walker had spent hours on the phone, calling airlines, hospitals and everyone else they could think of. All their efforts had produced no trace of their angry, disappointed leader. His bed had not been slept in. Did that mean he had left the previous night? If he had, by now he could be anywhere. He might have even bought a false passport and left the country.

That left a gap; who would wave the Candle Runners' flag to start the race? Who would light the first candle and introduce the chairwoman to the delegates to open the conference?

Such a mess, even before things got started, was not a good omen. Blowtorch knew that. He'd done it purposely . . . knowingly and willfully he had put them in this hideous quandary. Had it even occurred to him that once they got back home he would have to face them?

They didn't want to admit to Gopa's bunch that their leader had deserted them. Not yet. He had never done anything like this. Despite all his faults, where the association's work was concerned, he had always shouldered his responsibility to the last T. Was he testing their patience? If they waited just a few more minutes would he turn up with that famous broad grin on his face?

Mao Ki Tung had been hovering at the periphery hoping they would invite him to join them. He had been feeling like an outsider. No one had insulted him, but no one had expressed any friendliness either. They had left him alone, as one would a superfluous sculpture.

From the snatches of conversation he had heard, Mao Ki could guess something was not working according to plans. He dared to approach them. "Fine morning for the race."

Ignoring the remark would have meant insulting this pompous communist leader. They'd have done it, but Opal Fire felt sorry for him. He was alone and feeling lonely in a foreign country on a beautiful morning when everyone was having fun with their bunch. "I've known better," she said indifferently. "You going to observe our race?"

"Your leader mentioned finding a place for me in his boat, but I don't see him around."

"He iz late," Snow Flower said quickly.

Too quickly, Tung thought. Something was wrong. Was Blowtorch sick? His heart sank; amongst the thousands of people assembled here, Blow was the only one who had cared to say hello to him.

Wall Walker had a brain wave — their leader had deserted them because of the maneuvers of Gopa's co-workers. What a sweet revenge it would be if they could get the convention inaugurated by this outsider.

He glanced at his friends. If he asked them, they would refuse. No, they would insist, absolutely not, not even over their dead bodies!

"Blow had to go somewhere," he said, deciding to take the matter into his own hands, at his sole responsibility. "He tole us to get someone to open the convention. Would ye like to do it?"

"I'd be honored." Very much aware of the dark surprise written on the faces around him, afraid they might change their minds, Tung quickly added, "if you'll tell me what's to be done."

"Las' night, your president was callin'," Snow Flower said and asked in the same breath, "When are ye leaving?"

"I'm not."

"Ye are not?" The prompt reply shook them up. He was going to be a permanent spy? Would they allow that?

"Yes. You see, I've been catching up on my reading. Blowtorch helped me select. He gave me 'Lady Windermere's Fan' by Oscar Wilde. Last night I kept thinking about it all night."

"Really?" Opal Fire's eyes popped like two big saucers. She couldn't imagine Blowtorch hobnobbing with this lousy communist. Something had gone wrong in his mind, she thought, and asked, "It iz so good?"

"Well, you've read it many times no doubt and don't think it's worth a second thought. But it was my first exposure. And its words I can't seem to forget . . . 'In this world there are only two tragedies. One is not getting what one wants and the other is getting it. The last is much the worst; the last is the real tragedy!' And I couldn't sleep last night. I kept thinking, if the Soviet Alliance enslaves Japan, it'd be like Hitler's eating Poland. I don't want to be a part of it."

"You're wise," Snow Flower said, "and one of us. Let's go find Gopa."

In the small conference room, Gopa and Pooja were sitting

with their backs to the large sat-vision screen so that the disturbing news about the gathering U.S.-Soviet military confrontation wouldn't disturb their concentration.

Worried about missing breaking news, they hadn't switched it off, but they had switched off the sound, as if by not hearing it perhaps they could forget it for a while.

To a bystander, against the background of speeding warships, aircraft carriers and tanks and soldiers eagerly marching to entrench themselves, the two young faces and golden heads bent upon their expectant files would have seemed a heartrending sight. But on the sat-vision screens no one was looking down. No one had time to think that the fate of those two, and millions like them, was under the thumbs of faraway politicians itching to make Mars their first space colony at any cost.

"You're worrying too much, sis," Pooja said, firmly closing her file. "There will be hundreds of people there, whispering and gossiping, their minds busy imagining the fun waiting for them outside, bent upon getting out of that session as soon as possible. Half of them won't even hear you."

"Yes. But the other half will. And if I make one mistake . . . just one . . . " She sighed. "I wish mom was here. Then I wouldn't have to worry so much."

"Mom has only one child," Pooja said firmly. "Her Earth Reality. Remember? You're the one who used to say that. She doesn't care for us." She looked at her sister, older only because she'd been born a few minutes earlier. "You never liked her. Why now, suddenly, all the time . . . "

"I dunno. It just seems such a shame. No doubt Earth Reality is her baby. But working here, I've realized how, using it she made it possible that many tormented sideshows don't continue running around in circles, like fraternities of dope addicts — all those whom the politicians lovingly call *the critically maladjusted.* Chronically unemployed. And, now, when time's here . . . "

"Here? Or flying away?" asked Rahul's cheerful voice from behind them. "Why are you guys still here?"

Turning, they saw Rahul and James Miskovitz, their arms loaded with morning newspapers. Gopa smiled. "Did you buy the whole newsstand?"

"Where's Cheenoo?" Pooja asked.

"No, to the first question," Rahul said. "We were too late. Others were before us."

"And to the second, why ask us?" Miskovitz demanded. "Isn't it your job to keep track of that roving fiddler?"

Pooja smiled. "Fiddlers take all the liberties they can."

"Ludwig van Beethoven," Rahul said. "Only he said, *musicians.* Why is everyone quoting ancient wisdom today?"

He glared at the sat-vision screen, editorializing mutely about the latest Soviet missile launchers.

"So right!" Miskovitz said, flipping the pages of a newspaper, pitching red headlines and grisly blowups of the previous century's chemical warfare. "Seems no one can think of anything original. Look here. Our president is quoting Washington and Lincoln. The British are remembering Winston Churchill.

"And, here. The Japanese are paraphrasing our own Abraham Lincoln. Listen to this. 'All the armies of Europe, Asia and Africa combined, with all the treasure of the earth . . . with a Bonaparte for a commander could not by force take a drink from Ohio (our seashores) or make a track on the Blue Ridge (our Hiroshima and Nagasaki) in a trial of a thousand years.' And the Russians? Listen to this . . . "

"Can you admire these later?" Pooja complained. "We're getting late."

"Let's take my Blue Thunder," Miskovitz said. "I'll pilot. Rahul will read — "

"No, he won't," the twins retorted in unison. Snatching the papers, they dumped them under the table. "We're not going to let these bloodsuckers darken our day. What's the U.N. for? Let them worry about it."

"Let's go." Taking hold of Rahul's and Miskovitz's hands, Pooja pulled determinedly.

Deprived of their prized material, they grabbed her, swinging her, as if to throw her away. She giggled, broke free and ran ahead.

In Miskovitz's Blue Thunder, purchased only yesterday, it

took them only a few minutes to reach the river where the boats were lining up at their assigned places. To have a bird's-eye view of the kaleidoscopic pageant, Miskovitz circled once then dived to park on the spot he had rented, even before buying the craft.

Moving toward Cheenoo, waiting for them in ECO's catamaran, they saw Sun Flower and his gang. Miskovitz was surprised to notice Blowtorch missing. "Blowtorch in your boat?" he asked.

"Nope," Sun Flower grinned. "He had to go. Some emergency. He ask his friend, Mao Ki here, to take his place." He pushed the grinning communist leader forward.

Gopa looked at him dubiously. "His government is calling him. When is he leaving?"

"Not him." Wall Walker thumped his back. "He's a surefire Candle Runner. He don't throw missiles. On nobody."

"Is that so?" Miskovitz glared at him suspiciously. "OK, Mr. Surefire Barracuda, have these fellows told you — "

Opal Fire giggled. "Barracuda? I like that. Mao Ki the Barracuda. That's a good Candle Runner name."

Did that mean they had accepted him as one of them? Tung's eyes glowed with delight. "I like that. A good name. I couldn't have thought of one better."

His gang applauded. Not wanting to argue, Gopa started to move and Tung fell in step. "Miss A'Kash, I know I'm new here. But if you all have no objection, can I throw in a suggestion — mind you, just a suggestion — during my inaugural speech?"

Gopa looked at him suspiciously. "What?"

"I've heard about your reviving the bygone century's spherical structures. May I suggest adding one more?"

"I'm listening."

"I'd like to suggest, JESEC — Joint Earth Space Exploration Corporation."

"What for?"

"To unite the separate national efforts under one canopy. To establish an Earth academy for space research and the training of future astronauts. To control and launch all space vehicles — scientific, commercial and experimental. To — "

Miskovitz laughed. "Who'll accept it? Your people's republic will be the first one to denounce any such idea. They'll call it the imperialist plot to — "

"Wait a minute," Gopa said. "They won't accept it, for sure. But there's no harm in seeding the idea."

"Forget seeding," Rahul said, getting very enthusiastic. "I think we should push it, and this would be the best time to do so. comrade Mao Ki, if it's not just a Chinese ploy . . . "

"Not comrade," Tung quickly objected. "No more comrade. Now, only Barracuda."

They laughed and Rahul put his arm companionably around Tung's shoulder. "Fine, Barracuda, I'd like to believe you. Let's work on it. We've reserved a couple of sessions for late suggestions. I guarantee you, this will get top — no, topmost — priority."

Talking rapidly, the two of them moved toward the Candle Runners' dragon boat. Watching their backs, Miskovitz said, "Well, it seems we lost one member of our team."

Cheenoo had joined them. "In a good cause," he said. "I've also been dreaming about it. Our world's population is now more than a billion. If it's a nongovernmental, global effort and everyone contributes even a small amount to fund it . . . "

"Wow, Cheenoo," Pooja chimed in, "why didn't you draft a proposal?"

"Well, the idea seemed so outlandish . . . "

"You know what your problem is, Cheenoo?" Pooja asked.

"What?"

"You don't believe in yourself. You know what's been often said. 'Every great advance has issued from a new audacity of imagination.' When it comes to thinking about the future, no idea is too outlandish."

"OK Ms. Future-Thinker, does your outlandish vision foresee our winning this race?" Miskovitz asked. "If it does, we better move or the race will start without us."

Giggling, dropping Cheenoo's hand, Pooja raced toward their boat. Just then the gigantic screens lining the beach lit up, and on them, and they saw Buddhist monks anointing the inaugural dragon boat. Mao Ki Tung, the ex-comrade director of the

Chinese Space Control Sub-Section, stood behind them, eagerly waiting to unfurl the Candle Runners' flag.

Sam Oringer was staring at the outlandish painting over the mantelpiece, Rings Around the World, but his eyes were not really seeing it. His troubled mind was elsewhere; Gen. Stryker hadn't made it an order, but he rarely did. Those working with him knew that the only way to work for him was to take his words as more binding than any direct order.

So, unofficially, surveillance of Meera A'Kash was his overriding priority. And he had failed such a simple assignment.

He turned and stared at the uniformed messenger, who was tall and dark and stately as if he was a black prince. Oringer had never seen such a dark, ebony color. It was as if this human being hadn't just been dipped in black ink, he'd been boiled in it. For months and months, years and years.

"I know," he said softly, "you gave all the details to Mrs. A'Kash's son. But I'd like to hear them from you."

The messenger was staring at the muted sat-vision, depicting frenzied preparations for the impending war, as relaxed as if he were in his parlor. As if what the screen was portraying were happening on some other planet. It did not concern him.

Hearing the question, he turned his head and crossed his right leg over his left knee. Encountering the black man's gaze, Oringer thought his dark, black eyes seemed out of reach. Despite the words, the accent his thick lips emitted indicated Eaton's playfields.

"Not much to tell," the dark courier said. "This bloke gave me a letter for her. Reaching her office, I ask for her. She grab it an' tore it, impatient-like, not signing for it. 'Ma'am, signature,' I reminds her. She don't answer. Not even look at us — me an' her secretary — just gits up an' clip-clops fast to the elevator.

"I need her signature. Don't want to be fired from my job, see? So I follow. At the curb, I see this big, black limo waiting, all black-curtained. Your lady raises a hand to hail a cab. They grab her at pistol-point, push this here note in my hand and drive away. It all happen so quick like you blink. If you know what I mean."

"Why are you working as a messenger?" Sparky quietly
asked.

The question startled Neil and Oringer. They had forgotten
Sparky was in the room, but the query seemed valid. From his
regal bearing and intelligent eyes, one would expect this black-
soul-on-a-string to be presiding over a global corporation, not
running menial errands.

The fellow smiled. "Would any answer satisfy you? I doubt it.
The fact is, I don't believe in your rat race. Earn enough to feed
my body an' have fun, that's my free-born motto."

Oringer didn't say anything, simply answered his smile. He
again read the brief note.

As the messenger had said, the note didn't have much to say.
"Don't worry about Mrs. A'Kash. We are not kidnapping her.
When we are done with her, she'll be returned unharmed."

"We appreciate your bringing us the message," Oringer said.
"If we need you again, where can we reach you?"

"Self-employed. That's what I am," the regal messenger said
proudly. "Here's me card: The Impossible Messenger Service. I
keep no office. Work from home. If I'm not there, the
answering-video is." He got up to leave. Neil pressed a twenty
dollar bill in his hand and escorted him to the door.

Closing the door, the boy turned. "I bet he's not a messenger.
I bet he's one of them — the kidnappers. What did they mean,
not kidnapping? If you take someone at gunpoint, what's it
called?"

Oringer understood his anger, but he also knew that words —
any words — would only aggravate it. "Can I take this note,
Neil?" he asked, "Give it to the FBI."

Neil nodded. "They'll want it. Does the FBI work outside our
country?"

Oringer turned to look at Neil in surprise. "What makes you
ask that?"

"This fellow looked Caribbean. Or African."

"Good point, Neil. I'll also call the CIA."

"And Interpol?"

"And Interpol," Oringer agreed. "Meanwhile, neither of you

are to leave the house. Call your housekeeper. Give her a vacation. I'll send a housekeeper for you and a couple of plainclothes officers to watch your house."

Leaving his chair, he added, "Don't open the door to anyone, even me, without code words."

"Isn't that too dramatic?"

"No," Oringer said sternly. "It's not. If your mom doesn't cooperate, you may be their next target."

"That makes sense, Neil," Sparky said.

"OK," Neil nodded. "What code words?"

"Let's decide. What about . . . " Oringer's worried eyes landed on the weapons marching on the sat-vision screen. So far, it's a war of words, he thought. Any minute, it may erupt into a real war. Then all these worries would be meaningless, wouldn't they?

Pushing aside the morbid thought, he looked away and his eyes hit on the painting. "Rings Around the World," he whispered. "That's it. Rings Around the World. Sounds appropriate."

"And easy to remember," Neil nodded and looked at Sparky.

"Good." Oringer nodded approvingly.

He would not call the CIA, he decided. Instead, he'd report immediately to Gen. Stryker, who, no doubt, would be furious. Would probably give him demerits, but he'd earned them. No, it wasn't a question of his career. Neil's safety and Meera's life were the only things that counted. Stryker would be the best judge of what to do.

The general hunched in his workshop, brooding over the two annoying objects on his bench: a new prototype of Neil's invention that had arrived that morning and a twin of the robot that had gained additional mysterious pounds at its prelaunch weighing.

Did one or both of them have anything to do with the Titanic's disappearance?

It didn't seem possible.

Neil's invention was just what he had explained, a magnetic

device with a clever twist — push a lever and it pulled objects. Push another and it called Capt. A'Kash in Neil's voice.

Enclosed in its case, it couldn't have affected anything in the spaceship. Even if someone got curious and started playing with it, it would only have worked like a child's harmless toy.

The robot was enigmatic. Obviously, the boarding party had secretly stored something inside it. What could it be? Liquor? Forbidden food? Disallowed personal items that were considered unnecessary baggage?

Hand grenades? Weapons to deal with Japanese robots or Soviet cosmonauts in case they tried to board the Titanic?

The astronauts knew weapons were forbidden in space, but they were human. If they suspected Japan or the Soviet Alliance of violating the weapons rule, and wanted to protect themselves . . .

Had they turned the tables on themselves? Was there a fight, and, in the ensuing madness, had they used those weapons to annihilate themselves? But it couldn't have happened so suddenly, so instantaneously, that not even one of them survived to report it. He weighed a mixed lot of weapons — up to one hundred nineteen pounds. They didn't amount to much, but enough to cause substantial damage.

The beeper on his wrist watch beeped. "Yes, Mona?" he asked her ebony face, smiling up from the small crystal.

"Colonel Oringer is here, general. I told him you are busy."

"No, wait. I'll be there. Give him some of that coffee we received from my friend, Pablo Martinez."

He didn't feel like smiling; the honorable Martinez had, no doubt, done a great service to humanity by informing him about the Soviet intentions. When they met, he'd narrated with much gusto how the scientific imagination of his Martian timekeeper, the one and only Ray Bradbury, had helped him.

But only time would tell whether this early warning had been good or bad.

If we didn't know about it, he thought, the Soviet Alliance would have annexed Japan.

The world would have kept fighting about it in the United Nations. But war casualties would have been limited. Now, if the Soviet Alliance doesn't accept our ultimatum . . . He sighed and, locking the room, moved toward his office. Col. Oringer hadn't touched the steaming cup of coffee.

His eyes looked tired and worried in a face that was haggard and drawn.

Ignoring it won't help, Stryker thought. He picked up the coffee that Mona had brought as soon he took his chair and said, over the rim of the cup, "Worried about the president's ultimatum, Sam? The Soviets may back out. We still have about an hour."

"My worries are more of a personal kind, general."

"Oh. Your son?"

"Meera A'Kash." The colonel breathed hard. "Kidnapped."

Stryker slowly placed his cup on the nearby table. His fingers drummed the table top. "Ward's friends?" he asked softly.

"Maybe. Maybe someone else."

"What makes you say that?"

Briefly, quickly, Oringer narrated how he had received an urgent call from Neil. And how when he reached the A'Kash residence, what the messenger had told him. He handed the note to Stryker.

"When we are done with her." Stryker looked up from the brief note. "That doesn't sound like a blackmailer, does it?"

Sam Oringer didn't reply. Just looked at him.

"How's Neil taking it?" Stryker asked.

Oringer found his tongue, "Like his father would have."

"Does he realize he could be their next target?"

"He does. But he's not worried about that. He was asking if we could alert the Interpol."

"To guard his sisters?"

Oringer nodded.

"I'm really proud of that young man," Stryker said. "Despite his hot denials, I think he is going to follow his father. OK, let me give a note to Mona to get the wheels rolling. Then I want you to see that invention that got stowed away on the Titanic."

Quickly scribbling a note, he got up and stopped at Mona's desk to give her the instructions.

Waiting, Oringer stood in the doorway, staring at the muted sat-vision. No one wants to listen to this incessantly bombarding war hysteria, he thought. But no one wants to switch if off either, fearing that something could happen and they might miss it.

Something is bound to happen, he thought. And I'm going to miss it. As always.

"Coming, Sam?"

"Yes, general." He followed quickly, keeping pace with the general's long strides.

The workshop's door was locked, as Stryker had left it. When he inserted the key to unlock it, the tumbler seemed stuck and the key jammed. Impatiently, Stryker fumbled with it. Suddenly, the lock clicked. Opening the door, Stryker strode in. Just inside, his feet seemed to freeze.

"General? Something wrong?"

"Neil's invention! I left it there! No one else has a key to this room, not even Mona. Usually, I don't even lock it, but today because . . . "

He circled the spot where the innocent-looking, futuristic plaything had been sitting, as if by looking hard enough, he could make it reappear.

"Does Neil have another unit?" Stryker asked. "He told me he's conducting experiments in magnetic transference. Using that other unit, could he have whisked it away to surprise me?"

"I doubt it, general. But I can ask him."

"Let's go."

Again locking the room, Stryker strode back to his office and, without wasting any time, dialed Neil's number. The phone was picked up right away as if Neil were sitting right beside it.

"Neil, Stryker here. Can I ask you something, my friend?"

"Anything, general."

"Your invention? How may units have you made?"

"Just one, sir. The one I gave you this morning. Why?"

"Just curious, son. One more question. In addition to the functions you showed me, is it capable of doing anything else?"

There was a silence at the other end.

Then Neil's voice came, sounding the same, yet somehow different. "Is anything wrong, general?"

"I'm not sure, Neil. I was just wondering if it would have in some way affected the Titanic's instrument panels. For example, in certain conditions, can it disorient or disengage instruments?"

"Why?" Neil sounded very curious. "Has it affected something in your office? I better come and check it."

"Not right now, Neil. With the deadline on our Soviet ultimatum approaching, I can't spare any time. I'll call you."

"OK, general." The young voice sounded normal; no anxiety or fear lingered in it.

"I didn't want to lie to him," Stryker said. "Until we find out what happened to it, what can I tell him?"

Sam Oringer had no answer.

"If a staff member is a spy, he didn't have enough time."

"Should I alert security?"

"Too late. Whoever took it, he's not hanging around. What in God's name can one do with it?"

Oringer's forehead was furrowed. "Who knows its twin went with the Titanic?"

"No one except us."

Stryker stared at the package on his mantelpiece that hadn't gone with the Titanic, that had triggered Meera's memory and been instrumental in his learning about Neil's invention.

Neil's teacher had told him that if the prototype worked, it had lots of potential in many areas of space technology.

"Do you think," he asked as if talking to himself, "they've invented a machine capable of transferring objects? Through walls?" He glanced at Oringer. "Sounds preposterous, doesn't it?"

"As you sometimes say, general, until proven otherwise, nothing is impossible. I'll visit Neil's teacher right away."

Before he could move, Mona came rushing in. "General, you'll want to listen to this." She pushed the sound switch on sat-vision.

The anchorwoman's somber voice rang through the room. "Again, I repeat. It's not a rumor. The heads of governments of the following countries are missing: China, Japan the Soviet Alliance, the United States . . . "

"What?" Stryker pushed back his chair, sprang up and stood staring at the screen.

"The notes found on their bedroom doors are identical. 'You need not worry. They've not been kidnapped. When we're done with them, they'll be returned unharmed.' What does *done with them* mean? Who is responsible? How did they . . . "

Stryker lunged to his phone and punched in the number for the White House. "Stryker here. I want to speak with the president."

"General, sir," the operator's voice sounded as if she were on the verge of breaking apart, "haven't you heard? The president is missing."

15

Candle in the Wind

One of the toughest jobs they had tackled was the seating at the podium dinner table. Those over fifty were not saying it, but they expected it. Hadn't they earned the right? The younger ones were vocally backing out in favor of each other. The table, despite gracing the full length of the large dining hall, could not take more than seventy-five.

Gopa had tried her best to get her name removed, but she hadn't succeeded. At least she had managed to avoid being placed in the center and had gotten a corner seat.

After saying an indifferent *hello* her neighbor had gotten involved with the delegate on his other side. Delighted, Gopa relaxed; she'd be able to enjoy her dinner and think about the first day that, despite all her fears, had been a smashing success.

The dragon boat race had drawn huge, cheering crowds. Everyone had so much fun the winners had started crowning the losers.

Mao Ki, the Barracuda, had surprised everyone by his electrifying speech. His request inviting proposals for a *joint earth space exploration corporation* had been cheered and applauded. Later, debates and criticism, opposition and defiance, would undoubtedly come. But the seed had been planted. The idea had germinated. The sapling would grow.

Riding on this stimulating tide of approval, the other sessions had smoothly rolled by. If the remaining six days passed with even one-tenth of today's rapport and harmony, the candles lit each day would keep on burning.

A young waitress stood near Gopa's elbow and placed a piece of paper near her plate. Come on, guys. At least let me have dinner, Gopa thought as she picked it up. It simply said, "Your brother, Neil, has called three times. If we tell him a fourth time that you are busy, we're afraid he may start crying."

Surprised, Gopa looked at the waitress and at the phone held discreetly in her hand. Neil is not a crybaby, she wanted to tell her. Please tell him I'll call him later tonight.

But they had already told him that — three times. If he was calling again, something was wrong. Where was mom? Why couldn't she take care of him? Taking the phone, she spoke into it softly. "Neil, I'm in a meeting. Can I call you later, buddy?"

"Sis, just listen. Don't say anything. You and Pooja got to take extra care. Mom's been kidnapped and you guys could be next."

The phone almost fell out of Gopa's hand — mom kidnapped? Why? That wasn't part of the plan.

"I've got the CIA and Interpol alerted," Neil was saying. "Will keep you posted. Now, signing off."

"Wait," she hurriedly whispered. "Buddy, wait."

"What?"

"Remember that game we used to play when we were kids?"

"Rings Around The World?" he asked. "Funny, you're the second person to remind me of that today."

"Who was the first?" she whispered fearfully.

"Not important. What about it?"

"Nothing." She got scared. Perhaps she shouldn't tell him. Untimely knowledge can hurt. "I was remembering it. That's all. We're having a good convention. I'll see you soon."

"Bye, sis. Say my hello to Pooja."

"I will. Take care until I come back. I got a lot to tell you."

"Me, too, sis. Bye," he said and disconnected the line.

Returning the phone to the waitress hovering behind her, Gopa looked distastefully at her blueberry crisp. Her appetite was gone. Who had kidnapped mom? And why?

She looked at her watch. It was time. Already?

She glanced at the large screens depicting maneuvers in the global conflict and at the crowded dining hall decorated with fresh flowers and gulmohars twined with garlands of lights.

Everyone was having so much fun. The shattering world conflict, hovering in the shadows, was nowhere near their minds.

It would be so cruel to remind them of it. Oh, well.

Bracing herself, she pushed back her chair and stood up. "Invitees and fellow members," she said, adjusting the mike hidden in her dress collar, "may I have your attention, please."

Anticipating a new item, they looked up at her expectantly. Against the screens portraying the various war preparations their cheerful, laughing faces looked very incongruous.

"Do you feel we accomplished a lot today?" she asked.

"Yes," the cheering crowd roared.

"We were so busy," she said, "we forgot about Hiroshima Hoku. Before we adjourn, should we check what's going on?"

"Why not," "Sure," "OK," rose several voices. Those whose view of the sat-screens was blocked moved their chairs this way and that. Gopa signalled to a waitress to switch on the voice control, and the announcer's deep, somber voice filled the hall.

" . . . still not known. The American president lives a relatively unprotected life. Kidnapping him could be difficult, but not impossible. But how did they trap the leaders of China, Japan and the Soviet Alliance? And all at the same time. Who . . . "

Someone shrieked. Words got trapped in the confused babble that caught up the hall, fracturing the previous quiet. An ear-piercing babble punctured the rollicking, back-slapping harmony. It rumbled ominously and started to stretch and crescendo to higher and higher levels.

Feeling helpless and confused, Gopa glanced at Miskovitz sitting at the other end of the long table. He got up right away; activating the mike in his collar, he moved toward the front of the dais.

"Friends . . . Friends," he shouted, trying to be heard.

Cheenoo squirmed in his seat; should he join Miskovitz? Should he try to gain their attention by playing his guitar?

Rahul wondered if he should tell them the truth. Weren't there times when truth was the best shield?

He decided against it — with all his training, he should be able to control this mob. He moved and stood near Miskovitz. "Friends, you know me. Your anchor-reporter." He waved his press card. "Why don't we call my editor? Please, listen. Friends . . ."

A few people looked in his direction, but the pandemonium continued throughout the hall.

Mao Ki Tung was annoyed — enough was enough! It had to stop.

He moved, making a place for himself between Rahul and Miskovitz, and shouted at the top of his lungs: "Friends. Barracudas. Barracudas. What's wrong with you? Barracudas know how to swim against the tide. They can't be easily trapped. You remember that? For time's sake, answer me. You remember that?"

His booming voice registered. "Yes. Yes." Voices rose here and there. Those resounding 'yeses' reached the back rows and they turned. Here again was the maybe-spy who had made the morning session so much fun. They hadn't heard what he had just said, but if others were clapping, it must have been something interesting. "Yes. Yes." They added their voices to the clamor.

The mood spread. "Yes. Yes." Clapping, everyone in the huge hall joined the chorus.

"First, a statement. Then a question," Mao Ki grinned. "If I was a Chinese first, my reaction to these kidnappings would have been to shout *imperialist plot. Imperialist plot.* But — "

He had to stop because his voice was being drowned in roof-raising laughter and applause.

"But," he continued, "I'm a Candle Runner first. Therefore, I ask you: Should we feel sorry for the power-blind leaders? Or should we feel happy for the children who stand behind us?"

There was sudden silence in the cavernous hall.

Mao Ki glanced at their faces and continued. "Earlier today, I was helping a 6-year-old with her flimsy firefly wings. On the sat-vision, she was watching a battle cruiser churning through the ocean waves. You know what she asked me? Can you guess?"

Watching their eyes, he waited a few seconds, then continued. "Pointing at the candle we had lit this morning, she asked me, 'Uncle Mao Ki, I heard that if there is a war, the world as we know it would end. There will be no more mornings. Uncle, am I an evening candle or a morning candle?' Candle Runners, what is your answer?"

The question hit where it hurt the most. No one stirred. No one breathed. No one said a word.

Cheenoo had joined his friends. He twanged his guitar. Pooja came over to stand by his side and began to softly sing:
For God's sake, let us sit upon the ground
And tell sad stories of the death of kings:
How some have been depos'd, some slain in war . . .
Some poison'd by their wives, some sleeping kill'd;
All murder'd: for within the hollow crown . . .
Keeps Death his court . . .
Scoffing his state and grinning at his pomp . . .
Infusing him with self and vain conceit . . .
And humour'd thus
Comes at the last, and with a little pin
Bores through his castle wall, and farewell king!

"Bravo, Pooja . . . Bravo, first space daughter . . . Bravo . . . " they shouted and began taking their seats.

Their eyes again turned toward the screens and the announcer's voice again hit their ears. "Let's see what this note says. Oh, what lovely stationery. You see it? This tiny, blue wildflower? And under its shade, this robin feeding her chicks." The telephoto camera highlighted the piece of paper as she read the note. "Be assured. Your leaders haven't been kidnapped. They'll be returned as soon as we're done with them . . . "

"Blowtorch done it," someone shouted.

"Yeah, that's why he disappeared," another added.

They laughed, hushing each other so they could hear the announcer continue reading the note. "Those of you who are now ruling until your leaders return, remember that if you make any move, start any skirmish of any kind, you'll join your leaders. You'll hear from us soon."

"Yeah!" someone shouted, "and what do we do till then?"

Opal Fire raised a tattooed hand. "I have suggestion."

Gopa felt relieved. "Yes, Opal?" she said encouragingly.

"First, I ask," she began, glancing around defiantly, "who gave these high-flying turtles right to trap us so bad? Hoku won't reach Mars for months. What's their rush? Ours is a democracy. Is it not? So why didn't they have a referendum? They may be *big cheese* an' we're no Cromwell, but we're no slimy amoeba either.

"So I say, let's big cheese this nutty old boys' network straight from the shoulder. They can't go on livin' in clover an' take us for blinding rides all the time. We got to read 'em the riot act before they can jump start this war. It's now or never.

"Whoever got 'em, let's tell 'em what deals these bloody blue bloods must accept, fair an' square, before they're let go."

Saying all that, in almost one breath, she stopped and breathed hard, expecting jeers. But the response was applause that hit the high roof, and echoed. Some thumped their tables and chairs. Others threw napkins in the air.

Gopa waved her hands, trying to quiet the crowd. "Good, Opal, positive thinking," she said as soon as the noise level went down. "See? Everyone approves. Who else?"

She glanced at the leaders on the dais, sitting stonily with mixed expressions, then at the members crowded in the hall below. "Friends, what do you say? Should we postpone the morning's agenda and, instead, draft suggestions, finalize them after lunch and get them broadcast on the networks on the six o'clock news?"

Another round of applause, louder than the first one, hit the high roof and came back echoing. Heads began to bend together, whispering strategies. Some started pulling chairs and making circles, while others walked in groups toward the privacy of their rooms. The over-fifty generation on the dais, by tacit consent, moved as one toward their cocktail lounge.

Rahul decided it was time to call the elders. Feigning a headache and need to rest, he took leave of his friends and roared off in his Honda toward his apartment.

Halfway there, he changed direction and headed toward the deserted beach where, at a secluded spot, he unfolded and set up his inflatable tent. Going inside, he seamed the flaps and pressed the implant behind his right ear.

Within minutes, the holo materialized. "Rahul, you are breaking rules," the elder's eyes expressed disapproval.

Rahul bowed in greeting. "I'm confused, senior one. I don't know what to do. I need advice."

"You're forgetting. You're not supposed to do anything. You are an *observer*."

"But moving amongst them, I can't float like a dumb pillar," Rahul protested. "They demand things. They expect — "

"If you are feeling trapped — "

"No . . . No. It's not that. I like my job. But to handle it properly, I have a few questions."

The holo seemed to sigh. "Go ahead. Ask."

"Are you holding the Titanic?"

"What's the next question?"

"Why don't you tell me? Or, don't you trust me?"

The holo smiled. "You're learning to talk like them. When you return, you'll need to relearn your language."

"I'm sorry, senior one. It's just that — "

"I know. You're getting emotionally involved, which is wrong. You were told you would be given all the facts that you'd need to conduct your assignment. No more. No less."

The eyes in the holo softened. "You, who are now called Rahul, must remember that you cannot act upon what you do not know. Right now, you are a human, and knowledge of the future is closed to you as it is to them. If we do otherwise, it will jeopardize your objective. Your mission. Even your life."

Rahul didn't agree. But he knew that if he offered any more arguments, just one more, he'd be recalled. "OK," he nodded and asked, "can you tell me just one thing? Who has kidnapped the leaders?"

"Your friend Gopa knows. When the time comes, she'll tell you."

He glanced at Rahul speculatively. "You are underestimating her. She's very special. Remember what you were told?"

"I remember."

"Fine. Then from now on you should forget calling us. When you need to know something, we will call you."

Rahul bowed. The senior one's hand moved and hovered over his head. "Let me remind you of the *first rule*. Forget you belong to a different species. Behave like a human. In any situation, say and do what you think a rational human would say and do."

"A Lincoln Observatory guide," said Rahul, "only eight or nine, told me the other day that she's feeling like a 'candle in the wind.' Sometimes I feel like that, too. If I make a mistake — "

"Mistake is just a word. Remember, one thing can be good, bad or indifferent. Think of music. It is good for the melancholy, bad for the mourners and neither good nor bad for the deaf. Knowingly and purposely, you won't make a mistake. If, despite your precautions, you do, that's a part of your life. No one is perfect. One time or another, all of us make mistakes."

"If you are not worried, I am not worried."

"Spoken like a true observer," the senior one approved. "Now, you must go. Tomorrow's work is waiting for you."

The holo disappeared. Rahul didn't waste any time. Folding his tent, he picked up his Honda to return to Convention Hall.

Since receiving Oringer's password, Sparky had discovered the painting, Rings Around the World. He sat near it, staring at it. It seemed like another trap that he should remember.

The more he looked at it, the more it seemed he had seen it before. Sometimes, it felt as if he had painted it.

Aren't you something, he scolded himself; now you want to believe you were a painter? Ego! Ego! Give it up and you will remember who you were.

He tried to forget it, but the idea wouldn't go away. The more he tried to forget, the more strength it gained.

I'll try to . . . no, not try to, I'll paint it and get it out of my system, he thought, and asked Neil for canvas and paints.

Oringer wasn't pleased with the request. Painting might soothe his mind, heal his nerves. If that happened, he'd remember who he was. That would be disastrous.

Until this superpowers words' war was over — one way, or another — he shouldn't remember. It was important.

But he couldn't deny Sparky's request either. He decided to hand the problem over to Gen. Stryker.

"Funny," Stryker said, "you're the second person today who mentioned this painting!"

"Really," Col. Oringer's heart almost missed a beat; had someone discovered his password?

"Your Candle Runner called and he sounded very excited." Remembering, Stryker smiled. "When I gave him that 'copter with the tight phone beam I hadn't realized how useful it would be."

Oringer's eyes lost some of their anxiety. News about Miskovitz always cheered him up. "The newscasts are full of that puffy Chinese defector. Did he say anything? Is he for real?"

"According to Misko, he is. Seems he is an exquisite orator. Saved a couple of ticklish situations."

"So? Why did he mention Meera's painting?"

"Seems there are four of them. He said, now that the new leaders are controlling decisions, we'll be working out new compromises. During those, he absolutely insisted, we should make sure we get the painting hanging in the Chinese chairman's office. He sounded as if not just our victory, but our whole future depended upon getting it."

"Why be so greedy? We have one. Isn't that enough?"

"Not according to him. Seems they are not four separate units. They're four pieces of one painting. And when the four come together, something incredible is supposed to happen."

"What?"

"That he doesn't know yet."

"So? The Chinese have one and so do we. That makes only two. "

"He has located the third, which was the source of his excitement."

"He's been too long with those sun worshippers," Oringer sighed. "He better come back before his mind is totally addled."

"You don't believe there's something in it?"

"Do you?"

"I don't know." Stryker pulled open his top drawer, looking for something. "Since talking with Neil's science teacher — what's his name? Truex? — I don't know what I believe in." He pushed the drawer back and pulled out another one.

"Neil's teacher? He believes in the painting's — "

"No. Not about the painting. He lectured me a lot about magnetic fields."

"Magnetic fields?"

"Yes. Have you ever thought about the relationships between our Earth's magnetic fields and Jupiter's and our Milky Way's and our sun's — "

"General — "

"He says, during our evolutionary period, we failed to develop a mechanism to utilize magnetic cues. Take ocean-dwelling bacteria. They use it for guidance toward their food supply. Or the birds. They use it as a compass to navigate. According to him, the early astrologers who discovered this were disdained and laughed at by the others.

"This created a rift between the astronomers and astrologers. The astronomers, fascinated by the stars, viewed human beings as an accident in the chain of life, existing on one planet of an ordinary star near the edge of a spiral galaxy. Astrologers regarded each human being as a key component, directly linked to the nucleus of our universe through the connecting, rotating, galactic magnetic fields."

What did all of this have to do with that mysterious painting, Sam Oringer wondered.

"He explained to me that in the beginning, astronomy and astrology had existed side by side, like Siamese twins, both thriving upon careful observations of the changing positions of the planets, rotating against the backdrop of fixed stars.

"Not just in the East, but even in Europe, some of the greatest astronomers were also astrologers. He reminded me of Ptolemy in the second century A.D., and Copernicus, who followed him. And Johannes Kepler in the 1600s who, as an astronomer, surpassed all his peers and figured out how our moon causes the tides; he proved that the planets travel in elliptical orbits, not in circular ones. And,as an astrologer in the court of the Duke of Wallenstein, he churned out horoscopes, making political predictions."

Oringer wondered where all this was leading.

"I've done some reading," Stryker confessed, opening the book he had pulled out of his drawer. "Did you know it was Galileo's telescope that started the rift between the Siamese twins? The turning point came in the 1900s when the French psychologist, Michel Gauquelin, tried to seam the rift by putting the two sciences together. He was such a genius, he was casting verifiable horoscopes by the time he was twelve."

Oringer tried to change the topic. "General, if — "

"I'm telling you. I was really intrigued by Gauquelin's work that statistically proved there is more to astrology than what can be ascribed to mere chance. For example, investigating politicians' natal charts, he found that at the moment of their birth, Jupiter was either rising or reaching its zenith.

"Repeating his surveys, he found this phenomenon everywhere. Saturn was governing scientists and physicians; Jupiter was delivering actors, playwrights and politicians. Getting curious, he co-related the horoscopes of parents and children and discovered that planets tended to occupy the same positions across generations. Noting that both Ptolemy and Kepler had recorded this phenomenon, he called it, 'Planetary Heredity.'"

Oringer knew Stryker was a rational scientist and he could not understand his sudden, overpowering interest in this hocus-pocus. There could be only one reason. "General," he asked as soon as Stryker stopped for breath, "can one manipulate these magnetic fields to influence inanimate objects?"

"Sorry, Sam. I'm boring you."

"Not at all, general. I was wondering if, by manipulating the fields, one can trigger floods or earthquakes to destabilize political systems — when the four pieces of that painting come together."

"Well, you can forget that. That'll never happen."

"Why? You believe Beijing would never be willing to — "

"Beijing," The general seemed amused. "You are losing trust in our powers of persuasion? No. The reason is . . . You see, I happen to know where the fourth one is."

Oringer glanced at his boss, surprise playing hide-and-seek all over his face.

Stryker sounded unhappy. "I didn't know folklore was attached to it. If I had, I may not have let it go."

"Go? Where, general?"

"Commander Kodama insisted so much it seemed pathetic. He said, like the others, he was not taking any personal items. That was the only item he wanted to take. And that, only because it was his father's legacy. Said it was the last item his father had given him before their relationship ruptured."

"Oh!"

"So if someone had hocus-pocus planned, using those paintings, it's gone with the Titanic. No, when you mentioned Sparky, I remembered Gauquelin's ubiquitous magnetic cues and ancestral planetary heredity theory because, if his theory is right, that astrologer could have foreseen the probability of Sparky's injury. And warning him, tried to undermine the danger. And Meera could be his daughter. After all, we weren't shadowing him 'round the clock."

"Sir, I wouldn't buy that."

"Why?"

"If astrology was such an exact science, everyone would have their future forecasted and, learning the hazards, make sure — "

"Ah. But a professional astrologer wouldn't interfere with God's plans. They'd speak in generalities, or — "

"Wouldn't they? Wasn't Sparky told his future in such

graphic words that he never dared to marry?"

"Precisely," the general said. "That's why I want to find that astrologer. Why did she violate her professional ethics and forecast that accident? Why did she disappear when Sparky was injured? If there was a reason, does it link Sparky's accident, the Titanic's disappearance and the kidnappings of world leaders?"

"General, I was hesitant about meeting Sparky's request. Your logic makes me feel I was wrong. Perhaps he should be allowed to revive his memories."

"I agree," Gen. Stryker said. "Let's give him what he wants. If that's against that holy guru Mata's grand design, I'm sure we'll be stopped. This time, we will watch. And as soon as she interferes, we'll catch her."

"But, general, he may not have seen all the paintings. If he didn't, how will he paint them?

"Good question," Stryker said rubbing his chin. Then his eyes lit up. "Call our resourceful Candle Runner. Ask him to send a photo of that doctor's painting. The CIA will get a picture of the one in Beijing."

"How about Commander Kodama's?"

"I have a feeling we won't need it. When that mysterious guru Mata learns of our intentions, she'll try to stop us."

Col. Oringer stood up to take care of it right away. "General," he asked, "about planetary heredity? How can . . . "

"To appreciate it," Stryker said, as if his mind had moved to other problems, "knowledge of Gauquelin's basic theory is needed because later, like banyan roots, it kept spawning so many mind-boggling interpretations.

"In fact," he smiled, "his disciples cited material by others who hadn't even heard of Gauquelin as proof. One case I remember. When Sigmund Freud's great-granddaughter, Rose Boyt, published her first novel, critics compared her heroine's *father-love-imprisoned-psyche*, to Lucian Freud's paintings of dyspeptic lovers and naked children.

"Noting that both Lucian and Rose — father and daughter — were obsessed with compelling sexual relationships and secret, taboo workings of the psyche, the critics wondered if heredity was responsible, if their artistic styles and submerged

compulsions were handed down generation to generation —
from Freud to his son and granddaughter.

"Sam, I can't decide if Gauquelin was right. If he was, if
planetary heredity cues us at our birth, it's possible an
astrologer, who studies and understands these cues, influences
and patterns, can chart the course of a human life just as
accurately as an astronomer can predict the course of comets,
even the most rare and distant ones."

"Halley's Comet." Feeling intrigued, Oringer nodded. "When
you're finished reading them, can I borrow your books?"

"Why not? Meanwhile, read this one. My favorite. Now about
those photos . . . I hope Miskovitz is not sleeping."

Miskovitz and Cheenoo were worried; Gopa had impulsively
invited suggestions from everyone. Tomorrow's meetings could
turn into an ugly, chaotic storm. What could be done to stop
that?

Weapons and armed guards were not allowed in Earth
Sanctuary, Ayodhya, but this crowd was not your usual Earth
Sanctuary crowd. Should they call New Delhi to send
plainclothes guards? Considering New Delhi's stance, they
might refuse. Or, they might send troops to close the convention.

The more they debated, the more hopeless it seemed.

Miskovitz sighed and leaned back. "Let's sleep on it. We'll
find a way."

Cheenoo smiled. "You know, Kovi, you're a horrible
optimist."

"I've been accused of many things, Cheenoo, but not that."

"Look at you. We're standing at the edge of the final ledge.
The chances are that history is going to die forever. And all you
can think of are rowdy meetings and peaceful negotiations, as if
it's just a question of safely sequestering them. As soon as it's
done, both the terrorists and tyrants will bow down and the
world will re-balance itself on its curved keel."

Miskovitz grinned. "What makes you think they won't?"

"No ultimatum you can give will dissolve the traps and
threat-fields of the three *E*'s."

"The what?" Startled, Miskovitz sat up.

"You never heard of them? The three E's — Ecology, Ego, and Economic realities. One-way ladders that have brought us to the present peaks, demolishing routes of honorable retreat."

"You lost me."

"To understand some things, one must dig their roots. You remember what happened when Marxism-Leninism started changing orientations first in the Soviet Alliance, then in China?"

"What happened?"

"The chances of large-scale conflicts between blocks of nations started decreasing, leading to shifts in spheres of power, which in turn started opening new routes for increasing 'marketization' of sociopolitical relations on a global scale . . ."

Miskovitz smiled. "You're pouring oil into water, buddy. I'm not a professor of economics."

"Sorry. Let me put it this way. As threats of world wars declined, national interests shifted gears and world polities began to realign more and more on the fast-moving global tracks of newly developing, trading and manufacturing relationships.

"For the national systems, these changes didn't just mean cyclonic upheavals in their traditional roles. They were also plagued with new, tangled global equations, such as complex technical problems across national borders crying for endless solutions. Demands for luxury products escalated in the hungry, post-Communist nations. And, complicating it, were assaults by angry consumers concerned about environmental deterioration.

"You've seen the results, how these borderless problems have been fueling bloody conflicts on the various ethnic, intranational and international levels — "

"What you are saying," Miskovitz said, "is that the world wars didn't die. They just changed locale and shape to become ethnic and economic grab bag conflicts."

"Wars," Rahul said in a reflective mood. "Did your textbooks talk about them? Ours did. Quoting ancient European thinkers, they said wars were safety valves for letting out humankind's innate aggressions. Their demise left a vacuum, a void, that had to be filled because nature does not like a vacuum. It was filled promptly by the three E's.

"If you ask me, Kovi, I think the worst problem created by the three E's was they did not leave much room for rewarding — or, if your prefer the word, *motivating* — anyone for dedicating their lives to abstract causes, such as striving for excellence in nonfiscal areas like music and philosophy. I'm talking about pure, selfless dedication that is not for personal aggrandizement, but for a cause considered noble."

"Oh, I don't know," Miskovitz said. "In America, we have operas, concerts, people who devote their entire lives to writing songs, plays and novels."

"No," Rahul smiled. "No. I don't mean theater and music — their economics are not much different than any other business activity. I was talking about flights of fancy. About Michelangelo, Omar Khayyam, Hiroshige and Kalidas. About blind dedication . . . Joan of Arc, Martin Luther King, the Kamikaze fighters in World War II.

"Perhaps it's hard for you to understand. Consider this. In our times, the struggles for recognition compete in fiscal corridors. No one struggles any more for achieving purely abstract goals, devoting one's entire life to feats requiring daring and courage and imagination and idealism.

"Consequently, in pockets where ideologies survive, they create a powerful nostalgia for the way history had existed, painted by folklore and kept alive by fables."

"I think I understand," Miskovitz said. "You think the expansion of the Royal Samurai Society is a direct result of the uncontrolled global marketization created by the three E's."

"I know it's living in the past, lusting for something that is outdated. And, not trying for a better future. But sometimes, when I watch those eighteenth-century videos," Cheenoo's face and eyes acquired a faraway, dreamy and wistful look, "I myself feel nostalgic for those days when love and honor meant more than owning a private roof-copter and a robotic-house."

They didn't have roof-copters and robotic-houses in those days, Miskovitz felt like saying. But it sounded like a bad joke. Cheenoo felt like that because he was a romantic at heart, the American thought.

"I think there's a solution," he finally said.

Cheenoo looked up at him.

"We are proposing working councils. Let's propose one more — a heritage-sharing council, devoted exclusively to — "

"Good idea," Cheenoo's lost-in-thought face lit up. "I will work for it. Let it be my abstract goal."

"In the ancient days," Miskovitz remembered, "musicians and artists flourished because the kings and emperors patronized them. They've been replaced by our trading communities. If those guys can be persuaded to take over the responsibility . . . "

"We found a name for our ballet." Gopa's cheerful voice, demanding their attention, broke his thought.

Turning, they saw the twins surrounded by scores of giggling, laughing, pushing and shoving junior dancers.

Mao Ki Tung and Opal entered through another door. "We've found a way to avoid the riots in the morning session."

"You have? How?" Rahul asked.

"What have you been doing?" Gopa was asking Miskovitz.

"Wasting time, I bet," said Pooja, plunking down near Cheenoo. "Has he been telling you," she asked Miskovitz, "what kind of music is more appropriate at what time of day?"

"Uncle Mao Ki," A couple of fireflies wrapped themselves around his knees. "Fireflies Spark Arcs of Life."

"What?" he asked, trying to pick up both of them.

"The name of our ballet," they announced triumphantly. "How do you like it?"

"Great," Rahul applauded, coming in. "I've got good news."

"What?" They turned towards him.

"My editor loved our request. He promised he'll make sure that all networks reserve time to broadcast bulletins about our project. And he said they'll interrupt regular programming to make announcements so that we are sure to get the maximum possible audience."

"Wow! Rahul," Gopa said, "you're a real rope-from-heaven."

They cheered and applauded and Rahul continued, "So, let's go and celebrate. Martian cocktails on me."

"How about Sake?" someone shouted and others clamored, "Pina colada . . . raspberry juice . . . me, a Shirley Temple . . . "

"Nope. Only Martian cocktails. Whoever declines goes to bed thirsty. Come on, it's getting late. Then it's time for beddy-by and tucking you in. Come on." Putting his arm around Gopa's shoulders, he cheerfully herded them toward the late-night cafe.

16

The Conspirators' Trump

"Why do you want to paint it anyway?" Neil asked. "It looks like an ink blot."

"Ink blot!" Sparky was startled. "That's what I told her. 'You call it a painting? It looks like an ink blot.'"

"Told who?"

"That young girl with dark purple hair and midnight-sparkling eyes. I had never seen such black irises in anyone's eyes. I was fascinated."

"Making up stories again. Purple hair went out of style; no one sports — "

"That one did. A true rebel. Wanted to do everything her mother told her not to do."

Neil smiled. "Sounds like Gopa. When did you meet her?

Where?"

"Where? Near some caves." Sparky tried to remember. "Yes, it was an archeological tour. We were visiting caves. Ajanta? Elephanta? No. Some new digging site. Very important. Anyway, I got separated from my group and was trying to find them when I saw her sitting on the grass under a big banyan tree. She had a big easel and lots of paint tubes and was dabbing at this ink blot, the rough wind blowing her long hair all over her face. She stared at me as if she had never seen a human being before, so I asked her what she was doing and she bristled. 'What does it look like,' she said. I asked her what it was and she asked me what it looked like to me, and I said an ink blot.

"She was furious, sure that I was insulting her painting, and I said how could one insult something that wasn't there? And why was she calling it a painting, when it was just an ink blot?"

Neil was listening, fascinated, fearful that if Sparky stopped talking, he may not remember the rest of it. He quickly prompted, "Then?"

Sparky blushed. "You don't want to know the rest."

"Yes, I do," Neil complained. "Why are you blushing? I've never seen you blush before."

"I am not."

"OK, you were not. Tell me what happened then?"

"You are too young to know."

"Fourteen, going on fifteen," Neil reminded him. "If it's about birds and bees, I know about that. Dad told me, and, besides, we devoted a whole class to it in school."

"God! Schools haven't improved any since my days, have they?"

"OK, you don't want to talk with me. I'm just a kid. Not fit company. I'm leaving."

"Neil! Don't. You're the only friend I've got. You know that. I'm an old man, trying to learn the new ways the best I can."

"Hey, I was only kidding. Forget it. Forget the whole thing. Here, I'll help you with your easel. First, we must spread this plastic sheet, so mom's carpet — "

"But I want to tell you." Sparky took the plastic sheet and dumped it aside. "I think I blushed because, coming back so sudden, my memory got shocked. I didn't know her. She didn't know me. We just met. Spoke a few words. And the next thing I knew, she invited me to have sex with her."

Neil started laughing. "And you were complaining about our new ways!"

"I'm telling you! She saw the German-to-English dictionary in my hand, asked me if I was a German, and, as soon as I said yes, she said she had come to the caves only because she had heard lots of foreign tourists came there and she wanted to have sex with a German. If I was one, I'd do fine."

"Good for your ego, wasn't she?"

"I told her I was an exchange student, couldn't do anything to give my sponsors a chance to complain. And in America, we didn't do it that way. First, we went out places. And if we liked each other and wanted to get married — I didn't get a chance to say any more. She started to cry."

"Girls believe that's the best way to get things done," Neil commented.

"No. It wasn't that kind of crying. I could see that. I asked her why she was crying. And she said something very strange."

"What?"

"She said her father had arranged her marriage with his friend who was a German. She was scared. She was wondering if she should find out what it would be like or run away from home. And if I wouldn't help her experiment, no other German would either, so the only thing left for her was to run away."

"So what did you do?"

"What could I do? I didn't want to blame myself for the rest of my life, thinking that I forced an inexperienced girl to run away from home."

"And the painting?"

"She wanted to give it to me. I told her to keep it in memory of me and never give it to anyone. A stubborn, blue-blooded rebel, she said I couldn't order her not to give it away. However, because we would never meet again, she would compromise. She would give it, or sell it, only to the person who called it an ink blot."

Suddenly Neil's face grew very serious. With anxiety-dripping eyes, he asked, "What was her name?"

"I never saw her again."

"What was her name?" Neil insisted.

"Why?"

"Because," Neil hesitated, then blurted out, "you could be my grandfather."

"Oh, come on, Neil. I like you, too, but — "

"This is my Granma's painting. Only one she ever painted. She never separated from it. Wherever she went, it went with her. Until one day, teasing her, my dad called it an *ink blot*. She gave it to him right away and wouldn't take it back. Said he was the second person to call it an ink blot. That's why it was his. And he must promise her never to sell it or give it to anyone, no matter what."

"You are not making this up?"

"Space truth," Neil crossed his fingers. "Scout's honor!"

"Where's your granma?"

"She had a heart attack and doesn't recognize anyone. Just stares. Maybe you can revive her memory."

"She won't recognize me either. I don't look anything like I looked when I was twenty-two."

"There must be a way. I should ask Colonel Oringer."

"No. Don't. Don't tell him anything. Not a word."

"Why?"

"Because I can remember everything. I know who I am. But I don't want them to know that I know. Not yet."

"OK," said Neil, loving the conspiracy. " I won't tell him. Not a word."

Looking brutish and ferocious, like a creature from a savage world, Lt. Gen. Leon Kostyzn towered above Vladimir Grachenko, who was seated near his phone. "Can I trust you to make the call without using the wrong words?"

Grachenko bristled. "I love my country, comrade lieutenant. What do you think I am? A traitor?"

"If I thought that, you wouldn't be occupying this chair," Kostyszyn sneered. "But I do know you scientists have a secret brotherhood."

"Then why don't you call?" Pushing the phone towards him, Grachenko started to move from his chair.

Kostyszyn roughly pushed him back. "General Kikilo wants you to call. Now." Positioning himself on the opposite chair, he growled, "And don't activate the visual. He must not know I'm here."

Coward! Grachenko thought. How many times are you going to repeat that warning?

He didn't voice his thoughts. Insults slithered down Kostyszyn's hide like oil on a black buffalo's skin. Grachenko picked up the phone and dialed Stryker's number.

Stryker was leaving his office when he heard the phone ring. He retraced his steps and picked it up. "Stryker."

"General." Grachenko tried to make his voice sound as cheerful as humanly possible. "Grachenko, here. I'm glad I caught you before you went home. Hope I didn't disturb your dinner."

Stryker was tired and not in a mood for pleasantries. "What's on your mind?" he asked gruffly.

Americans! No manners! Kostyszyn squirmed in his seat, but Grachenko was secretly celebrating the fact that Stryker hadn't spoken in his usual *buddy-buddy, between-you-and-me* tone. Reciprocating the insulting style, he stated, "You know about the ones wasting their governments' money in Ayodhya. Should we take joint action and present our demands?"

Stryker was surprised. "To whom? The *money-wasters*?"

"Of course not!"

"To the kidnappers?" On the audio, Kostyszyn heard his booming, derisive laugh. "Don't you trust your president? Isn't he capable of making all the demands the Soviet Alliance can make?"

"General," Grachenko spoke as if his feelings were hurt, "it's not a question of trust. In a situation like this, support means victory. Wherever they are, our leaders need our support."

"Don't they know they have it?" asked Stryker derisively. "Anyway, our vice president is a caretaker executive. Without a clear signal from our president, he won't lift a finger."

Until when? Kostyszyn wrote on a piece of paper and pushed it toward Grachenko. Glancing at it, he said in the phone, "Caretaker or not, he is occupying the chief executive's chair. How long can he sit there without doing anything?" "As long as necessary," Stryker said pleasantly. "We have no desire to annex a free country and enslave its freedom-loving people. Since the kidnappers have stopped your guns, we can wait. Now, if you'll excuse me. I know you're up early, but I had a long day. Bye, comrade director."

Before Grachenko could reply, the phone was disconnected.

"And, I have a long day ahead of me," said Grachenko duplicating Stryker's icy cold voice. "Volga Two needs me. So, if you'll excuse me . . ."

Without waiting for Lt. Gen. Kostyszyn's permission, Grachenko, the director, left his chair and strode away toward his Mission Control office.

In the convention dining hall, the cocktail hour had begun.

The involved delegates knew their proposal would be aired only at the designated hour, but they were restless. The wait would be easier near the screens with one's friends. They had started drifting in and the staff had rushed to set up tables an hour earlier.

Drinks in hand, they were wandering from group to group, faces grim and anxious, wanting to sit down, but feeling uncomfortable sitting. There was so much to talk about, but none of it sounded appropriate. With drinks tasting unappetizing, nothing to say and nowhere feeling comfortable, time didn't seem to pass. If time can ever stop, it had done so.

Hoping no one would notice, everyone was looking furtively at their watches, wondering if the watch was working, not wanting to ask anyone the time so that no one would learn about their overwhelming, overpowering anxiety.

Suddenly it was time.

Someone turned on the voice control. As the World Coke ad that preceded the evening news waltzed in, everyone scurried to find a seat.

"Good evening, Candle Runners," said the suave and meticulous anchor. "We hope you are watching, wherever you are."

"You bet we are," someone shouted amid the general laughter that vibrated the hall and miraculously released their charged, churning anxiety. It was here. There was nothing more to worry about and they were ready for it.

"Before I read your suggestions, I have some good news for you. This morning, we got a call from the non-kidnappers . . . "

Non-kidnappers. The graphic word evoked spontaneous laughter in the anxious hall.

"We phoned them your manifesto and they've sent us their reply. It will be reported right after your — "

"We know what we said," someone shouted. "Just give us their reply."

"You dumbo, first the world has to hear our demands. Only after that . . . "

"Keep quiet . . . For Earth's sake . . . Guys, guys . . . "

"Our phones are waiting. Please call in your 'yes' or 'no' vote to let us know your opinion. Calls will be accepted for the next twenty-four hours. Tomorrow at this time, we will let you know the results of your votes."

"Good idea . . . Great . . . Wonderful . . . They do use their brains sometimes." The hall was full of cheers and applause, difficult to control. Because they wanted to listen, the crowd quieted down without anyone having to force the issue.

"The items requested are as follows. One, the identity of the kidnappers must be revealed.

"Two, if the leaders have been collected so that, instead of flinging missiles at each other, they can negotiate, it should be an open debate, broadcast on all sat-vision networks. If they ask for time to prepare their arguments, their goals must be revealed right away.

"Three, Japan is a sovereign nation. Its emperor's status is its internal matter. The people of Japan should be allowed to settle it themselves without any foreign intervention.

"Four, any space vehicle launched from now on should be an Earth vehicle. It should not fly any one nation's flag. It should fly the Earth flag. For funding and administering this planetary effort, a global corporation should be established. A name has been suggested: Joint Earth Space Exploration Corporation. Work on this project must start right away.

"It's urgent because this body must start functioning before any spaceship reaches Mars. Its first commands will be to the Titanic — if it's still out there somewhere — and to Hiroshima Hoku, to fly earth flags.

"And five, when humans establish settlements on Mars, it will be a free nation. It will not be a colony of Earth.

"There you have the suggestions sent by the people attending a U.N.-sponsored peace convention in Earth Sanctuary, Ayodhya. Your votes, world citizens, will decide your future. We will give you the non-kidnappers' reply after this word from our sponsors. Stay tuned."

Everyone in the hall started talking at once.

Spoken by a neutral, nonemotional voice, the demands had sounded better than they had on the floor. They thumped each other's back and cheered. The ruckus, however, stopped as soon as the First Roof-Copters' commercial faded away. As Opal Fire had asserted so graphically, it was now or never.

"And now, people of Earth," said the anchor resumed, "here is the non-kidnappers' reply. One, you all know them, but they cannot reveal their names yet because that might harm, even destroy, their painstakingly programmed effort.

"Two, the idea of an open debate is praiseworthy. And, may I add, we agree. The networks will give them time.

"Three, the Japanese emperor's rights are inalienable and the Japanese people should decide their own internal affairs. Your support proves that public opinion will not allow violation of those rights.

"Four, the formation of JESEC is a good idea. A comprehensive proposal must be submitted to the U.N., requesting that they establish a timetable for getting it approved by all the nations.

"Finally, questions concerning settlements on Mars — and on other planets — are the most difficult ones. No matter what is decided here, how will it be implemented there? Only the future will tell. What we can do is to find a leader, willing to dedicate his life to seeking workable ideas, based upon consensus . . . "

Instant pandemonium burst out in the hall. Suddenly, everyone was looking for Mao Ki Tung, the Chinese observer who had, at the last minute, replaced Blowtorch. "Barracuda," they shouted. "Barracuda . . . "

Miskovitz picked up the mega-speaker he had brought for just this kind of contingency. Trying to be heard over the ear-splitting din, he shouted loudly, "Candle Runners, Candle Runners, please watch the screen."

Finally, he was heard. Eyes, not anxious anymore, not worried anymore, but jubilant and hopeful, turned toward the screens. The World Coke commercial was ending and the anchor was saying, "And now, an unexpected treat. We've just been informed that the technicians are ready to give you a glimpse of your nonvacationing leaders. Are you ready?"

The screens dimmed. The voice control buzzed with the static of space. The hall waited, as if with one united breath. Before anyone could get restless, the screens cleared and they saw the president of the United States watching a news video, a steaming cup of coffee in his hand.

The picture changed to that of the president of the supreme Soviet playing chess with the chief of his combined armed forces, supreme Gen. Mikhail A. Kikilo.

The camera moved again to depict the Japanese prime minister and the leader of the opposition party sitting side-by-side but not looking at each other, playing solitaire.

And then it changed once again, showing the chairman of the Chinese Republic facing a portable video, his eyes staring somewhere else as if looking through an unseen window; his hand was playing a silent tattoo on his chair's arm.

Mao Ki was sitting in a remote corner with Opal Fire and Wall Walker. Seeing the chairman's vacant-looking eyes, his face turned pale. I know where he is, he thought and looked at the spellbound faces all around him. Should I tell them?

He decided against it — there were times when one must speak up, but then there were other times when one must not allow one's thoughts to even breathe.

The screens were repeating the kidnapped leaders' faces. But the anchor's words did not fall in Mao Ki's ears. Softly whispering to Wall Walker that he had to go to the washroom, he moved unobtrusively and disappeared through a side door.

Meera A'Kash had been allowed to watch. She was expecting them to introduce her after the Chinese leader. When the pictures started repeating without her being introduced, she started banging on the walls, cursing and shrieking.

"Damn you!" she hollered, "You can't hide me! My family's worried. Do you hear me? Where are you? Do you hear me?"

Finally, the phone attached to her chair's arm rang. She picked it up. "Why wasn't I included? You must call the networks. Right now."

"You are worried about your family?" demanded a gruff voice. "We believe it. We know you love them. Therefore, we'd like to do for you something better than just let people watch you on sat-vision."

He sounds like the messenger who delivered that fake note, she thought. "Who are you?" she demanded angrily.

"Would you like to know what we are willing to do for you?"

"Yes. You can return me to my family."

"That comes later. How about right now?"

Arguing with an invisible voice was not going to help, she decided. Just like I had to humor my Earth Reality misfits, I need to humor him. "What can you do?" she asked politely.

"We can let you talk with your family."

"Right now?"

"Right now. If you agree to help us out."

Despite her anger and frustration, she laughed. "Who'll believe you need help?"

"Believe it. We do. That's why we brought you here. As soon as the work is done, you'll be home with your family."

"You have not hurt them? They're OK?"

"What makes you ask that? Why should we hurt them?"

She mulled it over. If they hadn't thought of hurting them, had she made a mistake by putting the idea into their minds?

It was too late to worry about it now. A mistake once made is forever. But if she could somehow motivate them to reveal why they had kidnapped her . . .

"Mrs. A'Kash?" The invisible voice asked.

"I'm not going to negotiate over the phone," she declared. "You come over here. We can talk about it."

"That's fine," the voice replied. "Please, wait a few minutes. We'll be there."

Such a quick acceptance of her demand surprised Meera. She had never realized she had that kind of spunk. So it was not, she thought, only the dear, departed Vishu who knew how to put his foot down and get things done. She could do it, too.

She moved towards the closed window and looked at her reflection in its dark, tinted panel. "You know what's your problem?" she asked, placing her finger on her shadow's nose. "You don't just call yourself *rabbit-feet*, you behave like one. You are not just Vishu's shadow. You are a human being. Learn to behave like one.

"Give you an example," she told her scowling shadow. "They put you in this closed room. You are suffocating, but you didn't even try to open the window. Open it."

She tried to slide open the window. It resisted as if due to not having been used. It was rusted. She pushed. Suddenly it slid back and a gust of cool air ruffled her hair. That defiant success cheered her up. Suddenly the years rolled away and she was a student again, going on picnics, climbing the mountains that the others were scared of climbing.

Catching the wind in her right fist, she brought her lips near it, and slowly opening the fingers blew it away. "Yes," she whispered so that only the culprit wind would hear. "No more 'rabbit feet.' I'm Vishu's wife. Or widow. And, my kids' mother. But I'm also me." With firm steps, she walked back to her seat.

If they want me to do something I don't want to, she thought, I'll agree to it until I can talk with Pooja and Neil. Then I'll refuse it. One can change one's mind. Happens all the time. If they don't know that, I don't have to tell them.

She took her mirror from her purse, checked her face and felt ready for whatever it was that was coming her way.

Stryker had called an impromptu meeting of his staff and other officers. The first to enter the conference room, he selected a chair and was seating himself when Sam Oringer walked in.

"You heard about the meeting?" Stryker asked.

"I was coming anyway. Sparky has changed his mind."

"About what?"

"Painting. Says it was a foolish idea. Too tough — "

"That again torpedoes our chance."

"Of what?"

"Of catching that elusive astrologer."

"What worries me is that he seemed different."

"How?"

"Didn't have that sort of vacant look in his eyes."

Before Stryker could reply, his officers and staff walked in. Behind them were NASA administrators who happened to be in the building and heard about the meeting. The conference room filled as it rarely did.

Oringer took a chair; Sparky would have to wait.

Stryker waited until everyone was seated then spoke as if continuing a broken conversation. "Well, at least he's OK. Seems they all are. Nothing to worry about on that point. Not yet."

"They didn't give their location." The speaker glanced around. "Did the background indicate something to anyone?"

"They just showed chairs," a junior officer said. "They could be anywhere."

What about that static in transmission? Stryker wanted to ask, but decided against it. If they hadn't noticed it, it was best not to bring it to their attention. "I called this meeting," he said, "to discuss the demands and replies that — "

"What is there to discuss!" a NASA officer angrily interrupted. "Ridiculous, outlandish ideas, propounded by half-baked do-gooders. The president will never agree, I'm quite sure of it."

"I agree," said the chief of the joint command. "Short-term remedies don't work. A permanent solution is needed. There's only one way to get it. We haven't had a war involving major powers for almost a century. They're asking for it."

"But — " Stryker began.

"No ifs, ands or buts," the man holding the reins of naval, military and airborne forces thundered. "May I remind you what one of our most beloved chief executives, President Woodrow Wilson, told our Congress when asking for a declaration of war more than a century ago, on April 2, 1917, to be exact?

"He said, and I quote, 'The day has come when America is privileged to spend her blood and her might for the principles that gave birth and happiness and the peace which she has treasured. God helping her, she can do no other . . . The world must be made safe for democracy.' End of quote.

"That freedom, that democracy, gentlemen, which we have treasured since the birth of our nation, is again in jeopardy. If the Soviet Alliance is allowed to unleash nuclear hell, we'd be slipping back into the Dark Ages. That cannot be allowed. Since our president is not here, it's our job to plead his cause to our Congress. Therefore, I have much to do. If you'll excuse me . . . "

Ignoring the stunned eyes around him, the chief of joint command walked out of the conference room.

Lt. Gen. Leon Kostyszyn had thought it would be quite easy. But it was proving otherwise.

Grachenko's secretary, Tanya, stood erect and fearless, answering his questions without really saying anything. He hadn't wanted to ask a direct question because she'd surely report back. And Grachenko had his supporters. But he couldn't hold her forever and he was getting nowhere.

"Tanya," he said, making a supreme effort to keep his voice soft and neutral, "I'm sure you know one of my jobs is advising the supreme Soviet about those matters which are critical to assure that our country remains a major power. Our space ventures are a crucial part of that effort. That's why I need to know what they're saying in your office about the convention's demands."

Tanya had no love for either Kostyszyn or Grachenko, but she needed her job and that depended upon Grachenko. She replied without any hesitation, "Comrade, as I told you, I've been busy. I didn't get a chance to watch the sat-vision. And, I never gossip. I have no idea what anyone is saying."

"Fine," Kostyszyn said pleasantly. "You may leave. Tell your boss I'll be there in ten minutes." Pulling his drawer open, he found her file; before the day was over, he'd find a way to fire her.

As far as Grachenko was concerned, Kostyszyn wondered whether or not any purpose would be served by visiting him.

First, no matter how much they denied it, he knew these scientists had a kind of secret, global brotherhood. Sometimes, he suspected, they even had code words and secret language.

Second, although he didn't know why, it was obvious that Grachenko didn't like him.

He couldn't understand the reason. He was always extra nice to Grachenko and gave him more time and respect than what he had ever given to anyone else. Why did he always clam up and seem to be at swords and daggers whenever they were together, as if they were enemies and didn't work for the same government.

Third, what could Grachenko tell him that he himself might not have observed? The kidnappers hadn't provided much to be observed anyway — two chairs and a table. Could be a small room anywhere, even within Soviet Alliance borders.

From the setup, however, it was clear that the plot had been conceived by supporters of the Americas. That's why they had shown him watching the news, keeping up with world affairs, even in prison. And it had shown the Soviet president playing chess with the Alliance's supreme commander — to prove how uncaring and frivolous the Soviet leaders were.

How devious they were. How conniving.

The worst part of it was that the ignorant public would believe it, and there was no immediate, easy way to tell them they were being fed totally absurd propaganda.

This kind of injury could not be forgiven. The perpetrators would need to be punished, punished severely.

They believed themselves to be very cunning. Didn't they

know there were ways of tracing anyone when one is speaking? During that promised debate that was going to be space-casted, when Gen. Kikilo would be speaking, tracing the origin — and making sure the general was not somewhere where he could get injured — why not take it upon himself to order the attack? If he did that before the Americans could get an inkling of his intentions, who'd be able to stop him? Nobody.

Once Japan was annexed, they could debate the matter in the United Nations for centuries. It wouldn't matter.

He picked up the phone and dialed Grachenko's number. "Comrade, I've decided to launch Operation Space Sword."

Grachenko couldn't believe his ears. "Without the president's permission? When General Kikilo is out there? Without informing the supreme Soviet?"

"Good of you to remind me. I'll call an emergency meeting right now. If you have time to join us, you are invited." Without giving Grachenko time to reply, he disconnected the line.

In the crowded dining hall, which was emptying slowly, Miskovitz was trying to find Gopa and Mao Ki Tung.

Suddenly, he spotted her talking with her doctor. Worried that he might lose sight of her in the crush of people milling around, he started toward her at a rapid pace, not worrying about jostling anyone.

Reaching them, he grinned and extended a hand. "Doctor, how nice of you to come. I was trying to reach you."

The doctor shook his hand warmly. "Gopa forgot to tell you she invited me?"

"She told me, but with you being so busy, tough night duties and all, I didn't know if you'd be able to come. Anyway, I was calling you because I need to ask you a quick favor. I need your permission for something."

"Not for tying Gopa in ropes, I hope."

Gopa laughed. "My turn. He does need tying up."

"You dare! Just dare!" he threatened her mockingly. Putting his arm around her shoulders, he told the doctor, "I was calling you because I want to take a photo of your painting."

"Impossible."

"Come on. I'm serious."

"Do I look otherwise?" the doctor asked and smiled. "My friends accuse me of speaking like a steno. You see, I don't have the painting anymore."

"What happened to it?" Miskovitz felt the ground slipping away from under his feet. He had never, never, let down the general. Please, God . . .

"Its owner asked for it. I sent it yesterday."

"I thought she was on the Titanic."

"The painter, yes. Shakti, the ship's doctor. The owner is here. Her sister. I'm sure you've heard of her."

"What's her name?"

"Gopa, should I tell him?"

"Should we?" Her wide, aquamarine eyes danced mischievously. "Let me think about it. James, why don't you go find Mao Ki? He was looking for you frantically. Wall Walker and Opal Fire, too. What have you four got up your sleeve?"

Not giving him a chance to reply, she untangled herself from his arm. "Tell me later. Right now, we've got to go."

Grabbing the doctor's hand, dragging him, she walked away, leaving Miskovitz standing there, gawking at her vanishing trick.

17

War: the
Volcanic Guru

Sparky was helping Neil with his new experiment when the phone rang. "You want to pick it up?" Neil asked.

"Nope. No one calls me," Sparky said cheerfully.

"OK." Switching on the wall unit, Neil saw Meera's face.

"Mom," he shouted, "where are you? When you coming home?"

"Soon, son. I'm calling to tell you I'm OK and to ask you a favor."

"Say it, mom."

"You know your granma's painting, Rings Around the World? Someone's coming there to pick it up."

"Why?"

"I need it, son."

"You going to sell it?"

"Nooo! I can't do that. You know that. I'll bring it back."

"If something happens to it," Neil said, "if you lose it or something, you'll break granma's heart."

"How is granma?"

"No change. Mom, is someone listening or can I tell you something?"

"Important?"

"Like a serpent in the roses."

"Can it wait till tomorrow?"

"If you want to. Hey, you want to say hello to Sparky?"

"Not right now, son. I've got to go. The messenger will be there any minute. Don't give him a hard time. Bye now. I love you."

"I love you, too, mom," Neil said, but he wasn't sure if she heard him because the line got disconnected. At the same time, the front door bell rang.

Neil turned. Sparky was checking the door monitor. "Don't answer it," he said. "It's that mysterious impossible messenger. How did he bypass security? Let's call Oringer."

"Don't panic," Neil said. "Mom sent him. To pick up your painting."

"Could be a trap."

"Nope. They can maybe fake faces, but not mom's voice."

The bell rang again — harshly, angrily.

Neil deactivated the alarm and released the magnetic lock.

The black messenger strolled in as if he owned the house. Glancing neither left nor right, he went straight to the painting, took it off the wall, put it in the large bag he carried and walked out.

"How do you like that," Neil exclaimed. "Not even a hello."

"Why the painting?" Sparky wondered aloud.

"To raise funds, I bet. For her Earth Reality. Forget it. Let's get back to work."

But Sparky couldn't forget it. Staring at that empty space on the wall, his memory vaulted back forty years. He remembered the young woman with the disapproving face in whose cottage he had taken shelter with his one night's love, when outside it had started to rain. He pictured the event as if it had happened that morning . . .

"Don't worry," the purple-haired teenager, who was afraid of marrying a German but not afraid of making love to one, had giggled. "She won't squeal. She's my art teacher."

Unable to forget the runaway one's pouting lips, her laughter, her touch, her teasing, her quick temper that flared and faded so magically, he had gone to that cottage a few days later, seeking her address. It was then he had met the strange woman in yellow robes, who had laughingly volunteered to check his sun-signs, looked at his hand, his forehead, asked his birthdate and told him to keep away from his future daughter because he'd be mortally wounded by her.

Amused, thinking he had support because anger at her sister's antics must be the reason the cottage owner was wearing a disapproving face, he had asked her in his most beguiling voice — filled with innocence and respect — if her sister was a priest and fortuneteller, why wasn't she in the same profession?

The answer had surprised him as nothing could have. They weren't fortunetellers. She was teaching art and her sister was practicing astrology to earn their college expenses.

Now, remembering the discussion, he wondered. Did fortunetellers' predictions come true because they were destined to happen or because they were implanted in one's mind, influencing future behavior? If that student fortuneteller hadn't frightened him with a gruesome future, would he have married, had lots of children and never bothered to find Meera A'Kash? Then, how could she have hit him that day on that deserted road?

But if it wasn't supposed to happen, why had he gone on that archeological expedition, as if drawn by an irresistible magnet? No one had invited him . . . no one had recommended it. On the contrary, his friends had tried to discourage him, explaining it was a new find, not much to see there yet.

On top of their dissuasion, he had lots of paperwork on his desk that needed to be taken care of without delay. Nonetheless, as if pulled by unseen, magical strings, he had gone anyway. Rings Around the World or rings around me? he wondered. A clever trap for the sole purpose of snaring me? Who was pulling the strings?

"Neil," he asked, "do you believe in fortunetellers?"

"Granma does. My mom doesn't. I don't know about myself. I've never met one. Do you?"

"I didn't. Then I heard that prediction that won't leave me alone. Now, thinking about it, I can't understand why I began to believe in it. I met her only once, you know, the one who told me your mom would 'injure me mortally.' I remember that she had mesmerizing eyes — the kind you can't stop looking at. And a mesmerizing voice that made you want to believe every word she said, despite your best judgment."

He was looking at Neil, but Neil felt his eyes were looking at something far away. "I bet," he continued, as if coming back to the present, "hers is the hungry hand wanting your granma's painting."

"Why?" Neil was surprised. "And why would mom give it to her? She doesn't know her. Who is she?"

"I told you, I met her only once. But I've got a gut feeling she's the puppeteer juggling us by her invisible strings," he smiled. "Like your magnetic signals that you explained, you know. I'm wondering if we'll see her tonight, controlling, guiding that century-shaking debate."

"You keep saying *one, she, her*. Who is she?" asked Neil, feeling frustrated. "What's her name?"

"I, an atheist, an unbeliever, why did I always dream about that night, wherever I lived, wherever I went? Was it her words . . . the fear of unnatural death that she had predicted?

"Or was it your granma's all-giving love that I could never forget? Any woman I met after that night, no matter how eagerly, how flamboyantly they tried to hook me, no matter how much they connived to bond us, to me, they all looked so insipid. So drab. In every crowd, I searched for her laughing, midnight eyes, her prancing steps, her unforgettable face."

"People get over their first love. You didn't. It's as simple as that," Neil said matter-of-factly.

"Is it?" Sparky turned and stared at that blank wall again. "Is it really so simple? If I see that mercurial fortuneteller tonight, watch her mesmerizing act from the distance of space between us, would I be able to figure it out?"

Everyone was anxious to find a sat-vision before the debate began. Offices closed early. Commuter lines increased frequency. Roof-copters whirred. Doors clicked. Businesses that stayed open twenty-four hours, bars and coffee shops, made sure their sat-visions were working.

Even Stryker didn't feel like staying late at his desk, as he generally did.

Arriving home, he gave his housekeeper the evening off, ordered dinner from his favorite Italian restaurant and invited Sam Oringer, Herbert Caine and his friend, Pablo Martinez, to share it with him.

Oringer was the first one to arrive. Fixing a drink for him, Stryker asked, "What was it you were telling me about Sparky when we got interrupted?"

"Just my imagination maybe. But it seemed to me as if he was walking differently, talking differently."

"How differently?"

"I dunno. Like . . . like more confidently?"

Stryker smiled. "You're asking me? I wasn't there. But seriously, wouldn't it just mean he's getting used to living there?"

"Maybe. Or maybe it means he got his memory back."

"And he's not telling anyone?"

"And he's not telling anyone," Oringer agreed.

"He can't hide that. Arrange a check-up," Stryker said, dismissing it. "By the way, did you get a chance to scan that book?"

"On magnetic forces? Yes. Fascinating. Especially those diagrams and charts. The way they depicted all the planets going their separate ways, pulling at each other, raising tides and distorting orbits indiscriminately, falling into those striking geometric patterns, queuing up in a line, squaring off at right angles, ganging up on one side of the sun, and . . . I felt like an astronaut looking down."

Stryker nodded. "What about the logic — how changes in the magnetic field of the sun correspond to certain ascending or shifting aspects of the planets?"

"That part was beyond me, 'specially when they talk about items like opposition (180 between the planets), quarters of squares (90), and conjunction (O or close alignment). But, the other items I found fascinating, such as sunspots and geomagnetic storms and magnetic canals around the sun's equator. And how auroras disrupt items like telecommunications."

"So? What do you think?"

"Well. Their theory seems logical; when the impact of magnetic forces upon human behavior was first discovered, astrologers researching those influences could have assembled observable facts, discovered causes and means — relationships — that the astronomers, studying stars from a different viewpoint, may not have had the motivation — and reason — to investigate and understand."

"Exactly," Stryker beamed. "Scientists agree that in ancient India, after the concepts of zero and decimal were discovered, instead of devoting their minds to spiritual and social aspects of life, if they had pursued physical aspects of the sciences, they'd have discovered first what we discovered centuries later. But they were fascinated by the metaphysical and — "

"Discovered relationships between our galaxy's forces and living beings that were never written and were transferred to succeeding generations by word of mouth. If that's logical," Sam added thoughtfully, "I can understand how that guru Mata could have foreseen Sparky's getting injured by his unborn daughter."

"And, following the deductive logic of those ancient ones, I think I know who has kidnapped our world leaders."

"Really?" Oringer exclaimed. "Who?"

Just then the door-video announced the arrival of the other guests. Since Stryker had already punched in orders, the robo-lock allowed them entry and the next minute they were there, excited and beaming, ready to have an exciting evening.

It was breakfast time in the convention dining hall. Everyone was trying to gobble it up fast so that the waiters would leave and they'd have an unobstructed view of the screens positioned high on the walls, well above the tallest person's head. Eight more had been added overnight, so they could watch any wall facing them. Still, it was a cavernous hall, and those seated in the middle were worried about getting a good view.

Everyone knew the exact time when the debate would begin, but between mouthfuls they kept looking at the screens as if, should they forget to check, they might miss the opening remarks.

Right on time, someone turned on the voice control and they instantly applauded the bright and cheerful morning face of their favorite anchor, Bertha von Suttner. Always groomed perfectly, today, they could see, she had taken extra care. Her hair looked more regal, her dress more appealing. And, when she started speaking, her voice was even more charming than usual.

"Good morning. You all ready for your special program?" she smiled winningly at her audience. "Before we begin, I have two announcements: First, we won't be interrupted by commercials. We will have them right now, not during the debate." As if aware of the applause greeting her announcement, she paused and smiled.

Giving her worldwide audience time to settle down, she continued. "Second, computers have tallied your phone votes. We'll give you results after the debate because you wouldn't like the voting to influence the participants."

"Sure . . . Good thinking . . . Of course . . . " shouted voices in the convention hall.

"One more item." On the big screens, von Suttner was saying winningly, "We don't know where our participants are located. Although our technicians have done a wonderful job of synchronizing communication lines, if there are transmission problems, I do apologize in advance. Now, a break for our patrons, World Coke, First Roof-Copters and Robo-Houses Unlimited . . . "

The commercials were, in fact, welcomed for a last-minute dash to washrooms, for a cup of coffee, for changing places . . .

"And now, ladies and gentlemen, may I present the chairman of the Republic of China, the prime minister and opposition leader of Japan, the president of supreme Soviet and supreme general of Soviet military forces, and the president of the United States."

As she gave their names, faces appeared on the screen. A small table held a pitcher of water, silver cups and flowers. Tall plants were behind their backs. No flags. No background paraphernalia. Absolutely no way of telling what kind of room they were in or where they could be.

"And last, but not least," Bertha von Suttner smiled, "our moderator, one whom many of you know, a world leader in her own right. The president of Earth Reality, Mrs. Meera A'Kash."

"Omigod . . . earth alive . . . I'll be doggone . . . " A collective sigh rose in the hall. Faces turned toward Gopa and Pooja, who had jumped up shouting in one voice, "I didn't know about it."

"We know, we know," some shouted. Others clapped. Cheenoo and Miskovitz pulled them back to their seats.

Meera A'Kash was saying, " . . . and, you should know that I was given this job by someone I do not know. Suddenly. Unexpectedly. Therefore, I'm not prepared. I'll do the best that I can.

"First, the format. Our leaders have five minutes each to respond to your proposal. Then, five minutes each for rebuttal or clarification of their positions. The last twenty minutes will be devoted to suggestions for resolving the crisis. First, the honorable chairman of the Republic of China."

He looked old and frail, but his voice came strong and clear. "I yield the floor to our good friends, the mighty Soviet Alliance. Just as, in the bygone century, we made their ideology our own, so now, we stand by their side. Their position is ours."

"I wish everyone would make my job so easy." Meera smiled at him and at her audience. "Mr. Chairman, I'm sure you know that we can't change the format and give precedence to anyone, regardless of who makes the request. Therefore, now — " She stopped mid-sentence, as a robo-arm offered her a note.

Reading it, she looked startled. "I'm sorry, we do need to make a change. Please, don't go away. Please, listen carefully to this message. 'Friends, today, as perhaps never before, we're standing at the crossroads in more than one sense. I wonder if, like me, you've been feeling like students facing new life-roads. One such occasion I remember — a commencement address by an American, General Stanley Stryker. In his booming voice, he gave his charges a challenge. I wonder how many of them are listening now. And how many remember that challenge. What he asked that clear June day is even more relevant today. He said, and from memory I can only paraphrase: one day soon, you may find yourself in the shoes of a commanding officer, responsible for the protection of countless lives, even those yet unborn. That day, what will you remember? Will you remember that a general's job is not just to conduct a war? That it is also to frame strategies to contain a war.

'You are the pincers, the pioneers of this new century. Quite appropriately, you are proudly damning and breaking traditions all around you — in your social, political and economic lives. My generation's dreams gave us space flight. Yours may seed our civilization on planets far and wide.

'Since that first day, when a human picked up a stone to protect what he believed was his own, humankind has been busy devising better, more advanced, means of destroying each other. Like you, that innovative human was a pioneer. And I'm wondering, will you continue that Stone Age tradition? Or will you pioneer in some other direction and discover means and strategies to channel human aggression in some other direction?

'As you step out of these doors today to meet your destiny, I'd like you to take with you this thought. Is it better to sling back the Stone Age strategy where it belongs? To get rid of it? Or, is it better to lug it along endlessly, like Sindbad's demon, on your restless, itching shoulders, hindering your feet, your energy? Blocking your minds. Blocking and making you waste time that can be devoted to pioneering in some other direction?

'Fellow world citizens, I've taken your time to come along with me on this memory path, to hear these immortal, timeless words. Not to sermonize. Not to praise an American general. But to remind you that America has been a superpower, a major force in shaping our planet's history because of leaders like him.

'Before you accuse me of bias and start chanting "imperialist propaganda," let me inform you of this. Ignoring our warning that no violence will be allowed until our leaders are our house guests, the American and Soviet commanders decided to launch secret attacks. If we hadn't learned about it, at this moment, instead of this note, you'd have been hearing your networks telling you that the planetary war had begun and Moscow, Tokyo and Washington were smoldering, demolished by each other.'"

Stunned, unbelieving, the listeners glanced at each other. God Almighty! Was this a hoax to hook their captured minds? Or could it be true?

"'We have the speeches they intended to spacecast after launching the attack,'" Meera's controlled voice softly continued to read the note. "'In them, they swear their secret strategic decision was taken for the protection of their kidnapped leaders.

'That's not surprising. In any war, when weapons are unleashed, they're never for the personal glory of commanders. Never for winning those coveted, ego-boosting stars for their uniforms. They're always for protecting something. Always for the glory of a cause. When they throw their young ones into flames, they never tell them that war is a ferocious volcano. When it starts spewing burning lava, nothing lying in its path can be saved.

'What can we do about those two? We have put them under house arrest. But that is not a solution. Killing them is not a solution because that will only kindle the sleeping lava, making their blind supporters leap to take their place.

'What is your opinion, world citizens? Aren't there circumstances in which killing — no matter how obnoxious, how abhorrent — is the only solution? In the twentieth century, if Hitler had been killed before he started on his demonic spree, would millions of innocent lives have been saved?

'One tries to learn from history. Therefore, we are requesting the presidents of the Soviet Alliance and the United States to call their people right now to stop this volcanic holocaust that, if not stopped, will leave our planet in cinders, unfit for habitation, for any form of life, for millenniums.

'It hurts me to say it, but, like any surgeon, say it I must. If they won't stop this madness, they'll burn all their bridges, leaving us no choice. Just like in the unforgotten past, for the sake of freedom, French tyrants were guillotined by their people; right now, facing you on these screens, they'll be beheaded and their blood will be on their commanders' shoulders, on their peoples' heads, for all time to come.'"

In the convention hall, there was stunned silence. That same silence permeated Gen. Stryker's living room. Meera's living room. In bedrooms, living rooms, bars, restaurants and every place where people stared at their sat-visions, breaths stopped in disbelief at what had just heard.

Each viewer dreaded the blood about to be spilled on their sat-vision screens.

18

The Clairvoyant's Key

Stryker pushed away his dinner plate and glared at Caine. "Oh, no!" Caine said. "Don't cold-stare me! I had nothing to do with it."

"You knew about it," Stryker accused.

"Me? How would I know about it? If you think the military confides in me, you're nuts."

"You're nuts! What was it you had said, you'd recommend 'first strike'?"

"Yes, if the situation warranted it. If Congress asked my opinion," Caine blazed. "Blast those dumb CIA nitpicks. Why can't they find him? I shouldn't have left it to them."

During the slowly marching minutes, sitting in his living room surrounded by his friends, Stryker had sailed through bumpy, seismic spectrums of emotions. Seeing the president alive and unharmed, he had felt overjoyed. The narration of his commencement address to a worldwide audience had made him feel very self-conscious. Speculating about the kidnappers' identity, he had wondered if, should he call Meera, they would put him through.

Many problems had whirred through his mind, but not this. How could the commander and chief executive of the United States, the president of the most powerful nation on earth, be assassinated by a bunch of misfits? Were the kidnappers that stupid?

Did they really think they'd get away with it? That the people of America would let them commit such a ghastly act and do nothing?

No, sir! No way!

Seeing his face, his posture, no one had dared to say anything. Finally, Martinez ventured tentatively, "Stan?"

Stryker stared at him.

"I think there's a way."

"What?"

"Let's call them. Tell them we just heard from the Titanic. It has captured Hiroshima Hoku."

"What?" They all stared with amazement at the Mexican consul general, the soft-spoken diplomat they knew so well.

"You know we can't do that, Pablo," Stryker said. "I like to play poker, too, but what if they call our bluff? No. There has to be some other way. What if — "

"General," Oringer said respectfully, "isn't our worry premature, sir? You know the president. He'll be OK."

Stryker glared at him, saw what was in his eyes and suddenly all his anger, all his emotions, surged and burst forth. He started laughing. "You're right, Sam. I got so mad at Herb I wasn't thinking logically."

Pablo looked dismayed. "What are you guys talking about?"

Caine nodded, "We got so uptight we lost our nerve. Of course, he'll be OK. He's the best diplomat we have, Mr. Consul General, you just watch. See what kind of leader our people have elected to pull the nation through any catastrophe."

Sam Oringer nodded. "You can trust him."

Bertha von Suttner was beginning to worry about Meera. Sitting next to her, watching her body language, Bertha could see the effect of reading the non-kidnapper's ultimatum to her world audience. Although Meera's voice was steady, the strain and anxiety were beginning to take their toll on her courage.

If she collapsed . . .

As Meera reached the last sentence of the lengthy note, Bertha motioned to the camera man to move his camera away from her hand and slipped a note to Meera. "Time to take a breather. Go. Have coffee. Until you return, I'll hold the fort."

The camera zoomed toward Bertha. Looking at her gratefully, Meera quietly slipped away.

Bertha took a deep breath and thought of the audience watching her face. Pulling together her strength, she said softly, "Ultimatums! Sharper than licking swords . . . Sitting in their shadows, I've been wondering if I'm having a diabolical, never-ending, half-moon nightmare? Or is all of this true? Can it really be happening to our small little world, to all of us? And, I don't feel like smiling.

"But, as you just heard, when something's got to be done someone has to do it, smiling like a surgeon . . . As your world reporters, it is our responsibility to bring you all the news no matter how gruesome and bloodcurdling.

"I do not remember in the history of news spacecasting any massacre perpetrated on the news screen. God forbid! If it happens today, would someone wipe it off the pages of our history."

A robo-arm moved toward her with another note, and she grabbed it. Reading it, the light hiding somewhere deep down in her eyes sprang back. "There are only a few people in this world," she said in a voice chocked with emotion, "in whom I have unshakable faith. I have a note from one of them. I hope that today, of all days, my faith won't be broken. Candle Runners, friends . . . the president of the United States."

Suddenly, they saw the American president's face and heard

his razor-sharp voice, cool and poised, as if it would cut time into tiny fragments. "I am the commander of my nation's military forces, but I cannot trigger such a deadly trap. Only our Senate and Congress, acting jointly, can declare war. They did not.

"I hope the news we just heard is incorrect. If it is not, I am hereby ordering Vice President Louis Lockheart to immediately arrest the guilty officers. They will be court-marshalled according to the laws of our land," he declared firmly, "and those trials will be spacecasted. I guarantee you that."

The camera zoomed in on the angry faces of the Soviet team. Gen. Kikilo glanced at his president and stood up. "If you read your morning paper, you know that our supreme Soviet never declared war. If one of our officers was not able to stand the strain and went berserk, we demand his safe return. He'll receive proper psychiatric care."

Their faces were replaced by the Japanese leaders. "The fact that world opinion is with us," the prime minister said, "proves that our sovereignty rights are not negotiable. The item JESEC needs similar understanding. I request you to use your good logic.

"In western colleges, everyone is taught, 'East is East and West is West and never the twain shall meet.' How can we forget this inhumanly egoistic requiem? If we agree to JESEC, we will condemn our people never to be a part of any space venture.

"Mars? Who says we want to enslave it? With global warming and sea levels rising, our land is shrinking. We are trapped. We need additional land. Mars is the answer. When the Europeans grabbed the Americas and killed the native Indians, did anyone lift a finger? No! Then, why censor us?

"No! No indeed! We should not be blamed for doing what historically every nation has done, taking surplus land to keep its people alive. Particularly when it won't be an easy task. We'll be suffering unimaginable hardships, settling a barren, inhospitable planet. We won't be killing anyone like the Spanish and the Europeans and the British did when they decimated the native American tribes . . . "

The camera zoomed left because the Soviet president had started speaking in a voice breathing fire. "For time's sake! Who do the royal samurai think they're addressing? Kindergarten kids? Who doesn't know how globalization of commerce and trade requires that we conform to international norms? But the royal samurai want everyone to bow down to their rules!

"We don't enslave nations. It's against our ideology. But, if firm steps are not taken right away, we'd have to fight an interplanetary war. Proper administrative apparatus must be installed in Japan to make sure they do not grab all our wealth and send it to Mars to set up their colonies.

"With all due respect to the U.N., I must say that what looks attractive can be very unrealistic. JESEC falls in that category. Instead of taking such a risky step, it would be better to initiate joint ventures. As we get used to working together, in time, perhaps, efforts can be made to centralize the work in areas where we can help each other.

"Mars, as the honorable samurai just informed the whole world, is an open territory. According to the ancient, universally honored practice, anyone who conquers a territory keeps it.

"The Law of Territorial Conquest applies equally to all, not just to the royal samurai flag-bearers. Don't they know theirs is not the only country plagued by population pressure? When we reach Mars, the question of sovereignty rights will be handled by the settlers."

Replacing his image, the American president was on the screen. "The supreme Soviet's not pushing the war button is to be commended because at this decisive moment, if we clash, we will ruin this historic turning point. Can I commend Japan? No. And I don't understand why they keep flagging their sovereignty. No one is denying it. The problem is not their internal affairs, it's their international affairs.

"Who doesn't know that since the birth of our nation, we have believed in the preservation and protection of democracy. Any student of the discipline would attest that democracy is not an abstract ideology. It's a way of life. It is not a fantasy that can survive in isolation. It's an evergreen that must shield and bulwark neighborly interests because a fire ignited by a self-deluding leader, like Hitler, can destroy our planet.

"Speaking of leaders, is Japan the only nation boasting an emperor? Isn't Britain crowned by a hereditary king? The British were realistic. They made sure their rulers understood that the king's rights stop where the other nations' rights begin. That realism expects the royal samurai to enact a constitutional change. To prosper on a small planet, the basic rule is that an emperor's rights stop where another nation's rights begin.

"JESEC? I like the name. As our Soviet friends said, on a theoretical level, the idea sounds beautiful. But, would it work? I do not have the training to make a sound decision. I'll have to refer it to my specialists whose job it is to test the validity of such ideas. On the administrative level, to me it doesn't seem practical. We believe in free enterprise. We have private corporations actively engaged in space exploration. Their work is important. It has given birth to new products, new jobs. They'd need to be consulted. Our people would need to be consulted.

"Mars? Again, the idea is wonderful. Would it work? I think it's impractical to pass any resolution without analyzing all the aspects. Any hasty decision will not endure but will be torn apart by the currents of time."

Stryker turned toward Pablo Martinez. "What do you think of his speech?"

"Let's watch," Herbert Caine said. "We'll analyze later."

Meera A'Kash was back. "I've been taking notes. It seems to me that although we are facing three questions, they're stemming from one source — Hiroshima Hoku.

"All of us know the Soviet Alliance had no onerously unsolvable problem settling its business tangles with Japan, until they heard about Hiroshima Hoku's mission. America had no desire to attack the Soviet Alliance until it heard about their plans evoked by Hiroshima Hoku's mission.

"And, the emperor's Royal Samurai Society was a social club of a few elderly, honorable Japanese citizens, engaged in holding a meeting once a month to drink tea and sake and recite haiku, until the plans for launching Hiroshima Hoku materialized.

"Therefore, I'm going to throw out a suggestion and ask the leaders to use it as a launching pad. Technicians, would you please try to work out the miracle you promised?"

Faces wobbled on the screen. Suddenly they stabilized, freezing Meera's face in the center. Around her, in the four corners, appeared the four nations' chief executives.

She glanced toward the Soviet leaders. "Mr. President, if Japan agrees not to annex Mars, would you agree to let them work out their emperor's status and cancel your Yellow Alert?"

"Of course," replied the Soviet president. "Their sun god's status is their life. We cannot interfere in their internal affairs."

"Mr. President," Meera glanced at the American president, "may I please ask you the same question?"

The president smiled. "Mrs. A'Kash, I admire your style. I can see why Captain A'Kash talked so much about you. When we get back, I'd like you to visit with me . . . To your question, there can be only one answer. We believe in protecting, preserving and defending freedom worldwide, not snatching it from anyone. There are no exceptions to this rule. If Soviet forces hovering to enslave Japan are withdrawn, our warning to the Soviet Alliance is automatically canceled."

Meera turned towards the Japanese leaders.

"Mr. Prime Minister, to avoid a war that would not really solve anything, to save this century for humankind, to lay a firm foundation for free interplanetary commerce, would you be willing to solve your population problems through the United Nations and change Hiroshima Hoku's orders?"

The Japanese leaders looked at each other. Not getting any response, Meera prompted, "Mr. Prime Minister?"

"We are a very small, ocean-locked nation," the Japanese prime minister barked in an angry tone. "We cannot trust these major powers. It's now or never. If they wish to safeguard the world of their children, they must agree to our having Mars. Just as, in the past, we let them have the Americas."

The faces of the American, Soviet and Chinese leaders expressed shock and disbelief. But Meera didn't seem disheartened. Without missing a beat she asked, "And what is your reply to joining JESEC"

"As we explained before, we are a small nation. We cannot afford to be dwarfed by these major powers, Be it the U.N. or any international organization. Our membership does not mean anything. In any voting, they expect us to toe their line. Why worry about us? If they want to set up such a body, any help they need, we'd be most willing to give. But we will keep our space mission a separate venture."

"Obstinate, isn't he?" Pablo murmured.

Meera was gathering her papers. "Isn't it strange how people behave exactly as expected! All of you have rewarded us with the answers we were expecting from you.

"Therefore, I can throw away the speech that would have been used if the American and Soviet leaders had disappointed us, the speech that covered such items as the unregulated growth of space satellites, flying different flags, duplicating time, money and effort and ringing our world around the equator and around the poles, creating hazards in space that could lead to devastating economic and political wars.

"But, before proceeding, I should present the results of the phone poll. As you know, it's based upon the opinions of those who called. Many didn't call. And many callers may not have gotten through because the phones were so busy.

"Briefly, the majority of you said what we've already heard from the American and Soviet leaders. You'd like them to cooperate, to investigate, to find a middle ground to form a planetary space corporation.

"In fact, many of you cited twentieth-century space operas in which, for protecting galactic peace, Earth Federation spaceships battled alien species. We have many senior citizens who fondly remember growing up with those enchanting movies.

"Getting back, since the American and Soviet leaders are willing to cooperate, and the Chinese are willing to support them, they'll be released right away. For the Japanese, as we expected, we need additional time."

She turned toward the Japanese team. "Mr. Prime Minister,

you're forcing us to take this step. Therefore, we cannot keep your guest house a secret. You should know that the Chinese, Soviet and American leaders are our guests in the Egyptian president's guest pyramids. But you, sir? Let me show you where you are."

On the screen, the section imaging the Japanese leaders split in two. On the second half, it depicted a space satellite circling earth in a geocentric orbit. The camera zoomed to show a small section within the satellite.

"Mr. Prime Minister, do you see yourself? Do you recognize this Egyptian vehicle that your own industrial giant, Yamamoto, launched for us?"

Pablo guffawed. "What do you know! They helped kidnap their own leaders!"

"I'm sure you know," Meera A'Kash was saying, "that we can keep you there as long as necessary. In fact, if you wish, to give you company, we can send the other members of your space clique. If we do that, what do you think the people who elected you will say?

"As to Hiroshima Hoku, it's ours, any day we want. Let me show you how."

Stryker gasped. "Neil's toy! The one stolen from my workshop! She filched it?"

"This is a prototype of what we have at our control center. It's capable of hooking onto Hiroshima Hoku and bringing it back. You don't have to believe me now. You can wait until, relaxing in your circling guest house, you see your space ship resting in the Earth Spirit Park, in Earth Sanctuary, Ayodhya."

"So you are the one who destroyed the Titanic?" the Japanese Prime Minister shrieked.

"Titanic?" Meera smiled, a most charming, sweet smile. "I'm glad you reminded me of it. I'd like to take this opportunity to tell you that the Titanic is performing flawlessly. It should reach Mars on schedule.

"But," she glanced toward the American and Soviet leaders "it is flying the Earth Spirit flag. When it left, the idea of JESEC hadn't been born."

"Needless to say," she declared, "if the U.N. does not

cooperate, if they do not start working towards establishing JESEC, it will keep on flying this flag until it is established."

"Mrs. A'Kash," the American president interrupted, "you want us to believe that this toy's big buddy can bring back Hiroshima? And that the crew and captain of the Titanic are traitors?" He laughed. "You must love your fantasy and science fiction operas, Mrs. A'Kash. Or do you really think we are so . . . so gullible, that we'll believe your outrageous fairy tale? After doing such a fine job, in the end, you wish to disappoint us so poorly?"

"Earth forbid, Mr. President! How can you even think I can take such liberty? You know me better than that. Tell you what. I'll let you hear my husband's voice. You can talk with him later, when you reach the White House.

"But first, let me give you just one of the reasons why we believe your space specialists will support our idea. It will be to stop the kind of crisis you are witnessing just now. The Japanese prime minister is a hostage in his own country's satellite. Does that sound like a fairy tale, Mr. President?

"What else would you like to witness in the near future — criminal with a hydrogen bomb holding the world hostage? Other nations copying Hiroshima Hoku's mission? If private corporations are given the freedom to make space their playground, would any world leader, any industrial magnate, any freedom-loving person, be safe anywhere in our universe?

"You may trust the patriotism and the law-abiding nature of your private sector, Mr. President. That's your prerogative. But can you, with the same fervor, trust the motives of all the others? The economic barons . . . opportunists . . . terrorists . . .

"It's now or never, Mr. President. It's when required precautions are not taken during infancy that problems proliferate which cannot be controlled later. If corporations, only a handful now, find it difficult to work together — " She paused for dramatic effect, then continued. "What will happen during the coming years when other nations and their corporations start jumping onto the field?

"The problem is not Japan, Mr. President. We know what his august highness, the emperor of Japan, wants. That was the only reason Yamamoto Space, Inc., launched its own prime minister. When Yamamoto heard the suggestion about JESEC, they immediately called to let us know they'd like to work actively with the global committee to get the blueprints rolling.

"Now, my promise about the Titanic. Guru Mata, may I please have the paintings?"

A couple of robo-arms came into view holding three paintings. Seeing them, the chairman of the Chinese Republic shot up and shrieked, "That one is mine! The third one. How did you get it?"

"The same way you did," Meera replied sweetly. "You stole it from the Cairo Museum. We let you keep it till we needed it. You must know that these are not normal art objects. Camouflaged like paintings, they are astral magnetic panels, built upon the basic principles of the space-time continuum. Three here, one on the Titanic. Now watch."

Fascinated, the world's leaders and the viewing audience watched as she connected the three paintings, then hooked the unit to Neil's machine.

"A twin of this machine, which you were calling a toy, is on the Titanic," she explained. "When I turn it on, magnetic fields will be generated, connecting them. Awakened, the unit on the Titanic will let its captain know we're trying to reach him."

Suddenly, unexpectedly, her voice got caught in her throat. "By the way," she said, trying to mask her emotion, "I'm very proud to tell you that these spacemitters, the one on the Titanic and this one in my hands, were made by my son, Neil A'Kash.

"Neil, my son, if you're listening, you should know how sorry I am for all the misery you've suffered, but I wasn't able to tell you anything because I didn't know myself. Just as you didn't. We followed suggestions without knowing the reason.

"Gentlemen, I'm sorry to take your time for this personal message, but I couldn't help it. My son is only fourteen. And he suffered a lot. Now, with your permission, I'm going to switch on the magnetic signals." She threw a switch.

For a few minutes, nothing happened. She looked at it, tested the joints and said apologetically, "It's only a test-run. We never — "

294 Earth Trap: Rings Around the World

Just then, they heard Capt. A'Kash's voice, loud and clear, a voice that many recognized. "Titanic calling Mission Control. This is Captain A'Kash. Houston, do you read us? If not, because you weren't expecting us, we'll keep calling. Our channels are open to receive you. Houston, this is Titanic . . .

"Papa," Pooja whispered in Rahul's ear. "I told you. He's not worried. I told you. He's OK."

Gopa's head was hidden on Miskovitz's shoulder. He couldn't hear her, but he knew she was softly crying. He didn't touch her, fearing that if he did so, she would stop.

The voice from space was again calling. "Houston, do you read? . . . Houston, are you there?"

After the first shock, Stryker jumped up. "Yes, we are here. And we're coming. Let's go."

Forgetting the unfinished dinner on the table, all four of them moved rapidly, like one body.

On the screen, Meera was saying, "Honorable leaders, will you work to make JESEC a reality, like you do to win elections?"

Not receiving any answer, she smiled. "If Jefferson and Hamilton and Thomas Paine and all the other dedicated pioneers hadn't worked so hard, given it all they had, the United States of America wouldn't have materialized. The colonies would have remained thirteen small states, always torn by strife, just as Europe still is, despite all kinds of joint operations.

"America would never have become a superpower. The forces of democracy would have remained weak and ineffective or died. Is that the future you want for your home world when it faces an alien civilization? A savage planet, torn by a hundred and sixty national interests, ready to be colonized?

"Would you also consider this: If you won't accept the realities demanded by your century, won't you have to face perils like those suffered by others who refused to accept the changes demanded by their times, the tsars of Russia, the emperors of France . . ."

But the initial shock triggered by the Titanic's call was over and no one was listening.

In the convention hall, throwing napkins high in the air, people were dancing between the chairs, on the chairs, on the tables, spilling cups of coffee that were still there. From the dais, leaders were jumping down to join their friends. Was it freejam or the frogtrot? Why care? Dance, jump, holler . . .

Someone came running and whispered in Gopa's ears. She picked up a mega-speaker. "Candle Runners, friends," she shouted, "the fireflies are ready. They want to do a full dress rehearsal. Can we clear this stage for them? Would you help me move these tables?"

Willing feet moved. Willing hands cleared the dais in minutes. Junior artists, dressed in their firefly costumes, entered from the two sides. Someone switched off the lights. The recorded music was picked up by many voices in the hall:

Fireflies, fireflies
Life of our twinkling twilight.
Yours is this Earth,
Yours is this globe.

Your light is our life,
Your eyes are our dawn,
Keep on moving,

Loving and laughing.
Sparkling,
Arcs of Life,
That's all Earth is asking.
That's all our Earth wants.

Fireflies, fireflies.
Our breath, our lives.
Never gamble away our Earth.
This Earth is yours.

19

Only a
Bullet Away

In the unlit, subterranean room, the shimmering Fireflies Ballet threw shadows and lights on the three watching the 3-D screen. It didn't reach their faces, but they didn't need to see each other to feel comfortable.

"So," said Seven, "Eleven was right. We weren't needed. They sorted out their problems by themselves."

"Not my kind of planet . . . Brinkmanship games . . . Total annihilation just a bullet away." Nine stretched and yawned. "I'm glad we can go home."

"Not yet," said Five behind them.

The announcement surprised them. They had thought, closeted in his office, he was finalizing details for their return trip.

You found a way to stay! Eleven wanted to scream, but she controlled herself. Where Five was concerned, nothing worked. Not anger. Nor diplomacy. One of these days . . .

"The U.N. has decided to bring down the Japanese team," Five was saying. "Since the prime minister is not agreeing to anything, there may be a civil war. Therefore, we have to stay."

"Until when?" asked Nine. He was obviously tired of living here, cooped up, and was itching to return.

"Until Hiroshima and Titanic-Volga reach Mars."

"Oh no!"

"Are we going to have our own mini civil war?" asked Seven. It didn't seem like he was joking.

"Enough," warned Four. Tall and graceful as always, she stood behind Five. She rarely spoke. But when she did, even Five cringed. "Just because we weren't needed, doesn't mean our work is finished. The bullets that'll decide humanity's fate are not on Earth. They are on Hiroshima. Who has forgotten that?"

No one answered. No one spoke.

"Seven?" she asked. "Eleven?"

It's now or never, Eleven thought. "But Hiroshima is not a threat any more. Didn't that moderator, Meera, say they can bring it down any day?"

"Maybe they can, maybe they can't." The answer, crisp and clear, said more than her face would have, if it were not in the shadows and invisible.

Seven decided to risk it. "Meaning?"

Four moved toward a chair. "On this planet they play two games, chess and poker."

"So?"

"In the first one," Five explained, "although everyone knows the predetermined moves, no one can predetermine his own next move because it depends on the opponent's action."

"And in the second one," Eleven said, "they bluff to the *ninth sky*. I know that. But — "

"How do you know she wasn't bluffing?" asked Four.

"What if they can't capture it and, guessing that, Japan calls their bluff?" added Five.

"And Blowtorch?" said Four. "He's not a quitter."

"The conceptual term," said Seven, "is *life*. Meaning, problems. They solved this crisis. They will solve the next one also."

"If they do, that would mean they are qualified to join the ranks of others who have broken their planetary barriers. Wouldn't you like to submit a report recommending that status?"

In the silence that followed, Eleven tentatively ventured, "When you were talking with them, you could have explained how difficult it is to live cooped up in this two-by-four hell."

"I knew you'd say that." There was a hint of a smile in Four's voice. "We have new orders. We can get out and work in the field. They suggested, before leaving we should watch Rahul's tapes. To learn, and not repeat, his mistakes."

"Have they found out where he is from?" Nine asked.

"If they have, do you think they would tell you?" Seven slashed.

"Bicker! Bicker!" Four reproved. "Come on. Get ready. I don't want to stay here one minute more than I have to."

In the rooftop restaurant, watching the revolving Martian landscape, Caine was waiting for Gen. Stryker. Watching the shegota hunters, he was so fascinated that he was startled by Stryker's voice. "So, you like it?"

"You know what's most fascinating here? That one bullet. Every time it kills someone, the whole story changes."

"Like the bullet that killed Burt Ward. Now we'll never know if he was responsible for Sparky's accident." Signalling the waiter to bring his drink, Stryker asked, "So, what's the verdict?"

"About Meera A'kash? Everyone agrees, for the time being, we have to give her a long rope."

Stryker nodded. "She'll lead us to them. Since our second source has disappeared, she's our only chance."

"Second source?"

"Neil's teacher, Truex," Stryker explained. "He invented those astral spacemitters. And it was he who persuaded Meera to send it on Titanic without Neil's permission."

"Because he couldn't persuade Neil?" Caine smiled. "That boy has a strong mind. It needs to be nurtured."

"Colonel Oringer's job. He can do it," Stryker said smugly.

"What about Captain A'Kash? What kind of disciplinary — "

"He has to be given a long rope, too. At least," Stryker twirled his drink thoughtfully, "until he returns."

"Did you ask him what he took inside that robo-courier?"

"Weapons, he said. But, I think he was lying."

"Why?"

"When they called, the first thing the ground computers did was to take life readings. Of course, it's difficult to be accurate, but it seems there's an extra person on board."

"Why is it difficult to be accurate? I thought — "

"You've got to be kidding! With Volga attached? Our computers weren't ready for that."

"That bowled me over." Caine leaned back. "Volga attached itself to the Titanic, and the Russians don't even know. Have you told them yet?"

"Me? After Grachenko told me he knows what happened to Volga? That would start a war that no one would be able to stop."

"But they have to be told."

"Grachenko's problem. If Volga contacts him, he will have to convince his government that we didn't know anything about it."

"Tough."

"Tough is right." Stryker nodded. "If JESEC is established, the danger may — "

"You think it has a chance."

"It's up to us, isn't it? That's why I'm resigning."

"What!" Caine shot up in his seat.

"I consulted with the president. When times demand something . . . Remember the League of Nations? United Nations?"

Caine couldn't believe it. "You're going to organize it?"

"Heaven forbid! But as a private citizen, I can join the organizing committee. Take part in — "

"I get it," Caine's face suddenly looked wistful. "Do you think there will be room for an ex-intelligence specialist?"

"If I could get the formula I've in mind accepted, the American group can have a substantial — "

"Good." Caine looked pleased. "By the way, we feel sure about that Mao Ki fellow. He's genuine. He's not a Chinese spy."

"That may be, but one who changed once can change again. That's why I've got to lure Colonel Fong."

"Fong? Why?"

"You're the one who told me he has the uncanny ability of maneuvering Mao Ki. And I think I know what makes Fong tick."

Caine looked at his watch, "Well, I've got a dinner date. Before I leave, would you tell me something? As a personal favor?"

"What?"

"Did you ask Captain A'Kash about Neelam?"

"Are you kidding? With everybody — and, I mean everybody on every tracking station — listening? Why? I thought you had some leads in England?"

"Fizzled out." Caine got up. "We'll keep working. If she exists, we'll find her. Bye."

"Bye," said Stryker, calling a waiter to order his dinner.

Meera A'Kash was feeling restless. If she waited any longer, she'd miss her flight and that would mean missing the connecting flight that was bringing her daughters.

She had made up her mind to make them feel she loved them, cared for them, more than anything else, regardless of any sacrifices she might have to make. If she missed them at the airport, she'd fail even before she started. Feeling even more alienated, they'd again denounce her and contend that Earth Reality was her only child.

When the doorbell chimed, she ran. Sam Oringer! Her face fell.

"Am I such an unwelcome visitor?"

"Oh, no. Please." She looked very apologetic. "I was expecting someone else."

"Must be someone very special."

"Oh no, just guru Mata. She told me to wait for her, but she's more than an hour late. That's never happened before."

"You know where she is? Call her."

"Why not come in?" Meera moved back to let him enter, then stopped abruptly, as if struck by a sudden thought. "What are you doing here? Did you come to arrest me?"

"Arrest you? Why?"

"For working with terrorists."

"Now that you mention it — " He settled down in a comfortable chair. "I'm curious. Have you joined them?"

She sat on the edge of the chair opposite him, both hands on her knees, looking intense and anxious. "You know, colonel, I learned something from the past couple of days' trauma, something I never would have learned otherwise."

He looked at her but didn't say anything. She continued, "Guru Mata and her friends . . . they're not terrorists. We may not agree with their methods, but the only thing they were trying to do was to stop a global war."

"Aren't methods important, Mrs. A'Kash?"

"You know what she said when she heard that the U.N. had voted to bring down the Japanese team right away?"

"What?"

"She looked so sad. She said, 'It's stupid to try. I worked so hard to save the prime minister's life. All that work . . . '"

"But there is no danger to their lives. Getting down from the shuttle, they will pass through a bullet-proof corridor to the waiting copter. And their house will be guarded round the clock by carefully screened guards. The trial will be conducted via satellite. Whatever penalty they decide, it won't be the death sentence. I can assure you of that."

Meera settled back in her seat. "I hope you're right."

Oringer looked at her speculatively. "What about you? Are you going to work with guru Mata and wait for Captain A'Kash?"

"Are you kidding? No. A big no, to both," She laughed and

moved to fix him a drink.

"Why the big *no*?"

"Don't you know? Our civilization goes through phases. The Age of guru Mata is over. She's retiring. We are entering the Age of Space Runners. Of — "

"Of Captain A'Kash?" Oringer interrupted. "Are you going to work with him?"

"After what he did to me?" Her cheeks flamed with anger. "No. Hearing his voice that day freed me from the nightmare I'd been living since the Titanic was lost. Then I was thinking I wouldn't be able to live without him. What a mistake that was. Yesterday, I called my attorney and told him to rush the divorce."

Oringer considered the woman standing there, looking confident and determined. So fiercely independent. He remembered the trembling one who sat in the police station afraid of her daughter, trying to hide her tears.

He picked up his drink. "Where's yours?"

"No more drinks. That's gone, too." She looked at her watch. "I really can't wait any longer. I must catch my flight. I'll leave a note for guru Mata."

"You don't have to answer my question."

"Which one?" She looked puzzled. "I've nothing to hide. Oh, about my future plans? Well, right now, they center around my children. Making a home for them. And if you want the truth — "

"Yes?"

"I was hoping I'd have the help of a fatherly hand. When I was talking with Neil, he couldn't stop talking about you."

Sam Oringer glanced at her; she was an attractive woman. And if she was getting a divorce . . . "Why not?" he said.

"I'll call you as soon as I reach home."

"We can do better than that. I'm booked on your flight. Let me take you to the airport."

Picking up her purse, she moved beside him. "Colonel . . .

"Time for 'Sam'"

"OK." She took hold of his hand. "That day, just before the Titanic disappeared, going to my office, you know what I was thinking?"

"What?"

"That this would be a very peaceful, uneventful year. Nothing, absolutely nothing would happen to me."

"And the fellow who sort of triggered the events," said Oringer, holding open the door of his auto for her. "Sparky. He's waiting for you, to say good-bye before he leaves."

"Good-bye?" Meera exclaimed as they began to drive away. "No way. We will have to keep an eye on him. Me and you. We don't want him to get under my wheels again."

Oringer put his hand on hers. The auto raced as if knowing what they wanted.